Arthur Folkard

A Monograph of the Family of Folkard of Suffolk

Part I.

Arthur Folkard

A Monograph of the Family of Folkard of Suffolk
Part I.

ISBN/EAN: 9783744779494

Printed in Europe, USA, Canada, Australia, Japan

Cover: Foto ©Raphael Reischuk / pixelio.de

More available books at **www.hansebooks.com**

A MONOGRAPH OF THE FAMILY

OF

Folkard of Suffolk.

PART I.

Introductory.

VISIT paid some years back to the College of Arms, on which occasion my friend, the late Mr. Tucker, then Somerset Herald, kindly showed me very early records of the arms of Folkard of Suffolk, induced me to commence search for further memorials. An enormous mass of material had been collected by me in manuscript, when Mr. R. A. Baxter obligingly offered to print what I might select of it at his private press. It appearing to me that the ancient wills—as furnishing wider evidences than any other records—should be the first to be printed, they were therefore chosen for this initiatory instalment. Mr. Baxter having proceeded as far as page 30, circumstances compelled him to stop further assistance, and for the completion of this first part of "A Monograph of the Family of Folkard of Suffolk," I have been indebted to Mr. Richard Folkard.

The four pedigrees given in this part have, owing to the great cost of printing such work, been prepared by myself by a method and with appliances inadequate for producing finished workmanship. For a work intended only for family and gratuitous distribution, the heavy charge for printing these pedigrees properly must have wholly prevented their production. Indulgence may, therefore, be asked for their rough character.

During my researches it was found that there were in existence four pedigrees of the Suffolk family. The earliest was the compilation of the Rev. M. Gillett, *alias* Candler, probably about 1650. It is to be found on page 380 of No. 6071 of the Harleian MSS. in the British Museum Library. An amplification of this pedigree is preserved in the Bodleian Library (Tanner 180, 26, 27). A third is among Davy's Suffolk Collections, in the British Museum Library. This was compiled early in the present century, and relates to the Parham branch only, though very copious notes relating to the family in other localities of Suffolk and Norfolk are given in Vol. LIV. of the same work. The fourth was the work of Dr. J. J. Muskett, the well-known Suffolk genealogist, and was published in *The East Anglian*, Vol. II. (New Series), page 118. To that gentleman, as well as to Mr. F. A. Crisp, I am under great obligations for kind assistance in my researches.

It is scarcely possible to do better in the way of commencing a few observations respecting this ancient family than to quote the following prefatory remarks to the pedigree last named:—

"FAMILY OF FOLKARD, CO. SUFFOLK.

" The name of this family is derived from Folkward, *i.e.*, president of the local folkmoot. It is met with, in various forms of spelling, in the early chronicles of the continent. It was borne by the ancestors of the Dukes de la Rochefoucauld (Rupis Folcardi); the Counts of Anjou (Folcard and Folco of the Plantagenet line); the Marquises of St. Germain-Beaupré (Folcard and Foucault); and other noble houses of France, Spain, and Bavaria. It had, perhaps, a Danish origin, and appears amongst the mythological ancestors of the God Woden, and in the pedigree of Hengist and Horsa. The Suffolk family claims descent from Fulchard, '*prepositus*' of Thetford in 1130, whose descendants settled at Eye and Mellis and remained there well into the seventeenth century. The name occurs frequently in the Domesday of Suffolk. The earliest instance in the Eastern Counties is that of a King's Moneyer of Norwich, in the reign of Ethelred the Unready. There were moneyers of the same name at Ipswich in the reign of Canute, and at Thetford under the Conqueror. William Folcard, who seems to have been a Sheriff of Suffolk in 1130, may have been identical with the ' prepositus ' of Thetford.

" The Folkards of Suffolk bear as arms, by prescription, sa. a chev. betw. 3 covered cups or. An ancient sketch is preserved in the College of Arms. The assumption is they were granted to Walter Folcard, of Eye, who was Commissioner for the Queen mother's Suffolk estates, by Edward the 3ᵈ early in his reign. They were placed, at an early date, in the windows of Buxhall Church ; where a fragment of the shield with one of the cups is still to be seen.   They were quartered by Sir Edward Coke, Lord Chief Justice (see COKE), whose paternal great grandfather, John Coke of Ryston, Norfolk, married Alice, daughter and ultimately co-heiress of William Folkard.   The Earls of Leicester, his descendants, yet hold the Manors of Folkards and Sparham, which came to them through this marriage, and the Folkard arms are amongst their numerous quarterings.   Branches of the Folkard family still reside in the Eastern Counties.   Mr. John Folkard lived in the quaint old moated hall at Framlingham up to his death in 1823 ; and the last descendant of the Parham line, Mr. Thomas Folkard, died at Parham Hall in 1853.

" The Folkard pedigree, here given, is founded on that compiled by the Candlers in the seventeenth century.   The text of Harl. MS. 6,071, 380, collated with Tanner 180, 26, 27, is printed in italics.   The annotations in roman type are from the proposed edition of the Candler MSS., already sufficiently commented upon in the pages of the *East Anglian*.   This pedigree, it need scarcely be said, could be very greatly extended in every direction.

"J. J. M."

In extension of the above quotation, it is proposed to offer a few remarks under the several headings of which it treats.

𝔗𝔥𝔢 𝔑𝔞𝔪𝔢.

This is so abundant in the early chronicles, that it can only be said that the occasions of it go beyond the scope of reference here. It is to be found throughout all historical periods in those of nearly all the countries of the Continent of Europe, as well as in those of England, Ireland, and Scotland, from the earliest historic times.[*]   Only one authority on surnames (Camden) differs from the view taken of the meaning of Folkward by Dr. Muskett, and he maintains that its proper interpretation should be Prince or Ruler ; *i.e.*, the warden or guardian of the people.   But it seems more likely that Dr. Muskett's view is the correct one.   The name is undoubtedly of Danish origin, and not of that of the more northern races of Norway and Sweden, only one instance of it having been found by me in the Sagas, and that apparently referring to a Dane.

[*] In every country of Europe are also to be found many towns and villages bearing the name ; but the number of these is so great, that it is impossible here to state more than the bare fact.

The Ancestry of the Suffolk Family.

There has always been a family tradition that it owed its origin
to an abbot. Such traditions have very probably a strong basis, and
in my endeavour, made in Pedigree No. 2, to trace the source of the
Suffolk settlement, that origin has been hypothetically adopted. It
will be recollected that until Pope Hildebrand, who was elected in
1073, issued his Bull against marriage among ecclesiastics, the practice
of it was a recognised one; and it is on record that Abbot Folcard
of Marchiennes, Flanders, was deposed, because, among other evil
acts, he deputed the management of his monastery "to his wife." It
is quite possible, therefore, that the celebrated Abbot Folcard, of
Thorney, in Cambridgeshire, to whom the foundation of the Suffolk
family is assigned in pedigree No. 2, was a married man. In the
history of Thorney Abbey we read that he brought his relatives to
England from the Pas de Calais, and procured settlement for them in
England. Thorney being near to the borders of Suffolk, the theory
adopted that its abbot was the one of the family tradition is not a
far-fetched one. It is somewhat confirmatory of this theory, that a
family called "Fullard" has been resident at Thorney up to the
present time. Still, the name—as stated by Dr. Muskett—was certainly known in the Eastern Counties long prior to the abbot's coming
to England; but, on the other hand, the Norman origin of the family
is very conclusively determined by the fact of the early use by it of
both Christian and surname, as will be seen by the pedigree No. 2;
and that origin is further supported by the additional fact that the
Christian names used are quite Norman, and have in no case an
Anglo-Saxon character. Although admittedly this pedigree is largely
conjectural, it will be seen by it how firmly the line of descent was
established through and in one locality,—that surrounding the towns
of Mellis, Eye, and Thetford. This pedigree must be left to tell its
own tale without more lengthened remark upon it on this occasion.

Varied Forms of the Name.

I have written very fully on this subject in *The Antiquary* of
February, March, and September, 1886, and to my papers therein

appearing the reader must be referred for the full justification of my acceptance of the many forms appearing on pedigree No. 2, the only one of those published with this part in which the curious spellings met with have been maintained. The forms under which the name may be recognised are almost endless, and it would require more space than can be devoted to the subject here to give proof of their identity with Folkard. But since the papers above referred to were written by me, it has been my habit to preserve varieties of forms in which I have myself been addressed, and the following list is given of these. All bearing the name will have experienced the difficulty of obtaining correct nomenclature from those to whom it is strange; and they will therefore scarcely think this list an extraordinary one, or that it does not strongly justify my assigning kinship to the many cases shown on Pedigree 2.

Falcard (3 *instances*).	Folkraw.
Falkard (2 *instances*).	Foltyard.
Falkand.	Folward.
Falkhard.	Forkard.
Fallcard.	Fottrell.
Faukner.	Foukard.
Faulkin.	Foukeid.
Faulkland.	Foukhend.
Foijdard.	Foulchard.
Folnard.	Foulkard (4 *instances*).
Folcard.	Foulkhard (4 *instances*).
Folchard.	Foulkhend.
Fulckard (5 *instances*).	Fouzard.
Folkand (2 *instances*).	Fulcar (3 *instances*).
Folkarde.	Fulcard.
Folkaard.	Fulkherd.
Folkark.	Johnkard.
Folkart.	Okard.
Folkaut.	Polkatt.
Folkerd.	Rolkan.
Folkford.	Tolkard.
Folkhard.	Volkard.
Folkland.	Yolkard.

In further justification of the acceptance given by me to many varied forms of the name met with, it seems desirable to give the following extract from my paper on " The Multiplication of Surnames," which appeared in *The Antiquary* of September, 1886 :—

" The writer has therefore selected a few out of the many instances where the name of Folkward has thus received adoption as the name of a locality, and the citation of the different forms met with in ancient documents, and so applied, will form strong warranty for his assumption of similar variations in its use as a personal appellative.

" Out of 144 instances in his present possession wherein the personal name has so been the foundation of those of towns in various countries, four are quoted for the fulfilment of this object, though the two last have been associated, it having been found impossible to distinguish as to which of them the corruptions apply. The modern name of the town is that first given, and the older ones are arranged as they appear to vary in succession from the earliest to the latest form, some attempt at parallelism also being maintained :

FOCKERBY (Yorkshire).	FOGGATHORP (Yorkshire).	FAULQUEMONT AND FOUCARMONT (France).
Folkwardby.	Fulkwarethorpe.	Folcardi-Monti.
Folquardby.	Folkarthorp.	Fulcaudus-Montensis.
Folkardby.	Folkerthorp.	Fokardimonte.
Folkerdby.	Folkersthorp.	Fulcardemont.
Folkerby.	Fokkerthorp.	Folcarmunt.
Fokardby.	Fowkersthorpe.	Frocardi Monte.
Fokerdby.	—	Francquemont.
Foquerby.	—	Montes Fouquerannus.
Fookerby.	—	Foukarmount.
Fokerby.	Fokerthorp.	—
Fockerby.	—	—
Fawkeby.	—	Faukemont.
Folkesby.	Folkethorpe.	Falkemont.
Fulcherby.	Fulcathorpe.	Fulcharmunt.
Felcardby.	Follethorpe.	Facarmund.
Falgardeby.	Fulthorp.	Falco-Monte.
Fougerby.	Foggerthorpe.	Falconis Mons.
Folgnarby.	Fogathorp.	Falcmount.
Folnaiby.	—	Falkenstein.
Foceby.	—	Fontardi Monte.

It may also be mentioned that, from very early times, both Folco and Fulcher have been the recognised equivalents of Folkard. As one proof out of hundreds as to this, can be cited the fact that in the case of one important index all the Folcards given in it proved to be Folcos in the body of the work. Similarly, in Bohn's edition of Ordericus Vitalis, Abbot Folcard of Thorney is throughout referred to as " Fulcher," and not by the name, " Folcard," signed by that abbot to all his many literary works. Lord John Hervey, in his translation of the Domesday

Book of Suffolk, invariably translates "Fulchered" and "Fulkered" as Folkard, and in a law suit to which Benjamin Folkard of Beccles was a party, in 1650, his name is occasionally spelt as "Folkered" and "Folkerd."

It should be borne in mind that the ancient ch was the equivalent to the modern k, which only came into use about the fourteenth century, and was an adaptation of the old method of writing the c across the h, in the earlier times, to express a hard pronunciation. Thus Folchard should be read as Folkard, and Fulcher, Fulchar, Folcher, and Folchar, as Fulker, Fulkar, Folker, and Folkar.

But were an attempt made to give all the proofs in my possession of the identities, it would be an endless task, and what has been written above on this subject must suffice. Coupled with the alternative names given to the same individual, appearing on Pedigree 2, sufficient evidence will, it is believed, have been afforded. "No reliance," as is said in Cussad's work on Heraldry, "can be placed on the orthography of proper names, either of persons or places," in the earlier times.

Arms of the Family.

Mr. Tucker showed me a sketch of these, when the visit before referred to was made, of a date long antecedent to the institution of the College of Arms by Richard II., which, among its many records, has no reference to their grant. It is certain, therefore, that they were borne by "prescriptive right;" as, also, that at the date of the ancient sketch referred to being made, the family occupied a position of importance in Suffolk. I have suggested, on Pedigree No. 1, on which a drawing of the arms is given, that they may have been granted by Edward III. to Walter Folcard, of Eye, who was, in Edward's reign, commissioner for the estates of that king's mother situate in Suffolk. This, however, is mere conjecture, and it is possible, if any reliance may be placed on the assignment of arms on the ancient Roll of Battle Abbey, that they were borne at the battle of Hastings by Fauecourt (*alias* Folcard), who is placed contemporaneously, and as an alternative possible ancestor of the family, alongside of Abbot Folcard on Pedigree No. 2. The absence of the adoption of any crest by any branch of the family is significant of the great antiquity of the arms borne by it. All the armorials of Suffolk contain mention of them, and the most ancient of these refers to their appearing on the windows of Buxhall Church, Suffolk.

The Position of the Family in the County.

Pedigree No. 2 affords many indications that in the earlier times its members occupied important official posts. Its decadence into the ranks of the yeomanry of the county would seem to have commenced early in the 15th century, for none of the Herald's visitations contain reference to it, though about the middle of that century wealth began to be accumulated by some of its members, and the designation of " Armiger " appears on their tombs and brasses. But in all the instances of this accumulation known to me, the lines which possessed wealth eventually became extinct by failure of male heirs, and their property descended to the families into which the females had married. A special instance of this is noticeable in the case of the Sparham line (Pedigree No. 3), most of the lands and manors possessed by it passing into the possession of the ancestors of the present Earl of Leicester, and being still the property of his family.

Limit of space forbids my entering, in this Part No. 1 of the monograph, more fully into details. In subsequent parts it may be hoped that full references may be made to the individuals named in the four pedigrees this first one contains. It is regretable that opportunity has not yet occurred for me to search the registry at Bury for the wills it contains. All the other depositories of such documents, viz., those at Somerset House, Norwich, and Ipswich, have been fully examined. Very many of the Parish Registers of the county also remain unsearched as yet ; specially among which may be named those of Mendlesham, East Bergholt, Debenham, and Ratlesden. Where it has been possible for me to extract from these, they afforded reason for thinking that many branches of the family as yet undealt with may be fully traced out.

ARTHUR FOLKARD, M. Inst. C. E.
Ceylon Civil Service (Retired).

January 27th, 1890.

of the great antiquity of the arms borne by it.   All the armorials of Suffolk contain mention of them, and the most ancient of these refers to their appearing on the windows of Buxhall Church, Suffolk.

The Position of the Family in the County.

Pedigree No. 2 affords many indications that in the earlier times its members occupied important official posts.   Its decadence into the ranks of the yeomanry of the county would seem to have commenced early in the 15th century, for none of the Herald's visitations contain reference to it, though about the middle of that century wealth began to be accumulated by some of its members, and the designation of " Armiger " appears on their tombs and brasses.   But in all the instances of this accumulation known to me, the lines which possessed wealth eventually became extinct by failure of male heirs, and their property descended to the families into which the females had married. A special instance of this is noticeable in the case of the Sparham line (Pedigree No. 3), most of the lands and manors possessed by it passing into the possession of the ancestors of the present Earl of Leicester, and being still the property of his family.

Limit of space forbids my entering, in this Part No. 1 of the monograph, more fully into details.   In subsequent parts it may be hoped that full references may be made to the individuals named in the four pedigrees this first one contains.   It is regretable that opportunity has not yet occurred for me to search the registry at Bury for the wills it contains.   All the other depositories of such documents, viz., those at Somerset House, Norwich, and Ipswich, have been fully examined. Very many of the Parish Registers of the county also remain unsearched as yet ; specially among which may be named those of Mendlesham, East Bergholt, Debenham, and Ratlesden.   Where it has been possible for me to extract from these, they afforded reason for thinking that many branches of the family as yet undealt with may be fully traced out.

ARTHUR FOLKARD, M. Inst. C. E.
Ceylon Civil Service (Retired).

January 27th, 1890.

Wills of the Folkard Family.

Wills of the Folkard Family.

[1] 1416.

JOHN FFOKE (FFOKER), Rector of Frammingham Pigott, Norfolk, 1416. To be buried in chancel of the church of that place. To repair of chancel 40 pence, and for repair of church 40 pence. To leper hospital at Norwich 6 pence. Exors. Andrew Syre, Sibill his mother, and Richard his brother. Proved at Norwich, 1 July 1416.

(Exc. Orig. Lat.)   *Norw. Consis. Lib. Heringe 1416—27. Fo. 2.*

[2] 1451.

RICHARD FFOLKARD, Rector of the mediety of Pakefield, Suffolk, "*per parte Australi*," dioc. Norw., 9 November 1451. To be buried in Pakefield church. Legacies to that parish. To Henry Colayn "*cognato mea*" of Oxoma 40s, and remits a debt due by him. To John, son of Henry Colayne "*cognato mei*" 40s. To poor of Blyburgh one cuplyn *(?)* of silver. To Roger S—pwell and his wife six silver spoons, "*lapides*", and a horse. To Robert Stolys, perpetual vicar of Reydon, and to parishes of Carlton and Estonband certain robes and a cope of violett. To "Dominus" John Grigsbyfy *(?)* "three best togas of mine with a cope and 10s in silver", and condones a debt due by him. To John Hert, perpetual vicar of Cratfield, four of his togas and a capias. To "Dominus" Robert Elye, rector of Owleton, a toga of medley and a capias. Other robes to different clergy. To poor of Blythburgh 6s 8d. Several small legacies to individuals. All the rest of his goods to his exor. for charitable uses in Great Yarmouth. Carleton Colville named in a legacy. No relatives named. John Spyrlyng, perpetual vicar of Kessingland, exor. Proved at Norw., 18 Novr., 1451.

(Exc. Orig. Lat.)   *Norw. Consis. Aleyn 1448—55. Fo. 93.*

3

JOHN FFOLKYS (FFOLKEREDE) of Eye, Suff., 9 April 1456. To be buried in the church of St. Peter and St. Paul at Eye. To the High Altar therein 3s 4d. For expenses of burial 23s 3d. For the repair of the said church 20s. To the Guild of St. Peter the Apostle 6s 8d. No legacies to individuals. Residue of property to be sold and applied " for good of my soul". John Teylzor (? Taylor) exor. Proved at Eye, 3 July 1456.

Norw. Consis. Neve. 1456—7. Fo. 12.

————o————

[4]	1461.

THOMAS FFOLCARD of Heigham, Norf. (Rector of that parish.) To be buried in the chancel of the church of that place. For the reparation of the church 20s 8d, and to the Mendicant Friars of Norwich 4 pence. Other charitable legacies. To John ffolcard, his brother, 6s 8d, and one part of his best linen. To the Prior of the cathedral church at Norwich and his community, for his soul, 6s 8d. To Galfryd Smyth one part of his linen. A third part to Margaret, wife of Thos. Barthelmy. To the church at Sparham, Norf., 20 pence. To the High Altar at Norwich 12 pence. Several other legacies to churches in Norwich. Robert Sharyngton, chaplain, and William Amyott, chaplain, exors. Dated 8 Sept., 1461. Proved at Norwich " the penultimate " day of Sept., 1461.

(*Exc. Orig. Lat.*)	*Norw. Consis. Brosiard 1454—65. Fo. 252.*

————o————

[5]	: 1463.

JOHN FFOLKARD, " Citizen and Alderman of Norwich," 20th September 1463. To be buried in the parish church of St. Mary Parva in Norwich. To the High Altar of that church 40s ; to that of St. Trinity, Norwich, 3s 4d. Other legacies to various churches in the same city for the souls of himself and Beatrice his wife. Legacies to the Mendicant Friars and Celibate Sisters of Norwich, and to the Celibate Monks at Carhowe. To Margerie his daughter, nun at Carhowe, 40s. To Alice Supatus (?) three silver spoons and 3s 4d. To John Martyn, his nephew, 6s 8d. To Johan ffolkarde of Crosthweyte 3s 4d. To Alice Geyste, her sister, 6s 8d, with a mattrass and bolster, coverlets, platters, dishes, &c., and three silver spoons. To Margaret Wynce, sister of aforesaid Alice, 3s 4d. To Johan, daughter of John his son, 6s 8d. To Galfryd. Smyth, his servant, certain bedding, plates and dishes, and 10s in money. Further legacies to churches in Norwich and Crosthweyte. To the churches of Sparham, Attelbrigge, and Swenyngton, torches. Rest of property to be realized by executors, who are Roger Best, clerk, and John and William ffolkard, citizens of Norwich, drapers, his sons. To Roger Best for his pains 20s. Witnesses to seal, Robert Ball, John Marshall, John Gooe (? Goose), Jolpe Baly, William Cottyng and William Wellys.

By codicil of same date he leaves all his lands in Attelbrigge, Norfolk,

4

to Thos. Elye, citizen and alderman in Norwich, in trust for charitable purposes for the souls of himself and Beatrice his wife. Also his lands in
Swenyngton for like purposes. To his sons John and William certain lands
and messuages in the latter place. Further legacies to Alice Geyste and
others. Proved at Norwich, 15th March 1464.

(Exc. Orig. Lat.) . . . *Norw. Consis. Brosiard 1454—65. Fo. 350.*

---o---

[6] 1469.

JOHN FFOLKARD of Sparham, Norf., 11 April 1469. To be buried in
the church at Sparham, to the High Altar of which 20d. All his goods
to Johne his wife. His exor., Will. Amyett, to pay all debts. Sealed at
Sparham the day above named. Proved at Norwich, 24 April, 1469.

Norw. Consis. Jekkys 1464—72. Fo. 134.

---o---

[7] 1470.

WILLIAM FFOLKARD of Bedfield, Suff., 4 May, 1470. To church of
Bedfield 6s and 20s. To Robert his son 50 marks *(?)*. To Margaret
his daughter 50 marks. To "Hariot" his daughter 50 marks. To William
"fforkard" his son, who exor., the rest of his goods. Proved at Fressyng-
field, 21 July, 1471.

Ips. Pro. 1458—77. Fo. 206.

---o---

[8] 1483.

SIMOND FFOLKARD of Gressynhale, Norf., 1 April, 1483. To be buried in churchyard at Gressynhale. To the High Altar of the church
there 8 pence. To the repair of the bell of that church 6 pence. Legacies
to sundry guilds. To the repair of the church at Weybred 26s 8d. To his
wife Juliane, for the execution of these legacies, all his moveables. To Symond Bennett, his servant, in money and stuff 40s. His "place and all the
land thereto longing" to be sold, and divided between "me *(? him)* and my
wief, on peny and she anothyr." Wife sole executrix. (This will termi-
nates in Latin, though the main body of it is in English—a rare example.)
Proved at Hitcham by the relict, 25 September, 1484.

Norw. Arch. 1469—1503. Fo. 78.

---o---

[9] 1484.

MARGARET FFOKER (FFOLKARD) formerly wife of Roger ffoker,
of ffolsham, Norf., 16 March, 1484. To be buried at ffolsham. To
the High Altar of the church there 20 pence, and to its chaplain 12 pence.

5

Many charitable legacies, and others to religious guilds, including land called "Porkelyte." .To Agnes, daughter of William her son, a best "*zona*" and one pair of sheets. To Agnes her daughter 20s. To Cecilie her daughter 20s. To Margaret, Thomas, Robert, George and Alice Barker ; Alice, Thomas junior, John,. Henry and Richard ffox, 3s 4d each. To Agnes Edward's daughter, 3s 4d. To Margaret Horne 6s 8d, and a bedstead colored green, with blankets and sheets. To John Horne, Margaret Mayer and Agnes Edwards, 3s 4d each. To John and Nicholas Warne and William Allys, 12 pence each. To Nicholas Horne and Cecilie his wife, 6 "*papsides*"(?) of pewter and a candlestick. To Agnes ffoker 1 ....(*illegible*). To Margaret Horne 1 long coffer. To Cecilie.Horne, "my daughter" 1 "*sprowse clyste.*" Residue of goods to Thomas ffox and Robert Beaker (? *Barker*), who are exors. Nicholas Horne "to have 4s 4d. Proved at Baldeswell "last day of March 1489" by Thomas and Robert the exors.

(*Exc. Orig. Lat.*)   *Norw. Arch. 1469—1503. Fo. 153.*

---

[10]   1500.

THOMAS FFOLKARD of Horham, Suff., 29 August, 1500. To be buried in churchyard of Horham. "To the High Altar of said church for tithes negligently witholden, or not truly payed" 3s 4d. To Alice his wife all goods moveable, cattle, and stuffs of household. · His tenement in Horham, with all his lands.there, and his lands in Corton, Hoxne, and Denham, to his wife for life. After her decease the said tenement, with the "close lying by it, with the meadow and the close called Holton" unto,Thomas his son. To John his son, after his mother's decease, his close called the Long Close in Denham and Hoxne, and his close called Cullyng in Horham. Provided his said sons found a priest of good fame,to pray for his and his wife's souls. The priest to have a salary of 8 marks. Residue to exors., Alice his wife and sons Thomas and John. Proved 26 April, 1503. (*Date very illegible and uncertain.*)

Ipsw. Pro. 1501—6. Fo. 81.

---

[11]   1503.

PHILLIP FFOLPE (FFOLPER, FFOLPARD, FFOLKARD,) of Comeston, Norf., 23 July, 1503. To the High Altar of Comeston "a cowe bullock of three yeres." To Margery his wife "two kyne of the best." To Petyr and John his sons a cow each. His sheep evenly between his wife and two sons. Some sheep to William his son. To his wife, residue of all property and "a chamber to dwell in in my place." Also some land for life. A tenement called Durrante to his son.Petyr. Residue of land to his wife and son Petyr to pay his debts.—His wife and Thomas Nobes (? *Nokes*) of Castoris exors. Proved at Castoris, 19 October, 1503.

Norw. Arch. 1469—1503. Fo. 430.

6

[12]   1512.

JOHN FFOLCARD of Crosthweyt "by Norwich, "Norf., 10 Nov., 1512. To be buried in churchyard of "Crostwyk aforeseid." To High Altar there 6s 8d, and 20s to paint the "porke." (*i.e. porch*) of the church. To Margaret his daughter 7 acres of land in Horsted for ever and 40s in money. To Alys his wife all his other lands and tenements in "Crostwike" and other towns adjacent for ever. All other lands to be sold to make an estate for his said wife, and all other goods and debts to her. She and Edward Empson exors. The last to have 20s for his labour. Proved at Norwich by exors., 16 August, 1513.

Norw. Consis. Johnson 1510—13.   Fo. 233.

———o———

[13]   . 1513.

WYLLIM FFOLKARD of Bedfield, Suff., 14 December 1513. To be buried in churchyard of Bedfield. To the High Altar there for tithes forgotten 3s 4d. To Thomas his son all his houses and land, "free and bond" except Loders and Bernarde "which I will Robert to have, and he to bere the charge of my buryall." Son Thomas to pay £10 8s yearly to Juliane, testator's wife. "And after her decease I will Thomas shall pay 40.marks for peynting of ye Trinitye and masses for her soul.". To Nicholas his son 8 marks, 13s 8d yearly until fully paid. A priest to sing for his soul at Bedfield. To Agnes his daughter 5 marks after death of wife.—To the latter the house he lived in, with "a kowe and a pyggt and 2 loade of woodte caryed of the coste of my son Thomas." Wife to make her will "of the half yer next folowing here,doth " (*!*) To Worlyngworth Gylde 3s 4d. To each one of his belchildren (*i.e. grandchildren*) 6s 8d after death of wife. All difficulties as to will to be adjusted by Robert Denyo of Bedfyld and John Brooke of Monk Soham. Wife to have all moveables of household. Exors. to dispose of goods not specifically left. They are Nicholas and Robert his sons. The former to have £10 8s for his labour.—Witnessed by John Cooke, parson of Monke Soham, Alice Denny and Elizeabeth Brown, with others. Proved at Hressyngfield 6 Feby., 1513. (*Note—Apparent error in date from use of old style.*)

Ips. Pro. 1513—13. No. 34.

———o———

[14]   1514.

ALIS FFOLCARDE of Crostwyk "next Norwich," Norf., Widow. To be buried in churchyard there "by John folcarde late my husbond." To High Altar there 3s 4d, and 13s 4d "to buy an ornament for seid church." To Edward Empson, her son-in-law, her tenement called Caltis, "with all my fre londe and copye londe lying in Crostwyk, Horsted, Stannyngale and Spykworth for ever." He residuary legatee and sole exor., 8 October, 1514.—Proved at Norwich, 8 Nov., 15-4 (*Doubtless 1514.*)

Norw. Consis. Spurlinge 1514—16.   Fo. 34.

7

[15] 1533.

JOHN FFOLKARDE of Horham, Suff., "the elder," 30 April 1533. To be buried in the churchyard of Our Lady in Horham "before the porch door at the south side of the church." To the High Altar for tithes forgotten 12 pence. To the church of Horham 6s 8d. To the Anstin Friars, 20s to pray for his soul and all his friends' souls. A secular priest to do the same at Horham for half a year. To William his son the tenement the testator dwelt in, with all the land thereto belonging for life, he paying to exors. 20s yearly as a condition until will be fulfilled. After William's decease, the son of the said William, "my godson, shall have it." Should he decease without heirs, the property to go to his next eldest brother, or to the next heirs of him "that bears the name of ffolkard." If none of that name survive, all to go to church of Horham to pray for testator's soul. To each of his sons' children (not named) 6s 8d. To the children of his daughter Alice Sheppard 3s 4d each. To his godson John ffolkard "my frute garden lying in the wayside." Residue at disposition of exors. Appoints as his attornies William Brown of Warlingworth and John Gyrlyng of Horham. To each for their trouble, 6s 8d, besides all their costs. Witnessed by Roger Veci of Eye, Thomas ffermor, John Heyward and John Nycoll. Proved at Horham 3 November, 1533.

Ipsw. Pro. 1531—34. Fo. 131.

---o---

[16] 1535.

JOHN FFOLCHER (FFOLCHERD) of Reydon, near Diss, Norf., 24 May, 1535. To be buried at Reydon. Several legacies to churches. To Jone his wife, tenement and lands in Reydon for life, and at her decease to Reynold his son and Alis his daughter equally. To Nycholas his son 5 marks, 2 milch kyne and some land. His wife sole ext⁸. Proved at Norwich, 26 July 1535.

Norw: Consis. Attmer 1528—46. Fo. 247.

---o---

[17] 1539.

ROBERT FFOLKERD (FFOLKARD) of Monk Soham, Suff., "husbondman." 18 August 1539. To be buried in churchyard at Monk Soham. To the High Altar there for tythes negligently forgotten 2s, and 6s 8d "to be bestowed and layde in the waye leading from the house of the same Robert which he hath in fermie of Wyllyam Revett called Roggys unto Bedfield Crosse to be doon immediately after my decease." Similar legacy for the way between Ramneys Lane at Bedfield "Lyttyll grene to be doon Lykwyse immediately after my decease." To Johan his wife tenement and land called Ledders and Barnards, with all his other land in Bedfield for her life, provided she "kepe herself sole and unmarryd." If she married, to leave the land and have £20. At her death, or before if remarried, ex⁰ʳˢ. to sell the property, and the money to be parted equally between his seven daughters Agnes, Alice, Margarett, Johan, Ann, Elizabeth, and Margerye.

8

If any die before marriage, her share equally to other sisters. If all so die, the land not to be sold but to go to next of kin. To Alice, his eldest daughter, 5 marks at marriage, and a similar legacy to the other daughters, born in order above given. To wife all household stuff "as Brasse, pewter, lyning, mullyn and beddyng for life." At her decease, equally among his children. "To Margery my daughter my bed that I lye in " after wife's death. To his wife 12 milch kyne. To daughter Anne 2 kyne, daughter Margery 2 kyne, daughter Elizabeth 2 kyne, daughter Johan 3 heifers. Residue to ex^ors., who are Robert ffolkard of Debenham and Robert Romsey of Bedfield. Witnessed by Thomas ffolkerd the elder, Myles Kerryche of Bedfield, Richard Mayhewe, and John Mayhewe the younger. Proved at Horham before William Talmach, 1 September 1539.

Ipsw. Pro. 1538—43. Fo. 174.

———o———

[18] **1540.**

JOHN FFOLKARDE of Corton, Suff., Yeoman. 14 January 1540. To be buried in churchyard of St. Bartholomew's, Corton. To the High Altar there for tithes forgotten 3s 4d. In alms to poor folk in towns next adjoining Corton 5 marks. To each of his godchildren 4 pence, If his son Richard die before his mother without lawful male heirs "I will that my place, tenement, londes, pastures, medowe &c. in Corton or elsewhere which I lately purchased be sold, and the money disposed in almesse and merytoryous deedes for the helthe of my soule." To Anne his wife all other goods and chattels for life, " one halfe freely and the other halfe on her decease between my children Richard and Anne." Ex^ors, Sir John Jerningham, Richard ffolkard his son, and Miles Wynston of Blundestone. Signed in the presence of Sir Leonard Askewe, parson of Bradwell, William Baldwyn, William Jermye and Robert fforrows. Proved at Beccles 23 January 1541.

Norw. Consis. Beales 1555. Fo. 4., and Ipsw. Pro. 1541—43. Fo. 155.

———o———

[19] **1543:**

THOMAS FFOLKARD of Bedffylde, Suff., 16 January 1543. To be buried in churchyard of Bedfield. To High Altar there for tithes negligently forgotten 7s. " Alyce my wife to have all and singular my tenements and land whatso ere they be from ye daye of my deathe unto the ffeaste of Sent Michaell the Archaungell next after my decease and so from the said feaste one hoole yeare complete nexte and ymmedyatelye folowynge." To Thomas his son all his lauds and tenements in Bedfyld and Soham or "els where " for ever on wife's decease. " Notwithstanding I wyll that my said wyf shall have terme of her lyf naturallo a yearly poncion of 40s and also her dwellinge in my newe house." She also to have pasture for " 2 milch keen with summer meate and wynter meate and free keepyne of one swyne and fyve bennes." To wife 4 of the best milch kyne and two " calffs," with all moveables and implements of household stuff. His son Thomas to provide yearly for his mother's use 5 loads of " able fyerwoode." To Robert

· 9

his son £10, and to John, William, James, Thomas, and Agnes, children of
the said Robert, to each of them 20s at 16 years of age. To William his
son £10. To Anne his daughter £4, on marriage 20s, and the other £3 on
the death of his wife. To Elizeabeth his daughter £4 on similar terms.
To Margaret Candler one cow and a heifer of a year old. To Anne his daughter a cow, and to Elizeabeth his daughter one cow and calff. To Thomas
Drane, his godson, 6s 8d at 20 years of age. To each of his godchildren 13
ponce. Nicholas Drane of Tattington named. Residue of goods to wife A-
lyce. She sole ext⁣ˣ. Witnessed by Robert and John Dennye, Nicholas Drane,
William Lawnson, Richard Mayhewe, Robert Hervye and others. Proved
6 February 1549 at Bedfield.

Ipsw. Pro. 1544—50. Fo. 515.

————o————

[20] . 1550.

NICHOLAS FFOLCARDE of Monke Soham, Suff., 21 January 1550. To
the poor of Monk Soham 12 pence. To Juliane his daughter £13
"which Robert my son should pay as it do appear in some certain obligations." To John his son "my fether bedde with the boulstir." To son Robert and daughter Juliane all household stuff, to be equally divided. To
Edmonde his son his tenement in Monk Soham called Wyllferowyoos for
ever. To Robert his son his saddle. To his 4 children all his cattle equally.
Residue to John his son and Juliane his daughter, who are exᵒʳˢ. Witnessed by William Harrison, George Jeferye, Walter Gamage and John Bocher.

Ipsw. Pro. 1550—54. Fo. 21.

————o————

[21] 1552.

THOMAS FOLKARDE the elder of Horham, Suff., 11 November 1552.
To be buried in the churchyard at Horham. To the town curate for
tithes forgotten 12s. To Margaret his wife his tenement, houses, and lands
in Horham till Thomas his son be 21. She to find all necessaries "and
bring my children honestlye uppe." Thomas to have the property at 21.
Powter, easements and other necessaries to wife "for hor use and nedeful
hospitalitye." Son Thomas to pay wife 8s 4d a year. She to have to farm
all his lands and pastures called Holton lying in Hoxne until his son John
be 21. His wife to pay to his four daughters, Johan, Anne, Jane, and Alice,
5 marks each at marriage. Son John to have the land called Holton at 21,
but to pay 26s 8d yearly to wife. Son Thomas to give wife "kepe of a cowe
yerely with wynter meate and sumer meate" for life. If son Thomas dies
before 21, his legacy to go to son John. To Alice Cowper, testator's daughter, £3, and her three sons to succeed. All moveables and household stuff
to wife, who is extˣ with John Gyrling Junior of Horham. 8s to the latter
for his labor. Allusion made to Thomas ffolcarde and William ffolcarde
surrendering lands held of several manors. Witnessed by Thomas Kent &
John Gyrlinge 23 December 1552. Proved at Horham, 14 February 1557.
(*This year very illegible.*)

Ipsw. Pro. 1550—54. Fo. 439.

ROBERT FFOLKER (FFOLKARD) of Thetford, Norf., 6 August 1555. To be buried in St. Peters', Thetford. To High Altar there 12 pence. To "Nicholas ffolker my sone féther bed complight" at marriage. Similar bequests to his sons William and Richard. Residue to exors., who are Elizeabeth his wife and John his son. Proved at Thetford by the exors 12 December 1555.

Norw. Arch. 1553—6. Fo. 389.

THOMAS FFOLKARDE of Bedfield, Suff., husbandman., 21 August 1555. Tenement he dwells in in Bedfield to Margaret his wife. She to bring up his children and to keep unmarried until Thomas, his eldest son, be 21. If she marry,·however, "she to depart clerely from my said tenement and lands and to have fower marks yerely in lieu of dowery." Exors then to bring up his children. Lands &c. to Thomas his son when 21. Lawrence his son to have £40. If both sons die, "my lands to William ffolkarde, the son of Robert ffolkarde my brother." The said William then to pay William "my brother" £20, and £15 to the other children of his father and £5 to the children of Nicholas Drane. To Thomas, the son of Robert ffolkarde "my brother," a legacy. Exors are Margaret, testator's wife, Robert ffolkard of Debnam and Robert Grimbell of Bedfilde. Proved 21 September 1565.

Cur. Ep. Norw. Wills 1565.

JOHAN FFOOKE (FFOKER, FFOLKER) of Sparham, Norf. Widow. 23 August 1555. "Healthy of body." To be buried in the Holy Sanctuary of Sparham. To the poor there 12 pence. To Elizeabeth Chandler her daughter "all that my mere edifice with seven and one half acres custumary land and 1 acre of bond land in Sparham for life." She to keep house in repair, and it to go at her death to Thomas Davenye, son of the said Elizeabeth. He also to have "my cottage in the garden" in Sparham, paying to Robert and Alys Davenye and John Chandler, children of Elizeabeth Chaundler "my daughter aforeseid," 7 marks. Some other legacies to these children, and residue to Thomas Davenye, who is exor. Robert Ryner of Sparham, Supervisor, with 3s 4d for his trouble. Proved at Bawdeswell 11 May 1558.

Norw. Arch. 1557—8. Fo. 246.

ANNE FFAWLKER (FFOLKARDE. *See Will of her husband, No. 18*) of Lowestoft, Suff., "widow, late wife of John ffawlker of Corton." 9 November 1557. To be buried in the churchyard of Lowestoft. To her son

Richard ffawlker 40s. To Margaret, wife of said Richard, 40s. To John
Wheller and Margery his wife 40s. To Robert Waters and Anne his wife
40s. To Anne Waters "one olde fether bedde." Legacies of clothing to
different persons. Her son Richard ffawlker and Robert Walters ex[ors].
Witnessed by Richard Warde, Harry Coke, Janot Parye, and Robert Barge.
Proved at Beccles 28 September 1558.

Ipsw. Pro. 1557—9. Fo. 448.

---

[26]·   1557.

A LEXANDER FFAWLKE (FFAWLKER) of Aldeburgh, Suff. 22
   November 1557. To be buried in churchyard at Aldeburgh. To the
poor there £3. To the poorhouse at Holiers £14. Many legacies to variously named persons. Johan his wife named. To Alexander Smith, "my
daughter's childe," tenements &c. in Friston. To his daughter Emma legacies of "nettes" &c. and a "shippe called 'The Thomas'." "Towards building the kye" (? quay) £6 13. 4. To John Fox and Emma his wife, and to
Elizeabeth Foxe, "my daughter's childe," certain legacies. "To Thomas
Baker, the lame creature I have kept" a bequest. Proved at Norwich, 4
March 1557 (old style.)

Norw. Consis. Jerves 1557—8. Fo. 18.

---

[27]   ·   ·1558.

R OBERT FFOLSER. (FFOWKER & FFOWLCER) of Fretton, Norf.
   20 October 1558. To Emma his wife £40. To Margaret his daughter
£20. A legacy to the children of Anne Whytham. To his grandchild Henry Sporle £5 at 20, he being the son of testator's daughter Margaret. To
John ffolser the elder of Yarmouth, and to his son of 13 years, John ffolser
junior, "to go to schule," to each of them 33s 4d. Residue to wife. She &
Nicholas Stanton ex[ors]. Legacies to poor. Henry Sporle witness. Proved 11 June 1561 by the ex[ors].

Norw. Consis. Bircham 1560—1. Fo. 62.

(NOTE.—This will is purposely given before 28, because of the illustration these 3 wills give of the corruption of name.)

---

[28]   1558.

J OHN FFOLARGE (FFOLAD) the elder, of Bramfield, Suff. 11. February 1558. To be buried in the churchyard of St. Andrews, Bramfield.
For tithes forgotten 12 pence. To Alice his wife his tenements in ....
and Bramfield for the bringing up of his children. At her death to John
his son. To Henry his son £5. To Bridget his daughter 40s. To Susan
his daughter 40s. Until these sums be paid his son John not "to enter into
my legacy." Kine to sons and daughters. Wife and son John ex[ors]. Witnesses Anthony Wilkinson (? Williamson: see Will No. 29) of Bramfield,
Thomas Cross (?), John Moylland and Thomas ffolarge. Proved at Horham 10 March 1558.

Ipsw. Pro. 1557—59. Fo. 629.

1 2

[29]   1558.

WILLIAM FFOLKERDE (FFOLCARD) of Bramfelde, Suff., "husbondman." 12 January 1558. To be buried in churchyard of St.
Andrew's, Bramfield. For tithes negligently forgotten 12 pence. To Katheryn his wife his moveable goods for life. At her death to be equally divided among his four daughters, xpian, Grace, Agnes, and Marye, if of lawful
age. If not, then Thomas Wright, his brother-in-law, to be guardian of the
said goods, and to see his children "honestlye and accordyng to their degree
brought uppe." To wife his tenement in Cransford, "with all londs, me-
dowes, pasture and fedinge belonging to the same," for life. At her death
his eldest son William to have them, on condition that he pays Erasmus his
brother £10. Both sons then under age, and Thomas Wright to be their
guardian if wife be dead. Residue to ex^{ors}., who are wife and Thomas
Wright. Lawrence Rede of Laxfield, "my brother-in-law," supervisor. He
to have 20 pence for his pains besides costs. Witnesses—Anthony Williamson, clerk, Vicar of Bramfield, and John Amerell of Bramfield. Proved at
Blythburgh, 2 June 1559, by Katherine, the relict.

Ipsw. Pro. 1559. Fo. 235.

---o---

[30]   1558.

JOHN FFOWKERD (FFOLKARD) of Winston, Suff. 26 January
1558. To John "ffowkered" his godson, son of Edmund ffowkerd of
Hashfelde, his house in Wynston and all the lands belonging to it at the age
of 21. To Margarett, testator's wife, 20 marks, provided she relinquish all
right or title to the houses in Wynston or elsewhere. She to leave the
house immediately on testator's death, and the 20 marks to be paid out of
the yearly "ferm" till the aforesaid John "ffowkered" be of age. To wife
all household stuff and 2 "neate" (cattle). To the poor 40s. Residue to
be parted between his brother Edmund and his brother Robert in even portions. Edmund ffowkerd of "hashfelde" and Lawrence Mayhewe of Great
Cretingham, ex^{ors}, to whom 13s 4d. Witnesses—William Goodfellow, Vicar of Brandeston, writer of the will, Robert Moklett and Nicholas Johnson.
Proved at Coddenham, 11 December 1559.

Ipsw. Pro. 1559—60. Fo. 437.

---o---

[31]   1564.

WILLIAM FOLKARD of Eye, Suff. 26 June 1564. To his son John
a meadow of seven acres, he to pay to testator's two daughters, Ales
Page and Margerye fryer, each £6 13. 4., and to the children of Isbell Harvy, another daughter of testator's, £4 when 21 or on marriage. Sums of
money to Margery his wife. Household goods to son and 2 daughters. His
tenement and lands at Horham named. Legacies to Agnes, wife of Anthony
barker, and to Amy Chappell, "my daur-in-lawe." His son John to pay £6

13

yearly to wife, "or she to have the third part of all my land." Wife ext[x].
Refers to debts that he and his son John owe for land in Nedeham, Norf.
Proved 11 April 1565 by ext[x].

Cur. Ep. Norw. Martyn. Fo. 108.

---

[32]   1566.

MERGAYE FOLCARDE of Eye, Suff., widow. 27 August 1566. To
Mary her daughter, wife of John Warde, a legacy, and her husband to
"assure her goiniature" (*i.e. jointure*.) To her daughter Amy, wife of Robert Chappell, and to her daughter Anne, wife of Anthony Barker, legacies.
They to bring up Anthonie Woknawgh, their nephew. Bequests to the children of her nephew Thomas Sherman. Also to nephews Richard, ffrancis,
Henrie, and William Sherman. To Agnes, wife of said Richard Sherman,
and to ffrancis her son, money bequests. To the sons and daughters of her
said daughters Amye and Anne, and of her late daughter, Jane Wolnawgh,
when 21, bequests. Her nephew Richard Sherman one of ex[ors]. No other
named.—Proved 18 October 1567 by oath of Richard Sherman, and secondly, 24 July 1567, by procuration of the other ex[ors].

Cur. Ep. Norw. Martyn. Fo. 284.

---

[33]   1567.

THOMAS FFOLCAR (FFOLCARDE) of Brome, Suff. 29 July 1567.
To be buried "in the Sanctuary where I shall depart." To Margerye
his wife, tenement called 'Males' and land in Brodyshe and Thorpe for life.
Afterwards to his son John. He to pay Agnes Hendrye "my daughter"
.... To John Hendrye, son of Robert Hendrye, a bequest. To
Henry ffolcar "my son" £8. To Thomas "my son" £8.—Proved 5 March
1572 by ex[or] Thomas ffolcar.

Cur. Ep. Norw. Consis. Brigge(?) Fo. 668b.

---

[34]   1572.

EDMUNDE FFOLCARDE of Ashfield, Suff. Yeoman. 8 February 1572.
To be buried in the churchyard at Ashfield. His two tenements in Debenham to John his son, conditional on his paying within 2 years to John
Symer of Newton £7. If John die without heirs, or before the £7 is paid,
the same to go to Edmunde ffolcarde "my grandchild and godson." To the
poor of Debenham 5 marks. To "Margaret harvye which I brought
uppe of a childe," 20s when 20 years old. To Katheryn Clarke, "my wife's
daughter" £10, to be paid to her by his son Robert within two years after
the death of "Elizeabeth my wife." Also to Katherine Clarke 2 milch neat
and 40s at the day of her marriage. To Jane Clerke "my wife's grandchild,"
daughter of Walter Clerk, 31s 8d, to be paid by testator's son Robert out of
money "in which he is bound to me after my wife's decease." To John
Clerke, ffrancis Clerke, Robert Clerke the elder, Robert Clerke the younger,

14

and Edward Clerk, the children of the said Walter, to each 13s 3d, to be paid by the aforesaid Robert ffolcarde after the death of testator's wife. "To Robert my sonne one cowe and my mydle brasse potte." To Katheryn Clerk, "my wife's daughter, my cupboard standing in the Hall." All other household stuff &c. to Elizeabeth his wife and John his son, to be equally divided. "And whereas the seid Elizeabeth my wife hath estate of all my land and tenements lying in Ashfield aforseid during her natural lief, if she shall be minded to demise and leave it, I will that Robert and John my sons shall have it, paying for it as anie other would do." His wife Elizcabeth and son John ex^{ors}.—Witnessed by John ffolkarde, Roberte ffolkarde senior, John Bonde, William ffene, and Symond Jefferie.—Proved at Cleidon 30 March 1573.

Ipsw. Pro. 1572—3. Fo. 249.

------o------

[35] 1580.

ROBERT FFOLKERDE (FFOLKARD) of Debenham, Suff. 13 September 1580. "Being aged and sumwhat trobled with divers diacases and sicknesses." To be buried in the churchyard of Debenham. To the poor of that place 40s. To Ambrose his son the house he dwelt in, with lands in Debenham. If Ambrose die before Richard his son, then the latter to have them. To Nicholas and Richard his sons £40 each. "Whereas my seid son Nicholas has heretofore been given to lead a wasteful life (spending such moneys as have come to hys hands very careslye and wastefullye and therefore somewhat doubted of me whether there shall be any amendment in him hereafter yea or no)" if it appeared to two impartial men that after receiving the first £20 of his legacy he had not done well with it, then the other £20 to be void. Residue to be equally divided between testator's three sons, Ambrose, Nicholas, and Richard. Thomas ffolkarde of Bedfield, and Richard, testator's son, ex^{ors}. To said Thomas 20s for his pains.—Proved at Norwich 11 October 1580 by the ex^{ors}.

Norw. Consis. Moyse 1581. Fo. 69.

------o------

[36] 1581.

THOMAS FFOLKARD of Horham, Suff. 28 February 1581. To be buried in the churchyard at Horham. To Anne his wife his lands and tenements for life, "to keep same in repair and bring up my children decently." Wife to pay to ffrances, William, Anne, Elizeabeth, and John, his children, £5 each when 21. To Thomas his son the full reversion at death of wife. She to pay to said Thomas 40s a year, beginning when he is 21. A post bed and bedding to ffrances his daughter, and similar bequests to his daughters Anne and Elizeabeth. Sundry other legacies to his children. His horse mill and stones, with his lands, to go with the tenement. Anne his wife and Gregory Rous his brother-in-law ex^{ors}, the latter to have 6s 8d. John Stannard, his father-in-law, supervisor of will.—Witnessed by William Mullin, John Park, and John Keene.—Proved at Laxfield 30 March 1592.

Ipsw. Pro. 1592—3. Fo. 59.

[37]   1599.

JOHN FFOLKARD of Horham, Suff. 2 June 1599.   To Edmund Genn
  and Ann, wife of the said Edmund, all his copyhold lands in Horham,
"sometime Jarningham's"; with a tenement and 4 acres 3 roods of pasture
"sometime Durkittle's."   To Margerie, testator's wife, his cattle, household
stuff, and all moveables.   " There is £100 due by Ann, now the wife of Edmund Genn, to be paid after my own and my wife's death, according to a
bond.   My ex^ors shall receive it, and pay it to the poorest of my kindred as
it shall be thought best."   Wife ext^x, and Thomas Moise and William Porte
(i.e. Porter) ex^ors,—Witnessed by Thomas Howlet and John Lellye.   Proved at Beccles 20 October 1600.

                                              Ipsw. Pro. 1600—1.   Fo. 184.

———o———

[38]   1612.

HENRY FFOLKARD of Carleton Colville, Suff., Potter.   28 January
  1612.   To Thomas his son his houses and lands in Beccles which testator purchased of Robert Spooner, and "now in the occupation of the said
Thomas ffolkard."   The latter to pay to Cicily, testator's wife, £5 a year,
"and she to have her dwelling in one room of the said houses during life."
If these conditions are failed of, the above property to go to wife.   To ffrances ffolkard, daughter of the said Thomas, £10 when 21.   To Robert, son of
Nicholas ffolkard, late of Carlton Colville, deceased, £10 when 21.   To Anne,
daughter of said Nicholas, £5 when 21.   To Elizabeth, " one other daughter of the said Nicholas," £5 when 21.   To Margaret Hayward, "the daughter of one John Hayward, late of Rushmere, £10 when 21"; and to Ann,
another daughter of the said John Hayward, £10 when 21.   To Robert, son
of Robert Gayford of Beccles, £5 when 21 ; and to Henry, another son of
the said Robert Gayford, £10 when 21.   To Martha Gayford, a daughter of
the said Robert Gayford, £10 when 21.   A post bedstead to the aforesaid
ffrances ffolkard.   Cows and other legacies to Gayfords.   Residue to testator's son Thomas, who is ex^or.—Witnessed by John Carson, Henry Parish,
and "me Robert Hornbye."—Proved at Beccles 5 March 1612.

                                              Ipsw. Pro. 1612.   Fo. 115.

———o———

[39]   1614.

HENRY FFOKER (FFOLKARD) the elder of Newton-Flotman, Norf.,
  husbandman.   22 April 1614.   " Being sick."   To be buried in churchyard of Newton-Flotman.   To Dorothie his wife all his tenements, houses,
and lands in that place for life.   The reversion of the same to John his eldest son " on condicion he payes unto my children such legacies as follows."
To his son Henry £5 after wife's death.   To Agnes, Frances, Johan, Lydia,
and Dorothie, his daughters, 40s apiece.   His wife sole ext^x.   She to bring
up his children and made residuary legatee for that purpose.—Proved at
Norwich 23 April 1614 by executrix.

                                              Norw. Arch. Liber 41.   1613.   Fo. 192.
                          16

JHON FFOKARD (*Heading of Will destroyed.   A Norf. will.*)   To Ann ffokarde his wife all chattels, goods &c. for life.   At her death to pass to Hester ffolkarde, "my only grandchild," for ever.   His wife sole ext[x]. John Woodward of Sylome, Suff., Yeoman, his brother-in-law, to be supervisor of his will.   Proved at Brockdish by Anne ffokard.   (*Date destroyed, but in 1617.*)

Norw. Arch. Orig. Wills 1617.   No. 2.

---o---

[41]   1618.

WILLIAM FFOULEKARD of Earl Soham, Cooper.   17 April 1618. To Alice his wife all lands and tenements in Earl Soham for life, with reversion to his son William.   Wife to have use and occupation of cattle & household stuff for life, and at her death the same to go to son William. To the last-named, all his bonds and ready money, "with all my timbre, planke, and bord."   Wife sole ext[x].—Mark of testator.—Witnessed by John ffacebrowne and William Stebbinge.—Proved at Soham 17 May 1618.

Ipsw. Pro. 1618.   Fo. 6.

---o---

[42]   1620.

JOHN FFOKER of Fakenham, Norf.   To Samuel Browne and John .... 22 stone of wool for the education and bringing up of William his son until 14 years old, and then the remainder to be for his use and benefit.   To Andrew his son a tenement called Blackbornes in Holt till 15 years old, and 2 loads of hay for his education.   Another tenement and residue of property to be divided among his children, Margaret, Katherine, Mary, Christopher, Andrew, William, and N(*icolas*) (? *Destroyed in orig.*) To John his son all his "shoppe tooles."   John Goods and Walter Cowell ex[ors].—Date destroyed.—Proved at Norwich 6 April 1620.

Norf. Arch. Orig. Wills 1620.   No. 8.

---o---

[43]   1623.

ALICE FFOLKARD of Earl Soham, Widow.   26 December 1623.   To Rose Wyard of Earl Soham, her goddaughter, 20s.   To John, son of Randolph Wyard, 20s.   To Alice Smith, her servant, £2.   To John, son of Humphry Wyard of Saxted, 20s.   To Elizeabeth "Wyot," daughter of Humphry Wyard of Saxted, 20s.   To ffynett "Wyett" of "fframlingham at the castel widdowe" 40s.   To John "Wyett," son of last-named, 40s.   To ffrancis "Wyett," another son. 20s, and to her daughter Mary "Wyett," 20s.   To "Soperhe" (? *Sophy*) Wyard and Edward Wyard of Wickham Market 20s each.   To Elizeabeth Dumfrey, wife of Lawrence Dumfrey of Framsden, 20s.   To Margaret, wife of Thomas Turner of Earl Soham, 10s. To Robert, son of John Drane of Earl Soham, 10s.   Many other legacies to

1 7

Jolleys, Smiths, more Wyards, Sparrowes, and Rumsey. To William ffolkard of Sweffling, "my son-in law," (? *stepson*) 50s. To the poor of Earl
Soham 20s. Clothing and bedding to Alice Smith her servant, and many
other legacies of the same character. Randolph Wyard and William ffare-
browne of Earl Soham ex⁰ʳˢ.—Witnessed by George Russla (? *Russell*), John
Wyett, ffrancis Woode, and Susan Cowpre.—Proved at Wickham 10 January 1627.

Ipsw. Pro. 1627—8. Fo. 78.

————o————

[44]   1624.

2⁸ JULY 1624. "A note of certain legacies due from JOHN FFOL-
KARD" (FFOKER. *See will of his father Henry ffoker of Newton-Flotman, No. 39.*) 1.—To "Francis" his sister a legacy of 55s. To Joane
ffolkard his sister a legacy of 55s. To Lidia his sister a legacy of 40s. To
Dorath(y) his sister a legacy of 40s. "Some is £9 10s." "Due to severall
pusons for manie severall debts as with the legacies aforeseid do amount to
£14 or thereabouts." "Noates how to draw the will of the seid John." To
pay the above legacies and debts all his lands and tenements in Newton to
be sold by Anne his wife within three years of his death with the assistance
of John Nichould, his brother-in-law. Overplus for maintenance of wife
and children. His wife to pay to John his son £6 when 21. To Anne his
daughter at 21 £5. Should his wife "prove to be with child," then the £5
legacy to his daughter Anne to be divided between the two children as they
attain 21 years. His wife to enter into a bond to John Nichould in £20 to
pay the children these legacies, and to her all goods and chattels whatsoever. His wife Anne sole ext*, and John Nichould to be supervisor. This
memorandum was proved as a will at Norwich 8 June 1625 by the oath of
Anne ffolkard, widow, the executrix.

Norw. Consis. Belward 1625. Fo. 97.

————o————

[45]   1626.

THOMAS FFOLKARD of Bedfield, Suff. 1626—Aged 74. To Francis
his son 16 acres of land called Bennitts, a pasture called Newhall Close,
5 acres of "molland" (? *moorland*) in Walgrave, 4 acres molland called
................., and other parcels of land. To 7 of the children of Edmund,
testator's son, "born at the time of my decease," 40s each. To 10 of the
children of Lawrence, testator's son, "being born at the time of my de-
cense," 40s each when 21. To 5 of the children of Anne "my daughter,
wife of Xtfer Clarke," 40s each when 21. To 4 of the children of Margery
"my daughter, wife of William Mitchell," 40s each at 21. £10 to testator's daughter Margaret. To 5 of the children of the "saide Margaret, the
wife of Lionel Russel," 40s each. To Thomas and Mary, children of Francis, testator's son, 40s each at 21. To Anne, daughter of Anthony, testator's
son, 40s at 21. Testator's son Francis to be bound to testator's son Antho-

18

ny for 200 marks for the payment of all legacies. The said Francis ffolkard to be ex^or.—Signed by Thomas ffolkard the testator, and proved 29 March 1627.

Norw. Consis. Orig. Wills. 1627.

———o———

[46]   1627.

ROBERT FFOLKARD of Sweffling, Suffolk, Yeoman : 8 June 1627. "Sick in body." To be buried at Sweffling. To his son William "a blacke cowe called Pilgarlike," a bedstead and other furniture. To his son John a black heifer and furniture. To his son Robert a cow and furniture. To "my son-in-law Graystone" a like bequest. To testator's daughter Mary some furniture. To his daughter Elizeabeth, furniture items and "the best gowne that was my wife's." His linen between his said daughters Mary & Elizeabeth. To his 3 sons, William, John, and Robert, £6, to be equally divided between them. To Robert and Briget Graystone, his grandchildren, 10s each at 16 years of age. To John ffolkard, his grandchild, 10s at a similar age. The residue of his monies between his 2 daughters Mary and Elizeabeth. His son William ffolkard and Robert Sawer to be ex^ors, and to have 13s 4d for their pains.—Proved at Norwich 6 Feby. 1627 by the ex^ors.

Norw. Consis. Orig. Wills. 1627.

———o———

[47]   1630.

THOMAS FFOLKER (indexed FFOLKARD) the elder, of Horning, Norf. Husbandman : 12 November, 6th Charles I. (1630.) To Katherine ffolker, widow, his daughter-in-law, all his goods and chattels and money ; but Elizeabeth his wife to have the use of them for her "naturel lyfe, soe that she make noe waste of them." The aforesaid Katherine ffolker to be ext^x. The marke of "Thomas ffolker ye elder."

Norw. Consis. Orig. Wills. 1630. No. 204.

———o———

[48]   1633.

JOHN FFOLKARD of Rattlesden, Suff., Yeoman : 10 April 1633. Very ill. To Elizeabeth ffolkard his mother "for her great love and extraordinary paines that she have taken with me in my long and tedious trobles," his lands, tenements, meadows, and pastures in Mendlesham. She ext^x. Sealed in the presence of Robert Muryell, Robert ffolkard, Dorothy Muryell, and ffrances ffolkard. Signed John ffolkard.—Proved at Norwich 2 October 1633 by Elizeabeth ffolkard the ext^x.

Norw. Consis. 1633. Fo. 346.

19

THOMAS FFOLKARD of Ashfield, Suff., Yeoman: 2 March 1636. To Thomas, his eldest son, "my lease of the farm wherein Susan Tuttell now dwelleth, and all that tenement in Ashfield and Thorpe on condition that he pay to Ann ffolkard his sister and to Richard ffolkard his brother the sum of £260, and to his brother John ffolkard £24, and £28 a twelve-month later, and £28 another twelvemonth on, and £20 in each twelve months." If Thomas leave no heirs, John his brother to have the house, lands &c. Should John die without heirs, then Richard his brother to succeed to the property. To Lidda, testator's daughter, £60, to be paid to her by Mary his wife when 22. To Elizeabeth Harsham, his grandchild, £10, also to be paid to her by wife when 21. All residue to wife, and she to bring up the children. Should she marry again she to give a bond to Thomas and John his sons for £60, and to Lidda his daughter and to Elizeabeth Hersham his grandaughter for the sum of £10. Wife and son Thomas ex^ors. No witnesses.—Signed Thomas ffolkard.—Proved at Ipswich, 5 May 1637.

Ipsw. Pro. 1635—7. Fo. 50.

THOMAS FFOLKARD of Horham, Suff., Yeoman: 21 January 1638. To Alice his wife all houses and lands whatsoever for her life if she remain a widow. Trustees appointed to sell the property after her decease. They to dispose of the money as follows, it being paid in the south porch of the parish church at Horham :— To John his son £100 : To Thomas ffolkard "my grandchild, son of Thomas my son late deceased, £60. If I surrender my copyhold of Occolte and Bromhall manors before my death the last legacy to be void, and in consideration of that I give to the aforesaid Thomas ffolkard the aforesaid house and lands holden of the manors of Occolt and Bromhall to him and his heirs for ever." To Elizeabeth, testator's daughter, £30. To William, Edward, Mary, and Ann ffolkard ; Giles, Elizeabeth, and Alice Barker, his grandchildren ; and to Ann ffolkard his daughter-in-law "to each one £10." Alice "my beloved wife" sole ext^x, and to her all moveables, chattels, household stuff &c.—Signed by Thomas ffolkard on all three sheets.—Witnessed by Richard Jerian, Jeffrey Cullum, and Guy Hayte (*i.e. Hayter*).—Proved at Stradbrook 28 September 1639.

Ipsw. Pro. 1638—9 & 40. Fo. 52.

WILLIAM FFOLKARD of Earl Soham, Suff., Yeoman: 28 July 1639. To William his son all his copyhold and customary lands, tenements, and hereditaments in Earl Soham. "Johan, my well beloved wife, to enjoy the use of the parlor where I now live in Earle Soham for her life." She to have all his freehold and other lands &c in Earl Soham and Cretingham. They to go to his son William at wife's death. To Elizeabeth, his eldest

THOMAS FFOLKARD of Ashfield, Suff., Yeoman : 2 March 1636. To Thomas, his eldest son, " my lease of the farm wherein Susan Tuttell now dwelleth, and all that tenement in Ashfield and Thorpe on condition that he pay to Ann ffolkard his sister and to Richard ffolkard his brother the sum of £260, and to his brother John ffolkard £24, and £28 a twelve-month later, and £28 another twelvemonth on, and £20 in each twelve months." If Thomas leave no heirs, John his brother to have the house, lands &c. Should John die without heirs, then Richard his brother to succeed to the property. To Lidda, testator's daughter, £60, to be paid to her by Mary his wife when 22. To Elizeabeth Harsham, his grandchild, £10, also to be paid to her by wife when 21. All residue to wife, and she to bring up the children. Should she marry again she to give a bond to Thomas and John his sons for £60, and to Lidda his daughter and to Elizeabeth Hersham his grandaughter for the sum of £10. Wife and son Thomas ex^{ors}. No witnesses.—Signed Thomas ffolkard.—Proved at Ipswich, 5 May 1637.

Ipsw. Pro. 1635—7. Fo. 50.

THOMAS FFOLKARD of Horham, Suff., Yeoman : 21 January 1638. To Alice his wife all houses and lands whatsoever for her life if she remain a widow. Trustees appointed to sell the property after her decease. They to dispose of the money as follows, it being paid in the south porch of the parish church at Horham :— To John his son £100 : To Thomas ffolkard " my grandchild, son of Thomas my son late deceased, £60. If I surrender my copyhold of Occolte and Bromhall manors before my death the last legacy to be void, and in consideration of that I give to the aforesaid Thomas ffolkard the aforesaid house and lands holden of the manors of Occolt and Bromhall to him and his heirs for ever." To Elizebeth, testator's daughter, £30. To William, Edward, Mary, and Ann ffolkard ; Giles, Elizeabeth, and Alice Barker, his grandchildren ; and to Ann ffolkard his daughter-in-law "to each one £10." Alice " my beloved wife " sole ext^z, and to her all moveables, chattels, household stuff &c.—Signed by Thomas ffolkard on all three sheets.—Witnessed by Richard Jerian, Jeffrey Cullum, and Guy Hayte (*i.e. Hayter*).—Proved at Stradbrook 28 September 1639.

Ipsw. Pro. 1638—9 & 40. Fo. 52.

WILLIAM FFOLKARD of Earl Soham, Suff., Yeoman: 28 July 1639. To William his son all his copyhold and customary lands, tenements, and hereditaments in Earl Soham. " Johan, my well beloved wife, to enjoy the use of the parlor where I now live in Earle Soham for her life." She to have all his freehold and other lands &c in Earl Soham and Cretingham. They to go to his son William at wife's death. To Elizeabeth, his eldest

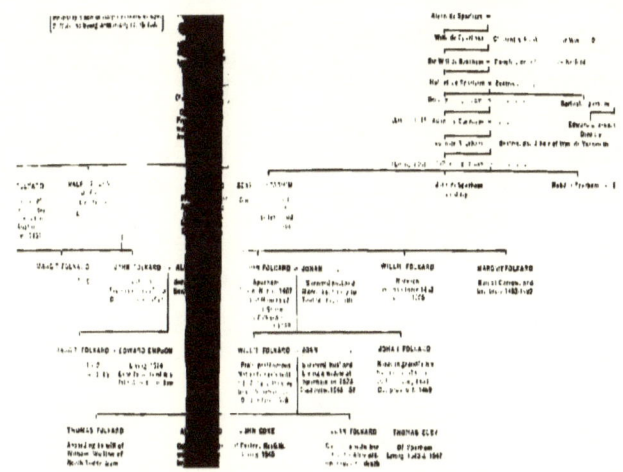

daughter, £30. To Brigitt his daughter £30. To Johan his daughter £30. These legacies to be paid by his son William after death of testator's wife. She and son William ex^ors. To them all cattle, household stuff, and goods and chattels, between them equally, except linen, all of which to wife.—Signed William ffolkard.—Witnessed by Bayliffe Atherton and Thomas Lingwood.—Proved at Ipswich 8 March 1644.

Ipsw. Pro. Orig. Wills. 1644—5—6. No. 42.

———o———

[52]   1640.

MARY FFOKER (*orig. will endorsed Marie ffokard*) of Kessynglond, Suff., Widow: 20 October 1640. "Unto Mary my daughter £10, whereof five pound was owing her from her father. Unto Margery my daughter the sum of five pound which my brother Thomas owned over me, which I will shall remayne in his hands for the good of her and her children, and that her husband may never getten it. All the rest to Klinghorn (?) my grandchyld, whom I make my sole executrix. To Thomas Passley (? *Paslew*) my brother's son, 20s. To Thomas Cripps, my syster's son, 20s."—Signed ffoker, her mark.—Witnessed by John Capps and Margaret Coan, her mark. Proved at Beccles 3 January 1640 (*old style*), and at Ipswich 23 January 1640.

Ipsw. Pro. Orig. Wills. 1638—40. No. 73.

———o———

[53]   1642.

FFRANCIS FFOLKARD of Bedfield, Suff., Yeoman: 20 October 1642. To Marie his wife all his copyhold lands whatsoever until his son William should be 21 "if she continue so long a widowe, and soe for long life, allowing the said William competent maintenance." All these lands to go to his son William when 21, or at his mother's death or remarriage. "To Marie my wife the bedstead in my parlor as it now standeth full furnished, a joyned chest with linen in it, and alle my other lynnen whatsoever, my litle table in the parlour, all my silver spoones, All my brasse and pewtre except my biggest brasse potte which I give untoe my sone William" with other household items. To his son William sundry furniture, his horse mill, "my long ladder, my cheese press &c., and all my bookes except my great bible, And all my Armour." To Marie and Anne his daughters all the rest of his goods, monies, debts, chattels and household stuff whatsoever not previously bequeathed, in equal shares. If either of them die before 21 the survivor to possess her sister's share. His said two daughters to be executors of the will.—Witnessed by William bacon and John Mayhewe.—Proved 14 February 1647 (*last figure very illegible*).

Ipsw. Pro. Orig. Wills 1647—8—9. No. 121.

21

MARIE FFOLKARD of Bedfield, Suff., Widow: 18 February 1647 (*a nuncupative will.*) To William, her son, 5s. All the rest of her monies, goods and chattels, and household stuff whatever, to her two daughters Marie and Anne equally. They to be executors. Declared in the presence of John Casson, clerke, Henry fuller, and Margarett Howell, widow.—Proved 24 February 1649 by the oaths of Marie and Ann folkard the ex^ors.

Ipsw. Pro. Orig. Wills. 1647—9. No. 119.

---o---

[55]	1653.

ROWLAND FFAWKARD. "Memorandum— That on the cleaventh Day of March in the yeare of our Lord God One thousand six hundred and fifty three, Rowland ffawkard, of the Parish of Saint Paule in Covent Garden in the County of Middlesex, being sick and weake in bodye but of very good and perfect memorie, did make and declare his last Will and Testament nuncupative, or by word of mouth, as followeth or to the like effect. That is to say he being desireis to make his will and to dispose of his estate, he answereis that his Wife Anne ffawkard had bin a very honest and carefull woman, and therefore he did and would give all his estate unto her and would give nothing from her, only he desires his said Wife to be carefull to bring upp his children in the feare of God, and if the Lord should blesse her with anything, that she would dispose thereof unto them as they should deserve. And the words therein by him spoken he declared with an inteut that they should stand for and bee his last Will and Testament in the presence and hearing of credible witnesses. Mary Harper her marke, Dorothy Appellger^tb."

"The Twelveth day of Aprill in the year of our Lord God one thousand six hundred fifty and foure, before the Judge for probate of Wills and Granting administrations lawfully authorized, Letters of Administration were granted unto Anne ffawkard, the Relict and universall Legatorie named in the last Will and testament by word of mouth of Rowland ffawkard late of the Parishe of Paule, Covent Garden, in the County of Middlesex, deceased, to administer the goods, chattels, and debts of the said deceased according to the Tenor and effect of the said Will, there being no executor in the said Will named, she, the said Anne ffawkard, being first sworne well and truly to administer ye same."

Cur. Prerog. Cant. Alchin 25.

---o---

[56]	1654.

THOMAS FFOLKARDE of fframlingham, Suff., Yeoman: 10 January 1654. "Whole of mind and of good and perfect memory."—"ffirst I commit and recommende my soule unto the hands of Almighty God my maker of whom I had my first being, and to Jesus Christ my Redeemer by whose bloodshed I trust to be saved, And my body to the earth to be buried in Christian buriall.   Item I doe annull and make void all other last Wills and Testaments by mee made before this time: Item— I give to ffrancis ffolkarde, to Samuell ffolkarke, To Jerimy ffolkard, To Richard ffolkard, To Timothy ffolkarde, my brethren, And to Martha, to Margarett, and to Sarah, my sisters, to every of them five shillings a yeere: Item— I give to Samuell & Richard my brothers all my wearinge apparell for my body of what kind soever, to be equally divided betwixt them (lynnen only excepted).   Item— I give to John Harmon, my wives grandchild, ffower pounds of good and lawfull money of England to be paid to him at his age of One and Twenty years and my bible."   To Mary wife of John Culner (? Culver) "one greate Coffer."   To John and Mary Negall "my wives grandchildren" 5s each. All above legacies to be paid within six months of his decease.   Residue of all kinds to Mary his wife.   She sole ext².—Signed and sealed by Thomas Folkarde.—Witnessed by John Calver, Paule Dade, and Mary Wade, her mark.—Proved at London 1 November 1655 by the oath of Mary ffolkarde the Relict and sole executrix.

Cur. Prerog. Cant. Aylett. 474.

———o———

[57]   1656.

ANTHONY FFOLKARD of Bedfield, Suff., Yeoman: 10 October 1656. To his wife Ann all his messuages, tenements, and lands in Bedfield & Monk Soham for life.   They to pass at her death to William Seaman of Monk Soham, Yeoman, and to his heirs, on condition that he pays £300 in the following legacies.   To Anne ffolkard, and to Mary, wife of John Tal-mage, daughters of Edmund ffolkard his brother, £15 a year, and to allow to Sarah their sister £15.   To the children of Lawrence his brother as fol-lows: viz., to "James ffolkard £20, to yᵉ children of George ffolkard, that is to say to George, Anne, Mary and Hannah, £10 to be parted equally among them, to Lyonell ffolkard £15, and to Mary and to Susan ffolkard £15 a-piece, but if any of the foreseid children of my brother Lawrence, or any of the children of the sayd George, shall die not leaving issue of their bodies lawfully begotten," their share to be equally divided among the survivors. To William Michell £15.   To Margarett Michell, the wife of Adam George, £15, "these being yᵉ children of Margery Michell my sister.   To the chil-dren of Margaret Russell my sister as followeth, that is to say to John, George, and Anne Russell, and to Mary Russell, £15 apiece, and to Thomas Russell £5."   To John Raynold of Wickham Market, his kinsman, £15. To Christopher Clarke, "my sister Clarke's son," £20.   To John Wade of Ratlesden, "my wife's kinsman," £10,   To Anne and Mary ffolkard, £10 between them.   To the children of James ffolkard, James, Anthony and Thomas, £15, and to the children of "ffrancys ffolkard, my kinsman, that is to say to Edmund, ffrancys and Thomas," £15 to be equally divided.   To his brother Edmund ffolkard £10, but if he should die before it be due, it to go to Anne, the said Edmund's daughter.   If William Seaman refuse to make the above payments, the tenements and lands to go to John Talmage,

23

the husband of Mary ffolkard, upon the foregoing conditions. All legacies to be paid at Bedfield Church. All moveable goods and three of his best milch cows to wife. To Anne, "the daughter of my brother Edmund," a feather bed and other items. To Mary, the wife of John Talmage, a bed &c. To Sarah, another daughter of his brother Edmund, a flock bed &c. To Lyonell ffolkard a table. To James ffolkard a brown cow, and to Christopher Clerk a heifer. All residue to wife, who sole executrix.—Signed by testator, and witnessed by William Gorlatt and Richard Glyn, Clerk.—Proved at Bedfield 27 January, 1663.

Ipsw. Pro. Orig. Wills. 1663. No. 113.

————o————

[58]   1662.

ROBERT FFOLKARD of Brundish, Suff., Yeoman: 12 January 1662. To Marie his daughter, wife of William Pantrye, of Dickelborough, Norf., sundry furniture items, including "one ketle called the middle ketle." To Robert ffolkard his son, furniture "after the death of Marie my wife." To Elizabeth, testator's daughter, "a livery bed as it standeth in the Buttery chamber" and other furniture after the death of her mother. More furniture to "John my son." Linen, brass, and pewter to be divided among "my three youngest children, Robert, Elizabeth, and John." To Roger his son 40s, to be paid to him by "Marie my wife if it has been demanded by himselfe." Residue of all kinds to his wife, who is sole executrix, to bring up his three youngest children.—Signed with a large R as mark of Robert ffolkard, and witnessed by John Crapnell and Robert Spurling.— Proved at Yoxford 3 July 1663, by Marie ffolkard the relict.

Ipsw. Pro. Orig. Wills. 1663. No. 47.

————o————

[59]   1663.

BENJAMIN FFOLKARD of Gillingham St. Mary, Norfolk, Yeoman. Sick in body. To Margarett his wife the tenement he dwelt in in Gillingham, together with the brewing office, until his son Benjamin be 24. The latter then to have it conditional on his paying "unto ffrances and Anne my two eldest daughters" the sum of £10 apiece when 30 yeares of age, and to "my two other daughters, Elizeabeth and Penelope," the sum of £10 apiece when 24 years of age. A house in Annelbridyg Street, Beccles, to his wife until his son Thomas be 24, when it was to pass to the said Thomas "provided she and he pay 40s a year to Hester Garrard, single woman, for life." To wife 3 parcels of medowe with a curtilage in Beccles and Worlingham, to be sold by her to pay testator's debts. All personal estate to wife to bring up children. Goods to be inventoried, and eventually to go to his daughters ffrances and Anne when thirty years old, and to Elizeabeth and Penelope when 24. His wife sole executrix.—Signed and sealed by Benjamin ffolkard 7 March 1663.—Proved at Norwich, 9 April 1665.

Norw. Consis. 1663. Fo. 5.

ANN FFOLKARD of Bedfield, Suff., Widow: 2 April 1664. To John Wade of Ratlesden, her kinsman, four dairy cows and "my husband's best clonk." To Elizeabeth Wade his daughter, "my great posted bedstead" &c. Also "my great cheste and deske in the chambre." To Mary, daughter of the said John Wade, many similar items. To Ann ffolkard, daughter of Edmund ffolkard, "all that money which is in her father's hands and due to me as executrix of my late husband." (*See will No. 57.*) Also "all the wheat in the house" and dairy items, "which I desire may bee for the benefit of herselfe and the olde man her ffather." Also to said Ann a cow and the fourth part of her hay, clothes, and furniture. To Elizeabeth & Mary Wade aforesaid several items of plate and furniture. To Thomas Russell of Kettleborough her cart, tumbrell, sledge, harness &c. To Charles Harrison of Wickham Market 20s. "which he oweth mee" and 10s. besides. To Anthony, son of James ffolkard of Worlingworth, her long table and other items. Legacies to Thomas Dyett of Dennington and to .... Manshipp, wife of .... Manshipp of Campsey Ash. All Residue to John Wade of Ratlesden aforesaid, who sole ex⁰ʳ. Mark of testatrix. John Jeffery one witness — the name of a second destroyed.—Proved at Wickham 15 April 1665.

Ipsw. Pro. Orig. Wills. 1665.

---o---

ANDREW FFOAKER (Ffoker, Phoker) of Glamford, Norf., 1 November 1665. (*See father's will No 42.*) To his son John his houses, lands &c. for ever. He to permit testator's wife Elizeabeth to enjoy part of the house in Glamford in which testator dwelt, as also a cow and a bullock. The said John further to pay to his mother quarterly during her life 25s., and she to have use of all household stuff, it going at her death to testator's two daughters, Elizeabeth and Mary. To his son, Caster ffoaker, £30 when 24, and in the event of his death before that age, that sum to two daughters aforesaid. To his daughter Elizeabeth 6s. per quarter after death of his wife. To his daughter Mary £10 when 21. If she die, the money to go to his son Castor. Appoints Robert Lowde, Rector of Eley, "my brother Christopher ffoaker," and William Reynolds of Glamford, exⁱˢ. Testator's mark. Proved at Walsingham 21 November 1667.

Norw. Arch. Ward. 1666—7. Fo. 388.

---o---

ELIZEABETH WARREN of Bury St. Edmunds, Suff., Widow: 3 March 1673. "To Anne ffokard wife of Thomas ffokard my kinsman and to Thomas ffokard his son and the daughter now living" many bequests. Many Tillots named. "To ffayth ffokard, widow, relict of John ffokard my kinsman."—"To Thomas, John, Elizeabeth and ffaith ffokard her children" sundry bequests. Cleggatts and Johnsons named, also the two daughters of Mathias Warren of Bury, Gent. Proved 1675.

Arch. Sudbury. Read. Fo. 254.

—o—

[63]   1675.

ROBERT FFOLKARD of Rattlesden, Suff., Linen Weaver. His loomes to Thomas and Robert his two sons. To Lydia ffolkard, his youngest daughter, £30. The rest of his goods to Susanna his wife for life, and after her to Robert his son and Elizabeth Bumstead his (testator's) daughter, or their children. His wife executrix.—Proved 6 December 1675.

Arch. Sudbury. Read. Fo. 288.

—o—

[64]   1676.

JOHN FFALKER of Hornyng, Norf., Husbandman: 20 January 1676. He being sick. To his wife Bridget two cows, one red the other brown, and his bedstead, feather bed, boulsters and pillows, coverletts &c. Other furniture, cattle, and farm produce to go to satisfy a bond given to Thomas Willson, late of Hoveton St. John, Norf., upon testator's marriage, for £10. To John Pidgeon his grandchild, son of Bridgett Pidgeon his daughter, £5 when 21. If he die, the £5 to James Jurden his grandchild, son of Ann Jurden his daughter. To the three children of Richard Reade and Susan his wife 20s. To the poor of Horning 10s. A sermon to be preached at his funeral by Mr John Sheringham, minister of Horning. To James Jurden aforesaid 20s. Residue to c:ors, who are William Pidgeon and Anthoney Jurden, "my sons-in-law." Fifty shillings to be spent on his funeral and burial.—Signed John ffalker.—Proved at Sutton by William Pidgeon 10 January 1680.

Norf. Arch. 1680. Fo. 217.

—o—

[65]   1678.

CHRISTOPHER FFOAKER (*indexed* PHOKER) of Brinton, Norf. Taylor, 13 January 1678. (*See Will No. 61.*) "Weake and sicke in body." To Roger ffoker his son all testator's land and estate in Brinton, Thorney, and Brinningham, "on condition that Roger Phoker my son shall pay my wife Sarah Phoker and Elizabeth Phoker my daughter together 30s per quarter for life of Sara my wife," and 52s a year at his wife's death to said daughter Elizabeth for life. Testator's wife to dwell in his house and have the orchard. To Clemence Multon his daughter £6, and to Sara Balls his daughter £20 at death of wife. Roger Phoker his son sole executor. Mark of C. ffoker. John foker a witness. No record of proof, but probably in 1681.

Norw. Arch. Makins. 1681—2. Fo. 458.

26

[66] 1678.

THOMAS FFOAKER of Little Harleston, Suff., Yeoman: 30 May 1678.
To Elizeabeth his wife and to Anne his daughter lands and tenements
in Cotton. If the latter die or marry before 24, then Elizeabeth his daughter to have her share. His daughter Anne to have all other and moveable
property and money to pay his debts. To Thomas his son *one shilling!*
To Elizeabeth his daughter £5 when 21. His daughter Anne executrix, &
Daniel Clarke of Wiverston Supervisor, the latter having 10s for his trouble.—Testator's mark.—No proof recorded, but probably in 1680.

Norw. Consis. Orig. Wills 1680. No. 165.

-----o-----

[67] 1681.

FFRANCIS FFOLKARD the elder of Parham, Suff., Clothier: 16 November, 1681. " Sicke and weake in bodye but of 'perfect mind and
memorey." Commends his soul to Almighty God after the usual formula.
" And as for that little worldly wealth wherewith it has pleased God to in-
trust me withall I thus dispose thereof." To Anne "my well-beloved wife "
the house he dwelt in with all appurtenances in Parham for life. At her
death the same to go to ffrancis ffolkard his second son and to his heirs for
ever. To Edward ffolkard his eldest son five shillings only. To Thomas
ffolkard his son £100. " Alsoe I give unto my sonne Thomas ffolkard my
gold ring with the seale engraven on it." To Alice ffolkard his daughter
£100. To his grandaughter Anne ffolkard £15 at 21. " Lastly I doe give
and bequeath unto my sonne ffrancis ffolkard All my goods and Chattles,
household stuffe, and all the moneyes due to me whatsoever, saving only
these goods hereafter mentioned." He to pay all testator's debts and legacies. Testator's wife to have " one bedd and everything convenient for her
to furnish a Roome, and my sonne ffrancis shall take an inventory of goods
as my Wife shall have for her use." Wife to engage that at her death all
said goods be returned to his three children. ffrancis, Thomas, and Alice, to
be parted between them equally. His son ffrancis to pay to Mr. Gregory
Damant £100, " that my house may be cleered of the mortgage." Should
he refuse to do this, then £100 to be given to testator's wife out of his stock
to pay Mr. Damant. His sons ffrancis and Thomas ex^ors. Signed and sealed by ffran. ffolkard the testator in the presence of William Wood, Robert
Whitlock (his mark), Henry Wyard, and Sarah Whitlock.—Proved at London in the Prerogative Court of Canterbury 20 January 1681 (New Style)
by ffrancis ffolkard, one of the ex^ors.

Cur. Prerog. Cant. 4 Cottle. 1682.

-----o-----

[68] 1683.

JOHNATHAN FFOLKARD of Letheringham, Suff., 3 March 1683. To
his son Thomas his house and lands in Crowfield, Suffolk, after the decease of testator's wife Margaret. To his son Johnathan his house and
appurtenances in Earl Soham when 21; the said son to pay to his brother

. 27

Thomas aforesaid 50s. a year while their mother lives. Also to the said Johnathan a piece of land in Ashfield when 21. To Margaret, testator's wife, £40 out of his goods and chattels. To his three youngest children, Elizeabeth, Joseph, and Samuel, remainder of goods and chattels, provided they do not amount to above £300, any overplus of that sum to be divided among his five children equally. All the said goods and chattels to be sold, and the money and rent of lands to be paid to wife to bring up the children. Samnel ffolkard of Cretingham and Thomas ffolkard of Cretingham ex^{ors.} Signed by testator and witnessed by Thomas Smith, Thomas ffolkard, and John Mathews.—Proved at Wickham Market 26 October 1683.

Ipsw. Pro. Orig. Wills. 1683.

———o———

[69]   1684.

JEREMY FFOLKARD of Gosbeck, Suff., Yeoman : 19 February 1684. To his son Thomas £10. To his daughter Mary, wife of Thomas Gilbert, 40s. To his daughter Susan £10. To his three sons, Samuel, Timothy, & James, 2s each. All residue to his son Thomas aforesaid, except to his daughter Susan a further legacy of a feather bed, bolster, and other items. Thomas ffolkard his son sole executor.—Signed with testator's mark, and witnessed by John Dove, William Dove, and John Colchester.—Proved at Ipswich 17 March 1684.

Ipsw. Pro. Orig. Wills. 1682—4. File 124. No. 431.

———o———

[70]   1684.

WILLIAM FFOLCKWARD (FFOLKARD) of Winston, Suff., Yeoman : 30 August, 1684. "Item—I give and bequeath to my sonne Sill Reeve, with Elizeabeth his wife, one shilling at or within three months after my decease, to be paid to him or his wife at the Church Porch of Winston by my executrix. To my son Ralph Sayer of Winston, my full coate, and to Susanna his wife the Tipt Jugg, unto Susan my loving wife all the rest of my goods." Wife sole executrix. She to give and bequeath to Rachel Sayer "my loving grandchild, all manner of goods whatsoever, hoping that the aforesaid Susan ffollikard, my Loving Wife and Executrix, that she will perform the same."—Signed William ffolckward "his marke," and witnessed by Josiah Smyth, Thomas Bolles, and ffrancis Lift.—Proved at Ipswich 18 October 1684 by the oath of the executrix.

Ipsw. Pro. Orig. Wills 1682—3—4. File 86. No. 406.

———o———

[71]   1686.

THOMAS FFOLKARD of Otley, Suff., Yeoman: 7 June 1686. "To my sister Susan (*see Will No. 69*) All my Pewtre and a Brasse Potte, one warming pann" and other items. "To Jeremiah ffolkard, my kinsman, 40s of lawfull money of England to be due unto him within two yeres after my decease, After which Two yeres I desire that my Executor should kepe it in his handes for seven yeres, Paying the Boy Interest for it, unless he see cause to pay it him sooner." Testator's brother Samuel ffolkard (*see Will No. 69*) executor, "paying himselfe woll for his troble." Residue to be divided between his two brothers and two sisters equally. Signed "Thomas ffolkard his marke," and witnessed by Robert Hill, Julia ffuller, and Richard Sallowes.—Proved at Ipswich 7 August 1686.

Ipsw. Pro. Orig. Wills 1685—8. No 145.

———o———

[72]   1684.

THOMAS FFOLKARD of Ashfield, Suff., Yeoman: 8 September 1684. To Johnathan, second son of testator's deceased son Johnathan, lands in Ashfield in full satisfaction of all promises made to the latter on his marriage to his wife Margarett. If the said Margarett declines to sign a release of such promises the lands to go to Thomas, eldest son of testator. To the aforesaid Margarett, and to Thomas ffolkard her eldest son, all his lands and tenements in Crowfield and Gosbeck, to be held firstly by the mother for life. "And whereas upon the marriage of Samuel my son with Susan his now wife I did settle upon the said Samuel and his heirs the reversion of all my tenements and lands lying in Framsden after my death and the death of Elizabeth my now wife, and did settle that during the life of my wife Samuel my son should be paid yearly £8 a year, and if the said Samuel should die (living the said Elizabeth my wife) that then the said Susan the now wife of the said Samuel my son should be paid yearly £10 during the life of Elizabeth my wife, for the execution of this settlement I gave unto the said Samuel my son I assign a rent charge to him of £8 yearly out of my properties in Ashfield and Thorpe St. Peter. If Samuel die while Elizabeth my wife and Susan his wife be then living, then the same property to be charged with an annuity of £10 to the said Susan to be paid in the Church Porch at Framsden." To Thomas, his eldest son, all properties undevised above in Ashfield. To Mary his daughter £50, to be paid "at or in the now Mansion house of mee the said Thomas ffolkard situate in Ashfield." To Joseph, the third son of his deceased son Johnathan, £5 at 21. To Elizabeth "my loving wife" £40 worth of goods and household stuff. To John, son of his daughter Lydia Savage deceased, £50 when 21, with reversion to aforesaid Joseph ffolkard, third son of his deceased son Johnathan, should the said John Savage die before 21. Thomas ffolkard, testator's eldest son, to be sole executor. All overplus after payment of legacies to be divided into 5 parts ;— 1 to go to Thomas his son ; 1 to his son Samuel ; 1 to be divided equally between Thomas, Johnathan, Joseph, Margarett and Samuel, the four sons and daughter of testator's deceased son Johnathan ffolkard, when 21 ; 1 part to Mary "my daughter," and 1 part to his grandchild aforesaid, John Savage, when 21. Written on seven sheets of paper, and signed by testator on each sheet in the presence of B. Gibson, B. Gibson Junior, and John ffrere Junior.

A codicil to this will dated 19 September 1684 revokes bequest of £5

29

to Joseph, son of testator's deceased son Johnathan, and gives it to Thomas, the last named's oldest son at 21; but the original bequest to stand if Thomas dies before 21.—The witnesses to codicil are the two Gibsons abovenamed and James Gibson.—Proved at Wickham Market 12 September 1689.

Ipsw. Pro. 1689—93. Fo. 25.

---o---

[73]   1690.

THOMAS FFOLKARD of Heaveningham, Suff., Grocer: 9 April 1690. To Joseph Cornish his son-in-law £60, "in performance of my promise on his marriage with my daughter." To his son-in-law Edmund Ludbrooke £40 for a similar reason. To his son-in-law Isaac Lock £150 in satisfaction of a bond given. Residue of estate to his son Samuell ffolkard. He to pay all debts and expenses and to be sole executor.—Signed by testator.—Witnessed by Ambrose Dopland, John Ellis, and ffrances Lowe.—Proved at Yoxford 6 May 1691.

Ipsw. Pro. 1689—93. Fo. 205.

---o---

[74]   1703.

WILLIAM FFOLKARD of Bedfield, Suff., Yeoman. Dated on or about 10 September 1703. (*Extracts from Will only.*) "Item— I give and bequeath unto ffrancis ffolkard of Parham in the County of Suffolk, my kinsman, all that messuage wherein I now dwell with all the lands, tenements and appurtenances thereunto belonging and lying in Bedfield, both freehold and coppyhold, to him and to his heires for ever." "Item— I give and bequeath unto Simon Rouse of Crosfeild in the County of Suffolke, the son of Ann Rouse my sister, that messuage with lands, tenements, and appurtenances thereto belonging situate and lyeing in Bedfield aforesaid called by the name of Bedfield Dogg and now in the occupation of John ffairweather or his Assigns during the term of his natural life, and after his death to be equally divided among his children, Mary, Simon and Anne." Appoints William Sewell, Rector of Holmly, Suff., and Samuel Rogers, Rector of Offley, Suff., ex^ors. No date of proof, but testator died 22 Oct., 1703.

Ex. Chancery Proceedings before 1714. Record Office. Mitford DXCII.

---o---

[75]   1704.

SAMUELL FFOLKARD of Helmingham, Suff., Yeoman: 14 February 1704. "Being aged." To his three children, Thomas, Penelope and Susan £10 each. To his wife Susan all his household linen, "my two ear'd cup and my three silver spoons," with all the rest of his goods and chattels, household stuff and implements of houschold, moneys, stock, and personal estate whatsoever and wheresoever. At her death his three children abovenamed to have £20 apiece in addition to foregoing legacy. To Anne Covell,

30

his grandchild 20s. Any overplus at wife's death to be divided between his three above-named children and his daughter Mary (wife of William Ladd). "And I do hereby declare that having formerly given to my son Samuell, my two daughters, Elizabeth (y⁰ wife of Benjamin Baldry) and Anne (y⁰ wife of Charles Covell) soe very considerably upon their respective marriages that I cannot doe so well by my other children (as they very well know) is y⁰ reason why I have no more to spare for them." His wife Susan and his son Samuell Exors.—Signed Samuell ffolkard, and witnessed by John Dove and Thomas ffolkard.—Proved at Ipswich 4 August 1704.

Ipsw. Pro. 1703-4-5. Fo. 19.

---o---

[76]   1706.

"I N the Name of God Amen. I, JEREMIAH FFOOKARD (FFOLKARD, see *Will No.* 71), late belonging to her Majesties Shipp ffly Brigantine, considering the uncertainty of this world and being of disposing miud and memory, do make this my last will and testament in manner following. ffirst and principally I commend my soul to Almighty God who gave it me, hoping through the merits of our Blessed Saviour to obtain pardon and remission of all my Sins. And as to the Temporall Estate wherewith it hath pleased Almighty God to bless me with, I give and bequeath as followeth. Thus I give and bequeath to my dear wife One shilling in full barr of all demands. And as to all other my estate either real or personall I give and bequeath to my well-beloved friend Samuel Scutt of the parish of St. Thomas, Southwark, Victualler, and of this my said last will do make the said Samuel Scutt sole Executor, revoking and making void all former Wills, Codicills, or Testamentary writings by me heretofore, and confirming this to be my last Will and Testament. In witness whereof I have hereunto sett my hand and seal this ninth day of November in the fifth year of the Reyne of our Soveraigne Lady Anne, over England &c., Annoii Dni. One thousand Seaven hundred and six."—The mark of Jeremiah ffookard.—" Signed, sealed, and published and declared in the presence of us William Hartwell, Henry Spencer, Ben. Hall."—This will endorsed "*in partibus.*"—Proved at London 8 September 1707 by the oath of Samuell Scutt the Exor.

Cur. Prerog. Cant. Poley. 204.

---o---

[77]   1706.

T HOMAS FFOLKARD of Cretingham, Suff., Yeoman: 29 November 1706. To his wife Margarett an annuity of £12 from his houses and lands in Ashfield-cum-Thorpe. The said houses and lands to his son Thomas when 21, conditionally on his paying the said annuity. He also to pay to Lydia, youngest daughter of testator, £100 when she be 21. His exors. to maintain and educate the said Lydia up to that age. Should she die before 21, the legacy of £100 to be equally divided among his other daughters, Anne, Elizabeth, Susan, Mary, and Priscilla. All these legacies to be paid in the south porch of the parish church of Cretingham. All his houses, messuages, and lands in Diss and elsewhere in Norfolk, to his wife for life.

They to be sold at her death, and his six daughters to share the proceeds equally. Wife to select "what she likes best of household stuff" to £20 value. To his daughter, the wife of James Clough in Ashfield, 10s. To his daughters, Susan, Mary, and Priscilla £100 apiece. Residue to exors. for payment of debts and legacies. Any overplus to be divided among his six daughters. His wife and son Thomas exors.—Signed by testator, and witnessed by Henry Hawer, Daniel Bigsby, and Elizabeth Molten.—Proved at Wickham Market 31 January 1706 (*the antedate due to use of old and new styles in this Will*).

Ipsw. Pro. Orig. Wills 1706-8. File 99.

———o———

[78]   **1706.**

ROGER PHOKER (FFOKARD FFOAKER, *see Wills Nos.* 52 and 65) of Brinton, Norf., Worsted Weaver: 30 July 1706. To William his son all his houses, lands &c., in Brinton "which were my fathers," and others in Briningham, he paying to testator's son Robert £3 yearly during the life of "my wife Catherine." To his daughter Sarah £30 and other houses and lands in Brinton. All household goods to wife. His son William aforesaid to be residuary legatee and exor.—Signed by testator, and proved at Gunthorpe 2 April 1707 by the exor.

Norw. Consis. 1707-8. Fo. 20.

———o———

[79]   **1709.**

SAMUEL FFOLKARD of Laxfield, Suff., Blacksmith: 21 May 1709. "Sicke and weake in body." To his sons John and Samuel all shop tools "save strakes and nailes." His furniture to sons John and Samuel. A legacy to Mary his wife. A cow to each of his daughters Mary and Elizabeth. His wife and John Dresser of Laxfield exors.—Witnessed by Edmund ffolkard, Thomas ffolkard, and James Krabbe.—Proved by the relict at Stradbrooke 22 July 1709.

Norw. Consis. 1709. Fo. 94.

———o———

[80]   **1709.**

THOMAS FFOLKARD of Woodbridge, Suff., Cooper: October 28 1709. "Being infirme." To Mary "my loving wife," sundry houses and lands in Gosbeck, Woodbridge, and Melton, for life. To his eldest son Thomas ("immediately after the decease of Margaret ffolkard my mother and Mary my wife) all my estate in Gosbeck;" but he to pay to Mary, testator's eldest daughter ("or to any person who will take good care of her, she not being able to take care of or provide for herself"), an annuity of £5. To Johnathan, his youngest son, land and houses in Melton, he also paying £5 yearly to the aforesaid daughter Mary. To Margaret, his youngest daughter, the house he dwelt in and all his other houses in Woodbridge at his wife's decease, she likewise paying £5 annuity to his daughter Mary.

32

To his son Thomas £150, and £100 each to Johnathan and Margaret his children when 21. Wife to select any household goods to value of £30. The residue, after paying £5 each to wife and Francis Rogers of Woodbridge, who are exors., among his children.—Signed by testator.—No date of probate, but this must have been in 1710.

Norw. Consis. 1710-1. Fo. 533.

———o———

[81]   **1715.**

THOMAS FFOLKARD (*see father's Will No.* 59), Rector of Uggeshall and Sotherton, Suff.: 28 March 1715. Described as " Clark " and of Uggeshall. To Augustus Palgrave, " son of my brother-in-law Thomas palgrave, of Brockdish, Clerk," all his lands in Pulham Saint Mary Magdalene, Norf., " providing he pay unto my niece Mary Vincent £40 " and to his sister Katherine Palgrave £100. To Rebecca " my beloved wife " all lands and tenements in Henham and Sotherton, Suff., for ever. Also all his lands in Uggeshall for her life, and at her decease these to go to his brother Benjamin ffolkard, of Gillingham, Norf., for ever. All his goods, chattels, and other personalty to his wife, " providing she pay to my niece Mary Vincent £40." Bequeaths £3 for a silk fringe to the pulpit in Uggeshall church, besides £3 to the poor there and at Sotherton, 30s. to those of Wangford; and 20s to those of Henham. His wife sole executrix.—Signed by testator, and by John Jefferson as one of the witnesses.—Proved 23 March 1719 by Rebecca ffolkard the relict.

Norw. Consis. 1720. Fo. 159.

———o———

[82]   **1721.**

CATHERINE PHOKER (FFOKARD, FFOAKER, *see husband's Will No.* 78), of Holkham, Norf., widow: 26 March 1721. To her daughter Sarah, " now wife of Thomas Magnes," lands and tenements in Great Snoring and Thurfford, Norf., for ever. To her son Robert Phoker of Brinton, Norf., 3 acres of land in Brinningham, Norf., he to pay to her son William Phoker £10. Sarah Magnes ext.—Signed by testatrix.—No record of proof, which must have been made in 1721.

Norw. Consis. 1721. Fo. 62.

———o———

[83]   **1721.**

THOMAS FFOLKARD of Starston, Norf., Yeoman: 30 April 1721. " Sicke in bodye." To Anne his wife houses, lands, and tenements in Starston. Also to her all household stuff. She sole ext.—Mark and seal of testator.—Proved 23 May 1721.

Norw. Consis. 1721. Fo. 62.

———o———

33

FFRANCIS FFOLKARD (*see his father's Will No.* 67), of Parham,
Suff., Clothier (*i.e., Cloth Merchant*) : 3 August 1722. To his wife "the
house wherein I now dwell, with the yards, meadows, and pastures lying near
the church there, and the four severall pieces of land and pasture environed
on all sides by the comon called Cuttings Green and the comon way
leading therefrom to the Church, and the Lauds late of John Pallant, for her
life. At her death to my son ffrancis ffolkard, as also to him all and every
my coppyhold and customary Lands and premises in parham aforesaid, but
wife to enjoy the profit of them during her life. But if wife refuse to give
my said son, or his brother or sisters hereinafter named, or any of them
requiring the same, a release or releases of all Dower and thirds out of the
estates devised, then bequests to be void. I give to the said ffrancis and his
heires the Advowson, Donations, and the Disposition of and to the Churches
of Clopton and Woodbridge-Hasketon. To wife the use of all and every my
household goods not herein specifically devised for life. At death to be
divided among her children iu such proportions as she may decide. To my
son Thomas my house and land in Bedfield and the goods in the parlor. To
my daughters Mary and Alice my messuage, farm, and lands in Persenhall,
Baddingham, Heveningham, and Sibton, as tenants in comon, and £100
each iu money after death of wife. I give to my daughters Sara and Elizabeth
one Guinea a piece to buy them a ring, the tankard, great copper, and furniture
in the Hall and Chamber. And all rest, land, &c., to ffrancis my son, who is
exor."—Signed and sealed by testator, and witnessed by William Damant,
Edmond Geater, and Robert Bentley.—Proved at Ipswich October 31 1722.

Ipsw. Pro. 1721-3. Fo. 119.

———o———

MARGARET FOKARD (FFOLKARD, *see husband's Will No.* 76), of
Pettaugh, Suff., Widow: 9 July 1725. All her messuages, lands, and
tenements in Diss, Norf., or elsewhere, to be sold, and the money to be disposed of as follows:—To Thomas Fokard and Ann Fokard, her grandchildren,
£6 each, " for the like sum I received on their account on the death of their
Aunt Welton of Framsden." To each of them in addition a further sum of
£5. To her five grandchildren, Mary, Joseph, James, Lydia, and Bridget
Godbold, £5 each at 21. To her daughter Priscilla Scotchmere £10. All
residue to Joseph Godbold, her son-in-law and exor.—The mark of testatrix,
and witnessed by Cha. Blomfield junior, John Mullett, and Samuel Sumonds
(? *Simmonds*).—Proved at Kettleburgh by the exor. 11 September 1727.

Ipsw. Pro. 1727-8-9. Fo. 276.

———o———

THOMAS FFAULKE (FFAULKER) of Happisburgh, Norf., Gentleman: 20 October 1729. To his wife Mary all his houses and lands in
Happisburgh for life, and at her decease to his son James, who is to pay to

testator's son Thomas £100. The aforesaid James also to pay to Ann, Mary, Martha, and Elizabeth ffaulker, "my daughters," £20 each. "My estate in Tost Monks, Gillingham, and Haddihee [? *Haddiscoe, Norf.*] to be sold, and money equally divided between my children at 21 years or at marriage of daughters." Residue to wife, who is to pay "any debts remaining of my Late father Thomas ffaulke." She sole ex*. "she consulting my brother-in-law John Wenn of Southrepps."—Signed by testator.—No proof recorded.

Norw. Consis. 1731 (Wills only). No. 73.

————o————

[87]   1733.

BENJAMIN FFOLKARD (FFOLKERED, FFOLKERD, FFOKER, FFAKIN, *see father's Will No. 59, and brother's Will No. 81*), of Beccles, Suff., Beer Brewer: 7 February 1733. To his son-in-law William Elmy, of Beccles, Maltster, "all my pieces of land called Neaves, lying in Beccles or in Higate-next-Beccles." To Elizabeth, the daughter of the said Elmy, the house testator dwelt in in Beccles, with all stables, gardens, &c. To "Rebecca Wake, my daughter, my house in Gillingham, Norfolk, wherein she now dwells, and all brewing utensils there, for life." These at her decease to go to George Wake, her son, for life, and then to such of the said George's children as may be then living. Also to the said Rebecca Wake "my house in Beccles known by the sign of *The Mariners*, for life, and then to Rebecca Wake my grandaughter. I give and devise all my copyhold messuages, lands, tenements, and hereditaments, situate, lying, and being in Uggeshall, late the estate of Thomas Folkard, Clerke, my deceased Brother, and all other property in Beccles and adjacent not otherwise disposed of, with all my personal estate, to be sold by Executors to pay debts and legacies, and all residue equally between William Elmy and Rebecca Wake my daughter." To the poor of Beccles 20s. William Elmy and testator's daughter Rebecca Wake exors.—Signed by testator, and witnessed by Thomas Rede, Ann Whitlock, and John Farr.—Proved at Beccles June 16 1737.

Ipsw. Pro. 1737. Fo. 210.

————o————

[88]   1735.

MARY FOLKARD (*see husband's Will No. 84*) of Parham, Suff., "relict of Francis Folkard:" 30 January 1735. "To be buried near the body of my deceased husband, the grave to be made large enough to contain both our Bodies and be Bricked from the Bottom, and a marble stone to be laid over our Bodies at the equal charge of all my four daughters." To her son Thomas Folkard "all the goodes in the ball." To her daughter Mary Punchard "£10 of lawful money of Great Britain, the Great Cheste of Drawers that stand in the Parlour Chamber, with all such goods as shall be in them at the time of my decease, and the bed there as it stands, and also the Clocke as it stands in the Kitchen." To "my daughter" Sarah Blomfield

35

a bed and other items, and £10. To "my daughter" Elizabeth Geater £5 and some furniture. To "my daughter" Alice Peachie a similar legacy. "To my son-in-law [*i.e.*, *stepson*] Francis Folkard the deal box marked F. Folkard with all in it." Goods not specifically disposed of to be sold for debts and legacies, and overplus to be divided among the four daughters abovenamed, who are appointed exors.—Signed by testator, and witnessed by Francis Stogdale, Elizabeth Calver, and Robert Pells.—Proof not recorded.

Ipsw. Pro. 1734-73. Fo. 215.

————o————

[89]   1742.

THOMAS FFOLKARD, of Ipswich, Suff., Ironmonger: 7 October 1742. "All my Real Estate, both in possession and Reversion, to my loving wife Elizabeth, and all my personal estate." Wife sole ext".—Signed by testator, and witnessed by Good Clarke, Ste. Clarke, and Pet Clarke.

"On y[e] 4 day of January, 1774, Elizabeth ffolkland the within-named executrix was sworn according to due form of law Before me George Routh, Surr. to y[e] County." (*See widow's Will No.* 98).

Ipsw. Pro. 1773-74. Fo. 117.

————o————

[90]   1744.

ROBERT PHOKER (FFOKER, FFOKARD), of Brinton, Norf.: 17 April 1744. To Mary, his wife, all his houses, lands, and tenements in Brinton, Brisingham, and ffoulsham, Norf., and she sole ext". and general legatee.—Mark R of testator.—Proved 14 January 1745.

Norw. Consis. 1745. Fo. 122.

————o————

[91]   1746.

SAMUEL FFOLKARD, of Wingfield, Suff., Linen Weaver: 8 April 1746. "Whereas my Daughter Elizabeth, having had a large Portion, can have no more but only a third part of y[e] blew Bed in y[e] Parlour Chamber, which part I value at twenty shillings. My daughter Sarah have.y[e] Chest of Drawers in y[e] parlour and y[e] Glass Keep hanging by it, and to have y[e] six black Chairs in y[e] Parlour," and other items of furniture. "The Red Bed in y[e] Parlour Chamber is my Daughter Susan's Proper own." Sundry other furniture to last-named daughter. "All temporal estate, indoors and out of doors, to be divided between my two daughters Sarah and Susan by an inventory." John Stollery sole exor., with two guineas for his trouble.—Signed by testator, and witnessed by Henry Counold, Elizabeth Daliston, and Henry Counold Junior.—Proved at Stradbrooke 23 May 1746 by John Stollery.

Ipsw. Pro. 1746. Fo. 22.

————o————

JAMES PHOKER (FFOKER, FFOKARD) of Salthouse, Norf.,
Yeoman: 9 April 1746. "Being Sicke." His houses and lands in
Salthouse to his wife Frances for life, and at her death to his son James
Phoker. Wife to maintain Martha Phoker, testator's daughter by a first
wife. His son James to pay to testator's daughters Martha and Mary 30s.
each at the death of wife. The latter ex". and residuary legatee.—Mark of
testator.—No probate.—Registered 1747.

Norw. Consis. 1747. Fo. 207

————o————

[93]   1748.

JOHN FFOLKARD of Laxfield, Suff., Blacksmith: no date. "To my
son Samuel my shop and Traverse with all iron and tools and half the
yard adjoining, and all household goods. And my House or Houses with
the appurtenances, except that given to son Samuel, now in the occupation
of my brother Samuel ffolkard, William Bishop, and myself, to be sold.
The sum of forty shillings in lieu of an anvil to my son John, and balance
equally divided among my four children, John, Samuel, Elizabeth, and Lydia.
Son Samuel and Edward Dowsing Exors. of this my last will." Added
afterwards: " Since I ordered my will to be written, and before signing and
sealing, have received a letter from my son Isaac, which before I believed
was dead in Battle. I therefore give him an equal share with my other four
children."—Mark of testator.—Witnessed by Charles Palmer, John Ward,
and Richard Bouiwell.—Proved at Stradbrooke 5 February 1747-8.

Ipsw. Pro. 1747-48. Fo. 67.

————o————

[94]   1750.

JEREMIAH FFOLKARD of Saxmundham, Suff.: 23 March 1750. To
Sarah, "my loving wife," John, his youngest son, and Elizabeth, his
daughter, all his goods and furniture in the parlour chamber, "and six of my
worst and six of my best pewter plates, and four pewter dishes, share and
share alike." His clothing to his eldest son Jeremiah, and some linen to his
son John. Residue, after payment of debts, to his wife, his son John, and his
daughter Elizabeth. Wife and Mr. Anthony Jenkenson exors.—Witnessed
by Mickleburgh Goldsmith, Richard Roberts, and William Toller.—Proved
3 April 1751 by Sarah ffolkard, ext'.

Ipsw. Pro. File 13. Fo. 335.

————o————

[95]   1753.

FFRANCIS FFOLKARD of Clopton, Suff., Clerk: 5 September 1753.
To be buried in chancel of Clopton Church. To his wife Deborah all
household goods, linen, and furniture (plate excepted), in lieu of £100
covenanted to her at marriage "about 21 May 1723." Wife to have use of

plate for life, and it then to go to his daughters Elizabeth and Deborah.
Wife to have use of £200 for life over and above all other legacies. This
sum is also to go at her death to his two daughters. "And whereas a
marriage is shortly intended to be had and solemnized by and between the
Reverend Mr. Montague North and my eldest daughter Elizabeth ffolkard,
spinster, Upon which said intended marriage, and as a part of the marriage
portion intended for my said daughter, I have agreed to settle and secure the
several Estates following, that is to say One estate at parham and another at
Wickham Markett." Should this marriage not take place, these properties
to go absolutely to his daughter Elizabeth. Several other estates are named
as included in the settlement referred to, one being at Clopton and another
at Wetheringsett. These are to be divided between daughters Elizabeth and
Deborah, and the share of the latter, failing issue of her, to testator's brother
Thomas ffolkard and his heirs. To the Reverend Montague North and
testator's daughter Elizabeth ten guineas each. To his brother Thomas,
"all the monies he owes me and one guinea in gold." To his brother-in-law
John Punchard, and to testator's sisters, Sarah Blomfield, Elizabeth Geater,
and Alice Peachey, one guinea in gold each. To Mary Service, "who was the
daughter of my cousin Ann Taylor," two guineas in gold. To the poor of
Clopton and Hasketon (of both of which places testator was rector), forty
shillings. Legacies to servants Girling and Woods. Residue to his
daughter Deborah. Appoints his wife guardian of the last-named till 21,
and in case of wife's death his daughter Elizabeth to assume such guardianship. His wife sole executrix.—Signed by testator, and witnessed by John
Sheringham, Justice Smith, and Benjamin Votier.—Proved by the relict
27 March 1754.

Ipsw. Pro. 1754-57. Fo. 21.

———o———

[96]   **1753.**

MARY PHOKER (FFOKER, FFOKARD) of Brinton, Norf., Widow:
3 August 1753. "Being weake in body." To her kinsman, John
Parker, all her "greasing" (? grazing) ground in ffoulsham. He to pay £8
to his sister Mary Leverington, and £100 to the children of the latter. All
houses and lands in Brinton to Thomas Rix, of Binham, Gent., and Ann his
wife. James Parker, her kinsman, named, and many legacies of linen, silver,
furniture, and clothing to persons before named. To be buried near her late
husband. Thomas Rix exor.—Signed by testatrix.—Proved 8 July 1755.

Norw. Arch. 1754-55. Fo. 565.

———o———

[97]   **1756.**

THOMAS FFOLKARD of Tannington, Suff.: 7 January 1756. "Being
sicke." A moiety of all property to wife Audrey for life. At her
death, one moiety to Audry Youngman, one moiety to Ann Hall, and one
moiety to Sarah Brook, testator's three daughters, and one moiety to William

38

and Elizabeth Daniels, his grandchildren. To Johnathan Hall of Horsham, his son-in-law, 2 guineas. To William Daniels, his son-in-law, one shilling. Wife and Johnathan Hall exors.—Proved 12 May 1756.

Norw. Consis. 1756. Fo. 96.

————o————

[98] 1776.

ELIZABETH FFOLKARD (FFOLKLAND) of Ipswich, Suff., Widow *(See husband's Will No. 89):* 25 November 1776. Appoints her sons Thomas and Benjamin Nathaniel ffolkard exors. To each of them £5 for their trouble. To them and their heirs, upon trust, the house in Ipswich in her own occupation, also lands in Ipswich called Cook's Fields. The whole to be sold. To her daughters Elizabeth ffolkard the younger, and Mary and Lydia ffolkard, £20 each. To her servant Mary Plummer, 2 guineas. To her sons William and Benjamin Nathaniel, and to her daughters Elizabeth the younger, and Mary and Lydia, all monies arising from sale of houses, lands, stock-in-trade, and personal effects in equal shares. Wearing apparel to be equally divided between her daughters.—Proved at Norwich 18 March 1777 by the exors.

Norw. Consis. 1777. Fo. 55.

————o————

[99] 1778.

JOHN FFOLKARD of Bredfield, Suff., Yeoman: 19 March 1778. John Keeble of Bredfield, who is appointed exor., to " hold and enjoy all my Messuage, Tenements, Lands, and hereditaments and premises in Bredfield, and now in his occupation, for ever, he paying £450 to discharge the mortgage on the said premises, and paying the remainder of that sum to the several children of my daughter Elizabeth, the now wife of John Burrows, as they arrive at 21." To Reuben, the son of the said Elizabeth Burrows, a messuage and land in Grundisburgh. Signed by testator, and witnessed by William Skeet, John Hood, and William Swain.—Proved 10 April 1778.

Ipsw. Pro. 1777-78. Fo. 50.

————o————

[100] 1780.

THOMAS FFOLKARD of Bedfield, Suff.: April 1780. To be buried at Parham. To Thomas his son, some of his wearing apparel, silver buckle, and wigs, and £5. 4s. a year for life "at 8 shillings per month to be paid into his own hand and nobody else." If this legacy be sold or transferred, it is to stand null and void. To testator's daughter Mary, wife of James Calver, £5. 4s. a year. " To my granson Thomas ffolkard my watch, silver spurs, and wearing apparel not before mentioned: All my grandchildren that I now have to be paid to them £5 each after decease of my son Thomas." Residue of all kinds to be sold, and exors. "to buy a small place and settle it on my grandson Thomas ffolkard for ever. And as Mr. ffrancis ffolkard of Clopton, my brother, did in his will leave a remainder of an estate at Parham to me if his daughters had no children, then I bequeath that estate to my grandson Thomas ffolkard and his heirs On condition that he pay to his father Thomas ffolkard, £4 yearly for life, and unto my daughter Mary Calver, and unto my grandaughter Mary, his sister, four pounds apiece yearly for life." Mr. John Russel of Woodbridge, Attorney-at-Law, and Mr. Joseph Clarke of Baudsey, Exors. and Trustees.—Signed by testator, and witnessed by James Farrer, John Bolton, and Edmund Applewhite.—Proved at Woodbridge 20 September 1783 by John Russel.

Ipsw. Pro. 1783-84. Fo. 99.

———o———

[101]   **1780.**

WILLIAM FFOLKARD of Ipswich, Suff., Joiner and Cabinet Maker: 7 October 1780. "To my son George ffokard, the house in my own occupation in the parish of St. Matthews." To testator's wife Ann, three houses in the parish of St. Nicholas, Ipswich, for her life, and afterwards to aforesaid son "George ffokard," and then to latter's son George and his heirs. In case of failure of heirs, one house to Benjamin the son of Benjamin Brame of Ipswich, House Carpenter, and another to George the son of George Brame of Ipswich, Maltster. Wife to choose goods to the value of £20. To John ffindoll of Ipswich, Gent., £50 to satisfy his loss through failure of "my son George ffokard," he giving a general release. Other legacies. Household linen between wife and son George. The last-named residuary legatee, and he with Benjamin Brame, senr., and Benjamin Page, a tailor of Ipswich, exors.—Signed by testator, and witnessed by Eliza Mary Long, John Mills, and B^w. (? Bartholomew) Long.—Proved at Ipswich 10 February 1780.

Ipsw. Pro. 1789-90. Fo. 12.

———o———

[102]   **1784.**

WILLIAM FFALJARD of Colchester, Essex, Gentleman : 16 February 1784. Everything, including £700 Government Stock, to "my ffaithful servant Elizabeth Andrews, Widow, in consideration of her long and faithful services." His friend Horatio Cook, Surgeon, of Colchester, and Elizabeth Andrews exors. £10 to the former. Signed by testator.—Proved 4 March 1784 at London.

Cur. Prerog. Cant. Rockingham. 134.

———o———

[103]   **1787.**

ROBERT FFOLKARD of East Bergholt, Suff., Carpenter: 8 January 1787. All his freehold messuages in East Bergholt to his son ffrancis, and a copyhold messuage in Capel St. Mary to another son, Jeremiah ffolkard. Nine copyhold houses in East Bergholt to testator's wife Sarah, for life, and then to his sons Thomas and James, but subject to payment of

£70 to his son John ffolkard of Manningtree, Essex, Innholder, and £30 to testator's son Robert ffolkard, of Dedham, Essex. Residue to be sold, and proceeds divided equally between his wife and his surviving children. Wife Sarah, and sons James and ffrancis, exors.—Mark of testator.—Witnessed by J. Phillips, John Ormes, and Thomas May.—Proved at East Bergholt 17 April 1787.

Ipsw. Pro. 1787-88. Fo. 38.

---o---

[104]   **1789.**

THOMAS FFOLKARD of Lowestoft, Suff.: 31 December 1789. All effects, including household goods, boats, vessels, debts, &c., to be equally divided between his wife Susannah, and his children, Thomas, William, Samuel, and Susannah, "my wife carrying on the business of the House where I now dwell, and to bring up and maintain my children." Should wife remarry, her share to go to children. Mr. Robert Palmer of Lowestoft sole exor.—Mark of testator.—Witnessed by Sarah Wiggins, Robert Palmer, and George Webb.—Proved at Lowestoft 27 January 1790.

Ipsw. Pro. 1789-90. Fo. 25.

---o---

[105]   **1801.**

ANN FFOKARD of Ipswich, Suff., Widow (*See husband's Will No.* 101): 25 May 1801. Benjamin Colchester of Ipswich, Merchant, sole exor. Everything to her son James Minter, for life, and at his death one third to Mary Ann, daughter of aforesaid James Minter, and residue to his other children, William, Edmund, John, and Elizabeth Minter. Mark of testatrix.—Proved 14 April 1803.

Norw. Consis. 1803. Fo. 67.

---o---

[106]   **1520.** (*Accidentally omitted.*)

ROBERT FFOLCARD (FFOLKARD) of Earl Stonham, Suff.: 13 March 1520. To be buried in the churchyard of Earl Stonham. A mass to be sung for him, and a priest to go on a pilgrimage to Our Lady of Mendlesham soon after his decease. To his son Roberd ffolcard, all goods moveable and immoveable, to pay testator's debts. Proved at Bramford 8 July 1521. (Endorsed "Robert ffolkard, Stonham Cornbust.").

Ipsw. Pro. 1518-1524. Fo. 133.

---o---

Administrations Granted.

[1]   **About 1375.**

NICHOLAS (?—*nearly illegible*) FFOLKARD of Stoleye, Norf., Deceased intestate. Egidia, his wife, administered.

(*Ex. Orig. Lat.*)   *Norw. Consis. 1370-83.*

———o———

[2]   **1555.**

ELIZABETT FFOLKARDE de Stybton, decessit intestat VIII° mens et annis suprscript. Admon. direct. Rose uxori Nichi Deane (? Drane), Thome ffolkard Robt°. ffolkarde et Will^mo ffolkarde sorori et fratribus natural. defunct.

           Act Books. Norw. Consis. No 2. Fo. 41.

———o———

[3]   **1556.**

THOMAS FFOLKERDE (FFOLKARD) de Bedfelde — intestat — 25 Novemb. 1556. Em^it tre ad colligend bona direct. Margaret nup-rel^e usque ad fest. Nativitatis S. Johnis bapt. prox.

           Act Books. Norw. Consis. No. 2. Fo. 141.

———o———

[4]   **1610.**

NICHOLAS FFOKARDE (FFOLKARD) of Carlton Colville, Suff. (*see Will* 38): 21 April 1610. Admon. granted to Dorothy ffokarde his relict.

           Ipsw. Pro. Sundry Books.

———o———

[5]   **1626-28.**

TOBIAS FFALLIARD (FFOLLIARD, FFOLKARD) of "Beatœ Mariæ," Colchester. Admon. granted.

           Deanery of Bocking. Somerset House. 1626-28.

———o———

[6]   **1628.**

WILLIAM FFOKARDE of Shotley, Suff.; 22 September 1628. Admon. granted to Marie ffokarde his relict.

           Ipsw. Pro. Sundry Books. Vol. 9. Fo. 16.

———o———

[7]   1631.

THOMAS FFOKARD of Dallingho, Suff.: 6 June 1631.   Admon.
    granted to Marie ffokard his relict.

Ipsw. Pro. Sundry Books.   Vol. 10.   Fo. 7.

———o———

[8]   1632.

GILIAN FFOLKARD of Dallingho, Suff.: 12 July 1632.   Admon.
    granted to Thomas ffolkard her kinsman.

Ipsw. Pro. Sundry Books.   Vol. 11.   Fo. 12.

———o———

[9]   1632.

RICHARD FFOLKARDE of Beccles, Suff.: 24 July 1632.   Admon.
    granted to Marie ffolkarde his relict.

Ipsw. Pro Sundry Books.   Vol. 11.   Fo. 11.

———o———

[10]   1636.

ANN EADE (*Nupt.* FFOKARD), Widow, of Sternfield, Suff.: 14 July
    1636. Admon. granted to John ffokard her kinsman.

Ipsw. Pro. Sundry Books.   Vol. 14.

———o———

[11]   1639.

EDMUND FFAULKE (FFAULKERDE) of Belton, Suff.: 2 April 1639.
    Admon. granted to Thomas ffaulke his son. And—
        Pro. feod. test ffaulkerde, Belton, 14 April 1640.

Ipsw. Pro. Sundry Books.   Vol. 17. Fo. 5. & Vol. 18. Fo. 4.

———o———

[12]   1664.

ROBERT FFOLKARD of Stowmarket, Suff. "The last day of August
    1664 John Bradley the universal creditor of Robert ffolkard formerly
of Stowmarket in Suffolk defunct had letters of administration granted to
him."

Cur. Prerog. Cant. Admons. 1664.

———o———

[13] **1675.**

MARGARET COLLINGS, *alias* FFOKAR, of Norwich, Norf.: 5 July 1675. Admon. granted to Priscilla Sherringham, *alias* ffokar, her sister.

Norw. Consis. Admon. Books.

———o———

[14] **1678.**

THOMAS FFOLKARD of Cookly, Suff.: 26 March 1678. Admon. granted to Elizabeth ffolkard, "widow and relict of defunct. Bondsmen of said relict, Sam. Manning of Walpole and William ffleet of Helmingham in £200."

Ipsw. Pro. Sundry Books, Vol. 30. Also Admon. Books, 1673 to 1708.

———o———

[15] **1684-89.**

LUCAS FFOLLIARD (FFOLKARD) of Colchester, Essex. Admon. granted.

Deanery of Bocking. Somerset House. 1684-89.

———o———

[16] **1694.**

ROBERT FFOLKARD of Pettaugh, Suff.: 26 August 1694. Admon. granted to Richard Sallowe, principal creditor, Maria ffolkard the relict having first renounced.

Ipsw. Pro. Admon. Books. 1673 to 1708. Fo. 119.

———o———

[17] **1697.**

JOHNATHAN FFOLKARD of Woodbridge, Suff., Bachelor: 10 September 1697. Admon. granted to Thomas ffolkard his brother, Margaretta ffolkard, his mother, having renounced (*See Will* 80.).

Ipsw. Pro. Admon. Books. 1673 to 1708. Fo. 137.

———o———

[18] **1699.**

SAMUEL FFOLKARD of Pettaugh, Suff.: 2 October 1699. Admon. granted to Elizabeth ffolkard his relict.

Ipsw. Pro. Admon. Books. 1673 to 1708. Fo. 145.

———o———

44

[19] **1719.**

ROBERT FFOLKARD of Tannington, Suff.: 6 October 1719. Sarah
ffolkard of Tannington, widow, Thomas Grome of Worlingworth, and
John ffolkard of Brundish, enter into bond that Sara ffolkard, widow and
relict of deceased, shall administer faithfully.

Ipsw. Pro. Admon. Rolls. *123.*

———o———

[20] **1722.**

JOHN FFOLKARD of Brundish, Suff.: 3 September 1722. Ruth
ffolkard of Brundish, widow, and Henry and James ffolkard of Brundish,
entered into bond that Ruth ffolkard, relict of deceased, will well administer
his affairs.

Ipsw. Pro. Admon. Rolls. *159.*

———o———

[21] **1728.**

RACHAEL FFOLKARD of Horham, Suff.: deceased intestate. 26
September 1728. Admon. granted to Arthur Cooper of Horham.

Ipsw. Pro. Admon. Rolls. *86.*

Index Nominum.

NOTES.

I.—Pedigree No. 1 refers to that of " Folkard of Suffolk," which has been issued separately without a number.

II.—The following Christian names in association with Folkard, Folcard, Folchard, Fulcard, and Fulchard, occurring as they do repeatedly on almost every page, have not been inserted in detail: *vizt.*, Ann, Elizabeth, John, Margaret, Mary, Robert, Thomas, and William.

III.—The old capital ff is invariably indexed as F.

IV.—The addition of a terminal e is not noticed.

Abbreviations.—For P read " Pedigree."   For " *Sæp.*" read " Often."

Index Locorum.

NOTES.

I.—Pedigree No. 1 refers to that of "Folkard of Suffolk" which has been issued separately without a number.

II.—Bedfield, occurring so frequently, is not inserted in detail.

III.—The old capital ff is invariably indexed as F.

IV.—The modern spelling of names of places has been followed where known.

Abbreviations.—For P read "Pedigree." For "*Sæp.*" read "Often."

MONOGRAPH OF THE F.

OF

Folkard of Suffolk.

PART II.

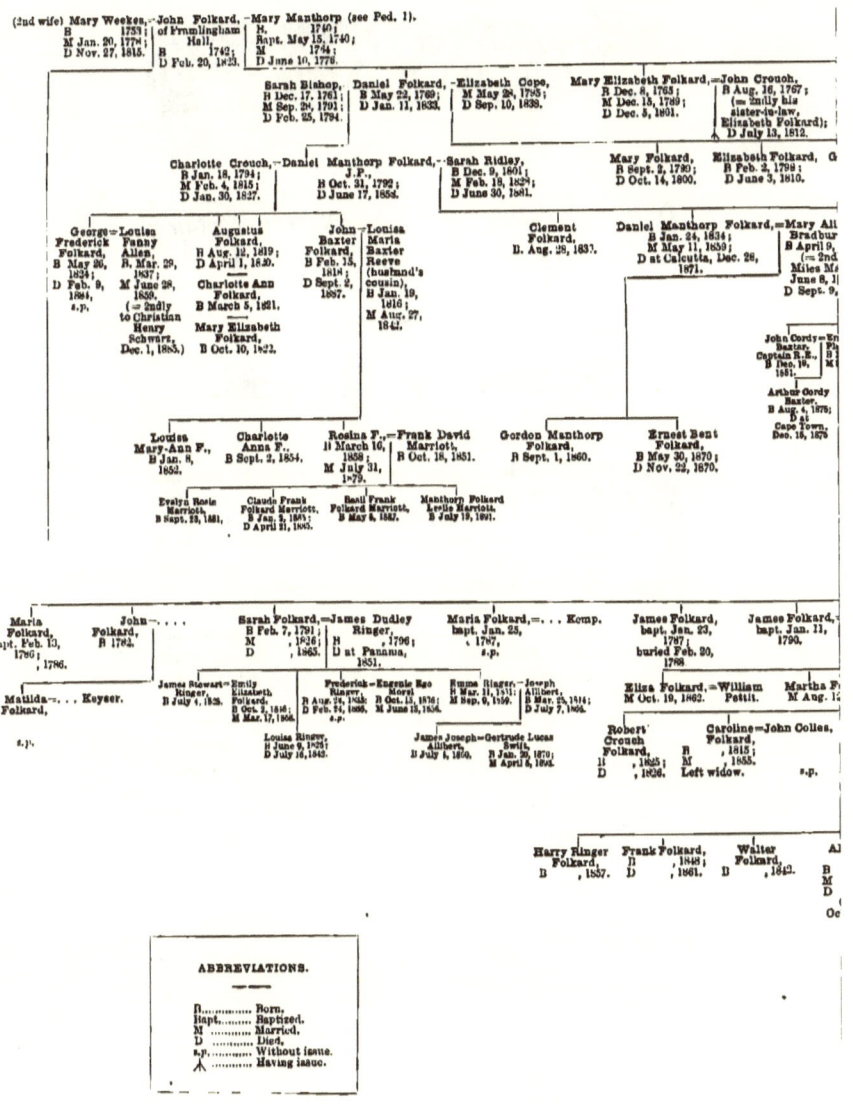

ABBREVIATIONS.

B............... Born.
Bapt........... Baptized.
M .... Married.
D .... Died.
s.p............ Without issue.
⅄ .... Having issue.

Notices relating to the Pedigrees contained in Part I. of the Monograph.

Introductory Remarks.

N order to avoid unnecessary work, the authorities quoted throughout the following notices are indicated by letters only, of which an explanatory list follows.

The smallness of the cash amounts left in the wills might, if unexplained, lead to misapprehension of the position in life of those devising them. In the first place, the purchasing power of money in the fifteenth century, in which these wills commence, was probably fully twenty times what it is in the present day. But secondly, and perhaps even more important to be considered when forming a judgment upon these wills, the great scarcity of coin in the earlier times should be remembered. Men who could probably bequeath to their descendants hundreds of acres of land, might not possess, nor be able to obtain, five pounds in money. For this reason the cash legacies were necessarily extremely small.

It is further desirable to bear in mind, in estimating the position in life of the testators, that to be engaged in trade was not in earlier days of the significance at present attaching to it. Thus it is no uncommon thing to find the younger sons of baronets so occupying themselves, and in one such instance, I have found the elder son succeeding to the title, while the youngest is described as a grocer.

Readers should understand that a yeoman was a man who farmed his own land. The line between that class and the gentry was extremely narrow. Intermarriage between the two constantly occurred, and, indeed, a man described in one deed as "*generosus*," or gentleman, is often named as "yeoman" in another. The husbandman was one who farmed land rented from others; but he was often, as are farmers in the present day, as substantially well-off as the yeoman.

The notices of the pedigrees are divided into the several main lines of settlement included in them, each one embracing minor branches deriving from those main lines.

The references to the numbers of the Wills and Administrations indicate exclusively those printed in Part I.

Where a line divides the notices of any particular settlement, it denotes the termination of the descent from father to son and immediate connections under treatment, and a following reversion to some earlier member of the same branch.

As Pedigree 2 is that embracing the earliest dates of the Suffolk settlement, it has been dealt with first in order that the references to it in Pedigrees 1, 3, and 4 may be the more readily made.

Abbreviations denoting Authorities quoted.

B.

B.	Blomfield's "Norfolk."
B.L.	"*Biographia Britannica Literariæ*," by Wright.
B.M.	British Museum Library.

C.

C.	Collections of Mr. F. A. Crisp.
C.B.	Chancery Bills and Answers (R.O.).
C.C.	"Collections des Cartulaires de France" (B.M.).
C.M.	Cottonian Manuscripts (B.M.).
C.P.	Chancery Proceedings (R.O.).
C.S.	Clerical Subsidies (R.O.).

D.

D.	Davy's "Materials for a Parochial History of Suffolk" (B.M.).
D.C.	Davy's "Miscellaneous Collections" (B.M.).
D.P.	Davy's "Suffolk Pedigrees" (B.M.).

E.

E.	Egerton Manuscripts (B.M.).
E.B.	"*Eboracum*," by Drake.

F.

F.	Feet of Fines (*Pedes Finium*) for Suffolk (R.O.).

G.

G.	"*Gallia Christiana*," by St. Marthe.

H.

H.	Harleian Manuscripts (B.M.).
H.A.	"Histoire des Auteurs Sacrés et Ecclesiastique."
H.B.	"*Historiæ Rei Literariæ Ord. S. Benedicti.*"
H.C.	Hardy's "Catalogue of Materials for a History of England to the reign of Henry VII."
H.L.	"Histoire Literaire de France."
H.M.	Historical MSS. Commission Reports.

L.

L.C.	Suffolk Leet Courts. Add. MSS. British Museum.
L.R.	"*Liber Regis*."
L.S.	Lay Subsidies of Suffolk (R.O.).
L.S.N.	Lay Subsidies of Norfolk (R.O.).

M.

M.G.	"*Monumenta Germaniæ*," by Pertz.

O.

O.	"*Ordericus Vitalis*" (Bohn's Translation).

P.

P.	"*Patrologia Cursus Completus*," by Migne.
P.L.	"Paston Letters."
P.R.	Plea Rolls. Queen's Bench (R.O.).

R.

R.F.	Rymer's "*Fœdera*."
R.O.	Record Office.

Pedigree No. 2.

Order in which the several Lines of Settlement, &c., are dealt with.

1. ISOLATED INDIVIDUALS (*i.e.*, unconnected with any distinct line).
2. MELLIS (includes branches settled at Eye, Thetford, East Bergholt, Rushall in Norfolk, Stoke Ash, Worlingworth, and Rendham).
3. DARSHAM (includes branches at Peasenhall and Dunwich).
4. LEISTON.
5. HONINGTUN (or CNOTINGTUN) (includes branches at Cavendish, Barton, Pakenham, Kersey, Bury, and Bacton).
6. THORNDEN (includes branches at Braham, Redlingfield, and Bury).
7. RICKINGHALL (includes branches at Mumpinton and Ereswell).
8. HOXNE (includes branches at Mendham, Weybread, Gressenhall in Norfolk, Syleham, Dickelburgh in Norfolk, Brent Eleigh, Carlton, Kelsale, Snape, Pakefield, and Knodishall).
9. GISLINGHAM.
10. HORHAM (includes branches at Corton, Lowestoft, Rendham, Redisham, Needham, and Brockdish in Norfolk).

Introductory Note.

HE assignment of the parentage of individuals on this pedigree during the earlier generations being, of course, very largely conjectural, the lines of settlement cannot be authoritatively defined. For the sake of clearness, however, it is desirable to adhere in the following notices as closely as possible to the lines shown, even where such have but a conjectural basis. Before commencing to deal with those lines which start from individuals named in Domesday Book, such men as are independently named in the first two generations will be treated of.

It seems desirable to explain the note on this pedigree: " All Domesday names perhaps identical." One man might have held all the properties named and entered under the different localities for which returns were furnished for the great survey. I do not think this was the case with respect to all the entries given, but the possibility of it should not be overlooked. Translations only will be given of the Domesday entries to save space, but their full correctness cannot be vouched for. It is a singular fact that but with one exception, that of Cornwall, the return of no county save Suffolk contains the name of Folcard. It is always given in the other returns either as Fulcher, Fulchered, or other variations.

Jsolated Individuals.

FOLCARD, Abbot of Thorney, Cambridgeshire. Also known in historical writings as Fulcard, Foulcard, Fulcher, Fulchard, Forcald, and Folcart.

My reasons for believing that, according to the family tradition, the Folkards of Suffolk derive from this distinguished ecclesiastic have been given in the Introduction to Part I. It is further confirmatory of this belief that the church of St. Gregory at Thetford, Suffolk, where we find the family first settled, was, on the authority of an ancient Papal Bull, the property of the abbey at Thorney.

Abbot Fulcard is said to have been of Flemish birth, and to have been a monk of the Order of St. Benedict. He was created abbot of Thorney by the Conqueror. The earliest reference to his career informs us that he was a monk at the monastery of St. Bertin at St. Sithieu (or Sithivens) in Normandy, where he was educated "from infancy" under the tutelage of Abbot Bavon, "who took particular care of his education, to which for some time he did no justice." St. Sithieu seems to have been either identical with, or a suburb of, St. Omer, in the Pas de Calais, then a town of Flanders. Froissart (II. 281) names the abbey of St. Bertin as being at the latter place, and Kingsley makes one of the characters in his novel, "Hereward the Wake," say: "I am the Abbot of St. Bertin of Sithieu and tutor of yonder Prince. I bring down at a word against you the Chatelain of St. Omer, with all his knights." We find Folcard made a priest of the church at St. Omer in 1060 (M.G. vii. 65). In the chronicles of that church, Folcuin (indexed as Folquin, *vel* Folcard; Folcwin, there is every reason to believe, being a Latin form for "the son of Folcard") is named as having collected in the 10th century most of the materials for the chronicles of St. Bertin, which we shall see hereafter Folcard of Thorney wrote; and in the same "Chronicles of St. Omer," this Folcard is further described as having been a monk of St. Sithieu and referred to as "Folquin the author."

Whether the two men were identical is, however, doubtful, as this Folcwin, though of the same monastery, is named as a monk of the 10th century and as having become Bishop of Morinensis, having previously been Abbot of Lambiens (G. iii. 484, 493), while it is elsewhere stated that Folquin commenced the Chronicles of St. Bertin in the 10th century

(P. cxxvi. Cartulary of St. Bertin). Whatever doubt may rest on the identity of the two men, it is certain that this abbot of Thorney was a priest of St. Omer in 1060.

Before proceeding further with any details as to this abbot's career, it may be named that from almost the earliest dates we find Folcards associated with or resident in the neighbourhood of the abbey of St. Bertin, and as donators to that monastery. In 666, Fulbert (*i.e.*, Folcbrat, *i.e.*, child of Folcard) witnessed a deed at Sithieu. In 770, Folchard is witness to another charter. Similarly, also, Folbert and Folchar in 811. Folcard the freedman and his wife Oderna and their children were assigned to the abbey in 883, while Folrad is named in 864 or 865. Folcar, a monk of the monastery, signed in 961 a deed binding the monks to practice self-flagellation, and in 1044 Fulcard signed a deed of gift to the monastery by his father Odo and his mother Ermengarde. It is not improbable that this may have been our future abbot. About 1066, we find William the son of Fulcard signing a further deed of gift, and it is noteworthy that it was a William Folcard who was Sheriff of Suffolk in 1130. These instances suffice to show the prevalence of the name in the vicinity of the monastery where the subject of this notice resided in his earlier years.

The authorities by whom this celebrated man is mentioned are so numerous, that I do not propose in his case to adhere to the system to be hereafter followed of citing them in detail. I shall, therefore, give a sketch of his career, and subsequently append a list of the authorities from which it has been compiled.

As we have seen above, Folcard commenced life as a monk of St. Bertin, and was, in 1060, made a priest of St. Omer. He probably came to England "to make his fortune" some little time before the Conquest, for we read that "Folchard, like most of the literary men patronized or encouraged by Edward the Confessor, was eminent chiefly as a writer of Saints' lives." But it would not of course follow from this that he was resident in England at the time he received the patronage of the Confessor, though one authority tells us he did come to England during the reign of that King. It is further added that he entered the monastery at Canterbury in 1060, the same year in which, as we have seen, he was made a priest of St. Omer. On the other hand, another writer states that he was summoned to England by the Conqueror immediately after the Conquest. He had been celebrated for his studious character as a monk, as which he had already achieved a reputation for his writings, and he is described by Ordericus Vitalis as "a man of deep erudition. He was courteous, pleasant, and charitable, and well-skilled in grammar and music."

On his arrival in England, he appears, as we have said, to have entered the monastery of the Holy Trinity at Canterbury, though this is disputed by some authorities, while by others he is described as of Dover in the same See. Another, quoting Baleus, states that Folcard was a monk of Durham, and the fact of his intimacy with Aldred, Archbishop of York, lends colour to the supposition that he may have proceeded from Canterbury to Durham before being appointed to the Thorney abbacy. At all events, he could not have remained long in either of these places, for the appointment last named was conferred upon him in 1068, though he does not appear ever to have been consecrated as abbot. The interest possessed by him with the Conqueror was probably due to the fact that the wife of the latter, Queen Matilda, daughter of Count Baldwin of Flanders, had for her first husband Gherbord, son of Rodolph de Warren, from whom she was divorced, and who was an *avoué* of the abbey of St. Bertin at St. Omer. This conjecture is heightened as to its probability by the fact that Abbot Folcard, in his dedication of the life of St. John of Beverley to Aldred, Archbishop of York, complains of the troubles of his monastery and of himself which had been relieved by the Archbishop, who had procured for him the assistance of Queen Matilda; for which aid afforded to him he expressed his gratitude.

Folcard ruled as Abbot of Thorney for sixteen years. He appears, not unnaturally, to have been disliked by the Saxon monks over whom he was appointed to rule in opposition to their charter, which gave them the right to elect their own abbot, and the Red Book of Thorney states that their dislike of him as a foreigner was deepened by the fear that he would alienate the abbey property " to his relations." Whether he had children of his own is not known; but it is a singular fact that a family named Fullard has long been, and is at the present day, settled at Thorney. Marriage among ecclesiastics was both permissible and common at that date, as witness the case of Abbot Folcard of Marchiennes referred to in the introductory remarks to Part I.

Our abbot appears to to have been on bad terms with the monks of his monastery during the whole of his term of office, and eventually, owing to some quarrel with the Bishop of Lincoln, he was deposed by Archbishop Lanfranc at a Council held at Gloucester at Christmas, 1084 (Quære; should this date not be 1082, when his successor in the abbacy, Gontier, was consecrated?). If Abbot Fulcard was, as we have conjectured, a married man, it is possible that the fact may have been the ground for his deposition, as it was Archbishop Lanfranc who most strenuously endeavoured to enforce the Papal Bull against the marriage of ecclesiastics. This Bull was issued by Pope Gregory VII. about 1080, only a very short time before Abbot Fulcard's deposition. There is some ground for the conjecture that William Folcard, Sheriff of Suffolk in 1130, may have been a son of this abbot, as the Pipe Rolls show us that his duties as Sheriff extended into Cambrigdeshire, in which county Thorney Abbey was situated. Historians tell us that the subject of this notice was, in consequence of the sentence of deprivation, " overcome with disappointment and grief," and that he returned to his old monastery of St. Bertin, after which no record of him has been preserved, except that some writers have referred to him as having been abbot of that monastery, which statement, if correct, must have applied to his career after leaving Thorney.

It has seemed to me to be not unlikely that he may have been the Folcard appointed later on to be Abbot of Lobbes in Cambray, who is statcd to have been a man of "distinguished learning and disciplinary power." There is no doubt that the abbot of Thorney answered at least to the first of those descriptions. One authority also says of him that "his knowledge was accompanied with an open and gracious air, with polished and agreeable manners." His chief writings were the "Life and Miracles of St. Bertin;" "A Review of a Record of some Miracles of the 10th Century;" "The Life and Miracles of St. John of Beverley," of which last there is a manuscript copy among the Cottonian MSS., though it is not known to be in the abbot's handwriting; "A Life of St. Oswald, Bishop of Worcester;" and "The Life of St. Botulph," whose remains were buried at Thorney. The Life of St. Andomari, Bishop of Térouenne, Pas de Calais, was largely added to by our abbot, and there were many other writings by him. A manuscript copy of one of these was recently sold by auction for £80. All of his works have been printed, and are to be found in the magnificent "*Patrologia*" of the Abbé Migne, a copy of which is in the British Museum Library. A very full account of his tenure of the abbacy of Thorney is to be found in Warner's "History of Thorney Abbey."

Following is a list of the authorities consulted for the foregoing sketch. ("*History of Thorney Abbey*.") (*P*. cxlvii. 1083, *et sæpe*.") ("*Historians of the Church of York and its Archbishops*," Fo. 239.) (*B.L.* i. 512.) (*H.C.* i. 423—427.) (*H.L.* xiii., iv. 49, 680, viii. 132.) (*H.B.*) (*H.A.*, *Table des Matières*.) (*Cottonian MSS. Faustina Liber*. iv. 156.) (*E.B.* 407, 413.) (*C.C.* iii. 461.) (*O.* iii. 422).

FAUECOURT ("In Latin Folcard"). The Roll of Battle Abbey contains this name as that of one of the knights who fought with the Conqueror at Hastings. In view of the liberal rewards in land distri-buted by the latter among his followers, it is not improbable that such remuneration was assigned to this man in Suffolk, and that some of the Domesday entries given on the pedigree refer to him. The name "ffauecourt" is one of the many French forms of "ffolcard" met with, and in more than one instance of the use of these I have seen the words "In Latin Folcard" appended.

Included on the Roll of Battle Abbey are also the names "ffouke" and "ffitz-ffouke." Fouke (pronounced Fouker) was also a very common form of writing Fulco or Fulcard, in the same way as Fouker or Foker has been long used in Suffolk, of which so many instances occur in the Wills printed in Part I. Three knights, therefore, who bore the name crossed from Normandy with the Conqueror. Ordericus Vitalis (i. 257) names Fulk the Lame as having furnished that invader with forty ships for the transport of his army, and it is not unlikely that in connection with such a service his sons might have embarked with the expedition. It would be apart from my present purpose to attempt any account of these men's progenitors in Normandy, but several noble families in that dukedom bore the name at the period treated of, and it may be that a son of this Fulk the Lame was identical with Fulcaud (also named as Fulcand, Focaud, and Fulcald), Lord of Arques in Normandy, in about

1150. This family was allied to that of Foucalt Desnier, Lord of l'Obroire in 1082, who is stated in " A Mésalliance of the House of Brunswick " to have been the ancestor of Eléonore d'Olbréze, married to George William, Duke of Zell, whose daughter Sophie-Dorothie was the wife of George I. of England and mother to that King's son, George II.

FULCERED of Framlingham, Suffolk. Of this man Domesday Book records under Framlingham as follows :—

" Fulcered holds of Robert Malet, one free man under the protection of Edric, ten acres : valued at two shillings. Edric of Laxfield held under the Confessor." (*See* Green's " Framlingham.")

FOLCARD (also FOLCIERD) of Thetford, was.a King's Moneyer, that is to say, a Master of the local Mint. There were in William the First's time several such Mints in Suffolk. From Sir Henry Ellis's " Introduction to Domesday " we learn that—

" A Mint was antiently one of the privileges of a burgh. In the Domesday Survey payments *de Moneta* for the privilege of coining are mentioned at Pevensey, Lewes, Malmesbury, Bath, Taunton, Oxford, Gloucester, Roelent, Nottingham, and Thetford. . . . . They received all their dies from the Exchequer, and they wrought under the inspection of officers who were called *Examinatores Monetæ* and *Custodes Cuneorum*, Essayers and Keepers of the dies, whose business it was to take care that their coins were of the standard weight and fineness."

The name of Folkard in association with this office of King's Moneyer is repeatedly met with in ancient records. In Hawkins' " Silver Coins of England" we find among a list of the moneyers of Eaured and Œthelred II., Kings of Northumberland, A.D. 808 to 848, the names of Folcnod, Folcno, Fulcnod, Fuldnod, and Fordred. Among those of King Alfred, A.D. 872 to 901, the name of Foleard occurs ; and as to the coins on which his name appears, Hawkins remarks that "these last may very possibly have been struck by the Danes in East Anglia or Northumbria in imitation of Alfred's coins." Under King Eadmund, A.D. 941 to 946, is to be found Eulcart, probably a mis-spelling of Fulcart. Such errors were common on the coinage, London, in one instance of A.D. 959, being spelt LVNNIP. It was no uncommon thing for the letters to be struck upside down. Folceard was a King's Moneyer at Norwich in the reign of Ethelred the Unready (*B*, iii. 6), a drawing of one of his coins being given in Blomfield's " History of Norfolk " on a map of Norwich. Golding's " Suffolk Coinage " informs us that the name of the moneyer on a penny struck at Bury, *temp*. Henry III., A.D. 1216 to 1272, is Fulke (pronounced Fulker): the same work tells us that on a coin of Canute, A.D. 1017 to 1035, struck at Ipswich, the moneyer's name and office appears as FOLKRD. MO. GIP. Abbreviation by the omission of the letter A was frequent.

It has seemed to me to be desirable to give the foregoing details in my account of this moneyer of Thetford. Under my notice of Abbot Folcard of Thorney I have referred to his monastery possessing the church of St. Gregory at Thetford. It is a singular fact that almost the first settlement of the family discovered should be at that border town between Suffolk and Norfolk; and it would seem no far-fetched pre-sumption that from this place the distribution of the family throughout both of those counties commenced. Davy tells us (*D.* xix. 247) that among 6500 coins dug up at Beaworth in Hampshire were found many struck at the Thetford Mint, some of them bearing as the name of the moneyer FOLCIERD and FOLCARD. In the "Norfolk Archæology" there is a further reference to these coins, stating them to have been engraved in Martin's plate (20 to 24) and in Rudings plate of the coins of William I. and II. One of this Folkard's coins bears on the obverse PILLELM REX, and on the reverse FOLCIARD MO DTFI, *i.e.*, Moneyer of Thetford. Another has a similar obverse, and on the reverse FOLCARD MO DTFI. The employment of P for W in William and of D for TH in Thetford was common, and is worthy of note in estimating the value of ancient spellings; indeed, the "Archæologia" (xxvi. 14) records William's name as appearing under twelve different forms among these coins.

It is open to conjecture that Folchard, Governor of Thetford in 1130, may have been son to this moneyer, but I have not proceeded on such an assumption in drafting the pedigree.

ROBERT FULCHERED of Sweffling. Domesday Book contains an entry of which the following is a translation:—

"Suffolk. Plomesgate Hundred. In Sueflinga one free man, Osbern, held under the protection of Edric 60 acres pasture and meadow in the time of King Edward. Then there were two ploughlands of pasture, and pasture and meadow for one. Robert de Clavilla holds it of Robert. In the same place, a free man held under tricnot 5 acres valued at tenpence. Now Robert the son of fulchered holds it."

FULCARD of Strandeston (mod, Thrandeston). The following is the translation of the Domesday entry referring to this man:—

"In Strandestuna there are two free men, Fulcard and Aluin, and in Mellis four free men and one half-attached, Leuric, Godric, Vluara, Leuuin the lucky(?), Furcard is the half-attached."

Thrandeston is close to Mellis, and only about two miles from Eye, and this Fulcard was almost certainly identical with Walter Fulcard of Mellis (No. 1 of that line).

FULKERED of Keduna. The name of this place cannot be recognized. It very probably referred to the modern Kenton lying between Eye and Debenham. Mention of this man has been accidentally omitted from the pedigree. The Domesday entry relating to him reads as translated:—

"Land of Richard, son of Count Gislebert. . . . . In Keduna 1 socman and 1 ploughland, and now there are 3 borderers and 1 female servant. One ploughland is in demesne, and there are 4 acres of meadow always worth 40 shillings. This is held by Fulkered."

FOLCHIER the Priest, of Suffolk. This man is not on the pedigree. The Pipe Roll of 12 Hen. ii. (1165) contains the note in Latin that "ffolchier the presbyter owes x marks," which he apparently did not pay, as the Roll of two years later, referring to this indebtedness, states that " ffolch the presbyter has fled into Norway."

EUSTACE DE FFAUCHERD, of Ubbeston, has not been placed on the pedigree. The occurrence of his name is, however, valuable, it being of so strong a Norman character. Davy (*D*. vii. *Ubbeston*) records that " Eustac de ffaucherd " was party, in 1206, to an agreement with the Prior of St. Neots about land at Ubbeston.

VIDALD DE FFONTARD, of Henham, is another instance of a Norman name early met with in Suffolk. I have been unable to assign him a place on the pedigree. That " ffontard " was a common mis-spelling of Folkard, many proofs exist. One reference here will, however, suffice. On folio vi. of Part I., Fontardi Mons will be found cited as a misnomer found for Folcardi Mons. The letter k and t were often used interchangeably. Thus, among the Cottonian MSS. (*C.M. Galba,B.* v. 39*b*) will be found written "ffonkleroy" for "ffauntleroy;" and in the Lansdown MSS. (175—186) " Foucault " is indexed as " Foncault," this being one among many instances of the use of n for u.

The " *Rotuli Literarum Clausarum* " (1) informs us, as to this man, that he was one of twenty-three inquisitors assembled in 1214 upon the death of Osborn, son of Walter de Coleville and Matilda his wife, who held a military fief at Henham.

The foregoing includes all names not brought under fixed lines of settlement on the Pedigree, and attention may now be directed to these last.

Settlement at Mellis.

(Includes branches at Eye, Thetford, East Bergholt, Rushall in Norfolk, Stoke Ash, Worlingworth, and Rendham.)

---

1. (WALTER) FULCARD (also Furcard), of Mellis. The only ground on which the Christian name of Walter is surmised for this man is that his presumed son, William Folcard, is several times mentioned as " Fulkered, son of Walter," and it therefore seemed justifiable to suggest that name for the subject of this notice. The Domesday entries referring to him read when translated thus :—

" Radinghefelda. In Mellis 1 free man, Fulcard, holds a moiety under the protection of Edric, 27 acres and 1 borderer and 1 ploughland and 1 acre of meadow, and a moiety of the Church (lands) of 8 acres, valued at 10 shillings."

I have suggested as almost certain, that the entry relating to Furcard of Mellis, given above under Fulcard of Strandeston, applies to this individual. The probability is, that the returns as to Mellis were made by separate officers and referred to distinct manors.

2. WILLIAM FOLCARD (also Fulchered), Sheriff of Suffolk. This man would seem to have been the channel by which taxes collected in Cambridgeshire and Suffolk reached the Exchequer. It is difficult to decide upon his precise office. I rather think that, at one time, he must have been an official of the Exchequer in London. There are many entries in the Pipe Rolls which refer to him. On the earliest Roll extant, which is thought to be of 1117, we find as translated :—

"Fulchered, son of Walter, paid 40 shillings as a gift by order of the King."

This gift has reference to Rutlandshire. On the same Roll :—

"Fulchered, son of Walter, rendered account of £209. 15s. 7d. of the old farm (i.e., rented taxation) at London. Into the Treasury he paid it. And he is quit. And the same Fulcher (with mark of abbreviation) owes 120 marks of silver of Gersoma for the Vice-county of London."

Again :—

"London. In discharge by order of the King. Fulchered, son of Walter, paid £12 in composition of County Normandy, and he owes £15. 7s. 0d."

Also :—

"London. Fulchered, son of Walter, pays in 20 shillings for pardons, by order of the King." And :—

"William son of Fulchered (indexed as William Fulchered) 18 shillings for pardons, by order of the King."

And again :—

"Fulchered, son of Walter, 5 shillings on a like account."

Further entries on a later Pipe Roll of 1156—57 read :—

"William, son of Folcred, owed 40 shillings for having a plea, 1156."

Under Kent :—

"William Folcard (indexed Folcred) 40 marks of silver for war horses by the brevet of the King, 1156."

Under Middlesex :—

"William, son of Folcred, rendered account of 40 shillings. He paid into Treasury 20 shillings and owed 20 shillings."

In 1158, in the account of Gervase of Cornhill, London, "William, son of Folcred, owes 20 shillings;" and in 1159, "William, son of Folcred, rendered account of 20 shillings and is quit."

In Stubbs' "Constitutional History of England" we are told that it was the Sheriffs of counties who paid in the contributions to the Exchequer or Treasury, and this William Folcard probably late in life filled that office for Suffolk. I think that both father and son may have resided in London as officials before settling in Suffolk, or they may only have held lands in that county, for we find constant references to William

Fulcred, son of Fulcred, Chamberlain of London, who was living in the 12th century. I shall not deal here, however, with the history of the latter on this mere hypothesis as to identity. I believe this William Folcard to have been the same man as the Governor of Thetford dealt with hereafter.

3. TERRIC FULCHRED, of East Bergholt. His sonship to the individual last above dealt with is purely conjectural. Mention found of him and of his son John is exceedingly scanty. The Register of the Abbey of St. John the Baptist at Colchester (*Add. MSS.* 294, *Fo.* 178) contains allusion to them both under the date of 1154, and apparently refers to them as holding lands of that abbey at East Bergholt.

4. —— FOLCARD, the Deacon, was of Mellis. In a charter of William, Bishop of Norwich (*D.* xiii. *Eye*), relating to the possessions of the Priory of Eye, there occurs mention of " the land which Folcard the Deacon held in Mellis." There is no date to this deed, but it is probably one of William Turbeville, who was Bishop of Norwich from 1146 to 1174, the order in which the dated charters are given corresponding to such a date. It is fairly presumable that this man was a son of the Fulcard of Mellis named in Domesday Book.

5. FOLCHARD, Governor of Thetford. The earliest Pipe Roll preserved of either 1117, or, according to Hardy, of 1130, contains the following :—

" Fulchard, *prepositus* of Tietford (mod. Thetford), Suffolk, owes £32. 2s. 8d. on the plea of G. de Clint(on)."

Hardy copies this entry in his "*Magnum Rotulum Scacarii,*" *i.e.,* " The Great Roll of the Exchequer." Stubbs, in his " Constitutional History of England," tells us that, according to the Norman lawyers, *Prepositus,* as used by them, meant the town reeve or chief magistrate. Shire reeve is the origin of Sheriff, and there seems some probability, from the fact of his contemporary payment into the Treasury, that this Folchard was identical with the William Folcard (No. 2) to whom I have assigned the latter office. It is also not an unfair assumption that this man was a brother of the King's Moneyer of Thetford before dealt with. Evidence is rare as to a continuance of residence of the family at this place ; but in 1340, a William ffochs, a not uncommon abbreviation or corruption of the name, paid a subsidy (*L.S.N.* 149/18) for land in or near Thetford. Later on, too, we find in a Calendar of Charters and Rolls by Turner and Cox (Fo. 470), preserved in the Bodleian Library, the following entry :—

" Euston, Suffolk. Edward Rokewode, of Euston, Esquire, son and heir of Roger Rokewode, late of Euston, confirms to Master William Focer, clerk, the whole of his manor of Euston, with the advowson of the church. Given at Euston, 20th August, 5 Hen. VIII." (1513).

Euston is but three miles from Thetford, and this William Focer was probably of the line at the latter place. The Christian name of

William seems to have been common among the family of this settlement, as it was also at Bedfield (See Ped. 1).

6. HENRY FOLCARD (also Felcard), of Mellis was, I have presumed, a son of the subject of the last notice. If not a son, there is little doubt, from the circumstance of residence at Mellis, that he was closely allied to him. The references found to this man afford the earliest record of a wife's name that I have found. A Latin deed (*H. Charters* 50, *C.* 58), attributed to the 13th century, reads translated as follows:—

"I, Albreda, late wife of Henry folcard, have given and conceded, and by this my present charter confirm in my pure widowhood, to Robert Brutlee, for his homage and service, and for four shillings sterling that he has paid me in ———— (*illegible*), one piece of land which formerly belonged to me in Wattisham of the town of Gislingham, near the fields of Mellis. That is to say between the land of Robert Brutlee and the land of Peter de Fowerhalle, and which have one end of them upon the road which leads to Adburiye, and the other end abutting upon the land of Bartholomew de Brecbe, and lies as a close or as a middle piece between them, he has it more or less. To have and to hold of me and my heirs, he and his heirs as well as his assigns and their heirs to possess freely and quietly in fœdary and heirship, paying therefor by the year to me and my heirs four and a half pence at three terms of the year, that is to say, at the Feast of St. Edmund three half pence, at the Feast of St. John the Baptist three half pence, and at the Feast of St. Michael three half pence. And I excuse them from any demand for all service or custom that may be exacted. And I, Albreda, and my heirs by this my warranty will yield and defend the said piece of land to the said Robert, his heirs and assigns and their heirs as aforesaid, against anyone, as is conceded and confirmed by this my charter. To have and to hold firmly for ever. To this writing I have put my seal. These are witnesses—Galfrid of Ikeling, Edmund of Mellis, Bartholomew de Breche, Adam his son, Roger his brother, Herbert Aickman, Henry Coterel, John Burgoin, Robert the Long, Edmund Brico, with many others."

The foregoing deed is indexed as "Felcards" in the index to the Harleian Charters. Although this Henry Folcard's name is found attached to many deeds, these are, as was so usual at that time, wholly without date. It is stated, however, that "Henry Folcard of Mellis" lived at that place in the reign of Henry III. (*H. Code* 639, *Fo.* 65). Among a series of 81 deeds (*D.* xiii., *Eye*) concerning the priory of Eye, we find the following references to this man:—

. . . "tenet de Sacrista Sci. Eadm. per Henr. Folcard."
. . . "quam una pec. jacet inter terram Henr. Folcard et inter libam terram Ecclie de Melles."

He is further a witness to six of the deeds preserved, and in one of these he is named as "Henr. fil. Folcardi."

The following charter (*H. Ch.* 47, *B.* 43) is one which Mr. Sims of the British Museum assures me to be of the reign of Henry III., and certainly of not later than 1250. As translated this document reads:—

"Be it known in the present and in the future, that I, Andraz the Bretun, of Mellis, yield and give, and by this present charter have confirmed to Alfrid, son of Galfrid de Nikelmore, for his homage and service and for twenty shillings ———— (*illegible*), that he gave in ———— (*illegible*) one acre of land—be it less or more—lying in the field of Mellis between the land of Henry son of folcard, who holds of me land of mine, and abutting on the way above the free land of the church at Mellis and on the other against Grealcroft, to have and to hold of me and my heirs, &c., &c."

" Hendricus fil. folcard" is one of the witnesses to the foregoing charter. From the constant association of his name with lands in and about Mellis, it is fair to conclude that this Henry Folcard was one of the principal residents of that place. The mention in his widow's charter above given of his land at Gislingham (anc. Goldingham) serves strongly to prove his connection with the Fulkons or Fawkuns of that place to be hereafter mentioned.

7. AGNES FULCRED, of Rushall, Norfolk. My assignment of the relationship between this woman and the foregoing Henry Folcard is of course wholly conjectural. There was, however, a well-established settlement of the family at Rushall, which is only some 7 or 8 miles from Mellis. This settlement my notes show to have extended from 1198 to 1355, the name appearing there between those dates in the forms of ffoake, ffouke, and ffulke (pronounced ffoaker, ffouker, and ffulker). In Harleston, about 2 miles only from Rushall, a house called "Folkard's" is named in a will of 1553, evidencing a late continuance of this line in the neighbourhood.

The only mention found of this Agnes Fulcred is in a Norfolk Fine of 1198. Le Neve's " Abbreviation of the Fines of Norfolk of Richard I.," gives:—

" Between Agnes, daughter of Fulcred, petitioner, and Roger the Chaplain, touching 8 acres of land in Ruieshall 10 Ric. 1 " (1198).

8. MILO FOLCRED, of Rushall, Norfolk, may fairly be presumed to have been brother to the foregoing. Only one deed relating to him has been preserved. It is without date, but is certainly either of Henry III. or Edward I.'s reign. This deed (*H. Ch. Vol. I.* 45, *F.* 39) is a charter of gift by Roger Baxter to Henry of Rushall, of the homage and service which Milo, son of ffolcred, owed to the former for a piece of land at Alwinesbeg (or burgh). It is after the usual formula of such deeds, and is witnessed by John de Marisco, Henry the None, Walter le Brun, Alexander de Riveshall, Roger le Mun, Robert his brother, Walter Lincorne, Alan Lenald, and others.

9. ALURED FOLCLED has been placed quite conjecturally on this Pedigree. Of him only a single mention has been found. This is in the "*Calendarium Rotulorum Patentium*" (I. *Part* 1.). It is therein stated that King John, in 1208, by a charter granted at Gillingham, a place only a few miles from Rushall, confirmed a grant of land to Cristian, wife of Ralph Wac (Wace?). The land is indicated as "lying between the land of Eustace de Clopton and Alured, the son of Folcled, and John, the son of Folkelet." The last-named individual I have erroneously assumed to be identical with John Folcard, of Mellis, here-after treated of.

10. WILLIAM FOLCARD, of Mellis and Eye, there is a fair presumption, was a son of the *Prepositus* or Governor of Thetford (No. 5),

and a brother of Henry Folcard, of Mellis (No. 6). He is mentioned in a deed of gift to the Priory of Eye by Henry Cratepanne, along with his brother last referred to (*D.* xiii. *Eye*) as holding land in Mellis; the reference as translated reading: "and three roods in the same field which William Folcard holds," and "held of the Sacristy of St. Edmund by Henry Folcard." There is no date to this deed, but it bears full evidence of being of about the beginning of the 13th century. There can be little or no doubt that he was the father of the Walter Fulco who, in 1225, gave evidence relating to land at Eye, at a King's Court held at Westminster, the latter's name in the record being once given as "fulcon, son of William." It is also more than likely that he is the party named in a Fine of 1204 respecting land at Rendham, his name occurring thrice in that Fine as "William, son of Folcard," and once as "William focha." The abbreviation mark across the h indicates the omission of the letter l. Such abbreviations were common, a Fine of about the same date giving Eustač de faučbg̃ for Fauconberge.

10A. JOHN FOLKARD, of Mellis and Yaxley. It has been an error to state on the Pedigree the identity of this man with the John Folkelet named with Alured Folcled (No. 9) in King John's charter of 1208. The earliest mention found of him is in a series of undated deeds which undoubtedly range between 1263 and 1280, for there is full evidence that he was a contemporary of Walter Folcard of Eye and Mellis, who follows below. It was probably about 1270 that this man, as John ffaukun, witnessed a deed of grant to the priory at Eye, as well as several others of later date. In one of these, we read of "the land of John ffaukun," which deed he witnesses as "John ffaucun." Most of these deeds are charters of William ffichet. In more than one of them in which his name occurs, he is described as "John ffaukun of Eye" (*D.* xiii. *Eye*). In 1327, we find him to have paid a subsidy (*L.S.* 180/6) of 17 pence, as "John ffaukoner," for land at Yakesley (Yaxley adjoining Mellis) and, on the same roll, 12 pence as "John ffaucoun of Eye."

11. WALTER FOLCARD, of Eye and Mellis, from the evidence above quoted, was certainly a son of William ffolcard of Mellis and Eye (No. 10). That evidence (*D.* xiii. *Eye*) tells us that in 1225 he was summoned to Westminster to give testimony respecting land at Eye. I have only found his name correctly spelt once. Fulco was a recognized form of the name, and often used alternatively for it. Fulcon and Faukun were simply the Latin forms of this when writing in that language, and no such name appears throughout Domesday Book. In some of the charters of the priory of Eye above referred to, he is named as a witness as "Walter ffaukun," and they contain repeated reference also to "the land of Walter ffaukun" (also ffaukoun). The only one of these charters wherein he is mentioned in which the date is given, is a deed of gift to the priory executed at Mellis in 1263 (*D.* xiii. *Eye*). We find him named "Walter ffulcard" as the father of his son Robert ffulcard, in an order of King John, dated 1215, releasing the latter from the prison at Eye.

12. ROBERT FULCARD, of Eye, we know from the document which follows to have been son to the foregoing. This is to be found in the "Rotuli Literarum Patentium" (R.O.), and it reads as translated :—

"Winton, 30th June, the year 17 of Our reign (1215). The King (John) to the Keeper of the Honor of Eye Salutation. Be it known to you that we recommend to your quiet and private love our faithful Robert, son of Walter ffulcard, a prisoner, who is in Our prison at Eye. And we order you that he, Fulcard, the same Robert, the son of Walter, or he and all his messengers, have letters of defence (or protection) without delay to his liberty, and that he be permitted to depart quietly. And in this thing we command you. Given as above the same year."

Stubbs, in his "Constitutional History of England," informs us that "Prince John (afterwards King) held the Honour of Eye during his brother Richard's reign."

13. ROBERT FOLCARD, of Stoke Ash and Worlingworth. There is every possibility that the Robert ffolkered of Rendham, shown distinct on the Pedigree, was identical with this man, but there is no evidence to prove this. The only record we have of him is in a Subsidy Roll of 1327 (L.S. 180/6), wherein he appears as "Robert ffokaurde," paying 20 shillings and 2 pence for land in Stoke, and as "Robert ffolkard," paying 13 pence for land in Worlingworth. Stoke Ash is only three miles from Eye, a fact which, when coupled with his name of Robert, justifies the assumption that he was a son of the foregoing Robert Folcard of Eye. Worlingworth, also, is but a few miles only from Stoke Ash.

A reference to the preliminary remarks to the notices of Pedigree I. will show my reasons for believing this man to have been the immediate ancestor of the Folkards of Bedfield.

14. ROBERT FULKARD, the son assigned conjecturally to the individual last treated of, is so named on a Subsidy Roll (180/49) of 1380, as paying 9 pence for land, but the locality is illegible. He is also named on this Roll as being one of the collectors of the Subsidy.

15. WALTER FOLCARD, of Eye. The important position occupied by this man will be seen from the frequent mention of him found. It is a fair assumption that he was son to Robert Fulcard of Eye (No. 12).

That his wife's name was Johanna we learn from a charter of 1333 of Galfrid, the son of Peter de Burgate (Add. MSS. 14,850), respecting a piece of land called Pulliscroft in Rickinghall, containing 8 acres, which is stated to have been "conceded by Walter ffaukoun, of Eye, and Johanna his wife." It was probably a daughter of hers and of her husband who is named among the oldest testamentary references of the Norwich Registry, wherein she is designated as "Isabel fflokoun de Rykinghale Inferior," and stated to have died intestate in or about 1375. This Isabel fflokoun is also mentioned in a charter (Add. Ch. B.M. 10,319) as having, previous to that date, held land of Framsden Manor.

The earliest date found touching this Walter Folcard is 1299, when as " Walter ffaukon " he served as a jurat in the manor court of Eye (*D.* xiii., *Eye*). In 1313 (*H.M.* 10, *Appdx.* iv. 518) " Walter ffankum " and others gave evidence on an inquisition held at Eye as to the townships which were bound to keep in repair the palings of the park of the King's Honour of Eye, and the "*calcetum*" of the town of Eye. Next, in 1327, we find him paying a Subsidy (*L.S.* 180/6) of 3 shillings and 6 pence for land in Rickinghall (see above), 5 shillings for land in Hintlesham, 2 shillings for land at Coddenham, 2 shillings for land at Gislingham (*See No.* 6), and 3 shillings for land at Eye. In 1330, he was Bailiff (*i.e.*, *Mayor*) of Eye (*D.* xiii. Eye). In the same year an important letter was addressed to him by Edward III. (*D.* xxx. *Haughley*), of which the following is a free translation :—

"The King to Walter ffaucon, Salutation. Whereas Isabella, Queen of England, my dearest mother, has returned into my hands the manor of Eye-cum-Haulegh, with the park and hamlets of Dalingho, Thorndon, and Alderton, with their appurtenances, in the County of Suffolk, we order you that as former custodian of the aforesaid manors, et cetera, you be responsible to us."

Isabella, the wife of Edward II., is named in the list of lords of the manor of Haughley. It was on account of the official position occupied by this Walter Folcard (latinized through the equivalent Folco to Faukun, &c.) that I have been induced to ascribe to him the receipt of the grant of the family arms. If this be correctly assumed, that grant was most probably made by Edward II., and not by Edward III., as stated on the Pedigree and elsewhere.

It was probably the last-named king who, in 1345 or earlier, presented the subject of this notice with a manor in Rickinghall, known as Facon's Hall (*D.* xiv. *Rickinghall*). In the notice of this presentation he is referred to both as Walter ffacon and as Walter ffaukoun. It was probably on account of this and other grants that he became liable to military service, for in the succeeding year we find Walter ffaukon rated for such service at 2 shillings and 6 pence for lands in Yaxley (close to Mellis and Rickinghall), 20 shillings for land in Rickinghall, and sundry sums for land held by him in other places (*D.* xiii. *Hartismere Hundred*). No further notice of this man within his probable life-time has been found ; but a rental of the manor of Rickinghall of 1387 (*Add. MSS.* 14,849) refers to " Walter ffauken " having held land there, but whether at that date or previously is not apparent. It is scarcely likely that having, as we have seen, arrived at the age required for a jurat in 1299, he could have survived to 1387. In a later rental of the same manor (*Add. MSS.* 14,850) of 1436, the land " late of Walter ffakon " is referred to, and it also names a Thomas ffocour and ffoco" (*i.e.*, Foker) as holding land of that manor. This may very probably have been a son of Walter Folcard, though I have given him no place on the Pedigree.

15. JOHN FOLCARD, of Eye, may reasonably be presumed to have been a son of the foregoing. I have associated, as identical with this individual, John Folcard, who held land at Sutton. The identity

cannot be guaranteed, but the dates and conditions make it a probability. Of his marriage no trace has been found ; but as his daughters were sole heirs to his property in Sutton, it is almost certain that his wife had predeceased him. The earliest evidence found respecting him is as a witness to a deed signed at Framsden (*Add. Ch.* 10,197) in 1358 as " John ffaucoun," and in the subsequent year, 1359, he was also witness at Framsden to a deed relating to Ottley (*Add. Ch.* 10,197). As " John ffaukon " he was a jurat of the Manor Court of Eye in 1381 (*D.* xiii. *Eye*). In 1413 we find him both Esson. and Inquis. of a similar Court at Sutton as John ffolcard (*D.* xxxvii. *Sutton*). In a rent roll of Hollesley, of apparently about the same date (*Add. MSS.* 23,950), we find a statement that " ffolkard held 3 —— " (*illegible*). The manors of Sutton and Hollesley adjoined.

Several entries in the Sutton Court Rolls relating to his death and heirs have been preserved. One of 1416 (*D.* liv. 36) reads translated :—

"John ffolcard deceased. Agnes, Letitia, and Dulcia, his daughters and heirs, being of full age, admitted."

The same rolls have a note that in 1418 one of these daughters, Dulcia ffest, had succeeded. A further entry of 1421 records that :—

" John ffolkard is dead. Agnes, wife of John Busk, Letitia, wife of Ade (*i.e.*, Adam) ffete (or ffest), and Dulcia, wife of Roger ffete (or ffest) are heirs, are admitted, and surrender made to them."

Further we find that at a Court held on the day of St. Martin in Winter (" St Martini in Yeme ") of 1416 (*D.* xxxvii. *Sutton*) the following entry was made :—

" John ffolcard held a holding called Cogynes in Sutton. Agnes, Letitia, and Dulcia, daughters of the same, are heirs and of full age."

Shawe, who compiled extracts from the manor rolls of Sutton in 1605 (*Add. MSS.* 23,950), gives an entry to the effect that in 1416 the holding of " ffolkarde " was in possession of Thomas Cowle. This must have been other land than that to which the daughters before named were admitted. Shawe also tells us that allusion to " ffolkard's " former holding was made at a Court of 1475, and that at one held in 1488 Richard Cowle held the " holding of ffolkarde." Davy affords us yet more testimony from these same Court Rolls, giving an entry in Latin of 1418 (*D.* xxxvii. *Sutton*) which is to the effect that Dulcia ffest had succeeded to land at Harecroft. He also recapitulates the note of admission of 1416 given above. But he adds another note from the rolls of that year, that

" the same John Busk and Agnes his wife, and Letic (*i.e.*, Letitia) wife of Ad. ffete, and Roger ffete and dulcia his wife, surrender (the land) for the use of John fforthe (*i.e.*, fforther or fforker. Probably their assumed brother *John Folkard of Eye*), who is admitted."

The three daughters referred to in the foregoing extracts will be found on the Pedigree.

16. JOHN FOLCARD, of Eye, I have presumed to be the son of the foregoing, and have assigned him place as being brother to the daughters named above, and as the John fforthe to whom these let their

lands at Sutton. It may be remarked here, in justification of my doing this, that Forther, Forthard, and Fotard have been repeatedly met with by me as mis-spellings of Folcard. The final r, though sounded, was rarely written in ancient times. Thus "father and mother" were written "fathe" and "mothe," and this even as late as 1700 in cases under my own observation. This practice was similar to that now prevailing in Germany and France, *i.e.*, Folke pronounced Folker, Foulque pronounced Foulquer, and this enables us to recognize the name in old writings where it would otherwise seem unjustifiable to assume identity.

We know nothing as to this man having married. It is probable, however, that he did so, and that children of his succeeded to the land above referred to as held by his father at Hollesley, for in 1467 (*S.L.*) we find a John ffauchare, esson (*i.e.*, foreman of the jurats at a manorial court) at that place, and a Matilda ffauchare paying 4 pence fine for land held there. Also John ffoker, esson at a manorial court at Wantis-den (about 6 miles from Hollesley) in 1463 (*S.L. Add. MSS.* 21,051). These assumed children are not given on the Pedigree. In 1416 this John ffolcard served as a jurat at the manorial court of Eye as "John ffolkerede" (*D.* xiii. *Eye*). There is little doubt that the will (3) of 1456, of John ffolkys of Eye, is that of this man. It is true that it names no issue and leaves everything for charitable uses, but it was common in those days to assign property to children before death, to avoid taxation or after litigation.

No trace can be found of residence by the family at Eye until a century later, when some members of it deriving from the Horham settlement, to be hereafter dealt with, certainly lived there. This line is therefore brought to a close in this narrative. A family of Fulchers was resident at Eye from about 1558 until the commencement of the present century, but I believe this to have been descended from Nicholas ffulcher of Syleham or Hoxne, as shown on the Pedigree.

Settlement at Darsham.

(Includes branches at Peasenhall and Dunwich.)

1. FULCHERED, of Darsham. It seems a fair assumption from the fact that Peasenhall is but a short distance from Darsham, that the Fulcred of the former place was identical with this man, and it has therefore been acted upon. It will also be seen hereafter that these Folkards of Peasenhall were possessed of land at Darsham.

The earliest mention of this man is in Domesday Book. The entry, as in the "*Terra Regis*" given in the " Norfolk Archæology," reads when translated :—

" In Dersam Edric himself held 60 acres for a manor, which, when Domesday was compiled, belonged to Fulchered : valued in the time of King Edward (the Confessor) at 8 shillings, but at the survey at 10 shillings."

That this Fulchered had his residence at Peasenhall, though possessed of this manor at Darsham, seems conclusive from the many following references. In Henry 1. reign, say about 1130, " Fulcred of Peasenhall" witnessed a charter granted by Robert Malet, the celebrated Norman follower of the Conqueror, to the priory of Eye (*D.* xiii. *Eye*). That charter included a list of donors to the priory, among these being this Fulcred, who donates to it a tenth part of his land in Peasenhall and a tenth of the service of a serf " Unfrid, the son of Unney." The land of this man is also referred to in a further charter of Henry III. reign given by the same authority. Dugdale, in his " Monasticon," (iii. 401) also refers to these gifts. There is difficulty in distinguishing between this man and the William Fulcred whom I have presumed to be his son. I shall therefore include additional references met with when dealing below with the latter.

2. WILLIAM FULCRED, of Peasenhall. In a document of the reign of Stephen, probably about 1137 (*D.* xiii. *Eye*), the tenth of the land at Peasenhall stated above to have been donated to Eye priory, is said to have been given by " William of Peasenhall." The following translated extracts (*H.M.X. Appdx.* iv. 454) give much information as to this man and his family :—

" Confirmation by William, son of Fulcred de Pesehalle, and Beatrix his wife, and John his son and heir, of the gifts of Matilda, the daughter of Fulcred, his sister, to the church of Blythburg and the canons thereof, of lands, &c., at Dersam " (Darsham).

" Confirmation of the gifts of the said Matilda by her husband Walter, A.D. 1144."

" Confirmation by Sir Nicholas de Falshaw, Knight, of the gifts of his grandfather, Walter, and Matilda his wife, to the church of Blythburg."

" Confirmation by William de Folshaw and Alice his wife of the gift of his ancestors, Fulcred, William, John, and Matilda."

From these documents we learn that the wife of this William Fulcred was named Beatrix, that he had a son and heir named John, and a sister Matilda. The latter married a man called Walter, who we may perhaps conclude—from the fact further ascertained from the above extracts that their grandson was Sir Nicholas de Falshaw (a corruption common in Scotland and elsewhere of Fulcher)—also had Fulcred for his surname ; unless, indeed, he may have derived it from his possession of the manor at Darsham belonging to his great grandfather. The latter supposition is strengthened by the use of " de " Falshaw. The William de Folshaw mentioned was probably a son of Sir Nicholas de Falshaw. The wife of this William we learn to have been named Alice. It may fairly be assumed that " Fulch, son of William," who, in Henry II. reign (*Add. Ch.* 7209), witnessed a charter of Thomas of Mendham to Humfrid, son of Drog, of 20 silver shillings and land in Livermere held by Knight service, was the son John Fulchered above referred to.

E

3. CLEMENT FOCAURD, of Dunwich, from the near neighbour-hood of that place to Darsham, I have conjecturally placed on the Pedigree as a son of Fulchered of Peasenall (No. 1). The only reference to him found is in a jury list of about 1150 (*D. Darsham*), wherein his name is spelt as given.

No doubt he was regularly settled at that place, and left descendants there, to whom it has not been possible to give a place on the Pedigree. I shall deal with these as under, in order, as far as possible, to include a notice of the family settled at Dunwich, a place which more than any other on the east coast has suffered from encroachment by the sea, it having been three times swallowed up by it, and the town removed on each occasion further inland.

4. JOHN FFOLKARD (also ffoliard), of Dunwich (anc. Donewyc), was the first of these descendants that I have traced. In 1327 he paid a subsidy of 40 pence at Dunwich (*L.S.* 180/6) as John ffolkard. A little later on, we find the widow of John ffoliard of Dunwich paying 2/4 by the hands of Henry Skynner for land held of the Abbot of Sibton (*D.* vi. Rendham).

5. PETER FFOLKARD (also ffolcard), of Dunwich, was probably a grandson of the foregoing. In the *Norfolk Archæology* (v. Part iv. 457) there is given a " Release of a messuage in Dunwich from Peter ffolkard, dated 10 Henr. IV." (1409). In 1412 he was party to the following fine (*F. Norf.* 152):—

" John Wedewe of Gyssing and Peter ffolcard of Donewych plffs. *vr.* Peter Codon and Margaret his wife defts. of land, messuages, pasture, and half acre wood in Gyssing."

This land may not improbably have been that which is referred to in the following extracts:—

" Hastings Manor in Gissing was given to the Abbot of Bury, who was Lord at the Conquest, and immediately after the abbot assigned it for life to Fulcher " (*B.* i. 168).
" Fulco or Fulcher (*Reg. Pinchbeck* 182) held of the Abbot of Bury in Shrimpling and Gissing in Norfolk, 70 acres, and 4 borderers, being unfeoffed by Abbot Baldwin in the time of the Conqueror " (*B.* i. 158).

$\mathfrak{Settlement}$ $\mathfrak{at}$ $\mathfrak{Leiston.}$

1. FFULCHRED, of Leiston. Domesday Book contains the following :—

" In the same town (Lessefelda, mod. Leiston) there are eight free men with a carucate and a half of land, and here there are 3 carucates in demesne, formerly two, and one acre of pasture, always valued at 30 shillings. This land is held by Fulchred of Robert Malet."

The expression "Free Man" in Domesday Book had, according to Sir Henry Ellis's "Introduction to Domesday," a greater significance than would ordinarily seem to attach to it. He writes, that the term "*liber homo*" appears throughout the Survey to have been given to the greatest and most powerful Earls of the preceding time; and even to Harold himself. Also that the term often included "all persons holding in military tenure."

2. FFULKER, of Leiston, was probably son of the above. In a deed of grant of about 1154 to the Abbey of Leiston (*D.* v. *Leiston*) there occurs reference to "the land of Fulker." The writing is difficult to decipher, and the name may be read either as Fulker or Fulkon. The land was doubtless the same as that held by his father according to Domesday Book.

No further record of settlement at Leiston has been found by me, and it would seem to be probable that the above-named two persons were identical with the families living at Peasenhall and Darsham.

Settlement at Honingtun (or Cnotingtun).

(*Includes branches at Cavendish, Barton, Pakenham, Kersey, Bury, and Bacton.*)

---

1. FULCHER, of Knodishall. An error has been made in placing this man on the Pedigree as of Cnotingtun. He probably belonged to the Leiston family last dealt with, Knodishall being close to that place. The entry in Domesday Book records :—

"In Gnedeshalla holds Fulcher of the Abbot of St. Edmund, with 4 free men, 1 carucate of land, and 30 acres and 6 borderers."

2. FULCARD, of Honingtun. A fine of 1198 (No. 113) among those of Suffolk in the Record Office is headed thus :—

"Walter de la More against fucard son of John for 30 acres of land and pasture in Honingtun."

In the body of this fine the name is also spelt "fulcard" and "fucarde." The assignment to this man of a son John on the Pedigree is an error, he himself having been the son of John.

3. GOLDWYN FFAUKUN, of Cavendish, has only been conjecturally placed as a son of the above. In a list of the tenants of lands belonging to the Sacristy of St. Edmund in Henry III. reign (1216) (*D.* i. *Cavendish*) are included the names of Goldwyn ffaukun and Katerina his wife. A John ffaukun and a Nicholas ffaukon, presumably the sons of

E—2

there people, are also named in it as holding lands at Cavendish in the same reign. Faukun, it should be understood, was as much the common Suffolk pronunciation of Folkard in those early days, as is Fokud in the present day. Among the commonalty in that county, an inquiry now made for a Folkard would not be answered, whereas Fokud would be immediately recognised.

These Folkards of Cavendish would seem to have left descendants afterwards resident in that place. In 1327, Ayennus ffaukoun paid a subsidy (*L.S.* 180/6) of 2/3 there, Martin ffaukoun also paying a similar amount in the same town.

4. FFOLCARD, of Barton, has been conjecturally assigned as a son to ffulcher of Knodishall (No. 1). The following references to him and to his son Osbern have been found. The *Liber Niger* of the monastery at Bury, by Sir Simon d'Ewes (*H. Vol.* 294, *Fo.* 163), contains a Latin entry to this effect :—

"ffolcard, of Berton, lived at that place in the time of King Stephen and Henry II. Osbern, son of the said ffolcard, lived there in the time of Henry II. and Richard I., Samson being then Abbot of St. Edmunds."

The same book (120b) again refers to "Osbert, son of folcard of berton," and to a messuage belonging to him. The Abbot Samson above named, probably some 35 years later than the date given on the Pedigree (1154), conveyed to this son by the following charter in Latin (*H. Code, Vol.* 639, *Fo.* 8), the lands held by his father of the community at Bury :—

"The said Samson and his community confirm to Osbert, son of ffolcard of Berton, and his heirs, one messuage in the town of Berton, which ffolcard his father held before him in the same town, to be held of them in perpetuity with liberty to compound for all services for twelve shillings annually, and they concede to the same Osbert and his heirs certain lands lying in the fields of the said town, he paying annually on the 15th January three —— (*Quære*, marks) and a half for rent (*Quære*) and five shillings and three and a half —— and four and a half pence for all services upon it."

It is almost impossible for me to read Sir Simon d'Ewes handwriting, so the translation of the latter part of the deed is very uncertain, except as to the amounts payable.

By entries, of which I have unfortunately made no copy, in an old MS. (*H.* ccixiv. 163b) it would appear that this Folcard of Berton either lived at or held land at Pakenham, about 2 miles only from Barton. No record has been found of immediate descendants of this Osbern or Osbert ffolcard. Much later on, however, in 1523, a John ffolkard paid a subsidy (*L.S.* 180/184) at Barton of 7/6 for moveable goods valued at £11, so that it is possible the family was living there during the interval of more than three centuries.

5. LAWRENCE FFULCO, of Pakenham. (It may be desirable to mention here that the family name is constantly met with in the form of Fulcoard, of which Fulco would only be one of the customary abbreviations). From the fact named above that Folcard of Berton owned land at Pakenham, the descent of this Lawrence Fulco from him

may not unreasonably be presumed. The earliest mention found of him is in 1234, when, in a warrant of assize held at Pakenham (D. Pakenham), his holding there is referred to as that of Lawrence de Pakenham. A deed of the same date, given by the same authority, informs us that Lawrence de Pakenham held land called " Byshopcroft," opposite to the church at Pakenham. To a fine of 1275 (F. 4, Ed. I.) Laurentem ffitz-ffulco, of Pakenham, is a party. It may be believed that he left no descendants at that place, for on a subsidy roll of 1327 the name is not to be found among those paying the subsidy there.

6. GALFRID (i.e., GEOFFREY) FFAWKEWARD, of Bury, has been placed conjecturally on the Pedigree as a son of the foregoing. He, his wife Justina, and their son Richard, are named in the following instances. Kempe's register of residents at Bury (H. ccxciv. 170b) has in Latin :—

" Galfrid ffaukewarge, also called Galfrid ffawkeward, with his wife Justina, were both living, 8th Edward II." (1314).

The same MS. (Fo. 170, 59a) states further :—

" Galfrid ffanwarde. Richard. son of the said Galfrid, was in life at that place in the 10th year of King Edward II." (1316).

7. RICHARD FFAWKEWARD, the son just referred to, was probably identical with the Richard ffolkard who, in 1327, paid a subsidy (L.S. 180/6) of 2/7 for land at Kelseye (mod. Kersey). The use of the final " ward " to this man's name marks the recognition of the original derivation of the name from Folkward, and its use may also be noted in other instances, specially in that of Will No. 70 of a much later date.

Whether my conjecture as to the parentage of this man's father be correct or not, it is certain that members of the family had early settled at Bury St. Edmunds, though only recorded by corrupted or abbreviated spellings of their names. I shall deal briefly with the family settlement at Bury here, as being a convenient opportunity for doing so, though the following have no place on the Pedigree under reference. The earliest resident there found by me is—

7a. ROGER FFULCO, who is thus named in the list of residents at Bury referred to above (Fo. 163b).

" Roger, the son of ffulco. William, the son of the said Roger, whose wife was Agnes, lived there in the reign of Henry II." (1154).

In 1100, we find him as " Roger, the son of ffulco," owning land at Clopton. In the Liber Niger of Sir Simon d'Ewes before quoted (H. Vol. 294, Fo. 131) it is stated that—

" William, the son of Roger, the son of fulconis, held land in Menezeden " (probably Monewden)

As " Fulcher de Maynerie," he held land also at Redgrave, and Gilbert, his son, succeeded to it (H. ccxciv. 163b). The Liber Niger mentions several other ffulcos as living in Bury about the same date. Among these was certainly included—

8. FFULKE (pronounced FFULKER), a King's Moneyer.
Golding's "Suffolk Coinage" informs us that three coins bearing his name
have been preserved.   They are of either Henry II. or Henry III. reign.

9. NICOLAS, SON OF FFULCO (also Nicolas ffuke, *i.e.*, ffuker),
of Bury, is named in an ancient MS. referring to that city (*Add. MSS.*
7102, *Fo.* 681). By this he is described as Bailiff (mod. Mayor), there
during the 9th, 10th, 11th, 12th, 15th, and 17th years of Edward I. By
the same authority we further learn of him that in the 22nd and 28th
years of that King's reign, he was an alderman of Bury, as Nich. ffouke
(pronounced ffouker). In 1284, as "Nicholas filius ffulcon," he witnessed
a deed at St. Edmunds Bury (*H. Cod* 639, *Fo.* 47b). The Berengero
ffolè(ard)—the ffolc bearing the note of abbreviation—who, about 1272,
witnessed a deed of gift to Drayton Priory, Cambridgeshire, by Ranuelfus,
Count of Chester (*H.* 294, *Fo.* 249), may have been a daughter of this
Nicholas ffulcon.

It is elsewhere stated (*H.* ccxciv. 1703) that "Nicholaus ffouke"
was living at Bury in 1303, and that "Robert, son of the said Nicolas,
lived there at the same time as his father." Davy alludes to this
Nicholas in his Pedigree of Foake (pronounced Foaker), a name identical with the corruption of Folkard so constantly occurring among the
Wills in Part 1.

10. JAMES FFOUKE (also ffulco), born at Bury, and named in
the Pedigree as Sheriff of London, will be dealt with further on.

11. RICHARD FFAUKON, a priest, is named as paying a
Clerical Subsidy (*C.S.* 45/5b) of 3/4 at Bury in 1380. It is not
improbable, from the identity of the Christian name, that he was son to
the Richard ffawkeward named above (No. 7). It will be well here to
give further evidence as to the identity of Faukon as a corruption of the
corruption of Fawker in such common use.

In a note respecting a claim by Raphael ffulker for freight
(*Lansdowne MSS.* 150, *No.* 30, *Fo.* 57), dated 1586—93, the claimant's
name is written in the margin as "Raphael ffaukon."

12. GEORGE FFACON, of Bury, in 1565, paid a subsidy (*L.S.*
181/359) of 2/6 at that place on goods valued at £3; and in 1568 (*F.* 6
Pasch.) he was defendant to a fine sued by Henry Coppinger in respect
to land there.

13. GEORGE FFACON (or "ffawcon"), of Bury, is stated in the
Pedigree of the family of Reeve of Suffolk (*D.P.*) to have married, about
1650, Margaret, daughter of Edward Reeve, of Bury. It is extremely
likely that he was grandson to the foregoing George ffacon.

14. ELIAS FFAWKER was martyred at Bury, July 6th, 1583.
Among the Lansdowne MSS. (38—64) is the subjoined letter of that date
from Lord Chief Justice Wray to Lord Burghley. After referring to
certain dealings with sundry popish recusants, this letter proceeds :—

" Elias ffawker and John Coppinge (*i.e.*, *Coppinger*) and Thomas Gybson are convicted for distributing of Brown's bookes and Harrison's bookes, the first two executed in the time of the assize ; Elias upon Thursday, Coppinge upon ffryday. They both acknowledged her Majesty's Sheriff (?) *rular civilis*, for so is the terme, and no further, and although doctor Still and other travailed and conferred with them, yet they, at the very tyme of their death, recommended all things in these said books to be good and godly. There were burnte to the number of fortie bookes, some part at the execution of Elias, and the rest at Coppinge. And Gybson was also convicted for the poesy (?) he gave to be painted about her Majestye's armes."

The association of the name of Coppinger with this Elias ffawker may be considered in connection with its mention in the fine quoted above (*See No.* 12), as additional proof of the identity of the corruptions of ffawcon and ffawker.

15. THOMAS FFOLKE (indexed ffolker). The following fine of 1715 (*F.* xxxiv. *Hil.*) indicates continued connection of the family with Bury:—

"Between Thomas ffolke, *Armiger*, pplf., and Thomas Macro, *Armiger*, and Susannah his wife defts., of 4 messuages, 4 gardens, 4 orchards, 140 acres land, 100 acres meadow, 10 acres pasture and conpasture, with appurts., in Bury St. Edmunds, Welnetham *parva* and *magna*, Bradfield St. George, Bradfield St. Clare, Alpheton, Shrimpling, Stanton, and Hapworth. Plf. pays deft. £260 sterling."

16. WILLIAM FFOLKER, writing master, of Bury, advertised in the *Ipswich Journal* of January 8th, 1742—3, that he could supply assistants " skilled in accompts, particularly in the Mercantile way, that can show an elegant command of the Pen in the Despatch of Business."

It is not worth while to enter upon the residents of Bury bearing the family name within more modern times, when greater facilities for travelling induced members of other settlements to resort thither. In the western parts of Suffolk, the name was rarely found in its original form of Folkard, and the Fawkuns and Fulcos of earlier dates have quite disappeared from them. These may perhaps survive in the Fawke or Fawkes, Folke, and Folkes, yet to be found in the towns of that division of the county.

17. RALPH FFOLKARD, of Bacton, I have conjecturally placed as a son of Galfrid ffawkeward of Bury (No. 6). It is exceedingly diffi-cult to decipher the name of the locality given in this instance. I read it as Buccone, but the old writing of c and t is so similar, that it may be read Bucton. The Subsidy Roll containing it is dated 1327 (*L.S.* 180/6), and gives the name of Ralph ffolkard as paying 12 pence subsidy, and of Adam ffachare paying 9 pence, Margaret ffachare 1/3, Matilda ffachare 12 pence, and Roger ffachare 12 pence, all of them in this same place, Buctone.

It seems a reasonable conclusion that these were all members of one family, the difference of the spelling on the same roll being of no account when it is considered that the Rev. Mr. Candler spelt the name in six different ways on his Pedigree of Folkard, as late as 1650.

Settlement at Thornden.

(Includes branches at Braham, Redlingfield, and Bury.)

1. FOLCHER, of Thornden. In a Pipe Roll of 1165 "ffolch (with mark of abbreviation) de Torndis" is entered as paying 12 pence to the Exchequer. In the following year "ffolchered and his friends owe 20 shillings per pledge of William" (see William ffolkard of Mellis, No. 2 of that line). The fact that Thornden was a place of settlement of the family for nearly a century and a half justifies me, it may be believed, in assigning to this man the foundation of it. On the Pedigree he is conjecturally placed as a brother of the William ffolkard above named. Nothing is known of him beyond the entries quoted.

2. ROBERT FFAUKERED, of Braham-Thornden. It is most difficult to distinguish in the old records between this man and his son; and the mention of the names of both is so frequent, as to still further increase that difficulty. The repeated entries to be given will prove that both men—presumably father and son—occupied high judicial posts.

In Foss's "Judges of England" (iii. 21), we are told that Robert Fulcon was Judge of the Court of Common Pleas in the reigns of Henry III. and Edward I. In 1218, the third year of Henry III., "ffauker de Brame" appears on the Fines Nos. 13, 17, 18, 19, 21, and 22, as one of the King's Justices for Suffolk. On the last, the final r of the name bears the abbreviating sign indicating the full name of "ffaukered." These cases were heard by this judge at Ipswich and Dunwich; his name, in one instance of a further case tried, being given as "ffolco," and it appears in these varying forms on all the Suffolk Fines up to the 10th Henry III. (1225). Brame is a common Suffolk corruption or equivalent of Braham, and there is every reason to believe its use in this case referred either to a hamlet or land bearing that name lying close to Thornden and named in a Fine (xxii. 41) of about 1422. Blomfield (*B. Yarmouth*) informs us that in 1233 Robert ffulco was one of the itinerant Judges at Yarmouth, and he again refers to him as having filled the same office in 1239 (*B.* viii. 115). To a Fine of 1255 (*F.* 18) relating to land at Berkyng (*mod.* Barking), "Robin, son of ffulco of Radinges," is a party. Radinges is probably the modern Redlingfield (*Radinghefelda in Domesday Book*) situate close to Thornden, and no doubt reference is made in this Fine to both the father and son of the Pedigree. A further Fine of 1258 probably refers to the father, naming him as "Robert fulcon of Radingges." In a fine of 1266, Robert fulcon is named as the judge in the case, and in others of 1271 and 1273 he is also so indicated, the first one of these being brought by Robert ffulcon against Robert de Wyke and John Eye, respecting messuages in

Berdwell. The plaintiff in this case was doubtless the son. As the date of this fine brings the father's administration as Judge up to 1273, in which year he must have held the judicial office for 55 years, it appears reasonable to conclude that further mention of Robert ffaukered as a judge must refer to his presumed son next treated of.

3. ROBERT FFUKER (many aliases) was in all probability a son of the foregoing. Several references have been made to him in the preceding notice of his father. Continuing the evidences already cited, mention is found of " Robert ffitz-ffulk " in the "Chronicles and Memorials of Great Britain and Ireland " (*Annales Monastici. Index*), as an itinerant Justice at Oxford in 1284; while in the same Index, under the names of Fulcon, Fulcher, Fulke, and Fuke, he is referred to as filling the same office at Winchester in 1280, and at Dunstable in 1283 and 1284.

In 1285, we find him named in a Suffolk Fine as " ffulco." In 1286, he was, as "Robert ffulk," one of the itinerating judges presiding at Norwich (*B. Yarmouth*). In the " Pleas of the Crown " (*Quo Warranto, etc.*) " Robert de ffulconis " is named as one of the King's Justices in Suffolk, and after this, I have come across no mention of him until 1314, when the King's commission had been issued to " Robert ffuke " (pronounced ffuker) to be one of the King's Justices in Eyre (*B. Yarmouth*), it may perhaps be presumed as a sort of *honorarium* after his long services as an itinerating Judge. The " History of Great Yarmouth " mentions Robert Fuke as one of Edward the Third's Justices in Eyre in 1328; and as we have above found him party to a Fine in 1255, he must at that date have been little less than ninety years of age, a good specimen of the longevity which has ever been a special characteristic of the Folkards of Suffolk.

4. JAMES FFOUKE (pronounced ffouker). I have assumed this man to have been a son of the foregoing. The "Chronique de Londres," from MSS. in the Cotton Collection, states that " Jakes ffouke " was Sheriff of London in 1310 (*Add. MSS.* 5444, *Fo.* 153*b*), a footnote informing us that his name was " James, son of ffulco, of St. Edmunds."

5. ALICE FFUCHER, of Thornden. It is of course possible that this widow was the relict of some unknown son of Robert ffaukered, the first of the two judges. Her residence at Thornden would make such an hypothesis by no means a strained one. Mention of " William, the son of Roger, the son of ffulconis," in Sir Simon d'Ewes' Register of Merketon, Suffolk (*Fo.* 131), with reference to land at Monewden in the reign of Edward III., strengthens this conjecture somewhat; the descent going back from the son William of this widow, through his father Roger, to ffulco (*i.e.*, Robert ffaukered), the King's Justice, who would be a well-known man. If this may be accepted, the husband of the subject of this notice would have been Roger ffucher. This widow and her son William of the Pedigree are named in a Latin deed of 1310, of which the following is a free translation (*H. Charters* 45, *E.* 47):—

F

"To all the faithful in Christ. By the present writings, et cetera, both seen and heard of, I, Alice of Cotton, who was wife to Hugo of Auggerhale (*Quære, mod. Uggeshall*), given in my pure widowhood, concede and release for myself and my heirs in perpetuity unto William, son of Alice ffucher, of Thornden, his heirs and assigns, which conveyance is made for the sum of money the same William has given to me ———— (*illegible*) two parts of the garden lying near Cotton, which the aforesaid Hugo formerly held in feoffment, and of which he made me heir for life by his will, and neither I, the said Alice, nor my heirs, nor anyone acting for us, nor by our motion shall by any oath claim the aforesaid parts of the garden ———— (*illegible*). In testimony of which I have put my seal to this present writing. Given at Cotton the day of Mercury (*Quære*) after Pentecost, in the fourth year of King Edward, son of King Edward. These are witnesses to this writing :—Richard Champanye, John de Cumpeige, Richard de Hadlye, William of Auggershall, John Gothelard, John Iypcat (*Quære*), John Ganical (*Quære*), Silcare (*Quære*), and others."

Having met with none other of the name as having resided in Thornden until 1548, it may be concluded therefrom that residence there died out with this Alice ffucher. I have, however, conjecturally assigned to her son the parentage of the two men next treated of.

6. THOMAS FFALKODE AND STEPHEN FFALKODE.

The first of these paid 4 pence, and the second 12 pence, on a Subsidy Roll of 1378 and 1380 (*L.S.* 180/34). This particular Subsidy names no localities except the county Suffolk. There is some probability that a Thomas ffokat, who paid 6 pence on a Subsidy Roll (*L.S.* 180/6) of the reign of Edward III. for land in Framsden, was identical with the first of these two men.

𝔖𝔢𝔱𝔱𝔩𝔢𝔪𝔢𝔫𝔱 𝔞𝔱 ℜ𝔦𝔠𝔨𝔦𝔫𝔤𝔥𝔞𝔩𝔩.

(Includes branches at Mumpinton and Ereswell.)

Rickinghall Superior and Inferior lie but about five miles west of Mellis, and lands were held there by members of the family resident at the latter place and at Eye from very early dates, and certainly as late as 1333, when Johanna, wife of Walter ffolcard of Eye, held land there (*No.* 15 *Mellis Settlement*). The connection of this line with that of Mellis and Eye may therefore fairly be assumed.

1. ROBERT FFULCHER, of Rickinghall. The Pedigree assigns as his father, Walter ffulcard of Mellis (*No.* 1 *of that Settlement*). Whether he really resided in Rickinghall is open to some doubt ; but between 1135 and 1150 he gave, according to a Charter of Abbot Sampson (*Add. MSS.* 14,850), land in that place to the monastery at Bury as "Robert the son of Fulcher." Land was owned there by a Folkard as late as 1727, but it would be too much to assume its identity with that owned by the family in earlier times.

2. CHRISTOPHER FFULQ̄(ARD). The parentage assigned to this man on the Pedigree is wholly supposititious. The only record of him found is on a Pipe Roll of 1167, which states that—

"Christopher ffulq̄ (with mark of abbreviation), of Mumpinton, rendered account of four score pounds and 100 shillings for his right of hastening ——— (*Quære*, his marriage) with (or against) Ada, the daughter of Aluric (or Alured). Of this sum he paid into the Treasury ten pounds."

It does not seem to be unlikely that this Aluric or Alured was Alured ffolcled (*No.* 9 *Mellis Settlement*). The entry apparently relates to Suffolk, but I have failed to even approximately identify Mumpinton with any modern place name. It was important, however, to include this Christopher ffulq̄, because the abbreviation sign over the q in the original indicates that the full name was ffulquard or ffulqard, both of which forms of the family name were most common corruptions in early chronicles of the ancient and original ffolcward. The c and the w sounded together have their equivalent in q.

3. WILLIAM FOLCARD, of Ereswell, has been conjecturally placed on the Pedigree as son to the foregoing. The only reference to him and his son found are in a Latin Charter (*Add. Ch. B.M.* 5913), of which a translation is given below. This deed is undated, but the Museum Catalogue assigns it to the reign of Henry III. (1216 to 1272).

" Be it known in the present and future that I, William, son of folcard, of Eriswell, have conceded and given, and by this charter fully confirm, to Alexander my son, by his homage and service, that messuage with its belongings and appurtenances which lies between my messuages which I hold by customary tenure of the Abbot and Convent of Colchester, to have and to hold of me and my heirs to the aforesaid Alexander and his heirs, or to whomsoever he wishes to deliver, sell, or assign it [*the next sentence I cannot translate*], he paying for it annually to me and my heirs, thirteen pence at two terms of the year known as the Feast of St. Michael six pence and a half, and at Paschal six pence and a half for all customary services and exactions except the service of our lord the king. To wit for Scutage twenty shillings and two pence, and so more or less. And I the aforesaid William and my heirs will guarantee to the aforesaid Alexander and his heirs, or to his assigns, the aforesaid messuage such as is aforenamed and all its belongings. These are the witnesses :—Peter de Tusford, Henry Canerarun, Thomas son of William Bobo of Langholm, Richard of Cotton, Richard of Chebenhall, John son of Edward, William the Clerk, Ralph Spurner, Herbert Reginald, Maurice the Chaplain, with many others."

Endorsed—

" The Charter which William the son of folcard made to his son Alexander, and j——j—— custom and paying feoffment yearly 13 pence —s. Given at Ereswell."

It is possible that the above Alexander folcard left descendants who lived at Ereswell, for in 1565 we find a John ffoockes paying a Subsidy (*L.S.* 182/359) there of 3/4 for goods valued at £4.

Settlement at Hoxne.

*(Includes branches at Mendham, Weybread, Gressenhall in
Norfolk, Syleham, Dickelburgh in Norfolk, Brent-Eleigh,
Carlton, Kelsale, Snape, Pakefield, and Knodishall.)*

1. WILLIAM FFULCO is the earliest instance named in connection with Hoxne. On a very old deed, without date, but believed to
be of between 1200 and 1267 from grouped deeds (*D. Hoxne*), the land of
William ffulco in that place is alluded to. This reference may have
been to the William ffolcard of Mellis and Eye to whom I have assigned
his parentage on the Pedigree. From the close connection between the
adjacent lands of Syleham and those of Hoxne, I feel little doubt that
the ffolcard de Scilo (and fulco de Syelford) named below, met with in a
Fine of 1234, was identical with this William ffulco.

In a customary of the towns and hundreds by "fulcat made and
took" in 1278 (probably this same William ffulco), it is stated with
regard to Redgrave (about 5 miles N.W. of Mellis) that "ffolcard of
Scilo held 10 acres all of the same custom" (*Add. MSS.* 14,850, *Fo.* 4).
The same MS. (*Fo.* 6b) has further:—

"In Redgrave, ffolcard at Scigheli holds 10 acres, and Alfric of Scigheli holds 1½ acre
of the said ffulcard."

Other references to this man occur in the same customary. In
another of 1433 we find what is evidently the same land still "called
ffolcardes." In a rental of 1301 we also read that "Adam Joop held 8
acres and 20 acres of land formerly called ffolcard's." These holdings
in Redgrave and Hoxne may possibly have been those of a William
ffulco who lived at Syleham but held land in Hoxne, all three places
being contiguous.

With reference to the early possessions of the family in Redgrave, it
may be noted here that (*H.* 294, *Fo.* 136b) a Fulcher de Maynerie was
living there in the reign of Henry I. (1100 to 1135), and that "Gilbert
the son of the said Fulcher held it after his father."

2. ALAN FFULCHER (also ffolard), of Weybread, has been
hypothetically assigned place on the Pedigree as a son of the foregoing,
Weybread being within a mile of Syleham. In 1327, he paid a Subsidy
(*L.S.* 180/6) of 12 pence for land at Weybread. It is not unlikely that
this man was identical with the Alan ffaukun of Goldingham (mod.
Gislingham), dealt with hereafter under the latter settlement, who was
knighted as Sir Allan Goldingham. This, however, I have been unable
to verify. An account book of Sibton Abbey, under date 1456 (*D. vi.
Sibton*) refers to land at "Weybrede which was ffolard's." This doubt-

less was the land for which the Subsidy above named was paid, and which, it will hereafter be seen, probably descended to Simon ffolkerede, of Weybread.

3. SIMON FFOLKEREDE, of Mendham, has been given a place as a son of the individual above, that town lying only two miles from Weybread. Land had been held at Mendham by members of the Mellis or Peasenhall Settlement (see those lines) both in 1154 and 1228. The sole reference found as to this man is as a witness to a deed of 1397 of transfer of land in Mendham to John Cobold and others. He is described in it as being of that place, but would seem to have had no descendants living there.

4. SIMON FFOLKEREDE, of Weybread. From the continuation through three generations of the same Christian name, and from the contiguity of locality above named, it is no strained assumption that this man was son to the Simon ffolkerede last dealt with. In 1418, as " Simon ffolkred," he witnessed a deed of transfer of a house with croft adjacent at Weybread, and he was again a witness to a similar deed of that place in 1460 (*D. Weybread*) as Simon ffolkered. I have assumed as being probable that late in life he moved to Gressenhall in Norfolk, for the will of Simond ffolkard of that place (8) of 1483 contains a legacy for repairing the church at Weybread. By that will we learn that his wife, who survived him, was named Juliane. It names no children. He probably had some relatives previously living at Gressenhall whose connection with that place induced his own move to it, for in 1378 (*L.S.N.* 149/51), Adam ffulk paid a Subsidy of 4 pence there. This might have been the Adam ffachare of Bacton before referred to (*See Honington Settlement*).

5. SIMON FFOLKARD, Prior first of Hoxne and afterwards Prior of Lynn, Norfolk, may fairly be presumed to have been son to the above. What we know of him is almost exclusively derived from Blomfield's "History of Norfolk." We are told therein that Simon Folcard was Prior of Hoxne in 1473, and that he held that office for seven years. He is further named in a list of the Priors of Hoxne (*D. Hoxne*). In 1493 we discover him as " Simon ffolkarde " among the *Nomina Commonactorum* in the " Visitation of the Diocese of Norwich." Whether he was then Prior of Lynn does not appear, but it would seem from the entry that he was in that year of the Norwich Priory. Elsewhere (*B.* iv. 18) it is stated that " In the South Cross Isle or transept of Norwich Cathedral was a brass plate on a stone for Simon Folkard, first prior of Hoxne, and after of Lynn, which is now lost (*written about* 1718), but had this inscription on it :—

" Orate pro anima Symonis Folkard Prioris Lenne, qui obiit M⁰· CCCCCJ⁰."

Weever's " Funeral Monuments," printed in 1631, gives, at page 797, a slightly differing inscription. This has :—

" Orate pro anima Fratris Symonis Folkard, nuper Prioris Lenne, qui obiit MCCCCCI."

A translation of this last would read :—

"Pray for the soul of Brother Symon Folkard, formerly Prior of Lynn, who died 1501."

No trace of this brass has been discovered. On the walls of Norwich Cathedral, however, there are many marks of brasses removed and destroyed possibly by the iconoclasts of the Commonwealth at a date subsequent to Weever's writing.

6. REGINALD FFOLKERED, of Weybread, has also been placed as presumably a son of Simon ffolkerede of that place (No. 4). The earliest mention found of him is in a deed of 1423 (*D.* xv. *Freesingfield*), which reads translated from the Latin original :—

"I, Alice, late wife to Thomas Carter of ffresynfeld, in my pure widowhood concede to Reginald ffolkerede of Weybride, &c., &c., the second year of King Henry VI."

A second deed of much later date, 1453, is given by the same authority, and refers evidently to the land transferred by the first deed. Translated this reads :—

"Be it known to all Christian people that we, Reginald ffolkered of Weybred, John Dade of ffressingfeld, Senior, and Robert Noyse of the same, remit, relax, &c., to Alice Carter, formerly the wife of Thomas Carter of ffresingfield, to be freely held by her, the land which we hold jointly with Nicholas Duffeld and William Dalangho now defunct, &c. Given at ffresyngfeld 20th March, the thirty second year of King Henry VI."

7. JOHN FFOAKE (pronounced ffoaker), of Weybread. The will of this man is in the Probate Registry of Norwich. No copy of it has been obtained by me ; but a note on the index states that, although of Weybread, he died at Hoxne, his will being among those filed for 1564-5-6. His relationship to this branch of the family may therefore be assumed.

8. THOMAS FFULCHER, of Weybread, was not improbably a brother of the man last dealt with, and son to Reginald ffolkered of Weybread (No. 6). My belief in the identity of the name is strongly borne out by the entries, all apparently relating to this man, in which he is designated by the two names. In 1523 we find Thomas ffolkerd paying a Subsidy on movable goods at Syleham valued at £10. (*L.S.* 180/171). On the 3rd February, 1536, Thomas ffulcher witnesses a deed at Weybread (or it may have been at Wingfield, only a mile or so distant) (*Add. Ch.* 19364). In 1546 Thomas ffulcher is defendant to a Fine sued by John Goldyng respecting lands in Wingfield, Syleham, and Ersham (*F. Trin.*), and plaintiff to a second Fine of the same year against Robert Wolverston respecting lands in Palgrave and Wortham (*F. Michs.*). There would seem to be little doubt of the identity of the men holding land, &c., in Syleham.

I have assigned to this man's parentage two sons, William and Robert ffulcher, as both were residents of Weybread. Authority for the first of these is derived from a Chancery suit hereafter referred to (*See No.* 12), and the second is found to have paid a Subsidy in 1591 (*L.S.* 182/407) of 3 shillings for land in Weybread valued at £3.

On working through my notes for the purpose of illustrating this Pedigree, it has become evident to me that my assignment of a son John to the William ffulcher just above named was an error. That John ffulcher, I am now convinced, was identical with the man (*No.* 13) dealt with hereafter.

---

9. THOMAS FFULCHER, of Hoxne, has been placed on the Pedigree as a son of Simon ffolkerede of Mendham (*No.* 3). It has been extremely difficult to decide upon the identity of the ffulchers of the Middle Ages with the ffolkards, because in those times the names were certainly becoming of more distinct application. On the other hand, however, one fact is of particular significance. In very many cases, and notably in those of the family settlements at Debenham, Weybread, Eye, and Horham, as well as in this of Hoxne, the appearance of ffulchers in the records and registers has been contemporaneous with the disappearance from those documents of the name of ffolkard.

It would be impossible to account for these coincidences save upon the hypothesis that the customary provincial pronunciation of ffulker or ffolker for ffolkard had been adopted by many of the unlettered scribes of that day; and, as has been pointed out in the Introductory Remarks to Part I. of this Monograph, the ch was to a very late date the equivalent for k. For this reason I have formed the opinion that in the case of Weybread, as in the other towns above mentioned, the ffulchers were the immediate descendants of the disappearing ffolkards. In proof of the recognition of their identity by antiquarian writers, I would here quote from Anthony Lower's "*Patronymica Britannica.*"

" Folkard, Folkerd, Fulcher, or Fulcherus, a Domesday name, is doubtless the same as Folchard or Fulcard, borne by an eminent Flemish scholar, who settled in England about the time of the Conquest and became Abbot of Thorney."

Also :—

" Folker, *See* Folkard."

Of this Thomas ffulcher we know nothing beyond the facts that in 1432, in a roll of the manor of Syleham (*Add. Ch.* 16,562), ffulcher is named as holding land there, and that he made his will in 1481, in which year, according to the date of its proof, he must have died. The following is an abstract of that will (*Norw. Consis. Hubert* 1475—91, *Fo.* 89) :—

" Thomas ffulcher of Hoxne, 7th October, 1481. To be buried at St. Peter of Hoxne. Legacies to church there, and to that of Dickelburgh. To Johane Hylle 62 pence ; John Hyll 13/4 ; Thomas ffoulsber. Senior, 40 pence ; John Hyll 40 pence ; Thomas ffoulcher, Junr., 40 pence ; a further legacy to the church of St. Gregory for his own and his parent's souls. Thomas ffoulcher and John Hill, Senr., exors. Proved at Hoxne 10th February, 1481, by the executors."

The legacy to the church at Dickelburgh in Norfolk, 5 miles northeast of Diss, implies that the testator must have had some connection with that place. He probably held land there, and his sons, Thomas ffuleer and John ffolcer, hereafter dealt with, seem to have settled there. The latter, there seems good reason to believe, was the progenitor of the large family of ffolsar or ffolser settled later on at Diss, the records of that family found favouring such a conclusion. The only life reference to this man is in a surrender of land (*D. Hoxne*) wherein his son Thomas ffulcher is named as " the younger."

10. THOMAS FFULCHER (also ffulchar), of Syleham and elsewhere, was son to the foregoing, and is named in the latter's will above
given. His own will is dated 1499, but his death cannot have occurred
till many years later, as we find him as "Thomas ffulcer (note approach
to ffulser above referred to) paying a Subsidy (*L.S.N.* 150/282) of 12
pence for land in Dickelburgh, Norfolk, valued at 20/. The date of this
Subsidy has been lost, and though ascribed by the Record Office
authorities conjecturally to 1525, it may have been levied somewhat
earlier in the century. By a deed of 1479 (*D. Hoxne*) Robert Greys
surrendered to—

"Thomas ffulcher the younger a deed of awarde given up in wrightingè by Humphry
Wingfield, Esqr., of landes in variance between Robert ffulcher and Exors. of Edmund
ffulcher."

This Robert was probably the brother shewn on the Pedigree. We
know nothing of Edmund ffulcher deceased, but he was probably also a
brother. In 1500 (*D. Hoxne*) the subject of this notice surrendered to
"Alis, my wife, all my lands for her life;" these, after her death, to go to
his son Edmund. On the Pedigree, by a misprint, the date of this
surrender has been given as 1546. These facts are from the accounts of
the manor of Syleham, and doubtless refer to lands in that place.

Allusion has been made above to this man's will. It is to be found
in the Norwich Consistory (*Gyles* 1517-18, *Fo.* 54). Only the first few
lines are entered in the books. An abstract of these reads:—

"Thomas ffulcher, of Hoxne, the elder. 15th year of Henry 7th (1499). To be buried
in the churchyard of Saints Peter and Paul, Hoxne. Several church legacies."

Why this will was not fully entered is unaccountable. The date of
its inclusion indicates its writer's death in 1517 or 18, and the Norfolk
Subsidy above named as being conjecturally assigned to 1525 was therefore almost certainly of an earlier date.

11. EDMUND FFULCHER (also ffucher), of Hoxne, was a son
of the above. Davy (*D. Hoxne*) gives two fragmentary copies of this
man's will of 1514. Amalgamated and abstracted these may be read
as under:—

"I, Edmund Fucher, of Hoxne. To High Awter for tithes forgotten 5/. Sir John
Weete shall sing for my sowle by the space of a year, and to have 8 marks and 6/8. Item,
I will have six masses songe at *Scala Cœli* in London if yt may be borne of my goodes, or
als three masses. A priest to synge for my sowle and my father and mother, and Rychard
my brother in the church of Hoxon. To Elizabeth my wyff all lands and tenements in
Syleham and Hoxton (*i.e.*, Hoxne) for life, and then to be sold and go to the church of
Hoxon or to a priest's service, or els to both, a part to the payntinge of the Image of St.
Peter of Hoxon, or ells any other thinge necessarye or most expedient for the weale of my
soule and all my frynds soules. All goodes, cowes, and catalls to wife. If she marries, she
to give security for the payment of debts and legacies. Sir John Wyett (see above "Weete"),
John Turston, and Will. Everard of Hoxne, exors."

Before 1523 the wife named in this will must have re-married. In
that year (*D. Hoxne*)—

"Elizabeth Colman, late the wife of Edmund ffulcher, did surrender and release divers
pieces of land (at Syleham) to the exors. of the above will."

12. ROBERT FFULCHER, of Hoxne, has been named above in the surrender of lands at Syleham by Robert Greys in 1479. He is named also in a Chancery suit, together with the several other ffulchers named on the Pedigree, who have been included on it mainly from the depositions in that suit. My abstract of these reads:—

"Chancery Depositions, Charles I., F. No. 2, 31 Henry 8 (1539). Bill of Complaint opens:—'William ffulcher, son and heir to Nicholas ffulcher, cousin [i.e., nephew], and the heir unto the said John, that is to say, son of John fulcher, brother to the said William ffulcher, one of the complainants, that whereas the same John ffulcher possessed certain lands in Palgrave, Suffolk.' After his death, these came to complainant. One Clement Cowper [also Coup] had entered on the lands without title. One Thomas fulcher, son to said John, father to said William. John ffulcher had two sons, William the eldest, one of the complainants, and John, father to the said Nicholas; and that the 'said William and Nicholas be heirs to the disputed lands.' One Thomas fulcher had four sons, John, father to the said William, one of the complainants, Robert, Simonde, and William. 'Agnes ffulche was the wife of Thomas ffulche.'"

The Simonde ffulcher (also ffulchar) named in the foregoing depositions as a son of Thomas ffulcher (No. 8) has been accidentally omitted from the Pedigree. It is possible that he was Simon ffolkard, Prior of Hoxne and Lynn (No. 5).

13. JOHN FFULCHER, of Weybread, was son to the William ffulcher of the Pedigree. In 1606 he was defendant to a Fine sued by Roger Bale respecting land in Weybread (F. Michs.). His wife's name we learn to have been Frances from the following notes respecting her. These also contain the only other references found to her husband.

" Frances Fulcher, widow (1623), late wife of John Fulcher, gent., deceased, petitions that William Calthropp, Esq., deceased, was in his life possessed of certain lands and houses in Weybred, Suff., and had mortgaged them to William Fulcher and John Bame of Fressingfield. John Fulcher was one of the sons of William. Payment not having been made, the mortgagees took over the property" (C.P. Series 2, Part 8, No. 46, Fulcher vs. Sweet).

"23 April, 1636. William Crowne of St. Clement's Danes, London, Gent., petitions that whereas one Henry Mayes of Norwich, about 1624, laid title to the messuage and lands of John ffulcher, then of Weybred, Suff., Gent., situate in Weybred, the latter's friends advised him to compromise the claim, which he would have done by a great sum of money had not plaintiff hindered him, and the latter cleared the title for him some years his having promised good satisfaction for his pains by defendant. And whereas ffrances ffulcher, widow, natural mother of John ffulcher, had an annuity of £30 issuing out of the manor of Porter (Quaere) and other lands in Yorkshire, the property of the late Lord Ross, and 150 miles from Weybred . . . . there was £60 arrears due on this, and ffrances ffulche and the said John ffulche, 'her only child,' being afraid of not getting it, and Lord Rosse refusing to pay it, and being so powerful in those parts that no man dare destrain on his cattels, the plaintiff out of affection for defendants rode to Lord Rosse's estate and at the hazard of his life seized cattle to the value of the debt."

The answer of John ffulcher the elder, gent., dated 8 July, 1647, reads, abstracted:—

"Alludes to his 'late' mother and denies plaintiff's statements. Says that the latter is a lawyer, and that the annuity was regularly paid to the widow ffulcher so long as Lord Rosse lived; but on his death, the manor went to Sir Richard Cecil, who neglected the annuity. The complainant did not go specially to Yorkshire, but having occasion to go into Derbyshire, not far distant from the manor, he offered to look to the matter. Says complainant was his mother's kinsman by marriage" (C.B. Chas. I., C.C. 38(62).

G

14. JOHN FFULCHER, of Weybread, is named in the case above quoted, to which he was defendant, as the only child of the man last noticed. On the 16th January, 1628 [*C.B., A.A.* 31 (42).]

"John Algar of Weyghbread, Suff., Yeoman, complained that money due to him by a will is held back by a combination of John ffulcher and others of that place."

From depositions taken at New Buckenham, Norfolk, in this case (*Chanc. Depositions, Chas. I. A. No.* 7) we learn that John ffulcher was co-defendant to it with William Cooks. The case referred to the rights of the exors. of the will of Robert Everard, of Weybred, whose son and heir was "an idiott, very noysome."

This John ffulcher was further defendant to a Fine of 1649 (*F. Hil.*), indexed "Thomas Botebright, Gen., *vs.* John ffulcher, Senr., Gen., Waybred." As being described as senior, he must at that date have had a son of the same name. This son was probably the John ffucher whose marriage license (*C.*) of June 29, 1640, informs us of his marrying at Hoxne Phillippa Dickerson, single woman.

A Matthew ffulcher was living in 1599 at Hoxne or Syleham, but is not included on the Pedigree. A suit (*C.P. Miscellaneous, Series* i. 45) of 27th May, 1599, has as plaintiff Richard Cowper, of Hoxne, Yeoman, who sought to recover from this Matthew sundry property of William Baldwyn, of Syleham, deceased. This family had descendants at Hoxne as late as 1784, when James Fulcher of that place was included in a Poll List as voting for property at Eye. This fact supports my theory that the Fulchers of the last-named place were allied to those of Weybread and Hoxne above sketched.

14A. FFALCARE, of Illeigh (*mod. Brent-Eleigh*), has been placed on the Pedigree conjecturally as a son of William ffulco of Hoxne (*No.* 1). He is named as a tenant of the manor at Illeigh (*Add. MSS.* 6159, *Fo.* 188b) about the reign of Edward II. (1308).

---

15. ROGER FFAUCON, Rector of Brent-Eleigh, may be presumed to have been son to the last named. In a list of the rectors of that place (*D*1, *Brent-Eleigh*) his name is given as inducted to that office in 1355.

---

16. WILLIAM FFOLPALD, of Carlton. This peculiar writing of the name has been found by me in several instances of the early Folkards of the Continent. "Ald" is a common form for "ard," and in one case of this man's descendants the last form is used. The substitution of p for k must have been a lingual peculiarity, as it was preserved through several generations. I assume this man to have been a son of William ffulco of Hoxne (*No.* 1).

In a Latin "Extent of the Manor of Carlton" of 1334 (*D. Carlton*), William ffolpald is named as being a land tenant. With reference to some land, it is said to "abutt on Folpald's wall." Of other land the entry occurs that the "holding abuts before the gate of J. Wadlove and the holding next to Folpalds."

17. HENRY FFOLPALD, of Carlton, may be fairly assumed as a son of the above. Another roll of that manor (*D. Carlton*) refers to him as holding lands in the same neighbourhood.

18. JOHN FFOLPALD, of Carlton, has been presumed on the Pedigree to have been a brother of the last. The roll last quoted has (*ex. Lat.*)—

"Hugo de Scarnahagh (*Quære*, Scarning, Norf.) has the farther part, and one piece abutting on the holding of William Geffry with Aquilon, a quarter of the piece lying next to the holding of John ffolpald from the part of Aquilon."

The land of this John ffolpald is again referred to in the same roll as being on the road from Framlingham. On a manor roll of Sibton of 1366 (*D. Sibton*) ffolpald is named as a jurat, and as giving evidence as to certain tenures at Kelsale (close to Carlton).

19. ROGER FFOLPALD, of Kelsale, was probably a son of the foregoing. In 1450 he is named on several manor rolls of Kelsale (*D. xvi. Kelsale*). Most of the lands named in them seem to have been in Carlton.

20. WILLIAM FFALPOLD, of Kelsale, was very likely a brother of the last. In a manor roll of that place (*D. Kelsale*) of 1450 his name occurs twice as a tenant of land.

21. JOHN FFALPOLD, of Kelsale, may have been son to the foregoing. In the rolls named above he is repeatedly named as holding lands at Carlton (12 acres), and others at Middleton. In 1480 he did homage at the Manor Court of Kelsale, and in 1483 he and his wife are referred to as " John ffolpald and Emma his wife." In the first of the two years named John ffolpald was appointed joint Commissioner with Thomas Bysshop to render account, and " Alicia, relict of John Amys," is subsequently stated to have held one acre of land in Carlton belonging to John ffolpald. No man of this name signed the covenant at Kelsale in 1641, so probably the family was then extinct in that neighbourhood. In the Ipswich Probate Registry there is a record of administration being granted to the goods of " Henry ffokarde who lived at Carlton," dated 5th March, 1612, and the register of Carlton records the marriage of Thomas ffaulke (pronounced ffaulker) to Jone Goose, on July 10th, 1563. These instances make it probable that the name had reverted in this locality to its truer forms.

22. JOHN FFALPOLD, of Snape, may either have been identical with No. 21 or else a son of his. This man and his brother, Wat ffolpard, are named in a Roll, 20 feet long, relating to manors in and about Snape of 1485, not 1474 as named on Pedigree (*D. Snape*). This informs us that :—

" Item. Hew,Thorpe purchased of John ffalpold 1 acre of fre lond and paid fine 2 pence." " Item, Thomas Meikeby and Wat ffolparn purchased 7 rods lond of Botelers, Olyve, and Thynglove, and John Meikeby was his aye (*i.e.*, surety) and paid fine 2 pence."

In 1487 (*Add. MSS.* 21,054, *Fo.* 28) " John plokatt," of Tunstall near Snape, is entered as holding land of Blaxhall Hall manor. Other forms of the name, probably those of descendants of these ffolpards, occur in subsequent records relating to Snape and its vicinity. In 1523 Catherine ffakon paid a subsidy of 3 pence for goods valued at £6 in Snape, and Thomas ffakon one of 12 pence for goods there valued at £10 (*L.S.* 180/128). A few years later (1543), John ffawken pays 10 shillings and Matthew ffaukon (*Quære*, the Matthew ffulcher living at Hoxne in 1599, see No. 14) 4 shillings Subsidy for goods in the same place (*L.S.* 101/252).

It may be concluded from the fact that no form in which the name can be recognized found mention in the Manor Rolls of Snape from 1279 to about 1450, nor in that of 1602, that the residence there of the family was confined to between the two latter dates.

---

23. ALICIA FFOLKARD, of Hoxne. Although place has been assigned on the Pedigree to this lady as a daughter of Simon ffolkerede of Mendham (No. 3), she may possibly have been a member of the family settlement at Horham, which place is only three miles from Hoxne; some of these (See Wills 10 and 21) having possessed land in the latter place.

A Rent roll of Hoxne of 1453 (*D. Hoxne*) has :—

" Reve lands whych bersth Reve in Hoxne. Alicia ffoll:ard 1 rod in tenure of the seid Alice. John ffolkard of Horham on the part of the bridge there."

24. RICHARD FFOLCARD, Rector of Pakefield, has been con-jecturally placed on the Pedigree as having been also a child of Simon ffolkerede of Mendham (No. 3), but I have not been able to authenticate his parentage, his Will (2) affording no clue to any relatives of his. The earliest mention discovered of him is in the year 1438, and it is to be found among the "*Munimenta Academica*" (ii. 521) of the "Chronicles and Memorials of Great Britain and Ireland;" the name of "Ricardus Folcarde" being mentioned therein, in a list of the Principals of Halls at Oxford, as the Principal of "Haburdashe Hall" on the 9th September, 1438.

Suckling's "Antiquities of the County of Suffolk" (*Fo.* 284) informs us that "Richard ffolcard was appointed Rector (*i.e.*, of Pakefield) in 1445 by the patrons, Thomas Bardolph, Esq., and Alice his wife." ·

He made his will (2) as Rector of the Mediety of Pakefield in 1451, proof of it being made only nine days after its date. A fine brass to his memory still exists in Pakefield Church, and all works on the archæology of the Eastern counties refer to it. The finest presentment of this brass is published in Suckling's book above referred to (*Fo.* 284), and a copy of a rubbing from the brass itself is in my own possession. The effigy is represented in full canonicals; issuing from its mouth is a label bearing the words—

"*Misericordia Domini in eternum cantabo*" (*i.e.*, "Of the mercies of the Lord I will sing for ever.").

**Memorial Brass of Richard ffolkard, Priest, in
Pakefield Church, Suffolk.**

TRANSLATION

LEGEND.—"I will sing of the mercies of the Lord for ever."—Ps. lxxxix. 1

INSCRIPTION.—"Here lies Master Richard Folkard, formerly rector of a mediety of this church in the southern part, who died on the day of St. Martin in Winter, A.D. 1451, To whose soul may God be propitious. Amen."

Below the effigy is the following inscription :—

"Hic jacet Magister Ricardus ffolcard, quondam Rector mediatatis istius ecclesie in parte australi, qui obiit in die Sancti Martini in y'eme Anno domini ccccli. Cujus anime propicietur deus. Amen."

This translated, according to Kelly's Post Office Directory of Suffolk, in which work the brass is described under " Pakefield," reads :—

"Here lies Master Richard Folkard, formerly rector of a mediety of this church in the Southern part, who died on the day of St. Martin "in hyeme" (*i.e.*, Winter), A.D. 1451, to whose soul may God be propitious. Amen."

An error has been made on the Pedigree in having shown the year of his death as 1450. Respecting this brass, Davy (*D.* xxiii. *Pakefield*) wrote in 1832 :—

"In the floor at the West end lies the stone which had the brass of Richard Folkard : this brass has been torn from the stone and has been fixed on a piece of Portland stone against the East end, on the South side of the Altar."

Explanation as to this Richard Folkard having been rector of a " mediety," or half, of the church of Pakefield seems desirable. It was no uncommon thing in ancient times to build churches on the border line between two parishes, that line running through the centre of the building. As regards the death of this rector " on the day of St. Martin in Winter," that day was so called in contradistinction to the feast of St. Martin " the boiling " (from the heat of the weather) of July 4th. The day of St. Martin in Winter, according to the Calendar, is November 11th.

25. WILLIAM FFULKERD, Stipendiary priest of Knodisham (mod. Knodishall), has been entered on the Pedigree conjecturally as another son of Simon ffolkerede of Mendham (No. 3). All we know of this man is from his name occurring on a Clerical Subsidy (*C.S.* 46/150) of 1448, not 1428 as erroneously given on the Pedigree, which reads (*ex. Lat.*)

"William ffulkerd, Stipendiary Chaplain of Knodisham."

Settlement at Gislingham.

This place is only 2½ miles from Mellis. The relationship of the Folkards who early resided there to those of the latter place may justifiably be assumed; and the more so because, as has been written under the record of Mellis and Eye, more than one member of the family in those towns were possessed of land in Gislingham.

1. FFULKON, of Goldingham (mod. Gislingham), has been assigned as son to Walter ffolcard of Eye. It is, however, feasible that

he was identical with that man's son, Robert ffulcard of Eye. Davy
gives deeds in which he is mentioned as being Lord of the Manor of
Goldingham in 1316 (*D.* xiii. *Gislingham*), and further informs us that his
son took the title of Sir Allan Goldingham or "de Gislingham" on
receiving knighthood. The date of this knighthood seems uncertain.
The possibility has been elsewhere named that this son, Allan.ffaukun,
was identical with Allan ffulcher (and ffolard), who held land at Weybread. No further record has been found of him.

2. JOHN FFULCO, of Gislingham, was, no doubt, son to Sir Allan
de Gislingham named above, for he succeeded to that man's manor there.
In 1331 he witnessed, as "*Dominus John de Goldingham*," a deed signed at
Cavendish (*Add. Ch. B.M.* 9939). In 1363 we find him referred to as
"*ffulco de Goldyngham*" (*D.F.*), under the locality of Gislingham. The
title "*Dominus*" was that commonly given to Lords of Manors.

Settlement at Horham.

(Includes branches at Corton, Lowestoft, Rendham, Redisham, Needham in Norfolk, and Brockdish in Norfolk.)

1. —— FFOLCARD, of Thorpe near Horham, would appear
to have been the almost certain progenitor of the line which for so long
resided at the latter place. As this lies but five miles from Eye, the
derivation from the settlement there may fairly be assumed. Whether
or not this man was one of the family already named as resident there
cannot be said.

The only knowledge we have of his residence at Thorpe, a place
now erased from the map, but which old deeds place just north of Horham, is in a charter of about 1216 (*Add. Ch. B.M.* 7539), between
Hamond of Thorndon, Chaplain, and William his nephew, agreeing to
sell a tenement and capital messuage in Theberton, Suffolk, for twenty
silver shillings, this land being described as lying between the land of
"folcard de Thorp" and that of Henry Carpenter.

2. RALPH FFOLCARD, of Horham and Eye, may be presumed
to have been a son of the last named and successor to his land. He
held lands also at Horham and Ufford in 1346, according to a Rent roll
of that date (*D.* xv. *Hoxne*). In a roll of the lands of "*Dominus Edmund
de Thorpe*" of 1356 (*D. Fressingfield*) this man is named, as *Radulphus* (*i.e.*,
Ralph) ffauken, as being a free tenant in Allyngton (mod. Athelington,
close to Horham). It also includes allusion to his land as "one piece of
meadow containing 20 acres and worth yearly seven shillings."

A Rental of Rickinghall of 1387 (*Add. MSS.* 14,849) contains repeated references to land of this manor at Winston, apparently just vacated by Ralph ffocour (*i.e.*, ffoker). This land seems to have been known as "Southfield." There is every probability that the man named was identical with the subject of this notice. The Folkards connected with Rickinghall are generally referred to as ffaucon, ffakon, &c., in the rolls of that place, but reference has been made before to one of these of 1436, in which the name appears as ffocour and ffoco'.

I have assumed this Ralph ffolcard to have been the ancestor of the Sparham Settlement in Norfolk (Ped. 3), the name of Ralph being continued in that branch of the family, while the identity of the arms borne by it with those of Suffolk affords some further evidence of its descent.

3. JOHN FFOLKARD, of Horham, was, in all probability, son to the foregoing. In a list of Reve lands of Hoxne of 1453 (*D.* xv. *Hoxne*) the lands of John ffolkard of Horham are named. Entries (*L.C.*) of 1466 may possibly refer to this man and his wife. These tell us that in that year John ffoker paid fines of 8 pence, 6 pence, and 12 pence, and Agnes ffoker one of 6 pence, for land held at Stanton. An entry of the succeeding year states the rental of this land to be 20 shillings, and refers to Agnes ffoker as the wife of John ffoker. In a rental of Hacheston (*D.* xxi.) of 1485, there is an entry which also probably refers to this man. Translated this reads:—

"Rendlesham. John ffolkard holds freely one piece of land formerly Roger Hall's, namely, 1¼ acre lying between the Lord of Colvill's on the one side, and the holding of Robert Shyringham on the other, and abutting on the road leading to Tunstall, towards Eyke, and paying for it by the year four pence and one cock and two hens."

4. THOMAS FFOLKARD, of Horham, was probably son to the above. He is the only man to whom it would be possible to assign identity with the Thomas ffolkard of a Latin deed of 1474 (*D.* xxxv. *South Elmham*), whereby there were devised to him and others by Robert Brende, Senior, of South Elmham, certain tenements. The object of the deed is not discoverable, but it does not seem to create a trust.

No further mention of him has been found prior to the date of his will (10) of 1500, which was proved between that year and 1503. His wife Alice is named in it as then living, and allusion is made to lands possessed by the testator in Horham, Corton, Hoxne, and Denham, all of these places, with the exception of Corton, lying contiguous. He is very likely to have been the Thomas ffolcarde alluded to in his son's will (21) as having surrendered lands held of several manors.

5. JOHN FFOLKARDE (also ffawlker), of Corton, has not been included on the Pedigree, but from the fact of the above Thomas ffolkard having held land at Corton, I am inclined to the belief that they were brothers, though so many years divided their respective deaths. For that reason I hold that notice of this man and his descendants at Lowestoft should find place here.

His wife's name, we learn from his will (18) of 1540 to have been Anne, and it may be conjectured from the fact that her later days were evidently passed at Blundeston, that the Miles Wynston of that place, who was one of the exors. to her husband's will, was a brother or other near relative of hers. A Reginald Wynstone was living at Blundestone in 1438. The maiden name of this wife was, for the above reasons, very probably Anne Wynston. Several references to her in her widowhood are extant. In 1545 she sued the following Fine in the King's Court at Westminster (*F. Michs.*) :—

"Between Ann ffolkard, widow, plff., and William Kempston and Johanna Oxenden, defts., respecting a messuage, 6 acres land, 3 acres pasture, and 2 acres heath and broom, with appurtenances in Corton and Hopton, that the defts. yield the said property to the plff. and her heirs for ever."

In 1548 we find her paying on a Subsidy Roll (181/298) as "Anne ffolkard, Wydowe," 10 shillings on movable goods in "Bloundston," valued at £10. It may be deduced from this that in that year, ten years before she made her will at Lowestoft, she resided at Blundeston. Her will (25) of 1557 is curious as affording evidence of the use of the name "ffawlker" for ffolkard, her late husband being also referred to in it by that name. She probably died in the following year, in which 'the will was proved. I regret that a singular injunction of that will, to the effect that she be buried "as wormes' meate," has been accidentally omitted in the printed abstract of it.

Of her husband the earliest mention found is of 1521. In that year he was one of the plaintiffs to a Fine (*F. Hil.*) of which the following is a free translation from the original Latin, which is very illegible :—

"Between John ffolkard and John london, clerk, plaintiffs, and William Eberton and Marion his wife, formerly wife to Robert pratte, defendants, of one messuage, 7 acres of land and 1 acre heath, with appurts. in Corton and hopton as to which there was a former Concord between them in the same Court. Be it known that the aforesaid William and Marion recognise the aforesaid holdings, with the part which John ffolkard has, as those which the same John and John london has by the gift of the said William and Marion, and by them remitted and quitclaimed by them the said William and Marion and their heirs to the aforesaid John and John and to the heirs of John ffolkard in perpetuity. And further, the said William and Marion concede for themselves and the heirs of Marion by their warrant to the said John and John and his heir the aforesaid John ffolkard to hold that part against their heirs in perpetuity, and by this do recognise remittance, quitclaim, warrant, fine, and concord to the same John and John, they giving to the aforesaid William and Marion 20 pounds sterling."

In 1524 this John ffolkard paid a Subsidy (*L.S.* 180/141) of 6 shillings for "movabyll goodes" in Corton valued at £13. Nothing further regarding him is known prior to the date of his will (18) of 1540. In that will, and in that of his widow, only one son, Richard, is named, but this would not necessarily prove that the John ffolkard who, in 1545, paid a Subsidy (*L.S.* 181/270) at Gorleston of 5/3 on goods valued at £8 was not also a son of his. A daughter Anne is also named, apparently as then single, in his will. She was probably the Anne Waters named in the mother's will, to which her husband, Robert Waters, was exor,

6. RICHARD FFOLKARDE (also ffolchard, ffawlker, and ffolker), of Lowestoft, has been referred to as a son of the foregoing. A legacy to his wife Margaret is left in his mother's will (25) of 1557, in which he is also a legatee.

In 1542, as "Richard ffolchard," he paid a Subsidy (*L.S.* 181/233) of 2/8 for movable goods in Lowestoft, valued at £8; and in 1545 a further Subsidy (*L.S.* 181/271), as "Richard ffolker," of 6 shillings for land in the same town, valued at £3.

I believe we may conclude that a son of this man settled at Belton, a few miles only from his own birthplace at Corton and his mother's residence at Blundeston. The Ipswich Registry contains the Wills of Robert ffalke (pronounced ffalker) of Belton of 1567—8; of Thomas ffaulke of Belton of 1580—81; of John ffaulke of Belton of 1638—40; and the administration (No. 11) of Edmund ffaulke of the same place of 1639 granted to the latter's son Thomas. Reference to that admon. in Part I. will show that in the Ipswich Probate Sundry Books a copy made of this admon. is described as that of "ffaulkerde of Belton." ffaulke (or ffaulker) was a customary corruption of the name. We find an Edmund ffaulk, probably a gandson of the last-named Edmund, party to a Fine (*F. Michs.*) of 1705 respecting land in Belton.

It was very probably a daughter of this Richard ffolkard of Lowestoft who married in 1561; the Ipswich Registry issuing a license of marriage, dated May 28th of that year, between "Robert Allen and Margaret ffolker of Lowestoft," the latter being evidently named after her mother. The will (52) of Marie ffoker (endorsed ffokard), of Kessingland near Lowestoft, of 1640, is doubtless that of the widow of a son of this Richard ffolkard. She was evidently a Mary Paslew before her marriage, and left two daughters, Mary and Margery ffolkard.

Whether this line at Lowestoft was continued unbrokenly by the descendants of the subject of this notice cannot be established without examining the registers there; but the will (104), dated 1789, of Thomas ffolkard, of Lowestoft, indicates this as probable. It was most likely the last-named man who contributed a benefaction to the parish of Lowestoft, the list of donors in the church there (*D. Lowestoft*) recording "Mr. Folkard £4 : 4 : 0." Davy made this note in 1823. A note in Golding's "Suffolk Coinage" tells us that this "Thomas Folkard gave, in 1756, five shillings towards rebuilding Kirkley Church." Of the children named in his will (104), Susannah is the only one of whom we have no further record. Of the others the following inscription on a tomb in Lowestoft churchyard informs us as to the sad end of the son Thomas :—

"Sacred | to the Memory of | Thomas Folkard, | husband of | Elizabeth Folkard, | who was unfortunately drowned | 15th October, 1844, | aged 42 years. | Also | Elizabeth | his wife, | who died 21 August, | 1846, | aged 77 years."

In this case the wife must have been the senior of her husband by 33 years!

It was probably a son of the above who, as Thomas Folkard, was described in the Suffolk Directory of 1844 (*C.*) as "a spinner of rope and twine" at Lowestoft. A will in Somerset House, proved 21 January,

H

1872, was apparently that of this man, and we learn by it that he died August 26, 1872, the will being proved by his son Thomas Folkard of Lowestoft, whose own estate was administered to in its turn by his relict, Maria Folkard, her husband's death having occurred on the 19th May, 1878.

William, another son named in the will of his father (104), lived till 1850, according to the following inscription on his tomb in Lowestoft churchyard:—

"To | the Memory of | William Folkard, | husband of | Mary Folkard, | who died July 11th, 1850, | aged 72 years. | Also | Mary his wife, | who died July 19, | 1851, | aged 73 years."

This couple probably left children who lived in Lowestoft, for we find a William Folkard in the Directory for 1879. The remaining child of the will (104) yet to be noticed is Samuel, who appears as a "fish curer" in the Suffolk Directory of 1844 (C.). A license, dated 1st January, 1839 (C. licenses), authorises his marriage to Susanna Richardson Dance, single woman, of Lowestoft. A Samuel Folkard described in the Lowestoft Directory of 1879 as "fishing boat owner," was probably son to this couple.

----

7. THOMAS FFOLKARD, of Horham, was the son of Thomas Folkard of the same place (No. 4) and Alice his wife. He is named in that father's will (10) of 1500. From his own will (21) of 1552, we learn that his wife's name was Margaret, and that she was living at that date, but her maiden surname has not been traced.

The earliest mention of him found subsequent to the date of his father's will is of 1522, in which year, as Thomas ffolkerd, he paid a Subsidy (L.S. 180/127) of 12 pence for goods in Horham valued at £10. In the year following he was again taxed on a Subsidy (L.S. 180/172), paying £1. 13s. 4d. (again as "ffolkerd") for land in Horham appraised at an annual value of ——— (illegible in orig.), and on movable goods there valued at £10. But to meet the insatiable demands for the foreign wars of Henry VIII. he was mulcted a second time in the same year (1523) on a further Subsidy (L.S. 180/177) of 5/6 for goods in Horham valued at £5. 13s. 4d. One naturally inclines, therefore, to think that he had been obliged to sell part of his goods to meet the earlier exactions of that year. In the last roll he is named as "Thomas ffolcarde."

He seems to have held the office of bailiff (i.e., mayor) of several parishes or townships, for the "Valor Ecclesiasticus" (iii. 345) has an entry of 1534, which reads translated:—

"Thomas ffolkarde, bailiff of Carleton, Okkolt (mod. Occolt), Horham, and Rishangle, pays annually to the Prior of Bronholme 3/4."

In 1545 he paid, as Thomas ffolcard, a Subsidy (L.S. 181/273) of 6 shillings for his land at Horham, and this is the latest record of him until the date of his will (21) of 1552. This will names his children as given on the Pedigree, some of whom will be subsequently treated of in detail. One of his daughters appears from the will (36) of his son Thomas to have married Gregory Rous.

8. THOMAS FFOLKARD, of Horham, was son to the foregoing. The earliest mention of this man is in his father's will (21) of 1552. He was under age at that date. In his own will (36) his wife is named as Ann, daughter of John Staunard, who was supervisor of it. She was living at that date, and in 1591, almost certainly as a widow, she paid a Subsidy (L.S. 182/407), as " Anna ffolkarde," of 16 pence for land in Horham valued at 20 shillings.

In 1575 we find her husband to have paid a Subsidy (L.S. 182/370) of 2/8 for land valued at 20 shillings in Horham ; and in 1580 he was payee of a further Subsidy (L.S. 182/377) of 16 pence on land of the same value there. He made his will (36) in 1581, but as this was not proved till 1592, it is probable that he did not die until the later year, though the fact above named of his wife paying the Subsidy in 1591 may fix a somewhat earlier date for his death. His children named in his will will appear on the Pedigree.

9. THOMAS FFOLKARD, of Horham, is named in the will (36) of his father, the above Thomas ffolkard, as being at the date of it (1581) a minor. His wife's name we learn from his own will to have been Alice, but nothing further is known respecting her.

This man was probably the Thomas ffolkard referred to in a case named in " Proceedings in Chancery, Queen Elizabeth " (iii. 195), which is entered therein as " Richard Vinior, 1595, versus Thomas ffolkard. Discovery as to a private agreement. Personal Matters. No locality." Of this case I have been unable to discover further trace. In 1612 he paid a Subsidy (L.S. 182/475) of 2/8 for land in Horham valued at 40 shillings. There is much likelihood that we may recognize this man and his wife Alice in the following Fines :—

"4 James I. (1615). It was agreed between Thomas ffolkard, plff., and Thomas Wulves (prob. Wolsey) and Elizabeth his wife, defts., respecting one messuage and a garden with appurts. in Engate [mod. Ingate], Thomas ffolkard paying Thomas Wulves and Elizabeth his wife 40 pounds sterling " (F. Michs.).

"15 Charles I. (1639). Between Christopher West, Clerk, and Thomas Pells, plffs., and Thomas ffolkard and Alice his wife, and William Russell and Johanna his wife, defts., of 1 messuage, 1 curtilage, 2 gardens, and 10 acres pasture, with their appurtenances in Engate, Beccles, and Letheringham, the plffs. pay the defendants 41 pounds sterling " (F. Trin.).

His will (50) was made in 1638, and he probably died in the succeeding year, that in which it was proved, as thus recorded at the Ipswich Registry (Sundry Books xvii. 52):—

"28th September, 1639. Will of Thomas ffolkarde, late of Horham aforesaid, proved."

To judge by the amount of the legacies left by that will, its writer's position must have been a substantial one for those days. His son Thomas, who is named on the Pedigree, this will informs us to have predeceased his father; the Ann ffolkard, "my daughter-in-law," possibly being that son's widow, she also having a son Thomas who is named as the legatee of £60. It was undoubtedly this grandson of the testator who was defendant to the following Fine of 1654 (F. Easter).

H—2

"Between John ffolkard the younger, plff., and Thomas ffolkard, deft., of 1 messuage, 1 garden, 1 orchard, 4 acres land, and 4 acres pasture, with appurts. in Horham, John ffolkard pays Thomas ffolkard the sum of money between them accorded."

From the provisions of the will cited it would appear that the daughter Elizabeth named in it was either the wife or the widow of a man named Barker, to whose children, Giles, Elizabeth, and Alice Barker, legacies were bequeathed by it.

10. JOHN FFOLKARD, of Horham, one of the sons of the above, was probably the eldest surviving son at the date of the father's will (50) of 1638. Mention has been made above of the possibility of the daughter-in-law Ann named in that will having been the widow of the deceased son Thomas referred to. She may, however, and more probably, have been the wife of the son John now under notice, as in a Fine to be quoted below his wife bears that name, and the William, Edmund, Mary, and Ann ffolkard, also named in the grandfather's will, were probably their children.

The "John ffolkard the younger" named as plff. in the Fine last above quoted of 1654, was also very probably another son, though not named in the grandfather's will (50).

---

11. JOHN FFOLKARD, of Horham, who was a son of Thomas ffolkard (No. 7) and his wife Margaret, was a legatee under his father's will (21) of 1552, being at that date under age. We learn from his own will that his wife was named Margerie, and that she was living at the date of it, 1599.

The Subsidy Rolls indicate this man's continuous residence at Horham. In 1543 he paid a Subsidy (L.S. 181/253) of 20 shillings at Wilby, close to Horham, for goods there valued at £20. In 1575 we find him taxed (L.S. 182/370), as "John ffolcarde," 10 shillings for goods at Horham valued at £6; and in 1580 (L.S. 182/377) 6 shillings for goods of similar amount in the same place. In 1591 he was again amerced 6 shillings for land in Horham estimated at £6 (L.S. 182/407); and in 1596, being assessed 16 shillings for goods there worth £6 (L.S. 182/423), he paid that amount as "John ffolcarde, Senior." On a later roll of the same year (L.S. 182/430), Thomas Botwright paid on the same roll 4 shillings for land in Horham "formerly ffolkarde" estimated at 20 shillings.

In a law suit of 1599 (C.P. Elizabeth ii. 9) between Humfrey Howlett and ffrancis ffolkard, of Nedeham, Norfolk (this will be found given hereafter), there occurs this reference to the John ffolkard under notice :—

"Hearing that one John folkard of Horham, Suffolk, yeoman, a nigh kinsman of ffrancis, whose next heir ffrancis was, then reputed a man of good wealth, and would leave unto ffrancis all or most part of property reputed £30 a year, whereby he, the defendant, expected to be repaid."

In the same year as this suit was brought, 1599, this John ffolkard made his will (37), one of the witnesses to it being Thomas Howlett, probably a brother of the plaintiff in that suit. The name of ffrancis ffolkard does not occur in this will, and it may have arisen from the discovery of this fact by Thomas Howlett that the proceedings in Chancery were taken. Unless it may be assumed that the Ann Genn, named in the will as the wife of Edmund Genn, was a daughter of this man, there is no evidence of any issue to him; the sum of £100 left to this Ann Genn being devised for distribution among the " poorest of my kindred."

---

12. JOHN FFOLKARDE, of Horham, who was son to Thomas (No. 4) and Alice, was left lands at Horham, Denham, and Hoxne by his father's will (10) of 1500.

The next reference found to him is on four Subsidy Rolls of 1522 and 1523. In the first of those years, as " John ffolkard " (*L.S.* 180/127), he paid 3 shillings on goods in Horham valued at £11. In that succeeding he was taxed on land there worth 33/4 by the year, as well as on movable goods valued at £2 (*L.S.* 180/172), in both instances again as " John ffolkerd." A second time in the same year, as " John folcard," he paid 2/6 on goods in Horham valued at £5 (*L.S.* 180/177), and for a third time within the same twelvemonth, 3/- on goods there worth £6, as " John ffolkerd " (*L.S.* 180/127).

We have no record as to who this man married; but it is possible that he was the " John ffolkens " stated on the Gedding Pedigree (*D.P.*) to have married Elizabeth Geddings, whose husband would appear to have been born about 1450 or 1460. This John ffolkard's will (15) is dated 1533, and was proved in that year. It is singular as granting a conditional bequest to the next heir of his grandson, John ffolkard, " who bears the name of ffolkard." It mentions no wife, who may therefore be presumed to have predeceased the testator. Reference will be found in the will to his daughter, the Alice Sheppard of the Pedigree, and to her children.

---

13. WILLIAM FFOLKARD, of Horham and Eye, is named in the will (15) of 1533 of the foregoing man as being his son, and as having issue a son John at that date. He appears to have had all his interests in Horham, and probably lived there; though, as he and his wife both made their wills at Eye, he probably resided in that town late on in his life. His wife's name we know from both their wills to have been Margaret, and from that of the latter (32) of 1566 it seems evident that her surname on her marriage to this William ffolkard had been Margaret Sherman. This will leaves legacies only to her children by a first marriage of hers, none of those by William ffolkard who are named in his will finding mention in hers. This was proved in 1567, and she probably died in that year.

The first mention found of this William ffolkard is of 1522, when he paid a Subsidy (*L.S.* 180/127) of 3/11 for goods in Horham worth £6. In 1523 he is named on two separate Subsidy Rolls. On the first of these (*L.S.* 180/172) he seems to have volunteered a payment (amount not stated) for goods at Horham valued at £5, as " William ffolkerd."

On a second (*L.S.* 180/177) he is amerced as " William ffolcard " for goods there, the amount being defaced and illegible. We hear nothing of him, save the mention of his name in his father's will of 1533 above referred to, until 1543, when he was the only ffolkard taxed in Horham on a Subsidy of that year (*L.S.* 181/253), he then paying 10/- on goods there valued at £10. In 1545 he had again to submit to pay a Subsidy (*L.S.* 181/271), as " William ffolcard," of 12/- for land in the same place, and on another Subsidy (*L.S.* 181/278) of the same year he had to pay 10/- for goods there. It is probable that he left Horham to reside at Eye between the date of the last payment and 1562 ; for in the latter year he paid a Subsidy (*L.S.* 182/346), as " William folkard of Eye," of 10/8 for land at Eye valued at £4. His parting with lands held of various manors is referred to in the will of his cousin Thomas ffolkard (21) of 1552.

In 1563 his daughter Isabell died, her burial at Frostenden being thus entered in the register of that place :—

"1563. Was buried Isabell Harvie, wife of William Harvie, daughter of William ffroker of Horeham, the first day of April, the year aforesaid " (*Ex. Lat. Orig.*).

This daughter and her children are referred to in her father's will (31) of 1564, she being therein named as "Isbell Harvy." Two other married daughters, Margaret ffryer and Alice Page, are also named in that will. The only son mentioned in it is John ffolkard, though ffrancis ffolkard of Nedeham, Norfolk, was almost undoubtedly also a son of this testator, and must have been " the next eldest brother " referred to in the will (15) of John ffolkard of 1533.

This will also gives legacies to two stepdaughters, Agnes Barker and Amy Chappell, who are also named in their mother's will (32). The allusion in this will to the land at Nedeham, Norfolk, is of importance as aiding towards establishing the fact of the sonship to the testator of the ffrancis ffolkard above mentioned.

14. JOHN FFOLKARD, of Horham, was son to the man last dealt with, and is named in his will (31) of 1564. He is also referred to in the will of his grandfather (15) of 1533, he being therein named as the testator's godson, and as the child of his son William.

In 1540, as " John ffulkarde," he paid 20/- Subsidy (*L.S.* 181/219) for land at Stradbrook, close to Horham. From the fact mentioned in the will of his grandfather that he was possessed of land at Brockdish, Norfolk, it appears likely that the will (40), of which the heading has been destroyed, but proved at Brockdish in 1617, was that of this man. It is confirmatory as to this, that a Fine of 1571 (*Norf. Pasch.*), sued by John ffolkard against Thomas Cobbett, referred to a house in Brockdish, the plaintiff having to pay £40 sterling. In 1579 a suit was entered in the Court of Requests (*Bdle.* 6, *No.* 279) entitled " William Baldwin *versus* Anthony Selfe and John ffolkarde." The latter appears to have been described as then of Eye, and the suit related to the marriage of William Baldwin to Margaret Wyppe, and the legitimacy of their children. The pleadings are lost, and the interrogatories and replies do not refer to this John ffolkard. From the fact that Henry ffolkard of Brome married a

Dorothy Wyppe, I am inclined to believe that the line settled at that place, and not as yet dealt with, had its descent probably from the man now under consideration. Further mention of him will be found in the case of ffrancis ffolkard of Nedeham, hereafter to be quoted.

Assuming the above conjecture that the will of this John ffolkard is that printed (40), it is probable that he died in the year of the date of its proof, 1617. By it we learn that his wife was Ann Woodward, and that he had " an only grandchild," Hester ffolkarde.

15. FFRANCIS FFOLKARD, of Needham, Norfolk, was almost certainly a son of William ffolkard, of Horham and Eye (No. 12). The reference in the will (15) of John ffolkard of Horham to his godson John ffolkard's " next eldest brother " evidences at least one other son, though his father's will (31) does not name him. It may therefore be presumed, either that he was dead before the date of that will (1564), or that the difficulties which, as will be hereafter seen, forced him to leave the country, led to his being omitted from all mention by his father. The reference in that will to " the debts which I and my son John owe for land in Nedeham, Norfolk," establishes the conclusion as to the parentage of this ffrancis. The evidence will be seen to be strengthened by the fact —to be stated further on—that the name of John ffolkard, this man's grandfather, occurs with reference to a bond given on his behalf, and that of Alice his wife, with respect of these same lands purchased at Nedeham.

ffrancis ffolkard's wife, we learn from the case which follows to have been a daughter of Robert and Mary Dowsinge. Mention of her is also found in a reference to John Dowsing, who, according to the *Inquis. Post Mortem* (14th Chas. I.), died 2nd June, 1579. This authority states that—

"Grace, formerly wife of Stephen Gurney, and Alice, formerly the wife of a certain ffrancis ffolkard, were then of consanguinity and coheirs of the said John, that is to say, daughter and coheirs of Robert Dowsing, Senior, deceased, the son and heir of John Dowsing, Senior, deceased, the eldest son and heir of the John Dowsing first named. At the time when this John [*illegible*], Grace and Alice were both aged 20 years. Tightles and pastures in Keddenhall, Harleston, and land in Dickelburgg held of the Queen, &c."

There is little doubt that this wife survived her husband: the following bond (*D. Framlingham*) almost certainly refers to her, and it indicates the distressed condition in which she was left.

" 37th Eliz. (1594). Bond from Richard Boteman of Framlingham to indemnify the parish from Margaret, the daur. of Alice ffolkard, Wo., becoming chargeable to the Inhabi- tants of that parish."

The earliest reference found to this ffrancis ffolkard is in a Fine of 1586 (*F. Norf.* viii. *Trin.*). This Fine proves that he had married Alice Dowsing before that date. It reads:—

" Between ffrancis ffolkard and Alice his wife, and Stephen Gurney and Grace his wife, of 2 messuages, 2 gardens, 2 orchards, 5 acres of land, 9 acres of ploughland, and 10 acres of pasture, in Nedeham and Brockdish. ffrancis and Alice ffolkard pay Stephen and Grace Gurney £80 sterling."

The following petition of 1599 informs us that " twelve years before that date," *i.e.*, in 1587, this ffrancis ffolkard purchased certain lands in

Nedeham. It reveals to us the troubles which arose out of that purchase, and of his consequent flight from the country. We also learn, from the reply of John ffolkard to it, that the subject of this notice had a large family. What became of his children may possibly be traced among the Folkards of Norfolk, when I may attempt some account of them. The petition and answer referred to read, abstracted, as follows:—

(*C.P. Eliz. ii. 9*). "May 20th, 1599. Petition of Humfrey Howlett, Thomas Woods, and Mary his wife, late wife of Robert Dowsinge, for themselves and on behalf of John Dowsinge, an infant four years old. About twelve years past, one ffrancis ffolkard, of Nedeham, in the Co. of Norfolk, and Alice his wife, or one of them, purchased certain lands and tenements in Nedeham, valued at £30 a year, of one Stephen Gurney and Grace his wife, which said Grace and Alice were dars. and coheirs of one Robert Dowsinge, deceased, and the said lands and tenements purchased of the said Stephen and Grace were the part and purpart of the lands and tenements which descended or came unto the said Grace after Robert Dowsinge died. ffrancis ffolkard, not having the money provided, borrowed of divers persons £300, and Robert Dowsinge, the late husband of Mary, became bond for the amount. Finding himself unable to pay, ffrancis ffolkard assigned the lands over to Robert Shemynge for a small sum, far under their value, which being done, ffrancis ffolkard fled out of the country or kept himself secret, so that the petitioners could not find him; and so by that evil device and practise Robert Shemynge enjoyed the land. Robert Dowsing being brought into danger for the bond given, did also forsake the country, whereupon Humfrey Howlett, uncle of Robert Dowsing, asked Robert Shemynge to release Robert Dowsing from his liability, who consented to leave the matter to assessors. It was thereupon agreed that the liabilities of ffrancis ffolkard and Robert Dowsing should be cancelled, Howlett giving bonds for the debts of ffrancis ffolkard in this matter amounting to a great sum of money. Robert Shemynge, in conversation, agreed to give over a piece of land of six acres called Nattishill in Nedeham to H. Howlett in trust for Robert Dowsinge then absent. Agreement as to this was made Decr. Eliz. 18. Assurance was given of title to these six acres, and Robert Dowsing returning, it was handed over to him by his uncle Howlett. Three years before these proceedings, Robert Dowsing fell sick, and by will gave the land to Mary, then his wife, and now the wife of Thomas Woods, for life, and then to their son John Dowsing. The fruits were enjoyed by the widow and her second husband. But Robert Shemynge and one John ffolkard of Brockdish [*see ante*], after a great part of the debts of ffrancis ffolkard had been discharged by Robert Dowsing, having in their custody the original deeds of the land, had fraudulently conveyed them to Nicolas, the son of Robert Shemynge, giving out that ffrancis ffolkard had assigned the land to the said John ffolkard, and declared the conveyance to Howlett to be void. Prays that Nicolas and Robert Shemynge and John ffolkard may be compelled to deliver up the deeds and transfer, which, if it existed, must have been fraudulently made and obtained."

Robert Shemynge's answer and that of John ffolkard are filed. In the first, the family name is spelt throughout as ffolcard; in the second, always with the k. Abstracted, John ffolkard's answer may be read:—

"ffrancis ffolkard being greatly decayed. Among the creditors of the said ffrancis he, this defendant, John ffolkard, bearing a good will towards him, the said ffrancis, for the namesake, and being then willing to help him, lent him divers sums of money at several times, being £100 or thereabouts. For this, ffrancis executed a deed transferring the land, and John ffolkard, 'such was his affection and licking which he did then bear towards the said ffrancis, having at that time a wyff and meny children," and seeing that he was in great pains to live, and hearing that one John ffolkard, of Horham, Suff., Yeoman, a nigh kinsman of ffrancis, whose next heir ffrancis was then reputed, was a man of good wealth, and would leave unto ffrancis all or most part of property reputed £30 a year, whereby he the defendant expected to be repaid," &c., &c.

From the terms of the foregoing answer by John ffolkard it is most difficult to decide in what relationship, if any, he stood to this ffrancis ffolkard. I think the John ffolkard, of Horham, from whom the latter had expectations, must have been he who died in 1599 or 1600 (No. 10), but the connection must remain at least doubtful. In the printed volumes (ii. 9) of the Proceedings in Chancery of Queen Elizabeth's reign, the reference to the foregoing case is thus made :—

"Humphrey Howlett and others *vs.* Robert Shemynge, John Folkard, and Nicolas Shemynge, to be relieved against bonds as respects a purchase made by Francis Folkard and Alice his wife of certain lands in Nedeham, Norfolk."

If the assumption made above that the bond of Richard Boteman refers to this man's widow be justifiable, he must have died previous to 1594, though the child referred to may have been his and born posthumously.

Of any other children left by this ffrancis ffolkard we have no record. It is, however, not unlikely that the following license (*ex. Lat.*) may refer to the marriage of one of his sons, Wilby being close to Horham :—

" 12 June 1618. License of marriage between Gregory ffolkard and Johanna Grimsbie, of Wilbie, existing in widowhood. To the church of ———— [*illegible*]" (*Ipsw. Pro. Sundry Books*).

It is the more probable that this conjecture may be correct, as I have in no other instance met with the Christian name of Gregory in the family.

. I have been unable to find any residents of the name at Horham of a later date than 1728. In that year a Rachael ffolkard, of Horham, died intestate (*Admon. No. 21*). The following indenture (*D. Horham*) of 1699 shows that the family residence at Horham had been parted with before that date :—

" 29 December, 1699. By Indte. of Mortgage between Robert Adams, only son and heir of Thomas Adams, late of Stradbrooke, of the one part, and Elisbth. Alderman, of Peasenhall, widow, of the other part, the said Adams did bargain, sell, &c., All that mess. or tent, called ffolkard's situate in Horham, and all the houses, &c., and the home close cont. 10 acres," &c., &c.

From the above it may probably be concluded that the residence of male representatives of the family at Horham had terminated before 1699. A family of ffoulsier and ffoulgier, however, are found to have been living in that place and at Stradbrooke towards the close of the seventeenth century, and their name may have been, and very likely was, only a corruption of the original by the softening process from ffoulker to ffoulcer, of which repeated instances are found. The unfortunate loss of all the early registers of Horham has prevented any attempt to deal more precisely than has been done with the family settlement there.

———————————

16. ROBERT FFOLKERED, of Rendham, has been assumed on the Pedigree to have been a son of ffolcard of Thorpe, near Horham (No. 1), the founder of the line at the latter place. It has before been named that William ffolcard, of Mellis and Eye (No. 10 of that line), held land at Rendham, and this assumed great-grandson of his may well have continued that possession. In a list of the lands of the manor of

I

Rendham, of 1324 (*D.* vi. *Sibton*), are several entries which read translated : " Robert ffolkered owes two pence per annum for faithful service."
Again, " Robert ffolkered " (as a free tenant) " owes two days (service)
at Sareland."

He is further noted in the same list as being the owner of two pigs,
or probably having the right of pasture for them. In a list of dues
received from the manor of Rendham on account of the abbot of Sibton,
of about the same date as that above referred to, 1324, there occurs an
entry (*ex. Lat.*) " Of Robert ffolcred by Henry Prat one halfpenny." The
same old deeds contain many entries as to a John ffokelot holding
lands of the Abbey named at this date, who may not improbably have
been a son or brother of the subject of this notice. In an account book
of Sibton Abbey, also noted by Davy, there is a record of 1456 (*ex. Lat.*)
reading : " And of 2/4 of Ralph Lundenays for a tenement late ffolkreds."
This would seem to indicate the continuance of the family residence at
Rendham probably up to about 1450; but I have found no trace of it in
the Subsidy Rolls. The only other mention discovered of the subject of
this notice is of 1327, when he paid a Subsidy (*L.S.* 180/6) as Robert
ffolkred, of 9 pence at Rendham.

17. ADAM FFOKENELD, of Redisham, has been, wholly conjecturally, assigned a place on the Pedigree as son to the foregoing.
His name has been but once met with. In a deed written in old French,
transferring tenancy and services on the manor at Redisham of 1396
(*D.* xxxvi. *Redisham*), this man is mentioned as a tenant. The mis-
spelling of the name in this instance is curious and important. It is a
manifest compound of ffaukun and ffolkered, and as such useful as an
indication of the interchangeable use of those two forms.

Pedigree No. 1.

Pedigree No. 1.

Order in which the several Lines of Settlement, &c., are dealt with.

1. BEDFIELD (includes branches settled at Dallinghoo, Wickham Market, Aldborough, Ipswich, and London).
2. EARL STONHAM (includes branch at Thetford).
3. MONK SOHAM.
4. DEBENHAM.
5. FRAMLINGHAM (includes branches at Winston, East Bergholt, Gosbeck, Laxfield, Bramford, Ipswich, Saxmundham, and London).
6. EARL SOHAM (includes branch at Sweffling).
7. ASHFIELD (includes branch at Pettaugh).
8. MENDLESHAM (includes branches at Ubbeston and Walpole).
9. RATLESDEN (includes branches at Heveningham and Walpole).
10. STOWMARKET.
11. PARHAM (includes branch at Clopton).
12. WICKHAM MARKET (includes branches at Worlingworth and Darsham).
13. CRETINGHAM (includes branch at Hollesley).
14. HELMINGHAM.
15. LETHERINGHAM (includes branches at Woodbridge and Ipswich).

Introductory Note.

EFORE proceeding to deal with the several Lines of Pedigree 1, which is that embracing the descent of the writer's family, it seems desirable to explain the note at the head of it indicating the derivation of the Lines it records from an ancestor who was Lord of the Manor of Buxhall.

Mr. G. M. Gibson Cullum, who is possessed of the MS. notes of Thomas Martyn made about a century back, wrote me that, with reference to Buxhall, those notes contain the following entry:—

"Mr. Tho. ffolkard, of Bedfield, tells me his ancestors formerly liv'd here (*i.e.*, *in Buxhall*), and were lords of ye manor. Their arms [*with sketch*] : Field Sable, cups gold, but I think Argent."

Davy has included this note of Martyn's in his notice of the family. Tradition conveyed from father to son would probably have preserved the fact of such a descent correctly. In a list of the lords of Buxhall (*D.* xxx. *Buxhall*) the name of Folkard does not appear ; but the entries therein from 1316 to 1428 are left blank, as unknown. It must have been between those years, therefore, that the manor was held by the family, and we know that the Folkard arms were placed in the windows of Buxhall church at an early date, as referred to on page viii. of Part I. At a visit paid by myself to that church in 1886, I could still trace a fragment (about one half) of one of the gold cups on a part of the sable. field, which had survived the destruction of the painted glass at the time of the Commonwealth.

Now Buxhall Manor was a dependency of the Honour of Eye (*D.* xxx. *Buxhall*), and it would be natural, therefore, to look for the owner of it among the Folkards of the latter place. For this reason, in combination with the range of date above given as available, I have felt justified in connecting the Lines of this Pedigree No. 1 with the more ancient family settlement of Eye in the person of Walter Folcard, the Bailiff (equivalent to Mayor) of that place in 1330 (*See Ped. 2, Part* I.)

On the Pedigree last named there is assigned to this Walter Folcard a brother Robert, who had possessions, and perhaps lived, at Worlingworth. The will (7) of William Folkard, of Bedfield, of 1513 bequeaths a legacy to the guild of that place, which adjoins Bedfield. It is therefore feasible that the man with whom this Pedigree 1 commences was, as conjectured on Pedigree 2, a grandson of this Robert Folcard. The ancestry cannot be traced by me more authoritatively than upon the two facts just stated.

Most unfortunately, the registers of Bedfield church prior to about 1710 or so disappeared some years back, and no transcripts of them are known at Norwich. The only extracts extant from the earlier registers are given by Davy. These include several entries relating to Folkard that will be quoted in their proper places. The Candler Pedigree of the family referred to in Part I. has done much to provide the missing information due to the loss of the registers.

Settlement at Bedfield.

*(Includes branches at Dallinghoo, Wickham Market,
Aldborough, Ipswich, and London.)*

---

1. WILLIAM FFOLKARD, of Bedfield, held land at Dallinghoo
in 1463, for which he paid fourpence fine at the Leet Court there (*L.C.*),
and in 1466 he appears to have held land at Stonham (*E.* 2161). In the
latter instance he is described as of Soham, where he probably also held
land. He may have been identical with the William ffauchare who was
esson at a Leet Court at Walton in 1467 (*L.C.*)

His will of 1470 (7) makes no mention of his wife, who had therefore probably predeceased him. Judging from the date of proof of that
will, he may be assumed to have died early in 1471 ; so, if we assign to
him the customary length of life of other members of his family, he may
have been born between 1390 and 1400. His children named in the will
are Robert, who settled at Earl Stonham (*No. 1 of that Line*), William,
dealt with below, Margaret, and Hariot. Of the two last nothing can
be traced. His legacies to the church at Bedfield are liberal for those
days, and seem to indicate a comfortable position.

2. WILLIAM FFOLKARD, of Bedfield, is named in his father's
will (7), of which he was an exor. As being also residuary legatee to
that will, he was probably the eldest son. A Latin entry in a Court
Roll of 1500 of the manor of Woodehall in Stoke Ash (*D.* xiv. *Stoke Ash*)
probably refers to this man. Translated it reads :—

"In the sixteenth year of Henry VII. (1500), William ffolcard did fealty for a free
holding called Notekyns formerly held by Robert Ruste."

His will (13) is dated 1513, in which year he must have died. It
names his wife Juliane as then living ; also his sons Nicolas and Robert,
who both settled at Monk Soham (*See 1 and 2 of that Line*), Thomas, who
succeeded at Bedfield, and his daughter Agnes, who is not further
traceable.

3. THOMAS FFOLKARD, of Bedfield, was son to the foregoing,
and named in the latter's will (13) of 1513. In 1539 he witnessed, as
"Thomas ffolkerd ye elder," the will of his brother Robert of Monk
Soham (17). It was also probably this man who, as "Thomas ffolyart,"
paid on a Subsidy Roll of 1543 (*L.S.* 181/259) fifty shillings for goods in
Sprowston (*Quære mod. Sproughton*) valued at £15. In the latter year he
also paid 10 shillings for goods at Bedfield valued at £10 (*L.S.* 181/253),
and in 1545 he further paid 6 shillings for land there (*L.S.* 181/271).

His will (19) is dated 1543. It refers to his wife Alyce as then
living, to his sons, Thomas, William, and Robert, and to the five children

K

of the last, who settled at Debenham (*See No.* 1 *of that Line*). Mention is also contained in it of his daughters Anne and Elizabeth. Another daughter, Rose, who married Nicholas Drane of Tattington, is not named in the will, though her husband is. She is mentioned, as being then married, in the Administration (*Admon.* 2) of 1555 of her sister Elizabeth, who died at Sybton unmarried and intestate in that year. The children of this Rose Drane were devisees under the will (23) of her brother Thomas ffolkard. The daughter Anne above named married Reginald Eade, being named as his wife in a Fine sued against her nephew Ambrose ffolkard in 1600 (*F.* xii.). The admon. of this Anne Eade's effects (*Admon.* 10) is dated 1636, she being described in it as a widow.

    The will of this man, though dated 1543, was not proved till 1549, in which year his death probably occurred.

    3A. WILLIAM FFOLKARD, son of the foregoing, is erroneously entered on the Pedigree as of Earl Soham. He resided at Brockford, where his brother Robert also held property. He is named in his father's will (19) of 1543, and in that of his brother Thomas (23) of 1555. It is probable that the following entry in the Framlingham Register applies to the burial of this man's wife, of whom we have no other record :—

    " Ann ffolkard, wife of William, was buried ye — of November, 1579."

    In 1522 he was assessed for goods at Brockford valued at £11. 13s. 4d. (*L.S.* 180/126), paying on another Roll in 1523 on goods there valued at £6. 14s. 4d. only (*L.S.* 180/159). It was probably he who in the latter year also paid, as " William ffolkerd," 12 pence Subsidy on land valued at £10. 5s. in Elmsett (*L.S.* 180/158), which was probably part of the old family possessions in and about Buxhall. We find him named as a brother in his sister Elizabeth's administration (2) of 1555. In 1575—6 a William ffolkard (probably this man) witnessed the will of Thomas Crispe of Badingham. No further information likely to refer to him has been found ; but there is some probability that the following entries in the Framlingham Register may refer to the marriage and burial of a son of his :—

    "William ffolcard and Catherine Danford, wedowe, were married 6th February, 1575."

    "William ffolkard buried 30th January, 1632."

    4. THOMAS FFOLKARD, of Bedfield, was also a son of Thomas ffolkard (*No.* 3) above, and is named in the latter's will (19) of 1543. His wife Margaret, who survived him and then married his brother, Robert ffolkard, of Debenham, I have conjectured on the Pedigree—though, as I now think, incorrectly—to have been a daughter of a —— Keene, of Cretingham, on the authority of an entry at page 367 of miscellaneous pedigrees by Gillett *alias* Candler (*H.* 6071), which is to the effect that Robert Gillett *alias* Candler married

    "Margaret Mansfield, da. of Walderswicke and of Margaret, one of the two dars. and coheirs of —— Keene of Cretingham ; the other daughter of Keene was married to ffolkard of Bedfield."

Comparison of dates warrants the assumption that this "other daughter" may have been the wife of this Thomas ffolkard. Opposed to this is the improbability that both daughters would be named Margaret, though such cases not unfrequently occurred. I should think it more probable that this daughter of Keene was the first wife of this man's brother, Robert ffolkard, of Debenham, or she may even have been the mother, Alyce, of the subject of this notice.

This Thomas ffolkard is named in the Administration of his sister Elizabeth above referred to in 1555. The plaintiff in the following Fine of 1556 (*F. Pasch*) may not improbably have been this man :—

"Between Thomas ffolcard, plff., and Margaret Bartewe, widow, deft., respecting a messuage and 3 acres pasture in Thrandeston. It was agreed that Thomas should pay Margaret £40 sterling."

There is a difficulty respecting the will (23) of the subject of this notice. This, although dated 1555, was not proved till 1565. Administration of his goods, as having died intestate, was granted in 1556 (*Admon.* 3). The conclusions would seem to follow, either that the will was not found until ten years after his death, or that it was deliberately and fraudulently suppressed until then; the administration, on account of intestacy, being granted to the widow, who was executrix to the will afterwards proved. It suggests itself that the clause in this will in opposition to the remarriage of the wife may have induced its extraordinary suppression by her.

It is with this Thomas ffolkard that the Pedigree compiled by the Rev. Mr. Gillett *alias* Candler, about the year 1650, commences, but his Christian name is not thereon given. His will names Thomas, his eldest son, afterwards of Bedfield, and then under age, his son Lawrence, his brother Robert, and the sons William and Thomas of the latter. Reference is also made in it to the children of his sister Rose Drane, named above. His brother Robert, of Debenham, who subsequently married his widow, witnesses the will.

5. THOMAS FFOLKARD, of Bedfield, was the eldest son of the man last dealt with. His age, 74, is given in his will (45) of 1626, so he must have been born in 1552. He was exor. to the will of his uncle and stepfather, Robert ffolkard, of Debenham, of 1580. According to Candler's Pedigree, he married Anna (or Annie) Stannaway, daughter of —— Stannaway, of Laxfield. This wife is not named in her husband's will, and must have predeceased him, though, by some error, I have stated on the Pedigree that she was living in 1627.

In 1580 this Thomas paid a Subsidy (*L.S.* 182/377) of 4 shillings for land in Bedfield valued at £3, and another of similar amount and valuation in 1591 (*L.S.* 182/407). In 1596 he was further assessed and subsidized 12 shillings for land at Bedfield valued at £3 (*L.S.* 183/423 and 182/430). Then in 1609 he again paid on the same land (*L.S.* 182/471), besides a further sum of 4 shillings in 1610 (*L.S.* 182/472). We find him again mulcted in 1612 of 2 shillings and 8 pence for land at Bedfield valued at 40 shillings (*L.S.* 182/475). It is believed that the valuation in all cases of these Subsidies represents annual rental.

K—2

His will (45) of 1626 names his son Edmund, who founded the
Parham line dealt with hereafter, and that son's seven children ; his
son Lawrence, who settled at Wickham Market, and then had ten
children; his daughter Anne, who married Christopher Clarke, of Kelsale,
and five of her children, one of whom, Christopher, is named in the will
of his uncle, Anthony ffolkard (57) ; his daughter Margery, wife of
William Mitchell, and four of her children, who were all under age in
1626, and who are also named in Anthony ffolkard's will; his daughter
Margaret, wife of Lyonell Russell, and five of her children, also named
in Anthony ffolkard's will; his son ffrancis, and that son's children,
Thomas and Mary ; and another son, Anthony, with the latter's daughter
Anne.

His will was proved in 1627, in which year he probably died,
aged 75.

5A. THOMAS FFOLKARD, of Dallinghoo, I believe to have been
also a son of the foregoing, although not named in his will or included by
Candler on his Pedigree.   Such omissions from wills were common.
We have seen under No. 1 that land was held by the Bedfield family at
Dallinghoo as early as 1463, and the settlement of a descendant there was
more than probable. It is further an unlikely circumstance that his father
would have had no son named after himself. We find also a John
ffolkard, of Dallinghoo, who was bondsman for one of the Russell family
with which the Bedfield line intermarried, as also for other Bedfield
people.

All we know of this Thomas is from the Administration (7) of 1631
granted to his relict, Marie. The Gilian ffolkard whose administration
(9) was granted in 1632 to her kinsman (i.e., nephew), Thomas ffolkard,
was probably a sister of the subject of this notice. Not improbably both
were children by a first marriage of their father, which might account
both for their omission from the latter's will and from the Candler
Pedigree.   The Thomas ffolkard to whom was granted the administration
of this Gilian ffolkard was probably son to the man treated of, and
Marie his wife.

6. ANTHONY FFOLKARD, of Bedfield, was a son of the above
Thomas ffolkard, and named in the latter's will of 1626 as being then
married. According to the Candler Pedigree his wife was Anne,
daughter, and one of the three coheirs, of ―― Lind, of Netherden.
She survived her husband, her will (60) being dated 1664, and proved in
1665. Between 1663 and 1665 she paid, as " Widow ffolkard," a tax on
a single hearth in Bedfield (L.S. 183/612).

The only child of this couple appears to have been a daughter Anne,
who, according to Candler, died unmarried, and probably between 1650
and 1656. She is named, as then being a minor, in the will (45) of 1626,
of Thomas ffolkard, her grandfather.

Probably this man was the "Anthony Robert falkard" who, in 1628,
paid a Subsidy (L.S. 183/504) of 8 shillings for goods in Debenham valued

at 41 shillings. In 1640 he paid another Subsidy (*L.S.* 183/511) conjointly with his brother Francis of 18 shillings for land in Bedfield valued at 40 shillings. His will (57) of 1656 is a very voluminous one, containing many legacies to relatives, and indicating his position to have been a substantial one for those days. It was proved in 1663, the entry of proof (*S.* xxii.) being in the following terms:—

"25 January, 1663. Commission and *pro barone* of will of Anthony ffolkard, late of Bedfield, defunct, directed to Willm. Garnett, of Monk Soham, and —— Patrick Lindsey, of Soham Combust."

A further entry referring to this will, but quite illegible, is made under date 27th January, 1663.

7. FFRANCIS FFOLKARD, of Bedfield, was named exor. to the will (45) of Thomas ffolkard, his father (No. 5). Candler's Pedigree states him to have married a daughter of William Ketterick, of Bedfield. In her husband's will (53) of 1642 he refers to her as named Marie. She survived him, her will (54) being dated 1647, and proved in 1649.

Her husband is named as "ffrank ffolkard" on a Subsidy Roll (*L.S.* 182/489) of about 1630 (*date undecipherable*), and as taxed 4 shillings for either goods or land in Bedfield valued at 20 shillings. He further paid, in 1640, conjointly with his brother Anthony, 18 shillings for land at the same place valued at 40 shillings (*L.S.* 183/511).

His will names issue, William, Anne, and Mary, all of these being also named in their mother's will. He also had a son Thomas, who is named in the will of his grandfather (45), but this son was probably dead at the date of his father's will. A ffrancis ffolkard, who was buried at Bedfield in 1703, was probably another son. The will being proved in 1647, the subject of this notice probably died in that year.

8. ANNE FFOLKARD, of Bedfield, was a daughter of the foregoing ffrancis, and is named in his will (53) of 1642. She was then under age, but sufficiently old to be named executrix of the will. She was also executrix to her mother's will. The Candler Pedigree states that she married Johnathan Rewse (Rouse), of Crowfield, and this is confirmed by the will (74) of her brother William ffolkard. Dr. Muskett says in his Pedigree of ffolkard that he believes her husband to have been a son of Thomas Rewse, of Coddenham, Gent., "whose daughter Elizabeth was then married to Thomas Folkard, of Ashfield." In 1703 her son Simon Rewse was a devisee under the will of her brother William ffolkard (74), that son's children, Mary and Anne Rouse, being also legatees under it.

9. MARY FFOLKARD, of Bedfield, was sister to the foregoing Anne, and co-executrix with her to the wills (53 and 54) of her father and mother, dated 1642 and 1647. She is also named in her grandfather's will of 1626, and must then have been quite an infant, but evidently the senior of her sister Anne, who is unnamed in the grandfather's will. The Rev. Mr. Candler names as her husband George Tovell, but the entry was so doubtful and illegible, that the copy by the younger Candler,

in the Bodleian Library, omits all mention of her marriage.   In a
Chancery Suit of 1705 (*Mitford* dxcii.) her husband is referred to as
George Sewell, and from the fact that one of the exors. to the will of her
brother William ffolkard (74) was the Rev. William Sewell, Rector of
Holinly, Dr. Muskett concludes that he was son to the latter.

10. WILLIAM FFOLKARD, of Bedfield, was brother to the
foregoing Mary, and a son of ffrancis ffolkard (No. 7), in whose will of
1642 (53) he is named as then under age.   He is also named in his
mother's will (54) of 1647.   I am in much doubt if the marriage assigned
to him on the Pedigree be correct.   In the lost Bedfield registers there
was an entry (*D.* xv. *Bedfield*) of " Old William ffolkard buried 1650."
This man I have been unable to trace or place on the Pedigree.   The
license for the marriage assigned to him reads thus (*S.* xv. 28) :—

" January 12th, 1637. Marriage license between William ffolkard, of Bedfield, widower,
and Anna Gyforde, singlewoman, of Bedfield. To church at Bedfield 5/. Signed Thomas
Gyforde."

Now, if this marriage was that of the subject of this notice, he could
scarcely have been a widower as described, for, as he was under age at
the date of his father's will of 1642, he could not have been above 16
years old when the license above quoted was granted.   So there would
seem to be little doubt that it was the unrecognisable William, who
died " old " in 1650, to whom this license referred, and the Pedigree is
in that respect in error.   But the Register of Bedfield above referred to
contained a further entry of " William ffolkard and Anne, married 1640,"
and this probably refers to the marriage of the William under treatment,
though he could not even then have been more than nineteen years old.
His wife's surname is therefore unknown.   The Candler Pedigree
assigns no marriage to him, but this was doubtless due only to want of
information.
In early life it was probable that he resided at Coddenham, for a
Hearth Tax paper of Charles II. reign (*L.S.* 183/612) taxes " William
ffokard " for two hearths in that place.   It seems likely that he was the
defendant in a suit of 1664 (*P.R. Hil.*), in which Robert Stebbing the
elder, and Robert Stebbing, Apothecary, of Ipswich, obtained judgment
against William ffolkard for £100 owing to them.   The sealed bond had
been first put in suit at Framlingham, and Richard Porter appeared as
ffolkard's attorney when the case was tried at Westminster.   In 1682
this William ffolkard was bondsman for £200 to the marriage license of
his brother ffrancis.   By some error the name of William is inserted in
the entry of this license, instead of ffrancis, as the intending bridegroom ;
but this is known to have been a clerical error, as will be seen under the
succeeding notice of the latter.
The will of the subject of this notice of September 10, 1703, has not
been found, but an extract from it (74) is given in the pleadings in a
Chancery suit.   In this pleading he is described as a yeoman, and as of
Bedfield, " being at the time of his death possessed of property (lands,
houses, &c.) in Bedfield and elsewhere in Suffolk."   It seems evident
from the extract from the will that his wife had predeceased him, and

that he himself died at the age of 74 or thereabouts, the pleading referred to informing us that his death occurred on the 22nd October, 1703. Judging from the disposition of his property, it may be concluded that he left no issue.

11. FFRANCIS FFOLKARD, of Bedfield. Although it cannot be proved, owing to the loss of the Registers, there can be no doubt that this was also a son of ffrancis (No. 7), and brother to the William last dealt with. He is not mentioned in his father's will (53), but this affords no guide, proved instances of such omissions being frequent in ancient wills. The fact that the William above named was his marriage surety to the extent of £200 adds to the probability that he was his brother. Davy's extracts from the missing Bedfield Register (*D.* xv. *Bedfield*) include "ffrancis ffolkard 1630." This probably indicated the date of his baptism, he, on the authority of the age given on his tomb, having been born in that year. Nothing is known of his earlier years, and he appears to have remained single until 52 years old, when license for him to marry was given in the following terms:—

"19 September, 1682. License between William (*Quære*) ffolkard, of Bedfield, single, and Martha Humphrey, of Soham Combust, single. Marriage to be celebrated in church of Ashfield Thorp, or Bedfield, or Monk Soham. Held by William ffolkard, yeoman, in £200" (*S.* xxxiv.).

Miss Humphrey was of good family, her long descent from the Dukes of Gloucester ("Good Duke Humphrey") being traced in a Pedigree among those prepared by Davy. This ends with her two marriages recorded on the tomb of herself and her first husband, this ffrancis ffolkard. This tomb is in Bedfield churchyard, and is in a fine state of preservation. As to it, the rector told me that a farm is now held by Mr. Humphrey, the present greatest landowner about Bedfield, on condition that its possessor maintains the tomb. It consists of a very large and fine slab of black marble or granite (I forget the exact material), on which the Humphrey arms—*i.e.*, a lion rampant, over his head a ducal coronet—are impaled between those of Folkard and those of the second husband, the last being 3 roundels, on each a squirrel seiant cracking a nut. The following inscription is deeply and clearly cut on the slab, and tells us all that is further known of this ffrancis ffolkard.

"To the Memory of | Mrs. Martha Croshold, Relict of | the Revd. Mr. John Croshold, | late Rector of Grasham, | in the County of Norfolk, | and daughter of | Charles Humphrey, | of Earl Soham, in the | County of Suffolk, Gent. | She died July ye 2nd, 1740, æt. 79 | By her desire she was interred here | by her first husband | Francis Folkard, Gent., | who died October ye 22nd, 1703, æt. 72."

No will of this man has been found, and his wife is stated, in Davy's Pedigree of Humphrey above named, to have died without issue. With reference to the entry of William for ffrancis in the marriage license, it seems possible that this man held both names, being those of old family use. It is somewhat confirmatory of this conjecture that in the following Fine (*F. Michs.*) of 1686, four years after the date of the above-quoted marriage license, the names both of William and Martha appear:—

" Between Ambrose Chapman, Clerk, and William Baker, plffs., and William ffolkard and Martha his wife, Jeremiah Rust, Edward Rust, and others, defts., of a messuage, 1 garden, 1 orchard, 12 acres of land, 13 acres pasture, with appurtenances, in Buxhall, Ratlesden, and Drinkeston. Defendants receive £60 sterling."

It seems probable that it was either this man or his believed brother William (No. 10) who owned land, part, very likely, of the old manorial possessions of the family, in Buxhall. In 1662 the following Fine was sued (*F. Trin.*) :—

" Between William ffolkard, plff., and Robert Moore and Anne his wife, defts., respecting a messuage, a garden, and orchard, and 12 acres of land, with appurtenances, in Buxhall. William ffolkard pays defendants £41 sterling."

In 1676 the name of William ffolker appears in a list of the custodians of " foote armes " (*D.* xxx. *Stow Hundred*), being therein stated to have " charge of a muskett in Buxhall." Some of the land in Buxhall appears to have remained in the ownership of the family till a comparatively recent date, the name of Folkard as owning land there appearing in a list of landowners of 1792 or 1798, given by Davy in his " Papers relating to Suffolk."

With the foregoing ffrancis ffolkard ends the direct line of family settlement at Bedfield, the property held by it then passing mainly into the possession of the Parham line. Residence was, however, continued by a presumed son of Lawrence ffolkard, of Wickham Market, who has been named before as a son of Thomas, of Bedfield (No. 5). His name was also

12. LAWRENCE FFOLKARD. I cannot find proof of his assumed parentage, but the Registers of Wickham Market might afford it. His presumed father had ten children according to Will 45, but only five of them are named in Will 47, and Lawrence may be supposed to be one of those who are unmentioned.

About 1663 or 1667, according to Hearth Tax Roll 133/612, he paid, as " Lawrence ffokard," for his residence in Bedfield, but the particulars have been burnt off the Roll. The only further notes possessed respecting him are contained in the Bedfield Registers which still exist. The entries run :—

" Joane, wife of Lawrence ffolkard, buried August 30th, 1715."

" Lawrence ffolkard, Buried August 14th, 1724."

12*a.* GEORGE FFOLKARD was also a son of Lawrence ffolkard of Wickham Market, and is named as such in the will (57) of his uncle Anthony of 1656. At that date, according to the will, he had four children, George, Anne, Mary, and Hannah, the first named of whom will be dealt with below. No further information respecting this man has been found, but from the fact of his descendants having subsequently settled at Ipswich, it is more than likely that the following license referred to a daughter of his born subsequent to the date of his uncle Anthony's will :—

"17 February, 1682. License between John Bird, of Ipswich, single, and Elizabeth ffokard, of Ipswich, single, to be celebrated at St. Margarets in Ipswich" (*S.* 1680, *Vol.* 34).

12*b*. GEORGE FFOLKARD, of the Pedigree, was son to the foregoing. It is probably to his marriage that an entry in the now lost Bedfield Register referred (*D.* xv.). This read :—

"G. ffolcard et Elizabeth ux. marrd. 1670."

From the rarity of the name of George at that time, and from the further circumstance of the dates fitting in, it may be fairly concluded that the George ffolkard subsequently met with as resident at Ipswich was identical with this man, and it is desirable, therefore, to deal here with his descendants. If the entry as to marriage named above does refer to this man, the wife therein named had doubtless died, and the husband remarried to a wife named Mary before 1702, the Register of St. Matthew's, Ipswich, containing the following entries :—

"Rose, daughter of gorg folkard and Mary his wife, was Baptized August ye 10th, 1702."

"1704. gorg, son of gorg focker and Mary his wife, was Baptized January ye 12th."

"1707. William, son of George ffaker by Mary his wife, bapt. Mar. 30th."

From documents in a Chancery suit (*Vol.* vi., *Part* 505) entitled "ffokard *vs.* Whincall and Wyatt," we find that "Mary, the wife of George ffokard," had received a legacy under the will of 1703 of Sarah Isaac, widow of Robert Isaac, of Barham, and resident at Ipswich, the legacy being couched in these terms: "I give the sum of thirty pounds to Mary ffokard, wife of George ffokard, of Ipswich." This wife was also residuary legatee under the will. The proceedings in this case are too lengthy to be quoted. They refer to a house at Barham, and possess little or no interest, The interments of this man and his wife are thus noted in the Register of St. Matthews, Ipswich :—

"1722. George ffolcard was buried April the 6."

"1743. Mary ffolkard, Oct. 24th " (*Under burials*).

Their son George, whose baptism has been noticed above as occurring in 1704, seems to have died as a young man, the same Register having the entry :—

"1722/3. George ffolcard was buried April ye 13th."

12*c*. WILLIAM FFOLKARD, of Ipswich, we have seen from the above given Register entry to have been a son of the foregoing, and to have been registered as " William ffaker " in 1707. He was twice married, and both times to wives having the name of Ann We have no information as to the maiden surname of the first wife, but it may be conjectured from the number of Brames named in her husband's will that she was of that family. She died, as we learn from the inscription on her tomb in St. Lawrence churchyard, Ipswich, in 1766, her age being obliterated.

L

We know only of two children born to this marriage, viz., George ffolkard, hereafter dealt with, and William ffolkard, born in 1734. Apparently there must have been two monumental inscriptions in St. Lawrence churchyard to this second son, for Davy (*D.* xvii. *Ipswich*) gives the following copy of one such as on a separate tomb as follows :—

"In Memory of | William Fokard Junr. | who departed this Life | the — of May 1763 | Aged — years " (*Rest gone*).

The Rev. Mr. Haslewood, Rector of St. Matthew's, Ipswich, sent me, in 1884, the inscription given below, which must have been on a tomb erected subsequently, and from this we learn that this son died at the age of 29 years.

The second wife of the subject of this notice we know from her will (105) of 1801 to have been a widow when he married her, and that her name was then Ann Minter. She survived her second husband, in whose will she is named, and her own will having been proved in 1803, her death probably occurred in that year.

We find the earliest mention of this William ffolkard in an advertisement of a house in Ipswich in the *Ipswich Journal* of February 18, 1744, application respecting which is to be made to " Mr. Folkard, Joiner, in Brick Street, Ipswich, who fitted up the said apartments." In " A List of the Subscribers of the County of Suffolk for the Support of His Majesty's Person and Government and the Peace and Security of the said County in particular, on occasion of the Rebellion " (*B.M.*), dated October 14, 1745, we find included "William Fokard, Ipswich, £2. 2s.od." In 1766, as noted above, he lost his first wife. By 1773 he had evidently remarried, for in that year he was party to the following Fine (*F. Michs.*):—

"Between Johnathan Worrell and Robert Lawton, Esq., plffs., and William ffokard and Ann his wife, defts., 1 messuage, 2 stables, 2 gardens, and 1 acre land, in Parishes of Saint Nicholas, St. Stephen, and St. Lawrence, in Ipswich, £60 sterling."

In 1776 he was plaintiff on another Fine (*F. Michs.*) which reads:—

"Between William ffokard, plff., and Lark Tarver, Thomas Swale, and Cordelia his wife, defts., 1 messuage, 2 curtilages, 1 garden, with appurts., in parish St. Lawrence, Ipswich, £60 sterling."

We find him voting as a Freeholder of Ipswich as William Folkard in a list of the poll for the Knights of the Shire, dated April 7, 1784 (*B.M.*), and in 1786 his name appears among the list of subscribers to Middleton's "*Biographia Evangelica*" as Mr. William Folkard. His will (101) is dated 1780, but the date of its proof, 1789, is consistent with that of his death recorded in the following monumental inscription from the churchyard of St. Lawrence, Ipswich. This includes the memorial both of his son William and of his first wife above referred to.

"In Memory of | William Fokard Junr. | who departed this Life | the 21st of May, 1763 | aged 29 years. | Also | Ann the wife of | William Fokard Senr. | who departed this Life | August — 1766 | — years | —— | —— | — Fokard Senr. | —— Life —— 1789 | Aged — years."

The Church Burial Register of 1766 has : " Anne, wife of William Folkard, August the twenty-seventh;" and that of 1789 : " William Folkard from S. Margarets, Feb. 10,"

Having been baptized in 1707, this man was probably over 82 years of age at death. It is curious to observe that although in his will, in the Parish Registers and other documents, his surname is given as Folkard, yet that his tomb bears that of Fokard. It may not improbably be that the following two entries in the Register of St. Matthew's, Ipswich, refer to children born of his first wife :—

(Burials) "1765. James ffolkard, an infant, April 22."
,, "1766. James ffolkard, an infant, January 29."

12*d*. GEORGE FFOLKARD was the son of the foregoing, and named in the latter's will (101). From the facts named in that will, which is dated 1780, only fourteen years after the death of the testator's first wife, it is certain that he was a son of his father's first marriage, as in that year he was a married man with at least one child, and had already failed in business. His bankruptcy is recorded in the list of bankrupts for the year 1772, given in the *Gentleman's Magazine* of 1773, in which he is described as "G. Fokard, of Ipswich, Suffolk, Mariner." He was probably master and owner of some coasting vessel, and this would lend colour to the belief that the following extracts from the London directories of 1778 and 1788 (*B.M.*) indicate that after failing in Ipswich he commenced business in London. The first of these entries reads : "George Fokard, Merchant and Slop Seller, 354, Hermitage Stairs, Wapping." The Directory of 1779 does not contain his name, so that he was probably unsuccessful in this second venture of his. We lose all sight of him until his name again appears in the London Directory for 1788 as "G. Fokard, Ship's Agent, 1, St. Catherine's, Wapping," and the same address is repeated in the directories for 1789, 1791, and 1792, but finally disappears in the issue for 1793 and subsequent issues.

We have no trace of his marriage, which must have taken place before 1780, nor do we know anything with certainty of his son George, beyond the mention of him in his grandfather's will (101), but it seems to be not improbable that he succeeded to his father's business as a Naval or Shipping Agent, and that he was identical with the George Folkard referred to in the following abstract of the pleadings in a Chancery Suit (*Surton Bills*, 1842, *No.* 1565).

"Christopher *vs.* Folkard. George Christopher, of Chiswick Mall, Esquire, and others, and the Attorney General, about the will of Robert Cleghorne, of Stepney Causeway, Merchant and Planter. Property in the island of St. Christopher (*i.e.*, *St. Kitts, West Indies*) referred to. Isabella Evans, one of the defendants in a previous suit, died leaving her husband, Thomas Evans, surviving. She had no issue, and she left Elizabeth Kynson, her surviving sister, Robert Ashington (a great nephew), and Alexander Lean, her coheirs at law. Her husband, Thomas Evans, died, and left George Folkard, of Lyons Inn, Navy Agent, and Gilbert Wells, Gent., of Fenchurch Street, exors. Prays therefore to have the proceedings that were instituted, and that lapsed by the death of Mr. and Mrs. Evans, revived against the exors., the said George Folkard and Gilbert Wells."

Residence at Bedfield was next resumed by a member of the Parham Line, which had issued from the parent stem three generations before. This was

13. THOMAS FFOLKARD, who resided both at Bedfield and Aldborough. He was son to Francis ffolkard, of Parham (No. 5 of that Line), who married Mary Porter. He was baptized at Parham, according to the Register there, as " Thomas ffolkard, the sonne of ffrancis and Mary," on the 25th June, 1700.

In a guardianship deed executed by his father 9th August, 1718 (See No. 5 Parham Line), he is described as being then " aged 18 and upwards." He is next named in his father's will of 1722 (84) as the legatee of a house and lands at Bedfield, and in 1726 he is described in the Parham Register as the husband of Mary, and as father to a son Thomas baptized February 28th of that year, who was buried as an infant at Parham 13th July, 1727.

I have found no record of his marriage to this wife Mary. She is named with her husband in deeds of sale of land at Bedfield in 1745 and 1761, and she was buried at that place in 1773, the entry in the Bedfield Register being :—

" Mary, wife of Thomas ffolkard, buried November 16, 1773."

In 1734 this man would seem to have been resident at Aldborough, and then holding land of the Earl of Stradbrooke either in Snape or Friston, for in a letter of account to the Earl at Friston Hall of May 21 of that year (*Add. MSS*. 22, 249, *Fo*. 99) there occurs the entry :—

" At Mr. ffolkards, a Bill for Thatching—0 : 19 : 4."

From the following extracts from letters from Mr. Benet, the then vicar of Aldborough, to the Earl, of June 4, 1734 (*Add. MSS*. 22, 248, *Fo*. 197), proposing among other matters that the latter should compound the vicarial titles of the Red House farm, this Thomas ffolkard appears to have held a confidential relation towards the Earl.

" If we agree together, I will be content to receive ye tithes of those marshes which are let off, and will discount for ye same either with Mr. Folkard, J. Aldridge, or with anyone else your Lordship shall please to appoint."

(*Ibid. Fo*. 200) " Mr. Folkard calls on me very often, and we consult as closely as we can, how to take ye best care of your Ldship's affairs here." . . . . " Mr. Folkard has sent for Bartram to give in his proposals all together. Mr. Folkard will bring him here to my house, but if he does not come in 2 or 3 days, I propos'd to Mr. Folkard that he and I shou'd ride over to Bartram, and so call upon him, not as designedly, but as tho' we had other business to transact in that neighbourhood."

In 1745 a Fine (*F*. xlii. *Pasch*.) was sued

" Between Catharine Alderman, plaintiff, and Thomas ffolkard and Mary his wife, and Crow Haws and Elizabeth his wife, defendants, of 1 messuage, 1 garden, 1 orchard, 10 acres land, 10 acres meadow, and 5 acres pasture, with appurtenances, in Bedfield, Earl Soham, and Shottisham. Plaintiff pays £60."

In 1753 this man was referred to in the will (95) of his step-brother, the Rev. Francis Folkard, of Clopton, who devised to him certain lands contingently on the testator's daughter Deborah dying without issue, and these lands are referred to in his own will. In 1756, as " Thomas ffolkard, of Aldburgh," he was named exor. and superviser to the will of his brother-in-law, John Punchard, and he proved that will on the 25th November of the same year. In 1761 he was sued on a Fine (*F*. xlvi. *Hil*.)

" Between Robert Haward, plff., and Thomas ffolkard and Mary his wife, and Thomas ffolkard the younger, defts., of 1 messuage, 2 curtilages, 1 garden, 1 orchard, 15 acres land, 15 acres meadow, and 10 acres pasture, with appurtenances in Bedfield. Plaintiff pays £60 sterling."

His name, as of Bedfield, is included in the County Freeholder's List of 1770 (*D.C.* iv. 175). His will (100) is dated April, 1780. It names his son Thomas, his daughter Mary Calver, and his "granson" Thomas, as legatees under it. Although this will was not proved till 20th September, 1783, he died in the year previous, and, as he was buried at Parham, probably at that place, the entry in the Register there being :—

" Thomas ffolkard, widower, buried 3rd October, 1782."

He must therefore have been 82 years old at his death.

14. MARY FFOLKARD, daughter to the foregoing, we know nothing of beyond the references to her in her father's will (100), of 1780, as being then the wife of James Calver.

15. THOMAS FFOLKARD was son to the last-named Thomas (No. 13). He is mentioned in that father's will (100) of 1780. I have no information as to date or place of his birth. As this is not to be found in the Registers of either Parham or Bedfield, it may be presumed that he was born at Aldborough. In 1761 he was old enough to be a party to the Fine last quoted. No particulars as to his marriage have been found, but this must have taken place before 1767, as his son Thomas was born in that year. It is very probable that he married a daughter of the Robert Haward, the plaintiff to the Fine referred to, and in or about 1761, as such proceedings were commonly taken with reference to marriage arrangements.

To judge by the terms of his father's will, this Thomas seems to have been a *mauvais sujet*. He probably had no fixed residence, for though his daughters lived, married, and died at Bedfield, the Register there contains no notice of their having been born at that place. I have found no record of their father's death or interment.

His son Thomas settled at Parham (*See No. 13 of that Line*). His daughter Mary is referred to in the following entries in the Bedfield Register:—

" Will Pepper, son of James and Mary Pepper, Spinster Folkard (*Quære*, baptized), February 27th, 1785."
" Lionel, son of James and Mary Pepper, Spinster Folkard, Born April 20th, 1787."
" Mary Pepper, widow, aged 54, Buried November 13th, 1807."

A second daughter, Elizabeth, is also thus named in the same Register:—

" Thomas, son of Will and Elizabeth Pepper, Spinster Folkard, Born June 2nd, 1787."
" Elizabeth, daughter of Will and Eliz. Pepper, Spinster Folkard " (*Quære*, baptized).

There is no date to this last entry, but it must have been in 1790 as witness

" Elizabeth Pepper buried 11th September, 1815, aged 25."

The mother's death is thus recorded :—

"Elizabeth Pepper, widow, Burd. Redfield, January 2nd, 1832, aged 69."

Probably these two daughters married two brothers. There was a third daughter, Alice Folkard, of whom we know nothing beyond the fact that she was living in 1783, according to an entry in the same Register.

There seem to have been no Folkards resident at Bedfield after the latest date above given.

Settlement at Earl Stonham.
(Includes branch at Thetford.)

1. ROBERT FFOLKARD, of Earl Stonham, was a son of William of Bedfield (*No.* 1 *of that Line*), and is named in his father's will (7) of 1470. As the father held land at Stonham, it was probably upon it that the son settled. In 1467 (*L.C.*) he paid, both as Robin and Robert ffolkard, £1. 5s 0d and 10/3 for lands held in Soham Combust. In 1502 (*F.* xxii.) John Purpet sued a Fine against him, as " Robert ffurch and Margaret his wife," with respect to lands at Ashfield-Thorp and Monk Soham. This wife has erroneously been placed on the Pedigree as the wife of this man's son Robert.

His will (106) is dated 1520, and was proved July 1521, in which year he probably died, being then certainly between 70 and 80 years old.

2. ROBERT FFOLKARD, of Earl Stonham, was son of the above and sole legatee under the latter's will (106) of 1520. Although he evidently possessed lands at Earl Stonham and Stonham Aspal, there seems to be very doubt that the residence of his later years was Thetford, no record of him in his age having been found in papers relating to Earl Stonham.

I conclude that the will of Robert ffolker, of Thetford (22), is that of this man. The mention in that will of a son Nicolas, named probably after his father's cousin, strengthens the ground for this conclusion. The will further informs us that this testator left his wife Elizabeth as his excecutrix. We know nothing more respecting the last named.

A Subsidy Roll (*L.S.* 181/253) of 1543 contains notes of payment by " Robert ffolyart " and " Robert ffolyart, Junior,"—the first of 25 shillings for goods in Stonham Aspal valued at 20 pounds, and the second of 20 shillings for land in the same place valued at 10 pounds. This is the only reference found to a presumed son Robert, and his name not being mentioned in the Thetford will, it is probable that he had died before the date of it. This will (22) is dated 1555, and was proved in the same year. The children named in that will are Nicholas, William, Richard, and John. We know nothing respecting the future of these sons.

Settlement at Monk's Soham.

1. ROBERT FFOLKARD, of Monk Soham, was a son of William of Bedfield (*No.* 2 *of that Line*), and named in his father's will (13) of 1513, by which he inherited lands called "Loders and Bernarde," both probably in Monk Soham, and also probably those possessed by his grandfather William (*No.* 1 *Bedfield Line*). The last named was certainly the first possessor of the family lands at Monk Soham, as the Court Rolls from 1379 to 1427 include no reference to the name of Folkard.

Reference is made in this Robert ffolkard's will to a wife Jone, who must have survived her husband. Nothing is known of her family. We find her, as "Jone ffolkard, widow," paying a Subsidy (*L.S.* 181/271) of 3/6¼ for goods in Monk Soham in 1545, while in the same place, as "Jone folihard, widow," she paid a second Subsidy (*L.S.* 181/281) of 2 shillings for land there in the same year. We recognise her, probably, in the "Johanna ffolkard, widow," who paid, in 1562, a Subsidy (*L.S.* 182/346) of 5/4 for land valued at 40 shillings at Bedfield, from which it may be concluded that she spent the later days of her life at that place, among her husband's relatives.

This husband, in 1523, paid 4 shillings Subsidy (*L.S.* 180/161) on goods valued at £8 in Monk Soham, and one of 13/4 for land there about the same date (*L.S.* 180/172). His will (17) of 1539 mentions seven daughters as then living, but no sons. Of the ultimate life of these daughters nothing is known to me. The Robert ffolkard of Debenham, who was exor. to their father's will, was his nephew.

2. NICOLAS FFOLKARD, of Monk Soham, was brother to the foregoing Robert, and also with him a son of William of Bedfield (*No.* 2 *of that Line*), and a legatee under the latter's will (13) of 1513. No mention occurs anywhere of his wife, who evidently predeceased him, and I believe my assignment to him on the Pedigree of a wife named Alice has been an error.

In 1522 he appears, as "Nicolas ffolkere," to have paid a Subsidy (*L.S.* 181/233) of 20 pence for goods at Debenham. Mention is found of him in an account of the manor of Monk Soham (*Add. MSS.* 21,049) which appears to have been prepared in 1596 by Lionel Tollemache, Lord of that Manor, to obtain Counsel's opinion in a dispute relative to its customs and rights, and to decide what land was "molland" (*i.e.*, moorland) and what "werkland" (*i.e.*, cultivable land). In this account, which is throughout in Latin, there occurs an entry which reads translated as follows :—

"In 1515, John Style surrendered a pightel called Hayman's Pightel, containing 9 acres and 1 10 d, to Nicolas ffolkard, 2/6 fine being paid."

Another entry records that in 1540 Nicholas ffolkard surrendered to his son, Edmund ffolkard, some land called Symons in Soham, with the pightel called Hayman's above named. And a further entry is to the effect that

"In 1550 Nicolas ffolkred surrendered to Edmund ffolkred, his son, 9 pightles, with a house built against a road, and 1 rood of land, paying a fine of 2/8."

This Nicholas apparently had either his residence, or possessed a farm in 1522, at Saxsted, for he paid in that year, as " Nicolas ffolkerd," a Subsidy (*L.S.* 180/127) of 3/7 for goods there valued at £10, while in the year following he further paid (*L.S.* 180/127) 4/6 for goods there valued at £9. He must, after that date, have gone to live on his land at Monk Soham. It is possible that he had a son Richard living at Saxsted in 1523, who has found no place in his will, being probably then dead, for I find that in that year a " Richard ffolkerd " paid a Subsidy in that place on movable goods valued at £9.

This Nicholas ffolkard's will (20) is dated early in 1550, but there is no record of it having been proved. It mentions the testator's daughter Juliane, of whom we have no further notice. Also his sons, John, Robert, and Edmond, who are referred to following.

3. EDMOND FFOLKARD, of Monk Soham, was a son of the foregoing, and named in his will (20) of 1550. The only other mention found of this man is in the account of the manor of Soham before referred to, two of the entries which include his name having been before given. A third entry records that in 1551, the year probably after his father's death, " Edmundus ffolwerde " surrendered to Robert Nicholls " 8 pictles, with the messuage he built contained in one acre and one rood." A Fine of 6/8 was paid on this surrender. In three recapitulations of this entry he is named both as above and as " Edus ffolkard." This is one of the several instances known to me in which the ancient spelling of Folkward is revived centuries after its comparative disuse. No will of this man, nor record of his ever having married, have been found. There is a probability that the following entry in the Register of Framlingham refers to his burial :—

" Edmund ffolkoad was buried the 8th January, 1608."

4. JOHN FFOLKARD, of Monk Soham, was brother to the man last treated of, and, like him, a son of Nicolas (No. 2). He is named in his father's will (20) of 1550. In 1545, as " John ffolcard," he was assessed for a Subsidy (*L.S.* 181/271) of 15 shillings for goods in Monk Soham, which he paid on a Roll (*L.S.* 181/281) of the same year as " John ffolchard." In 1548 he paid a like amount as " John ffolkarde " (*L S.* 181/317). No record has been found of his marriage or of any issue to him.

5. ROBERT FFOLKARD, of Monk Soham, was a third son of Nicolas (No. 2). He is named in the latter's will (20) of 1550. He is probably the man referred to in the following marriage entry in the Register of Carlton :—

" 1584. November 6. Robert ffowkard and Alice Simpson."

For we find " Alice ffolkard, widow," paying a Subsidy (*L.S.* 182/472) in 1610 for land at Earl Soham. A mistake has, it would seem, been made in assigning a first marriage to this Robert, as well as in the statement that he had four children living at the date of his father's will. The error arose from a misreading of his father's mention of his own four children as legatees of his cattle. The Court Rolls of Monk Soham (*Add. MSS.* 23,959) contain entries to the effect that on ·the 13th April, 1571, " Robert ffolkerde " was a jurat ; that on November 17, 1572, " Robert ffolkard (and ffolkerd) paid a Fine ; and that on May 16, 1574, " R. Folkard " was a jurat and paid a further Fine of 8/8 on Woodcroft Hall. Again, that on the 4th July, 1581, " Robert ffolkerd " paid a Fine of 6 pence. With this man the Line at Monk Soham appears to have come to an end.

Settlement at Debenham.

Only a single entry of this Line occurs on Pedigree No. 1. As yet I have not obtained copies of the Register entries at Debenham. As, however, the man treated of is the starting point of other important Lines, notice of the one individual named must find a distinct place here. This is—

1. ROBERT FFOLKARD, of Debenham, a son of Thomas, of Bedfield (*No.* 3 *of that Line*). There is reason to believe that land had been held at Debenham by this man's great grandfather, the first man on the Pedigree, and that it was known by his name, for on a rent-roll of the manor of Sackville-Debenham of 1470 it seems to be stated that Ralph Cheke held a messuage formerly held by Gilbert Barker, and before by John Gurdon, on land " vocat ffolcarde " (*D.* xxxiv.). This man and his brother head the copy of the Candler Pedigree of Folkard in the Bodleian Library.

Much interest attaches to his second marriage thereon indicated. We are aware of a first marriage by him from his father's will (19) of 1543, by which legacies are left to the children of this son Robert, viz., John (*see Winston*), William (*see Earl Soham*), Thomas (*see Framlingham*), and Agnes and James. Of the two last nothing further is known. All these children were, at the date of their grandfather's will, under sixteen years of age. Two of them, William and Thomas, are also named in the will (23) of Thomas ffolkard (brother to this Robert) of 1555.

There can be very little doubt that the following Fine of 1554 (*F.* iii.) refers to this man and to his first wife, as Wetheringsett adjoins Debenham. This runs :—

"Concord in the Court of the King and Queen [*i.e., Phillip and Mary*], at Westminster, between John Hyth, plaintiff, and Robert ffolkard [*indexed "ffoward"*] and Elizabeth his wife, defts., of a messuage and its garden, 4 acres of land, 1½ acre of meadow, and 26 acres of pasture, with their appurtenances, at Brockforthe and Wetheringsett."

As to this Fine, Robert Cheke seems to plead that he had the property as a gift from Robert ffolkard and his wife. Ultimately he

M

agrees to pay to the latter £80 sterling. The assumed identity is further almost absolutely proved by the fact that, in the same year (1554), Edmund ffolkard, of Ashfield (*No. 1 of that Line*), a son of this Robert is plaintiff in a Fine sued against the above-named Robert Cheke, respecting a messuage called Lowdhams in Debenham. This Robert's first wife should therefore have been named as Elizabeth on the Pedigree, and she must have died in either 1554 or 1555. I think it more than probable that this wife's maiden name was Elizabeth Keene, for reasons already given in the notice of his brother Thomas (*No. 4 Bedfield*).

Both this Robert and his brother William appear to have been living at Brockford in 1522 and 1523. In the first of those years he paid a Subsidy (*L.S.* 180/126) there on wages valued at 20 shillings, and in the second year 4 pence on the same valuation of 20 shillings (*L.S.* 180/159) he being described on the roll as a " cappar."

The second marriage before referred to was of a singular character, it having been to Margaret, widow of his brother Thomas, of Bedfield (*No. 4 of that Line*), and in the same year, 1556, as the latter died in. The license for this marriage is to be found in the Admon. Acts (*No. 2 1555—7, Fo.* 142 *Consis. Norw.*). It is in abbreviated Latin, and reads translated :—

" 21st of the month and year [*November*, 1556], to Charles Males (?) Curate of Bedfield, to solemnize marriage between Robert ffolkerde, of Debenham Markett, and Margaret ffolkerde, of Bedfield."

An account of this second wife will be found under No. 4 Bedfield Settlement. In 1539 this man was appointed exor. to the will (17) of his uncle, Robert ffolkard, of Monk Soham, being therein named as of Debenham. In 1542 his name occurs on a Subsidy Roll (*L.S.* 181/233) as paying 20 pence for goods in Debenham. In 1555 he and his sons William and Thomas are named in the will (23) of his brother Thomas, whose widow he married, and he is left exor. to it. In the same year he is given as one of the administrators of his sister Elizabeth, of Stybton (*Admon.* 2). We next find mention of him in 1562, when, for land valued at £5 in Bedfield, a Subsidy (*L.S.* 182/346) of 8/8 was paid by him, and in 1565 he again paid (*L.S.* 181/359) 4/2 for the same land. In 1572 he witnessed the will (34) of his son Edmund, of Ashfield, as " Robert ffolkarde, Senior." In 1575, as " Robert ffolcarde," he paid a Subsidy (*L.S.* 182/370) of 2/8 for land in Debenham valued at 20 shillings.

His will (35) of 1580, in which year he must have died, describes him as being then aged, and to judge by the mention of him as holding land in 1522 previously noted, he must have been quite 80 years old at death. It is singular that this will contains no reference to his first family. It may be presumed that his elder children were then sufficiently settled in life to need no help, as he only names in it the three children he had by his second wife, namely, Richard (*see Mendlesham*), Ambrose (*see Ubbeston*), and Nicholas (*see Stowmarket*).

Of the children of his first marriage (which is not given on the Candler Pedigree) five are named above, and the authority for his other children, Edmund, of Ashfield, and Robert, is derived from the will (30) of their brother John, of Winston, of 1558. The following entries in the

Framlingham Register probably record this son Robert's marriage and burial:—

"Robert fulkard and Margaret Buse were married the 7th October, 1603."
"Robert ffolkard buried 21 February, 1630."

Although, as stated above, I have not yet obtained the entries in the Debenham Register, it seems desirable here to record what has already been ascertained as to members of the family resident there, and not elsewhere dealt with. Of these:—

2. PETER FFLOCKERDE paid 20 pence for goods in Debenham on a Subsidy (*L.S.* 181/213) of 1542. I am quite unable to assign the parentage of this man.

3. CATHERINE FFOLCHARD is named in the following license in the Ipswich Probate Office (*C.*):—

"February 8, 1676. James Hayward, s.m., Debenham, to Catherine Ffolehard, s.w., Debenham."

The parentage of this woman has not been traced.

Settlement at Framlingham.

(Includes branches at Winston, East Bergholt, Gosbeck, Laxfield, Bramford, Ipswich, Saxmundham, and London. .

---

1. THOMAS FFOLKARD, of Framlingham, was a son of Robert, of Debenham (*No.* 1 *of that Line*), by his first wife, the earliest mention we have of him being as a devisee under the will (23) of 1555 of his uncle Thomas ffolkard, of Bedfield (*No.* 4 *of that Line*), he being at that date under 24 years of age. We have no further record of him until his marriage. The evidence on which I have concluded the entry of that event in the Framlingham Register to refer to this man is derived mainly from the mention of the several members of his family in the wills (30 and 34) of his brothers, the second naming his lands at Debenham, and on the further ground, that no other Thomas can be found to whom it would be applicable. This entry reads:—

"Thomas ffolcoad and Grace Moris were married ye 30th August, 1590."

A very numerous family sprang from this marriage, the entries in the Framlingham Register relating to baptism of its members being as under:—

"Thomas ffolkoad, ye sonne of Thomas and Grace ffolkoad his wife, was baptized ye 5th December, 1592."
"ffrancis ffolkoad, ye sonne of Thomas ffolkoad, was baptized ye 28th January, 1593."
"Johan ffolkoade, ye daughter of Thomas ffolkoad, was baptized ye 22nd of October, 1594."
"Marie ffolkoad, ye daughter of Thomas ffolkod, was baptized ye 26 August, 1596."
"Grace ffolkoad, ye daughter of Thomas ffolkoad, was baptized ye 7 August, 1597."

M 2

Also :—

"Grace ffolkod, ye daughter of Thomas ffolkod, was baptized ye 7 August, 1598."

(As to this second entry a note in the Register intimates that the first was in error.)

"Alice ffolkod, ye daughter of Thomas ffolkod and Grace his wife, was baptized ye fifth day of June, 1602."

"Ann ffolkod, ye daughter of Thomas ffolkod and of Grace his wife, was baptized ye 9th Februarie, 1603."

We know by the will (56) of 1654, of Thomas, the eldest son, whose baptism is above noted, that there were other children of whom we have no additional record. It may be that these were baptized elsewhere than in Framlingham, or that the Register there for the years of their baptism are incomplete, as are so many Suffolk Registers. It will be observed that the only one of these brothers and sisters named in the will of the son Thomas referred to is Francis, the others mentioned in it being Samuel, Jeremy (*i.e.*, Jeremiah), Richard, Timothy, Martha, Margarett, and Sarah. These last children must have been born subsequently to the last entry of baptism in the Framlingham Register, and may, with their brothers Francis and Thomas, have been the only surviving members of the family at the date of the latter's will, though the legacy to Mary Culner (*Quære*, Calver) in that will probably referred to the testator's sister Mary. The following entry in the Register of Petistree (*D.* xxxvii. *Petistree*) may refer to the marriage of the daughter Martha.

"Martha ffocard, s.w., married Edward Smith, of Marlesford, 10th February, 1634."

The death of the subject of this notice occurred in 1626, the Register of Framlingham thus recording it :—

"Thomas ffolkarde was buried 12 July, 1626."

No will of his has been found.

2. JOHN FFOLKARD, of Winston, near Debenham, was brother to the foregoing, and a son of Robert ffolkard of the latter place. He is named in his grandfather's will (19) of 1543 as being then under 16 years of age. The only further information respecting this man is given us in his own will (30) of 1558, in which he alludes to his brother, "Edmund ffowkered," of Ashfield. From the date of proof of his will, we may conclude that he died the year after it was written, and probably quite young. His wife Margarett is named in it, but it contains no reference to children of the marriage.

3. THOMAS FFOLKARD was the eldest son of Thomas (No. 1). The Register entry of his baptism has been given above. The only allusion to his marriage discoverable is the bequest left by his will to his wife Marie, who survived him. She must have been a widow at her marriage to this Thomas, as his will (56) of 1654 refers to "my wives grandchildren." This will has been above named to contain evidence as to his brothers and sisters. His burial at Framlingham is thus noted in the Register :—

"Thomas ffolkard buried July 7th, 1655."

No issue to him is named in his will, nor does the Register contain reference to any.

4. FFRANCIS FFOLKARD, of East Bergholt, was brother to the foregoing Thomas, the register of his baptism being quoted under No. 1. He was a legatee under the will (56) of his brother Thomas in 1654. On the Pedigree I have assumed him to be the man referred to in the following marriage license (*Sundry Books, Ipsw. Pro. xxxiv.*).

"26th November, 1686. License marriage between ffrancis ffolkard, of East Bergholt, and ffrances Browne, of East Bergholt. Surety, William Browne in £100."

This assumption is, however, on reconsideration, manifestly an error, as this ffrancis would, at the date of the license, have been at least 93 years old. Possibly it referred to the marriage of a son of his. I have assumed that the East Bergholt Line started from this man, so I may insert here the following extract from the will of the William Browne who stood surety for the marriage, which is registered in the Probate Office at Somerset House, and is dated 14th January, 1688. The testator, who describes himself as a "clothier" (*i.e.*, cloth merchant), bequeaths

"Unto ffrancis ffolkard, my sonn-in-Law, the sum of Tenn pounds, to be paid unto him by Executrix within one year after my decease."

As this will refers to Priscilla Browne as "my only daughter," the wife of this ffrancis ffolkard must then have been dead.

5. JERIMY (JEREMIAH) FFOLKARD, of Gosbeck, was another son of Thomas (No. 1), and the only remaining member of that man's numerous family of whom I have any information beyond the record of baptisms above quoted, and their mention in their brother Thomas's will (56) of 1654. That will is the only evidence possessed of this Jerimy's parentage.

From entries in the Register of Gosbeck, his wife appears to have been named Martha, and from that relating to the baptism of a son Thomas, it is evident the marriage took place before 1646. The death of this wife is thus recorded in the same Register:—

"Anno 1680. Martha Ffolkard, wife of Jeremy Ffolkard, buryed December 19th."

As, however, this entry is made upon an affidavit of December 22nd, it scarcely follows from it that the burial was at Gosbeck itself.

Two almost illegible entries on two Subsidy Rolls (*L.S.* 182/489 and 183/501) of 1628 record that "Jeremias ffolcard" paid 4 shillings on land valued at 20 shillings in Beddingfield. His will (69) is dated 10th February, 1684, and was proved in the following March, yet the entry of his burial in the Register of Gosbeck reads:—

"Jeremy Folkard was buried March 10th (1685)."

To the above entry is added a note:—

"Affidavit made before Mr. Candler, of Pettoway [*doubtless Pettaugh*] brought in March 15th."

The remark as to doubt of locality of interment made above as regards the wife probably applies also to the husband, and the place of his burial, it seems likely, was Pettaugh. The discrepancy as to date of proof of his will and that of burial may either have arisen from confusion owing to the use of the old and new styles, or, as the year in the entry is placed between brackets, it may have been added afterwards and mistakenly.

6. MARY FFOLKARD, a daughter of the foregoing, is named in her father's will (69) of 1684, as being then the wife of Thomas Gilbert. She had only been married the year previous, the entry in the Gosbeck Register being :—

"Anno Dom. 1683.   Thomas Gilbert & Mary Ffolker was married on the three & twentieth day of October."

This Mary was a joint legatee with her two surviving brothers and her sister Susan in the will (71) of her brother, Thomas ffolkard, of Ottley, of 1686.

7. SUSAN FFOLKARD was a sister of the last, and with her a daughter of Jeremiah ffolkard (No. 5). She is named both in the latter's will (69) of 1684, and in that of her brother Thomas (71) of 1686. At the latter date she was a single woman. In the year following she married, the license (*Sundry Books, Ipsw. Pro. xxxiv.*) reading :—

"13 April 1687.   License marriage between Lawrence ffosdike, of Ottley, single, and Suzanna ffolkard, of Ottley, single, at Akenham.   Bonds by Robert ffosdick de Clayden in £200."

From this license it is apparent that she resided with her brother Thomas at Ottley after her father's death.

8. JAMES FFOLKARD was another child of Jeremiah (No. 5). Nothing is known respecting him beyond his being named in the latter's will (69) of 1684, though he must have been one of the two surviving brothers who were legatees under the will (71) of his brother Thomas of 1686, the other brother, Timothy, as will be seen below, having died in 1685.

9. TIMOTHY FFOLKARD was also son to Jeremiah (No. 5), and brother to the foregoing. He is mentioned in his father's will (69) of 1684. He was probably named after his uncle. His death took place in 1685, the entry in the Gosbeck Register being :—

"Timothy Folkard, single man, was buried ye 4 '7ber.'"

To this entry is also appended the note :—

"1685.   Affidavit made before Mr. Stephenson of Winston.   Brot in ye same day he was buried."

10. THOMAS FFOLKARD, of Ottley, was another son of Jeremiah (No. 5) and brother to the last.   The Gosbeck Register has :—

"Thomas Ffokard, the sonn of Jeremy Ffokard, and Martha his wife, was baptized the 28th day of November, 1646."

He was evidently the best-loved son of his father, in whose will (69), of 1684, he is mentioned. His own death followed closely on that of this father, his will (71) of 1686 being proved in that year. The identity of this man is conclusively established by his reference to his sister Susan and his brother Samuel in his will. This document is of special importance as containing mention of his nephew Jeremiah ffolkard, so affording a clue for recognition of the latter's parentage which would otherwise be wanting.

11. SAMUEL FFOLKARD is the only child of Jeremiah (No. 5) remaining to be dealt with. Beyond the references to him in his father's and brother's wills (69 and 71) we know nothing of him ; unless, as I think it justifiable to believe, he was the Samuel, of Laxfield, whose will (79) of 1709 has been printed, and who will be found dealt with further on (No. 18).

The subject of this notice is the only member of his family to whom it is possible to assign the parentage of the "Jeremiah ffolkard, my kinsman" (invariably the expression used to denote a nephew), referred to in the will (71) of his brother Thomas ffolkard, of Ottley. The Jeremiah ffolkard therein named having died in 1706, his name would naturally find no mention in his presumed father's will (79) of 1709. What tends to support the assumption made of the identity of this Samuel with Samuel of Laxfield, is that a son John of the latter had as his partner, according to his will (93) of 1748, one of the Bishops of Saxmundham, in which latter place the son of this Jeremiah was brought up, an intermarriage with that family subsequently occurring. Everything, therefore, goes to suggest that this Samuel lived ultimately at Laxfield, and that he died there in 1709, although I have not acted on this presumption in drawing up the Pedigree. His descendants will be found dealt with later on.

12. JEREMIAH FFOLKARD I believe to have been a son of the foregoing Samuel for reasons above given. The first allusion found to him is in the will (71) of his uncle, Thomas ffolkard, of Ottley. It is probable that at the date of that will (1686), he was the only son of his father, who, being left exor. to it, would therefore have charge of the legacy devised to this son of his. From the terms of that bequest it is evident that this Jeremiah was, at the date of it, very young, probably not more than 8 or 10 years old.

The following entry of a license (*Sundry Books, Ipsw. Pro. xxxiv.*) probably refers to this man's marriage. It reads :—

"20 August, 1699. License marriage between Jeremias ffulkard and Maria Booth at Beccles."

At that date he would probably have been between 21 and 23 years of age. The parentage of this Maria Booth is doubtful; but from the after-connection of her son with Saxmundham, it is probable that she was either a daughter or sister of the Lionel Booth who, in 1725, sued a Fine (*F. Trin.*) in partnership with Jeremiah Aldrich against John Dowsing, and Elizabeth his wife, for messuages and lands in Saxmundham, and who was also plaintiff to a second Fine (*F. Trin.*) of 1751—2 against Peter Searles and Elizabeth his wife respecting other properties in the same place. This Maria Booth is referred to as living at the date of her husband's will (76) of 1706, but husband and wife had evidently parted on bad terms, and their child must have been born after the father left for service in the Royal Navy, as it has no mention in the latter's will.

From the date and circumstances of that will, it is evident that its author must have died abroad either in 1706 or 1707, and when about

29 or 31 years of age. I have searched what pay sheets, &c., survive at
the Record Office of H.M. Brigantine "Fly" among the Admiralty
records. The muster rolls are altogether missing, and the pay sheets
existing only cover from 1696 to 5th May, 1704, when this vessel was
paid out of commission at Harwich. She was probably recommissioned
at that port, and her crew, which is stated on the pay sheets to have
been nearly wholly of "pressed men," recruited from Essex and Suffolk.
It is probable, therefore, that this Jeremiah ffolkard was seized by a
press-gang in 1704 or 1705, and that he remained abroad till his death,
which probably occurred in some naval hospital, as he describes himself
in his will as "late belonging to her Majesty's Shipp ffly Brigantine."

13. JEREMIAH FFOLKARD, the son and believed only child of
the foregoing, must have been born after his father left for sea, *i.e.*, either
in 1705 or 1706. As above mentioned, he found no place in his father's
will (76). I have no record of his birth. The Register of Saxmundham
does not contain it. Judging from all the circumstances, there is every
probability that after the birth of her child, this man's mother went to
Saxmundham to live with her father (or brother) Lionel Booth. In that
place, no doubt, her son was brought up and settled. The baptism of a
son of his is thus entered in the Saxmundham Register:—

"Jeremiah, son of Jeremiah and Elizabeth Folkard, November 9th, 1733, baptized."

His marriage, of which I have no record, may probably have taken
place in that year, when he would have been 28 or 29 years of age. The
maiden name of his wife is doubtful, but from memoranda relating to a
legacy to her son John Folkard and her grandchildren hereafter to be
quoted, she was probably a daughter of the devisee, Henry Broom, of
Debach, whose believed father lies buried in Kelsall churchyard adjacent
to Saxmundham. The baptisms of the further issue of this man's first
marriage, viz., John and Elizabeth, are recorded in the Saxmundham
Register, and then follows the entry of the wife's burial as under:—

"Elizabeth Folkard buried May 21st, 1745."

In 1751 the same Register contains an entry which proves a subsequent second marriage.

"James, son of Jeremiah and Sarah Folkard, baptized October 1st, 1751."

Nothing is known of this second wife's maiden name, nor anything
respecting her beyond the fact that she survived her husband and proved
his will, of which she was executrix, in 1751. The son James above
named must have been born posthumously, as he found no mention in
his father's will (94) of 1750. This father died early in 1751, according
to the following entry in the Register of Saxmundham:—

"Jeremy Folkard buried March 27th, 1751."

14. JEREMIAH FOLKARD was the first-born child of the fore-
going by his first marriage, and is named in his father's will (94) of 1750.
The entry of his baptism at Saxmundham in 1733 has been given above.
We know but little respecting him beyond the fact that he was living in
London, and was a married man, in 1764. He returned subsequently
to Saxmundham, and was living there in 1782. These facts, and the

name of his wife and of his two only children, have been obtained from the memoranda given below, which were found among the papers of the late F. C. Brooke (*D.* liv. 36). His wife's name before marriage is not positively known; but from the fact of the name of Bream (or Brame) being given to her daughter, I conjecture this to have been her maiden surname. This conjecture is strengthened by the repeated mention of that name in the will of William Folkard (101). The memoranda referred to are as follows:—

" 21 May 1782. Release by Jenny Elisabeth Bream Folkard, of Madock's Street, Hanover Square, Midx., Spinster, one of the two children of Jeremiah Folkard, of Saxmundham."

' 21 May 1782. Release by S, (*Quære*, Susanna) Elizabeth Folkard, of Henrietta Street, Manchester Square, London, of her legacy under the above-mentioned will " (*i.e.*, that of Henry Broom, of Debach).

"These are to certify whom it may concern, that Elisabeth, dar of Jeremiah and Susanna Folkard, was born in the parish of St. George's, Hanover Square, in the County of Middlesex, upon the 7th day of May, in the year of our Lord 1764, and was baptid. upon the 9th day of June, as appears by the Register Book of Births and Baptisms belonging to the said Parish, and extracted out of the Register Book this 6th day of June, 1776. In Witness whereof I have hereunto set my hand. James Trebuck, A. M. Regr. of St. George's afsd."

The above-named will of Henry Broom of Debach is dated August 30th, 1780 (*D.P.*), and leaves to the children mentioned £90. 7s. They are also residuary legatees to it with their uncle John Folkard (No. 16). I have no record of their father's death, but did not search the Saxmundham Register to the probable date of it.

15. ELIZABETH FOLKARD was sister to the foregoing Jeremiah. Her baptism is thus recorded in the Register of Saxmundham.

"Elizabeth, daughter of Jeremiah and Elizabeth Folkard, baptized September 26, 1736."

Her father's will (94) of 1750 names her, but beyond this nothing is known respecting her.

16. JOHN FOLKARD, of Framlingham, was the younger son by the first marriage of Jeremiah, of Saxmundham (No. 13), and is named in the latter's will (94) of 1750. His baptism is thus recorded in the Register of Saxmundham:—

"John, son of Jeremy and Elizabeth Folkard, baptized Sept. 30, 1742."

He was first married, in 1764, to Mary, daughter of Daniel and Mary Manthorp, of Ufford, who was baptized at Saxmundham May 15th, 1740. Of this marriage there were born four children, whose baptisms are thus recorded in the Register of Framlingham:—

" Mary Elizabeth, Daughter of John and Mary Folkard, baptized 9th December, 1765."

"John, son of John and Mary Folkard, baptized 25 May, 1768."

" Daniel, son of John and Mary Folkard, baptized 29 June, 1769."

" Richard Manthorp, son of John and Mary Folkard, baptized 16 October, 1771."

N

The first wife died in 1776, the following being the record of her burial in the Framlingham Register :—

"Mary Folkard buried 13th June, 1776."

Her tomb is in the churchyard, and bears this inscription :—

"Mary, | the Wife of | John Folkard, | died June the 10th, | 1776, | Aged 36 years."

A second marriage of this John Folkard is thus entered in the same Register :—

"John Folkard, of Framlingham, Widower, to Mary Weex, S.W., of Framlingham, 20 January, 1778."

The issue of this marriage is thus noticed in the Register :—

" Elizabeth, daughter of John and Mary Folkard, baptized 20 June, 1779."

"John, son of John and Mary Folkard, baptized Feby. 5, 1784 (2 years old)."

" William, son of John and Mary Folkard, baptized February 5, 1784."

" Maria, daughter of John and Mary Folkard, baptized (privately) 13 February, 1786."

" Maria, daughter of John Folkard and Mary his wife (late Wicks), baptized 25 January, 1787."

"James, son of John Folkard and Mary his wife (late Wicks), priv. baptized, Buried 20th February, 1788."

"James, son of John and Mary Folkard (late Wicks, sp.), baptized January 11th, 1790."

" Sarah, daughter of John and Mary Folkard, priv. bap. August 29, 1795."

The burial of the second wife is thus registered at Framlingham :—

" Mary Folkard, of Framlingham, buried December 3rd, 1815, aged 62."

Her tomb in the churchyard has the following inscription :—

" In Memory of | Mary, the wife of | John Folkard | who departed this Life | November 27th, 1815, | Aged 62 years. | Also of | Louisa, daughter of | Michael Dennant | and Susan his wife, | who died November 30, 1822, | aged 11 weeks."

In 1782 this John Folkard was a legatee of £80, as also one of the residuary legatees, under the will of his (presumed) maternal grandfather, Henry Broom, of Debach, to which reference has before been made. His release for this legacy (D. liv. 36) reads :—

"21 May, 1782. Release by John Folkard, of Framlingham, of a Legacy given him by the will of Henry Broom, of Debach, Gent., dated 30th August, 1781."

In 1821 his nephew Richard Manthorp, when writing under date October 21 of that year to this John's son Daniel, remarked :—

"My uncle in an extreme weak state. He was in bed and prays for death, being quite worn out."

His death did not, however, occur till eighteen months later, his burial being thus recorded in the Framlingham Register :—

"John Folkard, of Framlingham, buried February 26, 1823, aged 80 years."

His tomb in the churchyard, which stands between those of his two wives, is thus inscribed :—

" In | Memory of | John Folkard | who departed this Life | February 20th, 1823, | Aged 80 years."

Davy (D. xx.) refers to his death and to his great age.

17. JAMES FOLKARD was a son of Jeremiah (No. 13) by his second wife, and must, as before remarked, have been born posthumously. The entry of his baptism at Saxmundham in 1751 has before been given. Papers came into my hands which show that he had practised as a veterinary surgeon at Beccles. From these we learn also that his wife Elizabeth survived him and administered to his will. He died April 12, 1820, apparently at Beccles.

I am not certain as to his issue, but there is every probability that Robert William Folkard, of Beccles, an artist, who died there 9th November, 1835, was a son of his. In that case, a sister of this artist, Louisa Folkard, who was living a spinster at Wells-next-the-Sea, Norfolk, must also have been one of his children. This Louisa, as late as 20th March, 1878, took out letters of administration to her brother's estate, it being probably necessary to do this, although forty-three years had passed, to complete some title to property.

---

18. SAMUEL FFOLKARD, of Laxfield, has been before dealt with under the No. 11 of this Line, he having been, there is much reason to think, identical with the son of the same name of Jeremiah ffolkard (No. 5), of Gosbeck. His presumed son, also named Jeremiah, has been previously dealt with. This Samuel is reintroduced here with the object of continuing the descent from him, although this is not given on the Pedigree. The will (79) of this man of 1709, in which year he died, names his wife Mary, who survived him, and his daughters Mary and Elizabeth, of whom we know nothing further. One of his two sons was

19. SAMUEL FFOLKARD, of Laxfield, who is named in his father's will, as also in that (93) of his brother John of 1748. The latter informs us of his partnership with the testator and with William Bishop, in Laxfield, at the date of it. We know nothing more respecting this man.

20. JOHN FFOLKARD, of Laxfield, was brother to the last. His name occurs in the will (79) of his father of 1709, apparently as the elder of the two brothers. The following license may refer to his marriage:—

" 10th June, 1684. License marriage between John ffolkard, of Woodbridge, single, and Ann Fletcher, of Woodbridge, single, at Woodbridge or Bealing's Magna (*Ipsw. Sundry Books, Vol.* 34).

He is also possibly to be identified with the man referred to in the following extract as to a Fine from the Court Roll of Culpho:—

" 1745. July 4. Of John ffolkard, on his admission upon ye surrender of Ann Rivett, £4 : 0 : 0 " (*D.C.*)

An entry in the Court Roll of Sutton and Hollesley also probably refers to land held by him.

" 13th October, 1727. John Furkard pays homage " (*Add. MSS.* 23951, *Fo.* 31).

N 2

His will (93) bears no date, and includes no reference to his wife, who had therefore no doubt predeceased him. It was proved in 1748, and names five children, John, Samuel, Isaac (a soldier), Elizabeth, and Lydia. Of only one of these, John, have we any later trace. It seems probable that the latter was identical with

21. JOHN FFOLKARD, of Bramford, who appears to have settled at that place—probably on account of his marriage connection—as an innkeeper. The following entry in the Register of Brundish would indicate that, prior to his marriage, he resided at that place, which adjoins Laxfield.

"1718. John ffolkard, of this parish, and Anne Downes, of Bramford, both single persons (married), by License, December 1st."

He was probably the man referred to in a curious quack advertisement in the *Ipswich Journal* of March 4—11th, 1721, which certifies that Benjamin Rose, of Hasketon, was grievously afflicted with " Fitts," but that Mr. Frost, of Ipswich, cured him.

"Witnesses who have seen him in his Affliction, John Carter, Minister, John Fockard" (and others).

In the Poll List for the Knights of the Shire of 1727 (*B.M.*), we find him voting as a resident of Bramford. The following advertisements made by him are extracted from the files of the *Ipswich Journal* (*B.M.*):—

"Advertisement. This is to give Notice to all Gentlemen and others—That on the 17th and 18th of this instant, April, there will be a Cock-Match fought at Mr. John Forckard's at the Angel, at Bramford, in Suffolk, for a Guinea a Battle, and ten Guineas the odd Battle. Note—There is 31 Cock on each side, and to be fought in silver" (*March* 23 *to April* 1*st*, 1731).

"There will be a Florists' Feast at Mr. John Folkard's at the Angel, in Bramford, in the County of Suffolk, on Wednesday the 20th day of April, 1743, when all Gentlemen that will be so good as to afford us their Company, will meet with a kind reception and a hearty welcome from their friends and servants, James Wilder, John Thorogood, Stewards " (*July* 30, 1743, *and ante*).

Similar advertisements are repeated in 1744 and 1745. Nothing certain is known to me, either of any issue to the marriage above quoted, or as to the death of the husband or wife. Bramford being, however, only 2½ miles north-west of Ipswich, it is far from unlikely that the following entry in the Register of St. Matthew's of the latter town may record the burial of both of them on the same day.

"1757. John and Ann ffolkard were buried Octobe 20th."

The omission of the final r in October is one of the very many instances of the kind which justify my conclusion that many names spelt with a final e were pronounced after the continental method, as in such a case as ffaulke for ffaulker.

If the identity of the parties buried at St. Matthew's with those of Bramford may be assumed, it may possibly be that, late on in life, this John ffolkard left Bramford (no record later than 1744 being there found of him) and resided in Ipswich. In that case the following further entry in the St. Matthew's Register may refer to a son of his :—

"1746. John ffolkard was buried (of the Small Pox) March 25th."

Ann Folkard, who was a tenant of land in Bramford in 1798, for which she was taxed 8 shillings (*D.* viii. *Hundred rating*), was probably a daughter named after the mother.

---

22. EDMUND FFOLKARD, of Laxfield, I conjecture to have been a son of Edmund, of Ashfield, by his wife Maria Salter (*No.* 4 *Ashfield Settlement*). On the 25th January, 1688, he stood surety in £200 with respect to the marriage license of John Mills, of Fressingfield, and Marian ffolkard, of Fressingfield, as " Edmund ffolkard, of Laxfield" (*Ipsw.* *Pro.* *Reg.*). He was again a bondsman to another marriage license (*Ibid.*) on the 18th October, 1692. If my surmise as to this man's parentage be correct, the Marian ffolkard of the license quoted might not improbably have been a daughter of his brother Robert, of Pettaugh (*No.* 6 *Ashfield Settlement*), the latter having married a wife named Maria.

The latest mention of this man's name found is as a witness to the will (79) of Samuel ffolkard, of Laxfield, in 1709. His kinship to the latter would have been remote—a fourth degree of cousinship only ; but residence in the same place would have stimulated intimacy and friendship. The Thomas ffolkard who was also a witness to the same will was probably a son of Thomas of Cretingham (*Nos.* 1 *and* 2 *of that Line*), given on the Pedigree.

Concluding Note.—As this Settlement has been noticed up to a comparatively modern date, there is no necessity for me to enter upon detail of the last two generations recorded on the Pedigree. As, however, all knowledge as to James, the son of John Folkard, of Framlingham (No. 16), who was baptized in 1790, seems to have faded out of family reminiscence, the following entries in the Kelsale Register, which have of late, and since compiling the Pedigree, come to my knowledge, may well be preserved here, as presumably applying to him and to his children :—

"May 10th, 1829. James Folkard and Eliza Spore, both single, married."

"October 19, 1862. William Pettit, son of William Pettit, and Eliza Folkard, 23, daughter of James Folkard, both single, married."

"August 12th. 1866. Edmund Page, widower, son of Francis Page, and Martha Folkard, daughter of James Folkard, spinster, married."

Settlement at Earl Soham.

(Includes branches at Sweffling and Winston.)

1. WILLIAM FFOLKARD, of Earl Soham, was a son of Robert, of Debenham (*No. 1 of that Line*), by his first marriage with Elizabeth (*Quære*, Keene). He is named in the will (19) of his grandfather, Thomas ffolkard, of Bedfield (*No. 3 of that Line*), of 1543, as being then under 16 years of age. He is further named in the will (23) of his uncle Thomas, of 1555.

By the will (43) of his widow we learn that he had been twice married; her stepson, William ffolkard, of Sweffling, being named in it. Who the first wife may have been cannot be traced with certainty, but the following entry in the Register of Gosbeck may refer to her and to the birth of the son William above named.

"Baptism of William, the son of William ffulkard and Borrit his wife, October 20th, 1611."

His second wife we know, both from his own and her wills, to have been named Alice, and, from the number of Wyards named as legatees by her, there is a fair presumption that she was of that family. She survived her husband—by whom apparently she had no issue—and died, probably, late in 1626, her will (43) being dated in 1623.

In 1603 her husband paid a Subsidy of 14 pence for land valued at 15 shillings in Earl Soham (*L.S.* 182/451). His deposition was taken as to the customs of that parish 4th April, 1609 (*Chanc. Depositions, Chas. I., No.* 20, *Bdle. F.*), in the case of ffrancis fookes *vs.* William ffolkerd and Nicholas Deve, the case relating solely to the payment of tithes to the plaintiff, who was the rector of Earl Soham. The plea of the defendants was that they desired to pay in kind, and not in money as demanded by the plaintiff. His will (41) is dated 1618, and he must have died in April or May of that year.

2. WILLIAM FFOLKARD, of Sweffling, was a son of the foregoing by his first marriage. The presumed record of his baptism in 1611 has been given above. He is named in his father's will (41) as also in that (43) of his stepmother of 1623, he being described in the last as of Sweffling, though his own will (51) of 1639 describes him as being at that date resident at Earl Soham. In that will he names his wife as Johan (or Joan), but nothing else is known respecting her. Reference is also made in it to a son William, and to three daughters, Elizabeth, Bridget, and Johan. Of these daughters we know nothing further, though, by an error, they have been entered on the Pedigree as living in 1657. In 1610 either he or his father paid a Subsidy (*L.S.* 182/472) of 16 pence

for land at Sweffling valued at 20 shillings, and in 1628 a further Subsidy (*L.S.* 123/500) for land there of 8 shillings.

In November, 1641, this man (described as a yeoman of Earl Soham) petitioned the Keeper of the Great Seal (*C.P. before* 1714, *Mitford* 48) to the following effect :—

"That 36 years since he was of great acquaintance and friendship with one Thomas Shemynge, then of Framlingham, and since dead, who had dealings with Francis Wood, of Harleston, great quantities of trees and wood being dealt in between them. In 1609 the petitioner went surety for 8 pounds for Shemynge for a payment of foure pounds to Wood. This bond he afterwards gave up to Shemynge, who died about twenty years after. Wood, after the death of Shemynge, fell into great distress and was in gaol for debt, and when he came out he got possession of the bond and other papers. He threatened to sue the petitioner on the bond, who pleads that Woods be summoned to prove how he obtained it. Defendant answers that he had lost the bond until about five years since, and that when he found it he applied to the petitioner for payment, who appealed to his forbearance and delayed payment. When a suit was entered against him the petitioner commenced this proceeding."

In 1642, two years before his death, this William paid a Subsidy of 8 shillings for land in Earl Soham valued at £1. No doubt, as his will, though dated in 1639, was not proved till 1644, he survived till the latter date.

3. WILLIAM FFOLKARD, of Winston, was a son of the last, and named in his will (51) of 1639. In 1657 he was defendant to the following Fine (*F. Easter* xxiv.):—

"Between Allan Catchpole, John and Thomas ffenn, plaintiffs, versus Robert Tovell, William ffolkard and Susan his wife, Samuel Symonds and Hanna his wife, defts., respecting 1 messuage and 1 orchard, 14 acres of land, 6 acres of meadow, and 34 acres of pasture, with appurts. in Cretingham, Earl Soham, and Crowfield   Plaintiffs paid defendants £100 sterling."

From the above we know that this man's wife was named Susan, and she is so named in her husband's will (70) of 1684 as then living. In 1679 he obtained judgment (*P.R. Trin.* 950) for a debt against Richard Thrower in connection with Soham. His name is indexed "ffulkard," and spelt both "ffolkard" and "ffolker" in the judgment itself.

The name of this man's wife, and the evidence above given that he was living as late as 1679, leaves no doubt in my mind that the will (70) of William ffolckward, of Winston, dated and proved 1684, was that of this man. This will (which has been printed in the "East Anglian" of 1885, fo. 63) affords a curious but by no means isolated instance of a return to the radical spelling of the family name, as well as of the not unfrequent corruption of "ffollikard." From it we learn that this man left two daughters, one, Elizabeth, married to Sill Reeve, and another, Susan, married to Ralph Sayer, of Winston. No sons are named in the will.

---

4. ROBERT FFOLKARD, of Sweffling. I have no direct evidence of this man's parentage. If he was, as seems to be probable, and as has been assumed on the Pedigree, a son of William ffolkard, of Earl Soham (No. 1), he is omitted from the wills both of his father and mother (41

and 43). This was, however, by no means uncommon. The fact of his residence at Sweffling coincidently with his assumed brother William, and his naming a son after his assumed father William, justifies to a great extent the conclusion arrived at.

Beyond the information afforded by his will (46) of 1627, we have no record of this man. From no mention being made in it of his wife, she had certainly predeceased him. Of his children, William, Mary, and Elizabeth, we know nothing. It has been assumed on the Pedigree that the last daughter named was the wife of "my son-in-law Graystone," but from the reading of the will it is at least possible that there had been another daughter who was the wife of that man, and who was dead at the date of it. The discrepancy observable between the date of the will and its proof was doubtless due to the use of the old and new styles. It seems probable that the grandchild, John ffolkard, was a son of the testator's son John named in the will, and this is so assumed on the Pedigree.

5. ROBERT FFOLKARD, of Sweffling, was a son of the foregoing, being named in the latter's will (46) of 1627. In 1629 we find him a party to the following Fine (F IIil.) which is almost conclusive as to his continued residence at Sweffling :—

" Between Robert ffolcard (also ffolkard) and Robert Otway and Elizabeth his wife, respecting 1 messuage, 1 garden, 1 apple orchard, 3 acres land, and 3 acres pasture, in Sweffling. Robert pays £41 sterling."

No other detail respecting this individual has been found, and apparently with him the Line resident at Earl Soham and Sweffling came to an end.

Settlement at Ashfield.

(Includes branch at Pettaugh.)

1. EDMUND FFOLKARD, of Ashfield, was a son of Robert, of Debenham (No. 1 of that Line), by his first marriage, and predeceased his father. The references to him and to his brother Robert, in the will (30) of their brother John, of Winston, to which he was exor., sufficiently prove his parentage, even if there was not the additional collateral proof of his having had property at Debenham.

He was certainly twice married, and the terms of the second wife's will given below would indicate that all his children were by the first marriage, as to which we have no particulars. His second wife, Elizabeth, is named as then living in his will (34) of 1572. It has been suggested on the Pedigree that his wife (who must have been a widow at her marriage to this Edmund) was named Clarke, and the legacy to Katheryn Clarke " my wife's daughter " in that will, as then unmarried, supports this. The legacies to the other Clarke must apply to the children of his wife's son, Walter, by her former marriage. This second wife appears to have lived at Thornden after her husband's death, and her will of 1581 from the Bury Probate Office reads abstracted as follows :—

"2nd January, 24 Eliz. Elizabeth ffoakerde, of Thornden, Co. Suff., widowe, being sicke. XXs. to the poorest of Ashfilde. To John Coates, the sonne of George Coates, wch. he had by my daughter Katherine XXs. To John Gynneryes children, Roberte and Jane, ——. To the children of William Clerke, namely, Ellis Clerke, Anne, Joane, and Grace, Xs. a piece. To the children of Walter Clerke, namelye, John Clerke, ffrancis, Roberte the elder, Roberte the younger [*N.B.*, *Two children named identicaliy, a very common case*], Edward Clarke and Laurence Clerke, XXXIIIs. IIIId. a pece. To Roberte ffoakerd's children, namelye, Edmund, Edeneye, ffraunces, and John, XVs. a pece. Item. To Edeneye, the wife of Robert ffoakerde, my beste petycoate and a square. Item. To Jane Gynnerye, the wife of John Gynnerye, bothe my best gownes, my beste cloake, &c., and my beste apron beinge blacke. Item. To Elizabeth Clerke, the wife of Walter Clerke, my best hatt, &c. Item. To Elizabeth Gyldingsleve, one of my worser smockes, &c. To my daughter Jane Gynnerye ——. To John ffoakerd's eldest child, Xs. To the porest of Thornden, Xs., to be payed at my buriall. Exors. John Gynnerye and Walter Clerke " —" *Probatum XX. die Aprilis*, 1582, *executorib.*" (*Bury Pro. Reg. Liber Browne*, 1579—82. *Book* 34, *fo.* 374*b*. *Endorsed* " *Elizabethe ffokarde, vid. de Thorndon.*").

While resident at Thornden as a widow she paid, in 1575, a Subsidy (*L.S.* 182/370) of 2/8 on land valued at 20 shillings.

Of the date of this Edmund's first settlement at Ashfield we know nothing, but we are aware that he was living there at the date of his brother John's will (1558). In 1543 we find him paying a Subsidy (*L.S.* 181/253), as " Edmund ffolker," of 10/- for property in Debenham valued at £10; and in 1545, or a little later, another Subsidy (*L.S* 181/293) for goods in that place valued at £9. In 1548 he was assessed 10/- for goods in Thornden (*L.S.* 181/298) which he paid in the following year (*L.S.* 181/301). These payments possibly indicate that he did not go to Ashfield till about 1550 or later. In 1554 he was a party to the following Fine (*F. Michs.*) :—

"Concord in the King's Court, Westminster, between Edmund ffolkerd, plff., and Robert Cheke and Margaret his wife, defts., of a messuage called Lowdham's, with appurtenances, in Debynham."

The plaintiff pleaded that the messuage had been made over to him as a gift by Robert Cheke and his wife. The decision was in his favour, he paying defts. 40 marks of silver, and it is probable that this was a marriage suit, and that one of his wives was a daughter of the defts. In 1565 we find him paying 6/- Subsidy (*L.S.* 181/359) on goods valued at £6 in Ashfield-cum-Thorpe. His will above referred to is a very full one, and is witnessed by his father, " Robert ffolkard, Senior." It will be seen by this will that he owned property in Debenham at the time of his death.

2. JOHN FFOLKARD was son to the foregoing by his first marriage, and is named exor. to his father's will (34) of 1572. He is also

o

a legatee under his uncle John's will (30) of 1558 as "John ffowkered my godson, son of Edmund ffowkerd, of Hashfelde," and is therein named as being then under age.   By this will he was devised a house and land in Winston, and under his father's will he became possessed of property in Debenham, and probably also of lands in Ashfield.   I have found nothing relating to any marriage contracted by him, but the mention of his "eldest child" in the will of his stepmother above given is conclusive as to his having married, and it is probable that the "John ffokard" who paid tax for one hearth in Gosbeck in Chas. 2nd reign (L.S. 183/612) was one of his children.

In 1565 he would seem to have been living at Ashfield, as we find him then to have paid a Subsidy (L.S. 181/359) of 5/10 for goods valued at £7 in that place.   Later on, in 1575, he paid 2/8 for land valued at 20/- in Ashfield as "John ffolcarde" (L.S. 182/370)   In 1586 he was a party to the following Fine (F. Trin.):—

"Between John ffolkard and Joseph Moyse and Rose his wife, — acres ploughland and 6 acres pasture, with appurtenances, in Wynston and Debenham. John ffolkard agrees to pay Joseph and Rose and Thomas Moyse £40."

I confess to some doubt if this Fine may not apply to John ffolkard, of Horham, whose will (37) of 1599 has for witness a Thomas Moise, but the locality of the lands would render it more probable that the Fine referred to the subject of this notice.   In 1596 he paid 4/- Subsidy (L.S. 182/424) on land in Winston valued at 20/-, and in or about 1603 he again paid 4/- for the same land and 4/- for land in Ashfield of similar value (L.S. 182/451).   We find no mention of this John subsequent to the latter date, about which it may be presumed his death occurred. No will of his has been discovered.

3. ROBERT FFOLKARD, of Ashfield, was brother to the foregoing.   His name occurs repeatedly in the will (34) of his father Edmund of 1572.   To judge from the fact named therein of his indebtedness to his father, he would certainly have been over age at that date.   Evidence of his marriage is afforded by this will, it naming "Edmunde ffolcarde, my grandchild and godson," who we also find mentioned in his grandmother's will above given.

That last will further informs us that the wife of this Robert was Edeneye, who was living at the date of it, 1581, and that the pair had then living issue, Edmund, Edeneye, ffrances, and John ffolkard.   In 1596 he paid a Subsidy (L.S. 182/425) of 4/- for land in Ashfield valued at 20/- as "Robert ffolkerd," and we have no later information respecting him.

4. EDMUND FFOLKARD was the son above referred to of the last Robert.   He is named in his grandfather's will (34) of 1572, and in that of his grandmother as above described.   The only further mention found respecting him is the following license for his marriage (Ipsw. Pro. Sundry Books x. 16):—

"Lic. of marriage between Edmund ffolkard, of Ashfield, and Maria Salter, of Bloxhall, widow, 15th September, 1631.   5/."

5. MARIA FFOLKARD I assume to have been a daughter of the foregoing Edmund and Maria, my only ground for doing this, however, being the name of her presumed mother, and the locality. Her marriage license (*C.*) reads :—

"October 7, 1674. Daniel Packard, s.m., of Framlingham, to Maria ffookerd, s., of Framlingham, at Easton."

By the same authority (*C.*) it would appear that the marriage took place four days later. Thus :—

"October 11, 1674—5. Daniel Packard, s.m., of Framlingham, to Maria ffookerd, s.w., of Framlingham, married at Easton."

We know nothing further respecting her ; but probably the following extract from the Framlingham Register refers to the burial of her husband :—

"Daniel Packard buried 13 April, 1728."

The following further entry in the same Register possibly refers to a son of this couple :—

"Daniel Packward married Martha Woodrow, single persons, 3 June, 1738."

The use of the w in the last entry of Packard is a return, as often occurs in the case of Folkard, to the original terminal syllable of "ward."

6. ROBERT FFOLKARD, of Pettaugh, I have assumed to have been also a son of Edmund (No. 4), and to have been named after his grandfather (No. 3). We have no reference whatever to him beyond the admon. (16) of 1694 ; his widow, Maria ffolkard, according to that document, surviving him.

7. SAMUEL FFOLKARD, also of Pettaugh, is a further assumption as being a son of Edmund (No. 4), and solely based on his co-residence with the foregoing at Pettaugh, at which place, also, his cousin Thomas's (*No.* 1 *Crettingham Line*) widow was living at the date of her will. From the admon. (18) granted to this Samuel's widow after his death in 1697, we obtain her name, Elizabeth. I see little reason to doubt that in early life he was resident at Winston, and that he was the man referred to in certain Chancery proceedings (*R.O.*), which state that in 1638

"Samuel ffolkard owned certain copyhold land and houses on the manor of Winston-con-Pulham, Suffolk, estimated to contain 15 acres. Wanting £200, he borrowed it of a money lender, Christopher Cooper, on security of the land, &c., at 6 per cent. Before repayment was due the lender died, and his heir, one Elizabeth Solby, declined to give up the property, though the money was offered. Samuel ffolkard brought the case against her to enforce restitution."

No further mention of this man has been found till 1684, an entry (*Ipsw. Reg. Sundry Books* xxxiv.) running thus :—

"4 October, 1684. Samuel ffolkard, of Winston, Yeoman, bondsman to a marriage between Peter Day, of Pettangh, and Elizabeth Scales, of Pettaugh."

The connection indicated here with the place of his death is very strong. It is possible that the following entry (*Ibid.*) also refers to this man:—

"27 July, 1694. Sam. ffolkard, a bondsman to admon. of Isaac Lock, of Yoxford, by his widow, Elizabeth Lock."

8. THOMAS FFOLKARD, of Ashfield. Although on the Pedigree I have assigned this man a place as a son of Edmund (No. 1), the first resident of the name at Ashfield, I am unable to give proof of his parentage. He finds no mention in his assumed father's will (34); but, as has before been pointed out, such a fact is no evidence against the parentage, and his residence at Ashfield may well be set on the other side. No proofs exist as to any other origin of birth, and the conclusion arrived at is a fair one. All that is known respecting him during life is contained in the following abstract of a Chancery Suit (*C.B. Chas. I.* cc. 44, *fo.* 24, and cc. 103, *fo.* 10):—

"14 May 1632, Martha Cutting, widow, and Susan Tuttill, single, dars. of Edmund and Anne Tuttill, of Ashfield, decd., complain that their father held a tenement called Games and 50 or 60 acres of land in Ashfield. The widow held this till expiry of lease, and then employed Thomas ffolkard, the husband of her daughter Mary, to treat with Sir William Marsham, Bart., for its renewal. A new lease of 21 years was obtained in ffolkard's name, but in trust and confidence for the widow, at a rental of £31. Before this was sealed the said Anne Tuttill fell sick, and on her death-bed told ffolkard it was her desire complainants should benefit by it. This ffolkard carried out for seven years, and then, with a "covetous eye," gave the plaintiffs notice to quit. The latter pray against this breach of trust."

"Thomas ffolkard replies that he denies any trust imposed upon him. Ann Tuttill, his mother-in-law, died before the old lease had expired, and the farm was relet to him at an advance of £1 on the old rental. This he satisfied from his own purse, but could never recover it from the petitioners, which was "very inconvenient" to him. Denies that Anne Tuttill desired that the complainants should have the benefit of a new lease. She asked him to be good to them, and as they were sisters to his wife, he allowed them to have the farm for six years. But they had not fulfilled the covenant of the lease as to repairs or ditching, and had cut down trees they had no right to fell, and defendant would be held liable. He, therefore, gave them notice to quit, intending to place some of his children on the farm, and the landlord had refused to seal the lease unless he would promise to remove the complainants whenever he might desire him to do so, and he was forbidden to assign the lease. The replication of the complainants declares this answer to be insufficient and untrue."

It will be seen from the above that this man's wife was Mary, daughter of Edmund and Susan Tuttill, of Ashfield. This wife survived her husband, being named in his will (49) of 1636, to which she was executrix. As will be proved by a suit to be quoted hereafter when dealing with her son Thomas, she remarried to Thomas Penning, the entry in the Framlingham Register being:—

"Thomas Penninge—Marie ffolkard, vid., married November 7, 1639."

By the suit last referred to we learn that she derived, under her first husband's will (49) of personal estate alone, the sum of £182. 6s. 4d., besides a considerable value in land. We further ascertain from this suit that in 1666 she was of the great age of 88 years. There is no record of any issue to her second marriage.

Thomas ffolkard's will (49) is dated 1636, and he probably died early in the next year, when it was proved. Of his children Anne and Richard we have only the mention in that will, but it is not unlikely that the " Ann ffulard " who *temp*. Chas. 2nd was assessed for three hearths at Mellis (*L.S.* 183/605) was the daughter named.

9. LIDDA (LYDIA) FFOLKARD was daughter to the foregoing and named in his will (49) of 1636. At that date, though under 22 years of age, she was married to ——— Hersham, and had a daughter Elizabeth, also named in the will. Reference to the payment to her of the legacy of her father of £60 will be found in the suit quoted below.

10. JOHN FFOLKARD was brother to the last, and a legatee under his father's will (49) of 1636. The suit to be quoted tells us that he died before 1666, and nothing further is known of him.

11. THOMAS FFOLKARD, of Ashfield, was brother of the fore-going, and eldest son to Thomas (No. 8). He is named in the latter's will. Judging by the expression used in his own will (72), " Elizabeth my now wife," I thought it fair to presume a first marriage, but of this there is no record. He married, in 1639, Elizabeth, daughter of Thomas Rewse, of Coddenham, whose son Johnathan married Anne ffolkard, of Bedfield (*No. 8 of that Line*), an illustration of the family connection being maintained, though separated by four generations. The entry of license for this marriage reads :—

"1 May, 1639. Marriage license between Thomas ffolkard, Ashfield, single man, and Elizabeth Reuse, of Cretinge. 5/-" (*Ipsw. Pro. Sundry Books*, xvii. 18).

He is repeatedly mentioned in the following abstract of the will of his father-in-law :—

"8 April, 1653. Thomas Rewse the elder, of Coddenham, Suff., Gent., £140 to son Thomas. To son Symon £110. To son Johnathan £80. To son Barnaby £180. To da. Margarett £130. To da. Rebecca £140. To da. Mary £130. To da. Anne £100; 'and £20 besides.' To his daughter Elizabeth ffolkard, the wife of Thomas ffolkard, £20 To his grandchild Mary ffolkard £5. To be paid in the South Porch at Coddenham. Many other legacies and properties. His silver spoons among his children, ' and if there be one spoon more than I have children, then I give one silver spoon unto my grandchild, Mary ffolkard.'—' Item, I doe hereby nominate and appoint my son-in-law, Thomas ffolkard, and my son, Symon Rewse, to be exors. of this my will. And I do hereby give unto the said Thomas ffolkard and Symon Rewse £10 apiece for their truble.' This Thomas and Symon are residuary legatees " (*Cur. Prerog. Cant. Berkly* 392).

One of the sons of this testator—but which I cannot say—was a Suffolk rector. In 1642 this Thomas ffolkard paid a Subsidy of 8/- for land in Ashfield valued at £1 (*L.S.* 183/529), while, in the year following, we find him to be a joint collector with John Jessop of a further Subsidy (*L.S.* 183/536) levied on the Hundred of Thredling. The following entry in the Register of Pakenham (*C.*) may possibly refer to the burial of a child of this man, no family of the name appearing—to judge by the absence of any other entry in the Register referring to it—to have

resided in Pakenham, and this daughter, of whom we have no other
reco:d, may have been simply a visitor to the place:—

"1657. Elizabeth ffowerde, ye daughter of Thomas and Elizabeth ffowerde, was
buried ye 26 day of October."

This partial reversion to the old form of spelling the name is noteworthy. In 1666 this Thomas entered an action (*C.P. before* 1714,
Mitford 163) against his mother and her second husband, Thomas
Penning, of the pleading and answer to which the following is an
abbreviation :—

"21 January, 1666. Thomas ffolkard, of Ashfield, Yeoman, petitions that his late
father owned freehold land in Ashfield and in Peter-Thorpe of about 4 acres. By the latter's
will, dated 2 March, 1636, he devised these to petitioner, and left to Mary his wife, now the
wife of Thomas Penning, of Ashfield, Yeoman, all his movable goods, &c., in lieu of dower
and thirds. An inventory taken of the personal estate amounted to £182. 6s. 4d., which went
to the said wife, as well as the lease of a farm in Ashfield (*see ante*) worth at least £200 more.
She paid £60 to her daughter Lidda in accordance with her husband's will. He (the petr.)
had held this freehold land for 30 years since his father's death, but his mother, the now wife
of Thomas Penning, having spent all her legacy, they sue for the dower and thirds, although
the legacy was expressly left in lieu of these. Prays for an injunction to arrest the suit by
Thomas and Mary Penning."

"The answer of the latter says that Thomas ffolkard, her first husband, left his grandchild, Elizabeth Hersham, ten pounds, and quotes the following extract from his will: 'And
my will and mind is, that if Mary my wife shall be married again to any other husband, that
then the said Mary shall before her marriage give good security to Thomas and John ffolkard,
my sons, for the true payment of three score pounds of lawful money of England unto Liddia
my daughter, and to Elizabeth Hersham, my grandchild, the sum of ten pounds —which
if she shall refuse to do, then it shall be lawful for my two sons, Thomas and John, to enter
upon the estate and sell so much as will pay the same. Also my will is that, if Mary my wife
shall be married again, that then shee, the said Mary, shall leave and forego this my lease
16 (*Quære*) years before the end and determinacion thereof, and that then those 16 yeres I give
and bequeath unto John, my sonne, his heirs and assigns, if hee so long live, and if he dye
before then to Richard my sonne."

"The testator died in 1636, and the defendant married three years afterwards. The
legacies she had to pay absorbed the whole of the personalty, and she paid her son Richard,
John being dead. Pleads her natural affection for complainant as 'hir sonne.' Also
that she is 88 years old, 10th October, 1666. Signed Thomas Penning and 'ye marke of
Mary Pennynge.'"

It seems probable that although nominally of Ashfield, the residence
of this Thomas ffolkard was in the adjacent village of Earl Soham, for
in a Hearth Tax Roll (*L.S.* 183/612) of Charles 2nd, we find him taxed
for six hearths in the latter place. This indicates a dwelling of considerable size for those days. We have no further record of him, except
his very long, lucid, and beautifully-written will (72) of 1684, which is
signed with the very clear signature of the testator on each of its seven
folios. Of the children named in this will, Thomas and Samuel settled
at Cretingham. Johnathan at Letheringham (*see those two Lines*), while Mary
is further named in the will of her grandfather, Thomase Rewse, above
given. It is possible that the following license (*C.*) relates to her marriage :—

"Septr. 16, 1720. Thos. Chisnall, s., of Higham, to Mary ffolkard, s., of Higham, at
Higham."

The remaining daughter, Lydia, is stated in the will to have married and to have died before the date of it, leaving a son, John Savage. The entry of the license for this marriage (*Ipsw. Pro. Reg.*) reads :—

" September 1, 1674. John Savadge, s.m., Woodbridge, to Lydia ffolchard, of Ashfield. To be married at Ashfield."

The record of the celebration of this marriage (*C.*) seems to be dated September 7, 1674. No later residents of the name at Ashfield have been traced, and the Line ceases with this Thomas, who, to judge from the date of proof of his will, must have died in 1689.

Settlement at Mendlesham.

(Includes branches at Ubbeston and Walpole.)

Since compiling Pedigree I., I have obtained copies of entries in the Register of Mendlesham which enable me to extend my account of the family at that place very materially beyond what is shown upon the Pedigree.

1. WILLIAM FFOLKARD, who appears to have been the earliest settler of the family at Mendlesham, and who in his later years either lived at or had lands there, we may recognize, I think, in the William of the Pedigree (entered erroneously thereon as of Earl Soham) who was son to Thomas ffolkard and Alyce, of Bedfield (*No. 3 of that Line*). He is a legatee of £10 in the will (19) of his father of 1543. The earliest mention found of him is of 1522, when he paid a Subsidy (*L.S.* 180/126) of 12*d.* for goods valued at 40/- in Thwaite, and 3/4 for goods worth £6. 13*s.* 4*d.* in Brockford, he also paying on the same Roll a second tax for goods valued at £10. 10*s.* 0*d.* in the first-named place, and a further one for goods worth £11. 13*s.* 4*d.* in the second one. It must be borne in mind that both these villages adjoin Mendlesham, and that this man's lands and farm stock might lie within all three parishes, and so be subject to different assessments.

In 1523 he paid a Subsidy (*L.S.* 180/159) of 3/4 for goods in Brock-ford valued at £6. 14*s.* 4*d.*, and 12*d.* for goods worth 40/- in Mendlesham. We have no further information respecting him, and know nothing either as to his having married or of his death. There is no entry of his burial in the Mendlesham Register, but it is not at all improbable that an entry which was contained in the lost Register of Bedfield (*D.* xv.) of 1580 referred to his burial at that the place of his birth.

2. WILLIAM FFOLKARD, of Mendlesham. This man does not appear on the Pedigree, information respecting him reaching me after it

was compiled. I assume him to have been a son of the foregoing, the Christian name being one strong ground for doing so, and there being in addition the facts that this man is the first of the name in the Register of Mendlesham, while his presumed father is the first mentioned in the Subsidy Rolls as having held property there, although these Rolls date from 1327.

In 1563 he married at Mendlesham as thus recorded :—

"Ano. 1563. William folkard and Mary Baldwyn were maryed Octob. 25th."

The following issue to the above marriage is also given in the Register of Mendlesham :—

"Baptism. Ano. 1566. ffaithe, ye daught of Willm. ffolkard, Julii 14.

"Baptism. 1568. William, ye sone of Uillm. ffolsarde, Junii 8th."

This child died an infant, according to the following entry :—

"Buryall. Ano. 1570. William, ye sone of Willm. folkard, Junii 4th."

"Baptism. 1570. William, ye sone of Willm. folkard, Junii 4th."

"Baptism. 1572. Henry, ye sone of Willm. ffolkard, Octob. 28th."

"Baptism. 1577. Edmonde, ye sone of Willm. ffolkard, Janu. 13th."

"Baptism. 1579. Marye, ye daught. of Uillm. ffolkard, Febr. 9th."

"Baptism. 1581. Robert, ye sone of Willm. ffolkarde, Augustii 27th."

In 1565, as "William folcard," he paid a Subsidy (*L.S.* 181/359) of 2/6 for goods valued at £3 in Mendlesham, and in 1575 a second one (*L.S.* 182/370) of 5/- for goods there of the same value. In 1596, the year of his death, he was again assessed on a third Subsidy (*L.S.* 182/423) for land in Mendlesham valued at 40/-, paying 8/- for it.

The burials of this man and of his wife are thus recorded in the Mendlesham Register :—

"Buryall. 1596. William ffolkard, Octob. 27."

"Buryall. 1596. Marye ffolkard, wid., Novemb. 11."

From all indications none of the children above named seem to have settled ultimately in Mendlesham, and we may now turn to a second branch of local settlement.

---

3. RICHARD FFOLKARD, of Mendlesham, was a son of Robert, of Debenham (*see that Line*), by his second marriage with Margaret, the widow of his brother Thomas. He is mentioned in that father's will (35) of 1580. In the Candler Pedigree he is described as of Mendlesham, but it appears probable that in early life he resided at Debenham, and I have accepted the Richard of the latter place as identical with the subject of this notice.

The only evidence we possess of his marriage is from the Mendlesham Register, which contains the following entries :—

"Baptism. 1598. Edward, ye sone of Rich. ffolkarde, Julii 10th.'

"Buryall. 1599. A child of Richard ffolkard, unbaptized, Maii 23rd."

Of these two children we have no other trace, and they do not appear on the Pedigree.

The following extract relating to a suit in Chancery (*C.P. Elizabeth R.O.* i. 367) reveals this man's occupation:—

"John Golde, *alias* Good, *vs.* Richard ffocarde, petitioner, of Wethersete, Suffolk, complains that he was indebted to Richard ffokarde, of Debenham, tailor, 23/6 for a cloake. Petitioner went to Her Maties warres, and gave an obligacion to double that amount. On his return he offered the original amount, which was refused, defendant demanding a penalty bond of £20. Plaintiff and his friends, 'in most gentell manner,' offered £5. The defendant 'Richard ffolkard' answers that the debt was incurred ten years or so back, and that he went to plaintiff, and in 'most fryndley manner' requested him to pay the 23/6, offering to return the bond. Plaintiff utterly refused to pay. Process was obtained, and plaintiff broke up the warrant and escaped the bailiff. This led to further expensive proceedings at Bury. In some instances defts. name is given as 'Richard ffockard.' Case settled 1592, but judgment not preserved."

On the 9th April, 1596, there is record of the demise (*H.M.* x., *Part* ii. 56) of a tenement called "Woodward," in Pettaugh, Suffolk, at a rent of £21. A man named Peache (*i.e.*, Peachey) to whom this was let for 21 years, "covenants to spend 20 marks on the house and buildings within 6 years according to the order of Edmund Strickland and Richard ffolkar." This Peache was of Debenham, and there can be little doubt that the man associated with him was the subject of this notice.

In 1600 he was party to the following Fine (*F.* xii. *Trin.*):—

"George Covell agai st Ambrose ffolkerd and Richard ffolkerd and Regi ald Eade and Anne his wife, of 2 messuages. 1 garden, 1 apple orchard, and 1 acre of land, with appurtenances, in Debenham. Covell to pay £40."

Ambrose was brother to this Richard, and Anne Eade (*see Admon.* 10) was their father's sister. We find no record of this man's burial in the Mendlesham Register. Possibly it is in that of Debenham.

4. AMBROSE FFOLKARD, of Ubbeston, appears on the Candler Pedigree as of "Upson," the local pronunciation of Ubbeston. He was brother to the man last dealt with, and a son of Robert ffolkard, of Debenham, by his second marriage, in whose will (35) of 1580 his name occurs.

According to Candler, he married Elizabeth, a daughter of —— Botteret (*probably Botwright*), of Laxfield. This wife is named, as then living, in the will (48) of her son John of 1633, and as having proved it.

I have found no additional record of this man's residence at Ubbeston, but his son Thomas eventually lived there. In 1600 he was a party to the Fine last quoted, and the title is indexed of a further Fine sued in 1605 by him against Nicholas Button for land in "Upston" (*i.e.*, Ubbeston). The Fine itself (*F.* xii. *Michs.*) is missing from the file. I have met with no will of his, nor entry of his burial. Of his children shown on the Pedigree, John, who, according to Candler, and to judge from his will, died childless and probably unmarried, lived at Ratlesden, and dated his will (48) of 1633 at that place, the Register of which has the following entry:—

"1633. July 3rd, John ffolkerd was buried."

P

Two other sons, Robert and Samuel, also settled at Ratlesden (*see that Line*). A daughter Elizabeth, according to Candler, married Edward Baldry. This marriage was celebrated at Ratlesden, the Register there having :—

"1633. January 14. Edward Baldry and Elizabeth ffolkerd were married."

It seems almost certain that later on this Elizabeth Baldry contracted a second marriage, and that the will (62) of Elizabeth Warren is hers, the reference to Thomas and John ffolkard "my kinsmen" (*i.e.*, nephews) demonstrating this. Another daughter, ffrances, Candler informs us, married firstly "Edmund Stockden" (*Stockdaile*), of Ratlesden, who was probably a brother of her brother Robert ffolkard's wife. Her second union was with "John Wallex" (Waller) of the same place. She must have been single at the date of her witnessing her brother John's will (48) of 1633. Her first marriage is thus recorded in the Ratlesden Register :—

"1637. Novr. 28. Edmund Stockdaile and ffrancis (sic) ffolkerd were married."

Another member of this Ambrose ffolkard's numerous family, Ambrose, who is dealt with hereafter, settled at Mendlesham.

5. THOMAS FFOLKARD, of Ubbeston, was, according to Candler, another son of Ambrose above. That authority informs us that he married a "Mary Wallex" (Waller), probably a sister of the Waller of Ratlesden who married his sister. There seems little room for doubting that he married again upon the death of his first wife, for in the Admon. (14) granted to his widow in 1678, the latter's name is given as Elizabeth. Cookly, named as the place of his death, adjoins Walpole and is not far from Ubbeston.

In 1665 he was one of the collectors of a Subsidy in Ubbeston (*L.S.* 183/586), and in 1674 he paid (*L.S.* 183/563) 12/- for land there valued at 30/-. It would appear that in 1672 he must have been living in Walpole, for in the Domestic Entry Books (*R.O.*), among the Preaching Licenses (xxxviii. 192), we find :—

"License to Thomas ffolkerd to be a Pr. (*Quare, Presbyterian*) teacher in his house in Walpoole, Suffolk."

And again :—

"The house of Thomas ffolkerd in Walpoole, Suffolk."

From the Admon. above referred to we may conclude that he died early in 1678.

6. AMBROSE FFOLKARD, of Mendlesham, Candler shows to have been brother to the man last dealt with, and a son of Ambrose (No. 4), of Ubbeston. Candler further informs us as to his marriage with Judith, daughter of the Rev. Peter Devereux, Rector of Ratlesden, and a grand daughter of Anthony Gissing, of Eye. The Register of Ratlesden contains the following entry :—

"1627. July 26. Ambrose ffolkerd and Judith Devereux were married."

This wife died, according to Dr. Muskett, in 1658. Her sister, Anne Devereux, married the Rev. Mathias Gillett *alias* Candler, M.A., the compiler of the Candler Pedigrees, the connection thus established accounting for the interest taken by the latter in that of the Folkard family. The marriage of this Ambrose is further vouched for by the will of his brother-in-law, which is to be found in the Archdeaconry of Suffolk (*Prideaux Fo.* 237*b*), part of which reads abbreviated as follows:—

"15 Decr. 1686. Robert Devereux, of Stonham Parva, Clerk. To Mary my wife beyond her Joynture, houses, &c., which were hers before our marriage, and moneys, rents, &c., due to her at Old Newton. To my sister Candler's five children, Philip, Nicholas, John, Anne, and Elizabeth, £100. To the children of my sister Judith ffolkard, of Mendlesham, deceased, £90, vizt., Ambrose, John, William, Samuel, Thomas, Benjamin, Elizabeth, Mary, and Sarah ffolkard." "To Ambrose ffolkard, my brother-in-law, the small farm I bought of him."

In 1665 this Ambrose was one of the collectors at Mendlesham of a Subsidy (*L.S.* 183/586) conjointly with John Cobbold. No record of his burial, nor of that of his wife, is to be found in the Mendlesham Register, and the baptisms of only two of his numerous children occur in it. I have no information as to the place of residence of his later years. It was very probably at Ubbeston.

Of the following, among this man's large family we have but limited information. Ambrose (*Candler Ped.*) died an infant. Elizabeth (*Ibid.*), named in her grandfather Devereux's will of 1640 and in her uncle's will above quoted, of 1686, was baptized at Ratlesden, the entry in the Register there reading:—

"February 15, 1629. Elizabeth, ye daughter of Ambrose ffolkerd and his wife, baptized."

Robert (*Candler Ped.*) is named in the Mendlesham Register as:—

"Baptism. 1634. Robert, the sonne of Ambros ffolkard, January 24."

Thomas, another child (*Candler Ped.*), died an infant. Samuel (*Ibid.*) was named in his uncle Devereux's will above given in 1686. This was probably the Samuel referred to in the following marriage license (*Sundry Books, Ipsw.* xxxiv.)

"29 July, 1681. License for marriage to be celebrated at Sibton between Samuel ffolkard, of Walpool, single, and Sarah Manning, of Walpool, single."

Another child, Mary, is also named on the Candler Pedigree, and is further named in her uncle Devereux's will. Sarah (*Candler Ped.*) died an infant, and a second child of that name (*Ibid.*) was living, according to her uncle's will, in 1686; another child, Benjamin, also given by Candler, receiving mention in it. The Candler Pedigree omits reference to a son William, who is, however, a legatee under his uncle Devereux's will. Another son, Ambrose, is also recorded by Candler, the burial of his wife Maria being thus notified in the Mendlesham Register:—

"1675. Maria ffolkard, uxor. Ambrosie ffolkard, Sepult. Octr. 11."

This Ambrose is also a devisee under the will of his uncle Devereux.

P 2

7. JOHN FFOLKARD, of Ubbeston, was a son of the man last treated of (No. 6). His baptism is thus entered in the Mendlesham Register :—

"1632.   John, the sonne of Ambrose ffolkard, March 5th."

This man is named both by Candler and by the will of his uncle Robert Devereux, of 1686. We glean further particulars respecting him from the will (62) of 1673 of his aunt Elizabeth Warren (*See under No. 4 of this Line*). That will refers to him as the testatrix's "kinsman" (*i.e.*, nephew), and as being dead at the date of it. It leaves legacies to his widow "ffayth ffokard," and to her children, Thomas, John, Elizabeth, and ffaith "ffokard." I have erroneously entered a date of 1702 and particulars as to marriage as relating to this John ffolkard on the Pedigree, but the dates and information subsequently obtained satisfy me that these particulars must apply to his son next dealt with.

8. JOHN FFOLKARD, of Mendlesham, was son to the foregoing, and is named in the will (62) of his great aunt, Elizabeth Warren, of 1673. Although he has no place on the Pedigree, it is desirable to briefly record here what is known to me of him and of his children. In 1702 he is named in a Suffolk Poll List (*D.* liv. 36) (*B.* viii. 258) as John ffolkard, of Ubbeston. I conjecture that the following entries in the Register of Henley may refer to a first marriage of his, and to the birth of a daughter to it :—

"1702.   John Fokard and Mary Simson were married October ye 8th, 1702."

"1703.   Mary, ye daughter of John Foakard and Mary his wife, was baptized December ye 27th Day."

If the above given marriage was contracted by this man, it seems probable from the baptisms named hereafter of numerous children of his by a wife, also named Mary, twenty years after the birth of his first child, that the first wife and her child must have died prior to 1720. In 1722 he and this presumed second wife were named in the following Fine (*F. Michs.*) :—

"Between John James, Clerk, plf., and John ffolkard and Marie his wife, Thomas James and Ann his wife. and Henry Gardner and Marie his wife, defendants, of 1 messuage, 1 garden, 1 orchard, 20 acres land, 10 acres meadow, and 20 acres pasture, with appurts, in Ubbeston and Thornden.   Plff. pays defts. £60 sterling."

This Fine, from its date—the birth of the children of this John ffolkard's second marriage commencing in 1722—was very probably connected with a marriage settlement, and, from the name of James occurring in it both as plaintiff and defendant, it is likely that the second wife was Mary, daughter of the Rev. John James. The entries of the baptism of their children in the Mendlesham Register are as under :—

"1722.   Mary, ye D. of John and Mary Folkard, Augt. 28."

This child died the same year, the entry being :—

"1722.   (Buryall) Mary Folkard Dec. 9th."

"1723.   Rebecca, the D. of John and Mary Folkard, Novemb. 27."

"1725. Susan, D. of John and Mary Folkard, March 28."

"1726. Deborah, D. of John and Mary Folkard, March 20."

"1727. Mary, D. of John and Mary Folkard, Octr. 15."

"1728. Sarah, D. of John and Mary Folkard, Dec. 26."

This child died in the following year, the entry being :—

"Buryall. 1729. Sarah Folkard, Jan. 2nd."

It is perhaps fairly conceivable that the following entry in the Mendlesham Register may refer to a son of this John Folkard by his first marriage, who was probably born at Ubbeston. I can find no other John to whom it could apply.

"1718. John Folcard, of Thraudeston, Singleman, and Margaret Bloyre (*Quære*, *Bloyse*) of this Parish, Single wooman, Septr. 15."

In 1734 the subject of this notice appears to have died, and, unless my last conjecture be correct, without any male heir. The entry of his burial in the Mendlesham Register is :—

"Buryalls 1734. John Focard, Dec. 23rd."

9. THOMAS FFOLKARD, of Mendlesham, was uncle to the foregoing John, and a son of Ambrose (No. 6) and Judith. Candler gives his name, and he is further mentioned in the will of his uncle Robert Devereux of 1686 (*see ante*) as living at that date. Among the " Papers relating to Suffolk" (*B.M. No.* 10,358), printed in 1647, is the following :—

"For 9th division Hartismere, next meeting appointed at Eye, to be joyned to the Ministries is Thomas Folkard, of Mendlesham. Date of their appointment, November 5, 1645."

I take this merely to mean selection as a parochial officer, or, perhaps, lay preacher, and as not referring to any clerical office.

This man was three times married, as will be seen by the extracts from the Mendlesham Register given below. His first wife was Francesca, who died in 1677, her burial being thus recorded :—

"1677. Francisca (*sic*) Folkard Sepult. Octr. 8th."

The second wife's name was Hester, and the entry as to her burial is :—

"1682. Hester Folcard Sepult. Novr. 27."

The name of the third wife was Sarah. She survived her husband and interment is thus stated :—

"Buryalls 1726. Wid. Folkard, Jan. 2."

The baptisms of the issue to these three marriages are entered in the same (Mendlesham) Register as under :—

"1672. Rob. filius Tho. Folkard et Francisca uxo, Bap. Novr. 28."

"1681. Beniaminus, filius Tho. et Hester Folkard, Bap. Jan. 2."

.This child died in 1683, the entry being :—

"1683. Benianimus Folkard, Sepult. Feb. 27."

"1683. Beniamin, filius Tho. et Sarah Folkard, Bap. Nov. 2."

This Benjamin also died, the burial being recorded:—

"1683.   Beniamin Folkard, infans, Sepult. Nov. 19."

"1684.   Samuel, filius Tho. et Sarah Folkard, Bapt. Oct. 22nd."

"1687.   Elizab., filia Thom. et Sarah Folkard, Bapt. Nov. 27."

"1692.   Maria, filia Tho. et Sarah Folkard, Bapt. Martii 29."

The last-named child died, the entry of her burial being :—

"1693.   Maria Folkard, infans, Sepult. Febr. 4."

Besides the above issue, I find in the Mendlesham Register the burials given of two children, the first of whom was probably by the second marriage, and the second by the third marriage. The entries read :—

"Buryalls, 1680.   Elizabetha Folkard, infans, May 9."

"Buryalls, 1688   Tho. Folkard, infans, Sepult. Mar. 24."

The baptisms of these two infants are unrecorded, and possiby were never solemnized.

About 1660—67 we find the father taxed, as " Thomas ffoulcard," for one hearth in Cotton (*L.S.* 183/612). His death is thus named in the Mendlesham Register :—

"1693.   Thos. Folkard, Sepult. April 30."

No will by this man has been found by me.

10.   WILLIAM FFOLKARD, of Mendlesham, brother to the foregoing, was another son of Ambrose (No. 6) and Judith. As he is not named on the Candler Pedigree, it is feasible that he was the youngest child, and born later than the compilation of that Pedigree. He was a devisee under the will of his uncle, Robert Devereux, of 1686, before given. From the following entries in the Mendlesham Register we learn that his wife's name was Maria, but beyond the information conveyed by these we know almost nothing either of her or her husband. The entries read :—

"1672.   Tho., filius Wm. Folkard et Maria uxo., Bap. Novr. 28."

This child died in 1686, the entry being :—

"1686.   Thom. Folkard, infans, Sepult. May 19."

"1675.   Georgius, fil. Wm. Folkard et Mari. uxo., Bapt. Dec. 29."

I believe this child died in the year after its birth, though there is a doubt about the entry following reading " gen." or " inf." in the Register which records :—

"1676.   Geor. Folkard, gen. (or *Quære*, ' inf.') Sepult. May 24."

"1677.   Maria, filia Wm. et Maria Folkard, Bapt. Aprill 4."

The burial of the last is thus entered :—

"1678.   Buryalls.   Maria Folkard, infans, Aug. 17."

Besides the above, I think that the child referred to in a further entry of the same Register must have been a son of this couple.

"1677.   Wmms. Folkard, infans, Sepult. April 24."

The entries above given bring the residence of the family at Mendlesham to a close in 1734. The descent may have been continued at
Ubbeston and Walpole, the Registers at these places not having been
examined. On July 6, 1778, however, a Hannah Folkard, single woman,
of Mendlesham, was married there to William Pleasants, single man,
also of that place; but I cannot identify her, and have no evidence of
her descent from the Line above treated of.

𝔖𝔢𝔱𝔱𝔩𝔢𝔪𝔢𝔫𝔱 𝔞𝔱 ℜ𝔞𝔱𝔩𝔢𝔰𝔡𝔢𝔫.

(Includes branches at Heveningham and Walpole.)

Since the Pedigree No. 1 of the first part of the Monograph was
compiled, the entries relating to the family in the Register of Ratlesden
have been obtained. I am, therefore, able greatly to extend my notes as
to this branch.

1. SAMUEL FFOLKARD, of Ratlesden, appears to have been
among the earliest of the family resident at this place. He was (Candler
Ped.) a son of Ambrose, of Ubbeston (No. 4 Mendlesham Line). The same
authority informs us that he married Elizabeth Swift, of Norwich, who
administered his estate in 1660. The Register of Ratlesden (Martin's
Church Notes i. 420-2) has the following memorandum concerning this
man:—

"1653. Whereas Samuel ffolkerd of the Towne aforesaid (Ratlesden) was chosen by the
Inhabitants of the same Town on the twoe and twentieth day of September, in the year one
thousand, six hundred, fifty three, to be Register for the sayd Towne according to the Act
touching Marriages, Births, and Burials, bearing date the 24 August, 1653, the sayd Samuell
ffolkerd came before me, George Grome, Esq., one of the Justices of the Peace for this County,
and have allowed the sayd Samuell ffolkerd, according to the sayd choise, to be Register for
the same Towne, and have taken his oath before me for the faythful performance thereof this
29 Octr., 1653."

Entries in the same Register inform us as to the baptism of his
children as under:—

"1633, Octobr. 13. Elizabeth, Daughter of Samuell ffolkerd and his wife, was Baptized."

"1638, April 8. Sara, the Daughter of Samuell ffolkerd and his wife, was Baptized."

"1640, Decr. 20. Thomas, ye Sonne of Samuell ffolkerd and his wife, was Baptized."

"1644, August 25. Benjamin, ye Sonne of Samuell ffolkerd and his wife, was Baptized."

"1647, May 16. Hanna, ye Daughter of Samuell ffolkerd and his wife, was Baptized."

Of none of these children, save Thomas, have we further record. It
seems almost certain from the terms of the following Admon. in the Bury
Registry (Admon. No. 5, 1660—1678, Fo. 9) that, probably late in life,

this Samuel resided at Wetherden, between two and three miles only from Ratlesden. Translated from the Latin, this Admon. reads :—

"3 February, 1660. Administration of the goods of Samuel ffolkard, formerly of Wetherden, deceased, granted to Elizabeth ffolkard, the widow and relict of the deceased."

He was, according to the following extract from the Ratlesden Register, buried at that place, the discrepancy of the date with that of the Admon. being due to the use of the old and new styles.

"1660. October 23. Samuel ffolkerd, a humble and exemplary Christian, was Buried."

2. THOMAS FFOLKARD, of Ratlesden, was son to the foregoing. His baptism, in 1640, has been above quoted. There is reason to believe that he was the " Kinsman " (i.e., nephew) alluded to in the will (62) of Elizabeth Warren of 1673. From that will we learn his wife's name to have been Anne. This wife was doubtless a daughter of Samuel Manning, of Walpole, the following entry (Ipsw. Pro. Sundry Books xxxiv.), coupled with the Fine given below, being almost conclusive as to this :—

"1678, 22nd January. Proved (will of) Samuel Manning, of Walpole, Gent. To my dear son-in-law, Thomas ffolkard, forty shillings and library of books " (Reference 78 Edgar).

Sarah Manning, almost certainly a sister of the above-named Anne Manning, married, in 1681, Samuel ffolkard, of Walpole (See Mendlesham No. 6), cousin to the subject of this notice, who, with his wife, is named in the following Fine (F. xxvi. Trin.) :—

"Between William Smith, Samuel Manning, Gen., and John Greenleaf, plffs., and Thomas Tansey and Anne his wife, and Thomas ffolkard and Anne his wife, defts., of 2 messuages and 20 acres of land, 20 acres pasture, with appurtenances in Westleton and Uppeston. Defts. receive £100 sterling."

Although entered on the Pedigree as of Ratlesden, where he was born, this man doubtless settled near his cousins of Ubbeston, as indicated by the terms of the foregoing Fine ; and it may fairly be concluded that he was identical with the Thomas Folkard of Heveningham (close to Ubbeston), whose will (73) is dated 1690. From that will it would seem that his wife predeceased him. The following entries in a rent-roll of the manor of Ubbeston, made 29th September, 1682, doubtless refer to him :—

"Of Thomas Folkard £1. 12s. 4d."   "Of John Greenleafe, late ffolkard's, 1/-."

From the date of proof of his will he would appear to have died in 1691, and, therefore, at the age of 51. It may be as well to notice here that the description of " Grocer " was used anciently as their designation by large importers of produce, such as were the Burroughs of Ipswich. Of the children named in the will, Samuel and Thomas are dealt with specially below. Of the three daughters named as married respectively to Isaac Locke, Joseph Cornish, and Edmund Ludbrooke, we have no additional record.

3. SAMUEL FFOLKARD, of Walpole, was the son of the foregoing and exor. to his will (73) of 1690. We know nothing more of this man than may be concluded from tokens issued by him ; one of these of

1670 being now in the possession of Mr. Richard Folkard. Davy (*D.C.* iii. 226) thus refers to these in a list of Suffolk tokens :—

"Samuel Folkard, of Walpole, Grocer, 1670. Obverse, a pair of Scales, 11 brass. Reverse, S. F."

Golding's "Suffolk Coinage" contains illustrations of two of these tokens, a half-penny and a farthing. The half-penny bears on its obverse "Samvell Folkard of," and in the centre a pair of scales ; the reverse having "Walpoole, Grocer, 1670." The farthing has on its obverse "Samvell Folkard, 68 ;" and in the centre "S.F." The reverse has "in Walpoole, Grocer," and in the centre a pair of scales. He, therefore, doubtless continued his father's business, the latter having probably retired from it and gone to live at Heveningham, only two miles or so from Walpole.

3*a*. JOHN FFOLKARD, of Walsham-le-Willows, was, I think, probably brother to the man last treated of, and with him a son of Thomas, of Ratlesden, Walpole, and Heveningham (No. 2), though he is not named in the will of the latter. The facts that he followed the same trade as his assumed father, and that his daughter bore his conjectured mother's name of Anne, add strength to this supposition. In 1727 he is included in the Poll list for Knights of the Shire as having voted for John Holt, Esq. His will is in the Bury Probate Office, and has been thus abstracted :—

"John ffolkard, of Walsham in le Willows, Co. Suff., Grocer, 2 July, 1728. Messuage I dwell in and lands to Ann my daughter, the now wife of Thomas Jenepe. of Bury St. Edmunds, Grocer, for life ; then to her children. She to dispose of it to them by will. To her my messuage in Rougham, Co. Suffolk. It to be sold on her decease, and profits divided amongst her children. All my books to the five children of the said Ann my daur. To Mr. Thomas Wickes one guinea to preach my funerall sermon. Residue to be put out to interest for use of said Anne my daur. My kinsman, Thomas Flowerdew, of Botesdale, Gent., sole executor " (*Clagett II.* 1727, *Fo.* 487)

Proof of the foregoing will is entered in these terms on the 31st July, 1729 :—

"Admon. bonor. concess. Anne Jenepe, fil defuncti, Flowerdew renunc."

3*b*. THOMAS FFOLKARD, of Little Harleston, near Ratlesden, I presume to have been another son of Thomas of Heveningham (No. 2) on the authority of the mention of him in the will (62) of Elizabeth Warren before referred to. If this presumption be admissible, his will (66), as "Thomas ffoaker," of 1678, would show that he predeceased his father, who did not die till 1691, a fact that would account for the absence of mention of this son in the will of the latter. From his own will we learn the name of his wife to have been Anne, and that he left behind him a son Thomas, and two daughters, Anne and Elizabeth, of all of whom we have no additional record.

4. ROBERT FFOLKARD, of Ratlesden, was brother to Samuel (No. 1), and with him a son of Ambrose, of Ubbeston. Candler's Pedi-

Q

gree names his two marriages, which are confirmed by the following
entries in the Register of Ratlesden :—

"1625, October 8th.   Robert ffolkerd and Elizabeth Stockdaile were married."

"1632, April 17.   Robert ffolkerd and Susan Sier were Married."

The first wife, whose name Candler gives as "Stockden," died,
apparently childless, in the year following her marriage, the entry as to
her burial in the Ratlesden Register reading :—

"1626, February 9.   Elizabeth, ye wife of Robert ffolkerd, was Buried."

The second wife survived her husband and was sole executrix to his
will given below, she dying in 1683, the Ratlesden Register having :—

"1683, March 22.   The wid. ffolkard was Buryed."

All the children of the subject of this notice hereafter named were
issue to the second marriage.   We find this man in 1633 witnessing the
will (48) of his brother John.   In the year previous he served the office
of Constable of Ratlesden, the Register thus notifying :—

"1632.   Robert ffolkerd was Constable for this year."

Constable was the term used as the equivalent to the mayor of a
municipality.
    In 1656 the same Register supplied the following :—

"Robert ffolkerd was Churchwarden this year."

His will, dated 1674, is in the Bury Probate Office.   An incomplete
abstract (63) of this is given in Part I. of this Monograph.   A fuller
abstract, since obtained, reads :—

"27 Chas. 2, 1674.   Robert ffolkard, of Ratlesden, Co. Suff., Linnen weaver.   To
Thomas and Robert, my two sonnes, all my Loomes, &c., to be equally divided.   To Lydia
ffolkard, my youngest daughter, £30.   All the rest of my goods to Susanna my loveing wife
for her naturall life.   And after her decease to be equally divided between Robert ffolkard,
my said sonne, and Elizabeth Bumstead, my daughter, or their children if they be dead.   I
have given Mary ffolkard, my daughter, £20 already.   Wife sole executrix.   John ffiske the
elder, of Ratlesden, Gent., and James Waller, Master of Arts (see intermarriage with his
family on Pedigree), to be supervisers.   Probat 6 Dec. 1675" (Lib. Read. 1674—77 [62] Fo.
288).

From the date of proof of this will it is manifest that this testator
died in 1675; but, strangely, the Ratlesden Register has no record of
his burial at that place.   Of his children we have the following notes
from that Register :—

"1633, May 12.   Anne, Daughter of Robert ffolkerd and his Wife, was Baptized."

This daughter appears to have died unmarried.   Thus :—

"1677, Decr. 1.   Anne ffolkerd was Buried."

"1635.   Elizabeth, Daughter of Robert ffolkerd and his Wife, was Baptized."

This Elizabeth is mentioned by her married name in the will above
given of her father, her marriage being thus noted in the Register :—

"1658, March 30.   ffrancis Bumstead and Elizabeth ffolkerd were Married."

"1638, April 8.   Thomas, the Sonne of Robert ffolkerd and his wife, was Baptized."

"1640, Septbr. 6.   Robert, ye Sonne of Robert ffolkerd and his wife, was Baptized."

"1643, March 2. Mary, ye Daughter of Robert ffolkard and his wife, was Baptized."
This daughter is briefly named in her father's will above.

"1646, February 21. Lydia, ye Daughter of Robert ffolkerd and his Wife, was Baptized."

In the father's will of 1674 this, his youngest daughter, is referred to as then single. Her subsequent marriage was probably that sanctioned by the following license in the Ipswich Registry (*C.*):—

"June 5, 1677. Nicholas Painter to Lydia Ffolkerd.'

4*a*. THOMAS FFOLKARD, son of the foregoing and named in his will, whose baptism has been above recorded, was, no doubt, from his relationship named with the Bumstead family, identical with the author of the following abstracted will in the Bury Probate Office :—

"Thomas ffolkard, of Great ffinborow, Co. Suff., Yeoman. To be buried in the church-yard of Ratlesden. Messuage in Great ffinborow in occupation of ffrancis Bumpstead to be sold by my nephew. Robert Bumpstead, of Ratlesden, and John Bumpstead, of Woolpit. To them my goods. They to be executors. Probate 8 May, 1722" (*Goodwin* vii, 1718—22, *Fo.* 535).

From this will it would appear that its author died at the advanced age of 84, and from the absence of all mention of wife or children in it, he would appear, did he ever marry, to have outlived both. No doubt the following Fine (*F. Michs.*) of 1709 was sued by this man :—

"Between Thomas ffolkard and Alexander Cooke, plfs., and John Smith and Sarah his wife, and Thomas ffuller and Abigail his wife, Richard Keyan and Robert Keyan, defts., of 3 messuages, 3 horries (*barns*), 3 stables, 3 yards, 3 gardens, 3 orchards, 12 acres land, 13 acres meadow, and 30 acres pasture, with apptces. in Wiveston, Drinkestone, and ffinborow Magna. Plffs. pay defts. £100 sterling."

Although this man's will directed burial at Ratlesden, the Register of that place has no record of this direction having been compiled with.

5. ROBERT FFOLKARD, of Ratlesden, was brother to the man last treated of, and son with him to Robert, of Ratlesden (No. 4). His baptism at that place in 1640 has been quoted above. We learn from entries in the Register there that his wife was named Mary, but her surname before marriage is unknown to us. According to the following entry in the same Register, she predeceased her husband by some thirteen years.

"1699, October 12th. Mary, ye wife of Robert ffolkard, was buryed."

This Robert paid a Subsidy (*L.S.* 183/550) in Ratlesden, as " Robert ffowker, Junr.," in the reign of Charles I. (1625—1649), and the following entry in the local Register informs us:—

"1703–-04. Robert ffolkard, Churchwarden."

His will in the Bury Probate Office has been abstracted as follows:—

"Robert ffolkerd, of Ratlesden, Yeoman, 6 Septr., 1712. To Robert ffolkerd, my grandson, house and gardens belonging wherein I now live. His education to be provided for, and maintenance, until he attain his age of one and twenty years. To Mary ffolkerd, my grand-daughter, when 21. Personal estate equally between Martha ffolkerd and Robert ffolkerd, my grandchildren. James Bumstead, my kinsman, sole executor. Probate 12 Novr., 1712. *Jurat Jacobs. Bumstead*" (*Goodwin* v. 1711—14, *Fo.* 230).

Q 2

Of this man's burial the Ratlesden Register records :—

"1712, October 20.   Robert ffolkard was buryed."

As to his issue we have but meagre detail.   The same Register has :—

"1670, September 1.   John, the Sonne of Robert ffolkerd and Mary his wife, was Baptized."

This son appears, according to the following entry, to have lived to 30 years of age :—

"1700. November 4.   John, ye son of Robert ffolkerd, was buryed."

6. ROBERT FFOLKARD was another son of the last Robert (No. 5).   The Ratlesden Register has :—

"1668, June 11.   Robert, the Sonne of Robert ffolkard and Mary his wife, was Baptized."

This was most probably the father of the children named in his father's will of 1712 above given.   We know nothing as to the birthplace of these children, and their father was, no doubt, living elsewhere than at Ratlesden at the time of their birth or baptism.   Neither he nor his wife are named in his father's will, nor have I found any record of the death of either of them.

Their son Robert, and their daughters Mary and Martha, are named, the two first as then being under age, in the will of their grand-father of 1712 above given.   As to a presumed third daughter of theirs, the Ratlesden Register has :—

"1713, Octob. 22.   Anne ffolkard was buryed."

7. THOMAS FFOLKARD, of Ratlesden, may also be believed to have been a child of the foregoing Robert (No. 6).   The entry in the Ratlesden Register gives us his age at death, and he was therefore born in 1715, after his presumed brother and sister who were named in their grandfather's will of 1712.

The entries in the same Register of the birth of his children informs us that his wife was named Mary; and from the fact of one son being christened Segrave, it is probable that she was a Mary Segrave.   A further entry in the Register informs us :—

"1796, Aug. 6.   Mary ffolkerd, wife of Thomas ffolkard, aged 81 yrs., was buried."

This wife must therefore have been born in 1715, the same year as her husband.   Of their children the Register has :—

"1760, Feb. 5.   Judith, daughter of Thomas ffolkard and Mary his wife, baptized."

"1770, June 17.   Thomas Segrave, son of Thomas and Mary ffolkerd, was baptized."

Their father's death is thus entered in the same Register.   He is the last of the name included in it as to which I possess extracts, though some of his descendants appear to be still resident at Ratlesden :—

"1800, January 7.   Thomas Folkard, aged 85 yrs., buried."

It may be stated, in conclusion of the notice of this Line, that as early as 1087 the name was known in connection with Ratlesden, the *Inquisit. Eliensis (Fo.* 522) informing us that Falè. (with note of abbreviation), a man of the Abbot of St. Edmunds, held land there at that date.

Settlement at Stowmarket.

1. NICOLAS FFOLKARD was the first resident of the name at Stowmarket discoverable. He was son to Robert, of Debenham (*No.* 1 *of that Line*), by his second marriage, and is named in the will (35) of the latter of 1580. The remark in that will as to this man's prodigal habits is a curious one. Candler's Pedigree informs us that he lived at Stowmarket, and that he married "the Widow Young." As his father's second marriage did not take place until 1556, he was probably about 20 ears old at the date of his father's will. I have found no subsequent traces of either him or his wife.

2. ROBERT FFOLKARD, of Stowmarket, is assumed on the Pedigree to have been a son of the last. He was named by the latter probably after the grandfather. Of this parentage there is no direct proof, the only mention of this man found being his admon. (12) of 1664, which would seem to indicate that he died heavily in debt, a tendency to extravagance having been probably inherited from his prodigal father.

3. TIMOTHY FFOLKARD, of Stowmarket, has his parentage also assumed on the Pedigree as a son of Nicolas (No. 1). The earliest mention of him is in a Fine (*F. Michs.*) of 1656, that reads as follows:—

"This is the final agreement made in the Court of the Queen's Bench at Westminster from the day of St. Michael in three weekes in the year of our Lord 1656. Before Oliver St. John, Edward Atkyns, Matthew Hale, and Hugh Wyndham, Justices, and others, and then present. Between Timothy ffolkard, plf., and Rowland Hodgson and ffrances his wife, defts., of 1 messuage, and 1 garden, with the appurtenances in Stowe markett. Whereupon a plea of covenant was sumoned between them in the said Court, that is to say, that the aforesaid Rowland and ffrances have acknowledged the aforesaid tenement with the appurtenances to be the right of him the said Timothy as those which the said Timothy hath of the gift of the aforesaid Rowland and ffrances. And those they have remised and quit claimed from them, the said Rowland and ffrances, and their heirs, to the aforesaid Timothy and his heirs for ever, &c., &c. Plff. pays £60 sterling."

It is a fair conclusion from the terms of this Fine, that this Timothy had married, about 1656, a daughter of Rowland and ffrances Hodgson, and that the property named in it was given as a dower on her marriage. We next find him defendant in a Chancery suit (*C.P. before* 1714 *Mitford* 190), of the pleadings, &c., in which the following is an abstract:—

"Bloome *vs.* ffolkard, 23 November, 1672. Mary Bloome, of Stowmarket, widow, and Joseph Crane, of the same place, Gent., exor. of Robert Bloome, deceased, who, on the 16th Oct., 1658, purchased of one Thos. Drap(er), of Melton, Woollendraper, a messuage in Stowmarket. Bloome sold it, 24 June, 1664, to Timothy ffolkard, of Stowmarket, Black-smith. On the death of Bloome, the absolute sale to ffolkard was disputed, and the action seeks to force him to disclose all deeds and writings in his possession. The answers filed possess no interest, though they are lengthy."

A further mention of this Timothy discovered is in a list of "Foote Armes" charged on the several towns of Suffolk in 1676 (*D.* xxx. *Stow Hundred*). It runs:—

"Timothy ffolker hath charge of a musket in Stowmarket."

This man's will has, since Part I. of this Monograph was printed, been found in the Probate Registry at Bury. It is dated 1696, and the fact of proof having been deferred until 1705 indicates the latter date as the year of his death. His wife Rose (*Quære, natus Hodgson*) was living at the date of the will, an abstract of which follows :—

"Timothy ffolkard, of Stowmarket, Co. Suffolk, the elder, Blacksmith. To Rose my wife messuages, &c., in Stowmarkett until 20 March, 1697. To son-in-law George Richardson, of Stowmarkett, Woolcomber, messuage with blacksmith's shopp in occupacion of Thomas Read, and other messuages in divers occupacons from sd. 20th March, 1697, for 99 years on trust. Rents to said Rose my wife for 30 years, if she shall live so long ; then to Timothy ffolkard my son. At the end of the 99 years all messuages to the heirs of my son Timothy. If he die sans issue, then to Rebecca Richardson my daur. To sd. George Richardson, husband of my said daur., and Rebecca his wife, other messuages in Stowmarkett. To my sister, Sarah Gill, of Debenham, widow, 40/-; if she be dead, this money to her two daughters equally. Goods to Rose my wife. She and son-in-law Richardson Executors. 29 April 8, Wm. 3d, 1696. Probate 18 April, 1705. Jur. George Richardson" (*Goodwin* iii. 1704—7, *Fo.* 233).

Of the children named in the above will I have found no further record. The "Court Booke of Stowmarket als. Abbottshall" contains the following entries relating to this man :—

"Cur. 5 May, 1671. Timotheus ffolker, Le Smith's Shopp and ter. lib. tenen."

"Cur. 13 Oct. 1674. Timotheus ffolkard, License to pull down and to build Smith's Shopp" (*No.* 11 1692—1727, *Fos.* 72b. 83).

4. SARAH FFOLKARD, according to the will above given, must have been a daughter of Nicolas (No. 1) and brother to the last. She appears to have married a man named Gill, who predeceased her, she living at Debenham as a widow in 1696, and having then two daughters.

5. FFRANCIS FFOLKARD, of Stowmarket, was also, it may fairly be assumed, a son of Nicholas (No. 1). We have no knowledge of his wife, who, as she is not mentioned in his will, must have predeceased her husband. The earliest reference found to this man is of 1650, when he sued a Fine (*F. Trin.*) as under :—

"Between ffrancis ffolker, plf., and Thos. Mounscall and Margaret his wife, and Thomas Rushbrooke, and others, defts., of 2 messuages, 2 gardens, and 2 orchards, in Stowmarket. ffrancis ffoulker pays £60 sterling."

The Court Book above named (i. 58b) has :—

"Cur. 15 Oct. 19 Car. 2, 1667. ffranciscus ffolkerd obijt., ffranciscus ffolkerd est filius senior et hœres."

The date of the foregoing entry is confirmed by the date of proof of his will found in the Bury Registry, of which the following is an abstract:—

"ffrancis ffolkard, of Stowmkett, Co. Suff., Yeoman. 2 April 1667. To Thomas ffolkard, my sonne, all my wearinge appel. My messuages and lands to be sold. I have received long since of Henry Locksume, of the Citty of London, Gent., the sume of ffive pounds, which was given vnto Anne ffolkard, my daughter. Exors. to pay the sayd sume vnto the said Anna (sic) ffolkard, together with Twenty Shillings for the vse thereof. Moneys that shall arise on the sale of my lands equally vnto my foure children, namely, ffrancis ffolkard, Thomas ffolkard, Anna (sic ffolkard, and Mary the wife of William Thoroughgood. Robert Greene and Peter Sare, of Stowmarkett, worsted weavers, to be exors. Probt. 1667, 18 April" (Liber. Edgar, 1666—1669, No. 60, Fo. 180).

Of the children named in the above will, ffrancis is thus referred to in the Court Book last quoted:—

"Cur. 19 Octr. 1669. ffranciscus ffolkard, nunc plene etatis, vendidit Roberto Glover."

He must therefore have been born in 1648. The other son, named Thomas, would appear to have lived at Combs, two miles from Stowmarket. The following abstract of proceedings in Chancery of 1681 seems to establish this, and informs us besides that he was then married to Elizabeth, daughter of Thomas Blomfield, of Baxhall (Buxhall):—

"Richer vs. ffolker. 3 Jan. 1681. Daniel Richer, late of Barking, Essex, Yeoman, was of Stepney. Wm. Lockwood, late of Combes, Suff., where he died, owned lands there called Lockwoods, and others in Finborough and Stowmarket, altogether worth £150 per annum. He died 1656, Margery ffrench, his niece, and da. of Robert Richer, being his heir. She was mother of petitioner, who succeeded at her death and he charges Thomas Blomfield, of Baxhall, since dead, with forging the will of petitioner's mother, and Elizabeth Blomfield alias ffolker, alias ffouker, his da., with combining with others in bringing action of eject-ment against petitioner on that will, which will was upheld by a jury at Bury, and the defendant lived on the land at Combes. The answer of the defendant and his wife is signed by Thomas ffolkard and Elizabeth folkerd" (C.P. before 1714, Hamilton 283).

In 1685 we find this couple concerned with the following Fine (F. Hil.):—

"Between James Waller, plf. and Thos. ffolkerd and Elizabeth his wife, defts., respecting 1 messuage, 2 barns, 1 stable, 1 garden, 2 orchards, 8 acres land, 7 acres meadow, and 20 acres pasture, with appurts. in Combe. Defendants receive £60 sterling."

---

6. JOHN FFOLKARD, of Stowmarket, is not included on the Pedigree. He was probably a son of Robert (No. 2), and would seem to have transmitted that name to his own son, who again continued it to a child of his. The earliest reference possessed to this man is in the will of Constance Browne, of Stowmarket, widow, dated 11th June, 1700 (Arch. Sudbury, Steward 26), an extract from which reads:—

"Messuage purchased of John Keble, of Stowmarket, Gent., and now in occupation of John ffolkard, my grandson-in-law, in Stowmarket, and to Elizabeth ffolkard, my grandchild, his wife, for their lives, and then to their children."

A Robert ffolkard, presumably a son of this John, witnessed this will. This presumption is, however, a doubtful one, owing to the omission of all reference to him in the will of 1718 of the latter, an abstract of which is here given:—

"John ffolkard, of Stowmarket. To ffrances, my dear and loving wife, garden lately purchased of Mr. John Parke, together with all household goods, &c. To my son, John ffolkard, my house I live in to him and his heirs for ever. He and my said wife to continue to live together, and carry on the trade. 8 May, 1718. Probate 14 May, 1718. Juramento ffrancisce ffolkard, executrix " (*Bury Registry, Goodwin* vi. 1715—18, *Fo.* 410ऍ).

This will proves that the first wife, Elizabeth, had died, and that the testator had, between 1700 and 1718, remarried to a second wife, ffrances, of whom nothing is known beyond this mention. Of the son John named we are similarly ignorant, though it is probable that the following Fine of 1743 (*F. Trin.*) refers to him and his wife :—

"Between Thos. Veale, plf., and ffredk. Cotton and Elizabeth his wife, John ffolkard and Elizabeth his wife, Ann Banks, widow, and peter ffugett and Sarah his wife, defts., of 2 messuages, 2 gardens, 2 orchards, 4 acres land, 4 acres meadow, and 4 acres pasture, with appurts., in Easton and Wickham. Plf. pays £60."

7. ROBERT FFOLKARD, of Stowmarket (not on the Pedigree) may possibly have been son to the Robert who witnessed Constance Browne's will above quoted from. We find him named in the several Poll lists (*D.*) for Knights of the Shire as of Stowmarket in 1770, 1784, 1790, and 1791 ; while, as the proprietor, he was assessed (*D.* xxx.) in 1798 at 8/- for land tax in Stowmarket on land let to T. Fuller, and at 16/- for land he himself both owned and lived upon in the same town. He was probably the Robert ffolkard, of Stowmarket, whose will of 1804 is in the Probate Registry at Bury, of which I have obtained no abstract.

𝔖𝔢𝔱𝔱𝔩𝔢𝔪𝔢𝔫𝔱 𝔞𝔱 𝔓𝔞𝔯𝔥𝔞𝔪.

(Includes branch at Clopton.)

PREFATORY REMARKS.—This Settlement is one of the best authenti-cated of all the Suffolk Lines. It died out in the direct descent with the Rev. Francis Folkard, the rector of Clopton and Hasketon. The house in Parham in which several generations of the family lived is near to the church and still standing intact. Davy alludes to it (*D.* xxv.), and remarks under date 1825 :—

"Under the window-sill of a house by the road side, a short distance northward of the church, carved on wood are the arms of Ufford. This house now belongs to, and is the residence of, Mr. Thomas Folkard."

This house, the parish clerk informs me, is reputed to have been built about 1400. The arms of the Folkard family appear on a shield on the end of one of the roof principals of Parham Church, the other principals bearing the arms of Valoines, Ufford, Corrance, Barker of Wickham Market, Bowtell, Warner, and Willoughby, all families connected with Parham. Residence at that place after the direct Line died out was continued by the Folkards, of Bedfield and by those of Dennington. The pedigree of this Parham Settlement compiled by Davy (D.P.) is inaccurate, and is evidently only founded on the entries in the Parham Register.

---

1. EDMUND FFOLKARD, of Framlingham and subsequently of Parham, was the first of the family to reside at Parham, no mention of the name occurring in the local records anterior to those having reference to him. He was a son of Thomas, of Bedfield (No 5 of that Line), and Anne (natus Stannaway). He is named in his father's will (45) of 1626, and according to it he then had seven children. Among the list of entries preserved (D. xv.) of the lost Bedfield Register, the name of ffolkard is found in 1580. This was, not improbably, the date of this man's birth. He would, if that surmise be correct, have been 86 years years old at his death. He may therefore well have deserved the description given of him as " the olde man " in a will (60) of 1664.

His first marriage, according to Candler, was to Susan, daughter of William Green, of Hadleigh. By this marriage, the same authority informs us, he had eleven childen. We have no record of this wife's death. In 1639 we find the following entry in the Parham Register, which doubtless records his second marriage :—

" Edmond ffolkard and Margerie Moorlinge marryed. 28th May, 1639."

At the foregoing date the husband would have been 59 years old, and it is therefore not surprising that we find but a single child of this marriage. The Parham Register has :—

" John ffolkard, sonne of Edmund ffolkard and Margerie, bapt. 19 April, 1640."

This child was evidently named after a son by the first marriage, who, according to Candler, died s.p., and therefore, possibly, young. This second John was assessed in 1663, as " John ffolker," for land at Bedfield valued at £2. 10s. (Add. MSS. 21,047). He would seem to have lived at Dallinghoo along with other members of the Bedfield family, the following entries occurring in the Sundry Books (Vol. 30) of the Ipswich Probate Office :—

" 10 February, 1678. Lic. between Tho. Russel, of Kettleburgh, and Susanna Baxter, de fframsden, to church at Dallinghoo, John ffolkard a bondsman in £200."

" 12 Janry., 1679. Marriage between Robert Smart and Phœbe Russel, both of Wickham Market. John ffolkard, of Dallingho, a bondsman in £200."

These Russels were probably children of this man's aunt shown on the Pedigree. The following further entry (Ibid. Vol. 34) also probably refers to this John :—

R

"11 Octr., 1683. John ffolkard bondsman in £200 for marriage between John Meadows, of Bedfield, single, and Hester Smith, of peasenhall, single."

It is not unlikely that he was identical with the "John ffoakard" included in a Suffolk Poll List of 1702 as a freeholder in Howe (Hoo) (*D.* liv. 36). From the fact, also, of his nephew ffrancis afterwards marrying Mary Porter, of Lavenham, it is no far-fetched conclusion that the following notification of bankruptcy in the *Ipswich Journal* of July 7, 1739, refers to a son of his settled in that town :—

"John Follyard, of Lavenham, Linendraper and Chapman, Dec. 29, 1739."

This mis-spelling of the name is of frequent occurrence. We have no further information as to this son of the subject of this notice.

Candler makes no allusion to the second marriage of this Edmund to Margerie Moorlinge, but his Pedigree does not enter upon the Parham Line. This wife was doubtless a resident of Parham, for we find (*Ipsw. Pro. Sundry Books* xxix.) the following entry :—

"7 Oct., 1675. Lic. ffrancis Mawling, of Parham, single, and Anne Church, of Hasketon."

In 1647 this Edmund ffolkard is referred to as under in the Parham Manor Rolls (*D.* liv. 35, *D.* xxv.), though he was at that date certainly resident at Framlingham.

"Chas. 23. Edmund Nelson surrenders to Edmund ffolkard, of Framlingham, who is admitted" (*ex. Lat.*).

"Thomas Alexander, Gent., admitted upon a forfeited conditional surrender of Edmund ffolkard to lands, &c., in Parham which said Edmund took up on the surrender of Edmund Nelson at a Court holden the 30th April, 1647."

Further references to these lands will be found under the notice of the son Francis. In 1656 the will (57) of this Edmund's brother Anthony refers to him and to his children, and both he and his daughter Anne are named in that (60) of Anthony's widow of 1664. Children of his were baptized at Framlingham in 1623—26—30, and in 1657 he is named as "ffolkod of Bedfield" in the same Register, when notifying the marriage of his daughter Mary. He seems to have changed his place of residence six times. Born at Bedfield, he first settled at Framlingham ; went, probably about 1635, to Bedfield ; was back at Framlingham in 1647 ; was of Bedfield again in 1657, and late in life settled at Parham, where he died in 1666, his burial being thus recorded in the Register of that place :—

"Edmund ffolkard buried 21 Febry., 1666."

No will of his has been found. Of his numerous family, Francis is dealt with hereafter at length. Mary was baptized at Framlingham as

"Marie, daughter of Edmund and Susan ffoliarde, baptized 2 Nov. 1626."

Of her marriage the same Register records :—

"The daie of publication between John Talmage and Marie ffolkard, both single, ffolkod of Bedfield, and were married ye 25 December, 1656, by me, B. Bowtell."

This daughter Mary is twice named in the will (57) of her uncle Anthony ffolkard of 1656, her husband being the conditional trustee of all the testator's property. The Register of Coddenham has :—

"Anne Talmach, daughter of John and Mary, da. of Edmund ffolkard, of Bedfield, born 1st July, 1657."

The Talmaches of Coddenham were a not remote branch of the Earl of Dysart's family, the name of that being Tollemache; their name in the Register of that place being variously spelt as Talomache, Tallemach, and Tollemach. This John Talmage was baptized at Coddenham, 7th July, 1617. His marriage to Mary ffolkard is recorded on the Candler Pedigree.

Of the other children of this Edmund's first marriage Candler names Thomas, John, Elizabeth, Susan, and William, who are all said by him to have died without issue. The last may have been the man referred to in the lost Bedfield Register as

"Old William ffolkard buried 1650."

The word "old" here probably only meant senior, as a younger William, who did not die till 1703, was then living at Bedfield. A second Thomas and a son Robert are also given by Candler. Of this Robert the Framlingham Register has :—

"Robert, son of Edmund and Susan Folkard, baptized 12 Feb. 1630."

Candler's Pedigree also names a daughter Sarah, whom we find further referred to in the will (57) of her uncle Anthony of 1656. The same authority also includes Anne, named in the wills (57 and 60) of her uncle and aunt. At the date of the aunt's will, 1664, she seems to have been unmarried, and to have lived with her father. The only child, John, of the second marriage has been dealt with above.

2. FFRANCIS FFOLKARD, of Parham, was son to the Edmond last treated of. The Register of Framlingham has :—

"ffrancis, sonne of Edmund ffolkard and Susan his wife, was baptized Nov. 4, 1623."

Some time before 1649 he married Ann, daughter of Barnaby Burrough, of Ipswich. Her father died, according to Dr. Muskett's Pedigree, in 1632. This Pedigree also states that she was "cousin to Thomas Burrough, of Ipswich, who entered pedigree in the Suffolk visitation, 1664." The Burroughs were of an old and good county family. In 1650 we find this wife thus alluded to in the will of her brother, Barnaby Burrough, Merchant, of Great Yarmouth (*Cur. Prerog. Cant. Ruthen* 407) :—

"Item   I doe give unto my sister Anne folkard. wife to ffrancis ffolkard, of Parham, in Suff.   All that my right and interest which I have by virtue of the last will and testament of my deceased ffather, Barnaby Burrough, in the several legacies or porcons of my two deceased sisters, Martha and Sarah Burrough, my severall parts of which porcons remayneth in the handes of my mother Anne Burrough, in Ipswich, widow."

That will was proved in London 12 Nov., 1657, by Anne Burrough and John Reeve exors. This Edmund ffolkard left by will to his wife the house at Parham for her life. She did not, however, survive him, the Parham Register recording :—

"Ann ffolkard, of ——, buried 4th August, 1681,"

R 2

Of her husband we have the following additional information. In 1656 he is named in the will (57) of his uncle Anthony, of Bedfield, three of his children being also therein specified. In 1660, on a Hearth Tax Roll (*L.S.* 183/610), he paid for five hearths in his house at Parham. In 1663 (*P.R. Hil.* 930) judgment was given whereby he recovered a loan of four pounds made by him to John Dawson, of Framlingham, with 26/- as damages, his attorney being Edward Colman. In 1665 (*P.R. Trin.* 1554) he sought recovery of a messuage and four acres of pasture in Parham let to Nicolas Cole. Richard Porter, who appeared at Westminster as his attorney in this suit, may not improbably have been a relative of the Mary Porter who married his son Francis. He is named as follows in the will of 12th Oct., 1667, of Thos. Burrough, of London, Merchant, of Goodman's Yard, Minories. This will (*Cur. Prerog. Cant.* 15 *Hene*) bequeathed £700 and property in Ipswich to the testator's son Thomas, with the accompanying proviso that

"Ne· ertheless, if my said sonne Thomas shall die before his said Age of One and Twenty years without any Children, then I give and bequeath One hundred and fifty pounds of the said sum of Seven Hundred pounds to Edmund ffoulkerd, Sonne of ffraucis ffoulkard, of Barham (*sic.*), in the said County of Suff." (Proved Feby. 14, 1667).

We find the following entries naming him in the Parham Court Rolls (*D.* liv. 35) in 1660:—

"Anne, wife of ffrancis ffolkard, son of Edmund ffolkard, admitted on regrant" (*ex. Lat.*).

"John Lambe·t, of Wapping, Merchant, admitted on the forfeiture of ffrancis ffolkard and Anne his wife to the tenure which the aforesaid Anne took on the reconcession of the lord at a Court held 27 April, 1660" (*ex. Lat.*).

In 1664 there occurs the following entry:—

"John Lambert admitted on the forfeiture of ffrancis ffolkard and Anne his wife (of land) which the aforesaid Ann became seised of in 1660" (*ex. Lat.*).

And later on, but of uncertain date:—

"Anne, wife of ffrancis ffolkard, son of Edmund ffolkard, admitted on the regrant of the lord to lands seised after the death of Thos. Alexander, Esq., and which the said Thomas Alexander took up on the surrender of said Edmund ffolkard at a Court held the 11 April, 1654."

In 1676 he was defendant to a Fine (*F.* xxv. *Pasch.*), sued by John Lambert respecting lands in Parham and elsewhere. These doubtless included the lands of John Lambert referred to in the entry above quoted. His will (67) is dated 16 Nov., 1681, and his burial is thus recorded in the Parham Register:—

"ffrancis ffolkard buryed 6th Dec., 1681."

His will, it will be seen, describes him as a "Clothier." This term was applied to those who dealt on a large scale in the cloth which was at that date the prime manufacture of Suffolk. The gold seal left by that will to his son Thomas is still in existence, but I have not seen it. The Rev. Dr. Punchard did so some years ago, when it was in possession of a daughter of the John Gray, of Parham, named on the Pedigree. To Dr. Punchard I am indebted for an impression from it, which shows the family arms very distinctly. This ffrancis ffolkard died at the age of 58, much younger than customary with the members of his family.

Of his children, Edmund, ffrancis, and Thomas will be found hereafter dealt with. Of Alice we know nothing beyond the mention made of her in her father's will (67).

3. EDMOND FFOLKARD, of Parham, was the eldest son of the foregoing ffrancis. His baptism is thus entered in the Parham Register :—

"Edmond ffolkard, son of ffrancis ffolkard and Ann, baptized 8 April, 1649."

But little is known to me respecting this man. He is left a legacy by the will (57) of his great-uncle Anthony ffolkard, of Bedfield, of 1656, and, contingently, in the will of 1667 of his uncle Thomas Burrough above quoted from. No record is discoverable of any marriage by him.

From the character of the legacy left him by his father's will (67) of 1681—his name has been erroneously printed therein as Edward—we may conclude that he was a *mauvais sujet*, the reference to him reading :—

"Item. I give and bequeath unto Edmond ffolkard, my eldest sonne, the sume of ffive shillings, to bee paid him within one year next after my decease."

This man lived only to the age of 52, and the following entry in the Parham Register records his interment :—

"Edmund ffolkard buryed 6 March, 1701."

4. THOMAS FFOLKARD was the third son of ffrancis (No. 2). He is named in that father's will (67) of 1681. He was probably the Thomas who is referred to in the following extract from the Framlingham Register :—

"Ann, Dr. of Thomas and Ann ffolkard, baptized 8 Novr., 1711."

It is not unlikely that the granddaughter, Ann ffolkard, referred to in will 67 of 1681 as then under age, was also a child of this Thomas, and that she had died before the birth of the Anne baptized as above. The Thomas ffolkard, who, in 1727, was on the Poll List of Suffolk for the Knights of the Shire (*B.M.*) as a freeholder at Rickinghall Inferior, was, no doubt, identical with this individual, of whom I have found no further mention.

5. FFRANCIS FFOLKARD, of Parham, we find described as the second son of ffrancis (No. 2) in the will (67) of the latter. He continued his father's business of cloth merchant at Parham, and lived in the same house, to which the following reference has been found in the *Ipswich Journal* of April 14th, 1739 :—

"A very good Dwelling House in Parham, with convenient Out-houses, Yards, Garden, and 1 Orchard, and about Thirty Acres of Land, late in the Occupation of Mrs. Folkard, and now of Mr. Henry Williams. For further Particulars Enquire of Mr. Peregrine Love in Ipswich, or of the Revd. Mr. Folkard at Clopton."

This advertisement names the occupation of the house by the widow of the subject of this notice, whose baptism is thus entered in the Parham Register :—

"Francis ffolkard, son of Francis and Ann, baptized 26 June, 1652."

He married twice. Of the first marriage we have no certain evidence beyond that afforded by his widow's will (88), in which the son Francis is referred to as her "son-in-law" (*i.e.*, *stepson*). The latter was therefore evidently the issue of a first marriage. There is much probability, I think, that the license of marriage between ffrancis ffolkard, of East Bergholt, and ffrances Browne, of that place (*See No. 4 Framlingham Settlement*), of 1686, may refer to this man's first marriage. The son of that marriage was born in 1688, and his baptism is not recorded at Parham. The will of this ffrances Browne's father before quoted is dated in that year, and may, not improbably, have been made consequent upon his daughter, ffrances ffolkard's, death in childbirth, she being certainly dead when the will was made. That this ffrancis ffolkard resided in early life elsewhere than in Parham seems certain, and it may have been at East Bergholt. What adds to the probability of my conjecture about this marriage referring to him is the fact that William Browne (the father) was, like the subject of this notice, a cloth merchant.

The second wife, we learn from a law suit (*C.P. before* 1714, *Mitford D.* xcii.), was Mary Porter, my extract establishing this from the case reading :—

"On the 27 Nov. 1705, Ffrancis ffolkard, Gent., of Parham, and Mary his wife, one of the daughters of John Porter, late of Lavenham, Suffolk, Clothier, decd., and Sarah Porter, of parham, singlewoman, the other daughter of the said John Porter, his only children, in Septr., 1683, the said John Porter being then a widower and having entered into a treaty of marriage with Elizabeth, *alias* Bettie, Wells, of Lavenham, widow, made certain monetary arrangements. The case (ffolkard *vs.* Snelling and Boughton) turns upon these."

The Sarah Porter referred to is buried at Parham, her tomb, still preserved there, bearing the following inscription :—

"Here lieth the Body of | Sarah Porter, who was | daughter to John Porter, of | Lavenham, who departed this | Life July ye 16, 1730.'

The first child of this ffrancis ffolkard by Mary Porter having been baptized in 1692, the marriage most probably took place about 1690 or 1691. She survived her husband, and made her will (88) in 1735, her death occurring in 1737, and her burial being thus entered at Parham :—

"Mary ffolkard, Widd., buryed 24 June, 1737."

The following inscription is below that of her husband on their joint tomb :—

"Also the Body of | Mary Folkard his wife, | who departed this Life | the 21 June, 1737, | Aged 71 years."

The succeeding mention to that of the baptism of the husband is in the will (57) of his great-uncle Anthony ffolkard, of Bedfield, of 1656, he being a legatee under it to a small amount, £5, though then but an infant of four years old. Next in order of date are the references to him in his father's will. His elder brother Edmund, having been almost disinherited by that will, the bulk of the property is left by it to this ffrancis, he being appointed exor. to it. In 1693, 1702, and 1709, he is named in the Court Rolls of Parham as " ffrancis ffolkard, Gentleman, Inhabitant of Parham " (*D.* liv. 35). In 1692 he was named in a Fine (*F.* xxix. *Trin.*) :—

" Between ffrancis ffolkard, plff., and John King and Margaret his wife, defts., of the fourth part of a messuage, a garden, an orchard, 10 acres land, 10 acres meadow, 70 acres pasture, with apptces. in Parham, Cransford, and Glenham Magna. ffrancis ffolkard pays £60 sterling."

In 1693 he was a party to the following further Fine (*F.* xxx. *Hil.*) :—

" Between ffrancis ffolkard and Thomas Botwright, plffs., and Robert Colvill and Margaret his wife, Charles Colville and Marie his wife, Henry Murdock and Mary his wife, and John Bradlaugh and Alice his wife, defts., of 5 messuages, 5 gardens, 5 acres land, and 30 acres pasture, with apptces. in Parham, Clopton, Ufford, and Orford. Plff. pays £160 sterling."

In 1699 we find him to have been concerned with a third Fine (*F.* xxxi. *Mich.*) :—

" Between ffrancis ffolkard, Joshua Paske, Charles Stanmer, and George ffrost, Plffs., and George Carew, Gent., and Alicia his wife, and others, of 3 messuages, 2 barns, 2 stables, 22 acres land, 34 acres meadow, and 52 acres pasture, with apptces. in Peasenhall, Baddingham, Heaveningham, Sibton, Stradishall, and Lavenham. Defendants receive £260 sterling."

In 1701 he and his wife are thus referred to in another Fine (*F.* *Trin.*) :—

" Between Henry ffauconberge, Doctor of Laws, and John May, plffs., and Joseph Cutleve, Clerk, and Susannah his wife, and ffrancis ffolkard, *generosus* [*i.e.*, gentleman], and Marie his wife, defts., of 2 messuages, 2 gardens, 6 acres meadow, and 1 acre pasture, with apptces. in Ipswich, Beccles, and Ingate. Plffs. pay defts. £60 sterling."

In 1705 he entered a suit in Chancery (*C.P. before* 1714, *Mitford D.* xcii.) of the pleadings in which the following is my abstract :—

" 2 May, 1705. ffrancis ffolkard, of Parham, Suffolk, Gentleman, showeth that William ffolkard, late of Bedfield, Suffolk, Yeoman, deed., was his uncle, and possessed of lands and houses in Bedfield and elsewhere in Suffolk. The will of the latter was dated on or about the 10 Septr., 1703, the orator benefitting by the following clauses of it " ((See Will 74).

" The testator died 22 October, 1703. The plaintiff entered upon the occupation of the properties, among them being three closes which he contends were part of the appurtenances devised to him. The defendants claim these as being part of their bequest. The plaintiff says the testator made a former will in 1693, and then only left to Simon Rous, the father, £100. The Rouse family entered action of ejectment, but would not produce the will at the trial of it. The defendants' answer describes Bedfield Dogg as a farm, and says (*which was true*) that the testator was not uncle to the plaintiff, ' as the compt in his said Bill pretendeth, but at the most some remote relation; but the defendants, Simon Rouse and George Sewell, were sisters' sonnes, and are heires-at-law of the said testator.' They claim the lands as part of the Bedfield Dogg farm."

The actual relationship between the complainant in the above cited case and William ffolkard, the testator named, was, as will be seen by the Pedigree, that of second cousinship only.

In 1716 we find the subject of this notice named in a list of the tenants of the manor of Kettleburgh (*D.* xxi.) as:—

"ffolkard, ffrancis, free tenant, formerly King's, formerly Haly's. 6/4." (*ex. Lat.*).

This land, however, appears to have been situated in Parham. In 1718 he appears, from some reason or other which I cannot even guess at, to have executed a deed constituting himself guardian of those of his children then under age. The entry as to this in the Admon. Rolls of the Ipswich Probate Office (245) reads thus :—

"ffrancis ffolkard, of Parham, Gent., by the election of Elizabeth ffolkard, aged 20 and upwards, Thomas ffolkard, aged 18 and upwards, and Alice ffolkard, aged 14 years and upwards, minors, the real and lawful son and daughters of the abovenamed ffrancis ffolkard, is admitted and sworn Guardian and Curator to them, the said Elizabeth, Thomas, and Alice, during their minorities. 9 August 1718."

In a marriage settlement of 1719 (*D. Parham*) allusion is made to

"All that Tenement or Cottage, with the yards, &c., &c., formerly in the tenure of ffrancis ffolkard and John Damont and now of Samuel Buttrum and Thomas Arnold, situate in Parham."

In 1721 (*L.R.*) there occurs the entry :—

"Clopton. ffrancis ffalkard, Patron of living."

This man made his will (84) but very shortly before his death. His burial is thus recorded in the Parham Register :—

"ffrancis ffolkard, Gent., buried 29th September, 1722."

The stone which covered his grave in Parham churchyard, it is evident from his widow's will, was placed upon it 13 years after his death. Davy, when describing it, refers to its having been at that date, about 1820, much broken. When I saw it in 1884 the slab had been removed from the former brick monument and laid on the ground close to the wall of the church. It was cracked in several places, and consequently the date of the death was illegible, but the other lettering is as clear as when first cut. The inscription reads:—

"Here lyeth the Body of | Francis Folkard, Gent., | who departed this Life the 23rd of — | — | ."

We know from the Register that the blanks above should be filled by September, 1722. Below this inscription is that of the widow previously quoted.

The Court Rolls of Parham (*D.* liv. 35) record :—

"1722. The death of ffrancis ffolkard, Gent., presented."

Of this man's issue, Thomas has been dealt with under the Bedfield Settlement (No. 13), and ffrancis, Mary, Sarah, Elizabeth, and Alice will be found separately treated of further on. His remaining children are noticed by these entries in the Parham Register :—

"William ffolkard, sonne of ffrancis and Mary, baptized 27 Dec., 1694."

"William ffolkard buried 15 May, 1695."

"Anne ffolkard, daughter of ffrancis and Mary, baptized 10 July, 1696."

"Edmund ffolkard, the sonne of ffrancis and Mary, baptized 7 October, 1701."

Punchard of Suffolk.

Arms: Sa. 6 plates 3, 2, 1.   Crest: An Unicorn's head erased gu., spotted with bezants and armed or.

PUNCHARD OF HEANTON-PUNCHARDON, COUNTY DEVON.

BY

E. G. PUNCHARD, D.D., Oxon.,

Vicar of Christ Church, Luton, Beds.

(Read at Torquay, July, 1893.)

[*Reprinted from the Transactions of the Devonshire Association for the Advancement of Science, Literature, and Art. 1893.—*xxv. *pp. 383–388.*]

PUNCHARD OF HEANTON-PUNCHARDON, COUNTY DEVON.

BY

E. G. PUNCHARD, D.D., Oxon.,
Vicar of Christ Church, Luton, Beds.

(Read at Torquay, July, 1893.)

[*Reprinted from the Transactions of the Devonshire Association for the Advancement of Science, Literature, and Art. 1893.—xxv. pp. 382-388.*]

PUNCHARD OF HEANTON-PUNCHARDON, COUNTY DEVON.

BY E. G. PUNCHARD, D.D., Oxon.,

Vicar of Christ Church, Luton, Beds.

"Heanton is surnamed Punchardon; the parish reserveth charily the old lord's name of long antiquity, and therewithal copious in some ages; for you shall peruse few ancient evidences in those parts, whereunto the Punchardons have not been witnesses; yea, sometimes two or three of them. I will not avouch a remainder of them yet in being (but it is very probable): if there be, they have lost their "don," and are now ycleped only by the name of Punchard."—WESTCOTE'S *Devon.*

Devon.—The name of Punchard appears first in England on the roll of Battle Abbey. Holinshed spells it *Punchardoun;* Duchesne *Punchardon;* and on the Dives Roll it is found as *Pontchardon.* This last form is the nearest to Pontcardon,[1] a village near Neauflla, in Normandy, where the family was noted in the ninth and tenth centuries.

Robert de Punchardon, who came over with William the Conqueror, received the Manor of Heanton (Haginton, or Hainton) at the hands of Baldwin the Sheriff. Other lands at Blachewilla and Mothercombe, amounting altogether to four and a quarter knights' fees, were added from the confiscated possessions of three unfortunate Saxons—Ulf, Brismar, and Alceric. Robert's descendants in direct male line were lords of Heanton-Punchardon till the end of the thirteenth century, when the last of the elder branch (Sir John Punchard) divided his estates between three daughters —Ermegard, Mabel, and Margery—who married respectively into the families of Beaumont, Ralegh, and Beauple. Ermegard's son, Sir John Beaumont, married Alice Scuda-

[1] The word has more than fifty variants. See an article on "The Multiplication of Surnames," by ARTHUR FOLKARD, in the *Antiquary,* No. 81, vol. xiv., p. 94. "Pinchard" however is not a form of Punchard. Its first possessor came also in 1066, and his name appears on the Roll next to Robert Punchardoun.

more; Joan, their granddaughter, married Sir James Chidleigh, but died without issue, and gave her lands to her cousin, another John Beaumont. The heirs male of this family also were extinct in the third generation; and Joan, the heiress, married a Basset, whose descendants were possessed of Heanton Manor down to recent times. Mabel Punchard, the second daughter, who married Sir John Ralegh of Charnies, succeeded to the Manor of Charles (in the hundred of Shirwell), and also to West Buckland. Margery, the third sister, though twice wedded, died childless. And so the direct line of the Heanton Punchards came to an end.

The continental estates at Avesnes and St. Germain, Roche and Cetrentost, were held till 1216, when they were confiscated by Philip Augustus of France.

But though the senior stock at Heanton ended in 1330, other descendants of the first Robert held lands at Little Bovey, Kentisbeare, and Clanbarrow down to 1413. One of these, Sir Richard Punchardon, distinguished himself in the French Wars of Edward III., and was made a knight banneret. During the campaign of 1356, which ended with the battle of Poictiers, September 19th, he was caught in an ambuscade, but fought his way through with great valour.[2] He stood high in court favour, and was entrusted by the King with lands in Essex, Cambridge, Wilts, and Herts on behalf of the infant heir of the de Bensteds. Under the banner of the Black Prince Sir Richard crossed again into France, and his Devon lands received the usual *fœdus de protectione*[3] during his absence abroad. Froissart speaks of him as Marshal of Aquitaine in 1366, at the birth of Richard of Bordeaux.

Various members of the family are noted in the *Testa de Nevill* and similar records. But from the middle of the fifteenth century there is silence concerning them for nearly a hundred years; and from 1540 the chief sources of information are parish registers and wills. Three or four distinct families are traceable at Pilton and Barnstaple from 1500 to 1800, only one of which retained its place among gentlefolk, ending with a girl (Elizabeth, born 1672), who married John Rowe in 1692, and left four children. Her father, Richard Punchardon, is described in his will, dated 1720, as a weaver, and died six years later, very poor. One member of this family—William Punchard, of Pilton—was

---

[2] FROISSART, *Chron.* ii. 296; iii. 16, &c.
[3] 33° Ed. III.

notorious in lawsuits, extending from 1630 to 1659, concerning the estate of Dorothy ffontleroy, with whom he eloped. Marriage connections were made with several other families of good name—Chichester, Luppingcote, Aishe, Harford, and Stukeley. But the later representatives of the Punchards gradually went down hill.

About 1550 Lewis Punchardon, presumably of Barnstaple, moved to Totnes, and founded a new family there, whose descendants still survive in that part of Devon. Wills of these Totnes and Dartmouth Punchards describe them as vintners, goldsmiths, farmers; and in one case a bookseller (Lewis + 1686).

The names connected by marriage are Staplehill, Flute, Flavel, Newberry, Aylwin, and Kennant.

It is not however to Devonshire alone that we must look for the story of this unfortunate family. Younger sons of the main line at Heanton settled in Somerset, Dorset, Wilts, Hants, Herts, Norfolk, and Durham; and solitary adventurers are found from 1100 to 1500 in almost every county in England, occasionally adding their names, as did their ancestor Robert, to the manors of which they became possessed.

Somerset.—Early in the thirteenth century a leading knight of Dunster Castle, under the fourth De Mohun, was William de Punchardon, of Devon; a grandson apparently of Robert. Amongst other fees received by him from the Earl of Somerset were St. Audries and Lydiard, known henceforth as Lydiard-Punchardon. The grandson of this knight, also called William, left an only child, Aubrea, who married Hamelyn le Deaudon. Here again male issue failed; and their daughter (Mabel) married Sir Baldwin Malet of Enmore, to whom the Somerset feoffs of the Punchards fell; continuing with his descendants till the time of Charles I., when Arthur Malet sold the estates.

Dorset.—The Dorsetshire family is less worthy of note. John, the son of Hugh Punchardon, by Lucy, daughter of Reginald Fitz-piers, succeeded to a small estate at Mapoudre in 1429, but was escheated shortly after. Hugh, the last of the line, conveyed his lands at Motcombe to John Toppe, of London, in 1627.

Wilts.—In Wiltshire the chief possessions were at White-parish, in the hundred of Frustfield, and remained in the name of Punchardon to the close of the seventeenth century. Richard, Vicar in 1638, was ejected from Whiteparish by the Puritans, in favour of one Charles Luke, a Presbyterian.

John, the latest of the family, lived till 1652; his widow, Margaret, died at Salisbury nine years afterwards, the principal legatee being "her beloved grandson Punchardon Roberts." Other daughters were married into the families of Goter and St. Barbe, and Punchard estates fell again to the spindle side.

Herts.—In Hertfordshire another of the Heanton family won his way to favour in the time of William II., and was seized of the Manor of Willian. Four generations followed him in peace; the last of whom, Geoffroy, was noted in 1275 by a grant of lands to Roger, twenty-fourth Abbot of St. Albans. The names of these Punchardons appear several times in similar grants or confirmations.

Hants.—Perhaps, however, for good fortune, certainly for valiant deeds of arms, and munificent gifts to the Church, we must turn to the Hampshire branch; the founder of which was Sir Robert Punchardon, lord of Faccombe and Ellingham, grandson to Robert the first of Heanton. Rymer's *Fœdera*, Inquisitions *ad quod damnum* and *post mortem*, Placita *de quo warranto*, *Rotuli litterarum clausarum*, &c., bear witness to favour and prosperity, at least for awhile; but all came to an end with Walter Punchardon, who succeeded to the manor of Faccombe in 1466, and died fourteen years after. His father, Sir Richard, was disseized of Ellingham by order of Henry VI., and its church of All Saints and chapelry of St. Mary were given to the King's new college at Eton.

An earlier Richard was ordered by Henry III., in a letter dated January 9th, 1233, to march with Philip de Heye to the castle of Devizes, against Hubert de Burgh, whose mother, as we shall see by the Norfolk records, was Joan Punchard.

Another of the family, Nicholas, was returned to Parliament as Knight of the Shire for Northumberland in 1297. Four years subsequent he was Commissioner of Array, the writ being tested at Linlithgow, November 21st, 1301. He survived the carnage of Bannockburn, and attended the Great Council of Edward II., at Westminster, in 1324. With him was his kinsman Oliver, who, after escaping from the Scots, was stripped of his feoffs in Berkshire by escheat in 1316.

A disreputable namesake of this Punchard was a favourite of King John, and often sent on secret service by him; in reward for which the Earl of Lincoln had a royal command, dated September 23, 1216, to effect seisin of lands at

Naseby—"*dilecto et fideli nostro Olivero Punchardon, sine dilatione.*"

Several of this active line took Holy Orders, and some attained to high rank; one (William) being made sixth Abbot of Rievaulx (1199–1203), and another dean of Kildare (+ 1260).

After 1480 the Punchards disappear from the ranks of the Hampshire gentry, their last enrolment being in the list compiled by order of Cardinal Beaufort in 1433. But in 1620 Margaret Punchardon received a sister's room in St. Katherine's, near the Tower; and in 1628 a Richard was glad to become master carpenter of H.M.S. *Warspite*. He dying childless and intestate three years later, administration of his poor estate was granted to Dorothy, his relict, August 17th, 1631.

Durham.—Of the Durham branch a weird story is told by Surtees, concerning Sir Hugh de Punchardon, identifying him with the Wild Huntsman of Gualtres Forest. He "for his evill deeds and manifold robberies had been driven out of the Inglische Court, and had come from the South to seek a little bread, and to live by stalinge." This "black Sir Hugh" was lord of Thickley-Punchardon. A soldier of this line, Evan, fought at Lewes in 1264; and a Richard appears as early as 1159, coming in all probability from Devon. The name in this county was, after awhile, contracted to Punshon; distinctive arms (see Appendix) being granted by Norroy, September 6, 1575.

Norfolk.—For strangest contrast of fortune there is one more branch to be considered—the East Anglian. At the opening of the twelfth century William Punchard held the manor of North Tuddenham, and after him John, his only son. Once again, in curious fatality, the lands fell to three daughters, Matilda, Alice, and Joan. The eldest wedded Sir Richard Belhus, who succeeded to her father's fief; their last descendant died in 1363, and left three co-heiresses, who married respectively L'Estrange, Bozun, and Oldhall. The second daughter of John Punchard (Alice) married Robert de Nerford, Warden of Dover Castle, and, being childless, founded the abbey of North Creyke. The third daughter (Joan Punchard) married Walter de Burgh, and became the mother of a famous race. Her eldest son (Geoffrey) was Bishop of Ely in 1225, and died three years later. The next born (William de Burgh) was steward to Henry II., and from him descend the Earls of Ulster and Clanricarde. The youngest boy was greatest of all, and is best known by his simple name of Hubert de

Burgh. He rose to be Earl of Kent, Governor of Norwich and Oxford, and Grand Justiciar of England. He was married four times; first to Joan, daughter of William Rivers, Earl of Devon, and widow of De Briose; secondly to Beatrice, daughter of William de Warenne; thirdly to Isabel, youngest daughter of William Fitz-Eustace, Earl of Gloucester; and lastly to Margaret, daughter of William, King of Scotland. Hubert died in 1243, and through him the ancestral line of Heanton-Punchardon was brought into union with noble and royal pedigrees. No other members of the Norfolk family, nor indeed any of the English branches, have a like renown, and the rest of the story is tame and commonplace.

Alexander Punchard of Apelton was manucaptor of Richard de Walsingham, Knight of the Shire in 1305; and again for Richard de la Rochelle in 1311. His descendants lived at East Dereham till the end of the sixteenth century; and their collaterals, in yeoman families, are scattered about Norfolk still. Some of them possessed fair estates, and their numerous wills are chiefly found in the Norwich Courts. About 1660 William Punchard, presumably from one of these Norfolk farms, emigrated to America, where he married Abigail Waters, at Salem, in 1669, and their descendants are at Boston still.[4]

Suffolk.—Several of the Norfolk Punchards came into Suffolk early in the fifteenth century. One died at Eye in 1496, another at Bedingfield in 1506. From this latter (William Punchard[5]) most of the Suffolk families descend; connected by marriage with Gynner, Hyske, Crane, Paton, Carter, Camborne, Peachey, Folkard, Symonds, and Elgood. Almost all of them, especially in the seventeenth and eighteenth centuries, were well to do; and their wills are more in number and interest than those of other counties. But on the whole the drift of the family, here as elsewhere, has been steadily downward. Manors are few and far between, lands become less, until the last fields are conveyed away, yeomen change to husbandmen and labourers, and whole families disappear. Few persons go into trade or merchandise; in fact, the absence of any calling is remarkable: one pedigree of thirteen generations being absolutely free from it. Perhaps the landed instinct of at least a thousand years was hard to eradicate;

---

[4] Genealogical notes of this flourishing American family are given in an appendix to a sermon preached at the funeral of John Punchard, February 16, 1857, by the Rev. S. M. Worcester. He was born in 1763, fourth in descent from William and Abigail, fought at Bunker's Hill in 1775—a boy of twelve—and became Town Clerk and Magistrate of Salem. (*Obit.* 1857.)

[5] The writer of the present notes is eleventh in direct descent from him.

and, for good or evil, these Punchards, gentle or simple, lived and died "with the land."

Strangely enough in the eastern counties, as well as in the north, a tradition of the race has been true, that it came originally from Devon. And to Robert of Heanton, it is fairly clear, Punchards and Punchardons, whether thriving or decaying, may look for their ancestral line.

APPENDIX.

ARMS.

Devon.	Sable, six plates; 3, 2, 1.
	Sable, ten plates; 4, 3, 2, 1.
Hants.	A fess sable, within a bordure gules, escallopée of the field.
	Argent, a fess within a bordure gules, charged with eight escallops of the first.
Somerset.	Argent, a cross sarcel, voyded gules.
Norfolk.	Argent, a cross moline azure.
	Argent, a cross potence gules.
Durham.	A fess embattled, between three sheep's heads erased,
(Punshon, 1575.)	argent.

CREST.

Devon.	An unicorn's head erased gules, bezantée and armed or.

MANORS OF THE NAME.

Ponte-Cardon, Normandy.
Heanton-Punchardon, Devonshire.
Lydiard-Punchardon, Somerset.
Thickley-Punchardon, Durham.
Punchardon, Northumberland.
Ponchardisland, Kildare, Ireland.

From the omission of the two last from the guardianship deed above cited, it may be concluded that they were dead before the date of it, 1718.

6. MARY FFOLKARD was daughter to the foregoing, and is named in his will (84) of 1722. She was the eldest child of her father's second marriage. Parham Register has:—

"Mary ffolkard, da. of ffrancis ff. and Mary, baptized 28 July, 1692."

There is ample evidence of her having married John Punchard, of Hasketon, but I have no particulars as to the date of her having done so. Owing to her not being named as Mary Punchard in her father's will, she was probably single at the date of it. In the will (88) of her mother of 1735, she is so described. Her husband, who survived her, was a legatee under the will (95) of her brother Francis of 1753. The Rev. Dr. Punchard informs me that she had two children, Rachel, born in 1725, and John, born 1728. The second named lived at Saxstead, and married, in 1766, Ann Symonds. His tomb is in Parham churchyard. He was great-grandfather to Dr. Punchard.

This Mary and her husband are also buried at Parham, their tomb bearing this inscription :—

"Here lyeth the Body of | John Punchard, | who departed this Life | October ye 4, 1756, | aged 70 years. | Also | Mary his wife | who departed this Life | March 7, 1738, | aged 46 years."

7. SARAH FFOLKARD was the next eldest child of Francis (No. 5) and his second wife. The Parham Register has:—

"Sarah ffolkard, daughter of ffrancis ffolkard and Mary, baptized 26 September, 1693."

Her name, as then single, occurs in her father's will (84) of 1722. In that of her mother (88) of 1735 she is mentioned as Sarah Blomfield. In the will of her stepbrother ffrancis (95) of 1753 she is similarly named, but has a complimentary legacy only. Nothing further is known respecting either her or her husband, but very probably the Ann Blomfield named in a Fine with ffrancis ffolkard, the rector of Clopton (*seq.*), was a daughter of theirs.

8. ELIZABETH FFOLKARD was a third daughter of ffrancis (No. 5) by his second marriage. Parham Register has:—

"Elizabeth ffolkard, daughter of ffrancis and Mary, baptized 26 April, 1698."

On the 9th August, 1718, the guardianship deed before referred to mentions her as then " aged 20 and upwards." She married later on Richard Geater, of Melton. We know of only two children of this union—ffrances, whose death is recorded on her mother's tomb (*see below*), and Ann, who married George Lord, of Campsey Abbey, and was buried at Melton in 1777, aged 35. Richard Geater survived his wife, and, dying in 1772 at the age of 72, was buried at Melton (*D.* xxxvii).

In the will of this Elizabeth Geater's mother (88) of 1735, she is named a legatee. Her stepbrother ffrancis's will (95) of 1753, also refers to her.

s

Her tomb is at Parham, near the church porch, and this, when seen by me in 1884, was in fair preservation, it's inscription as under being quite legible :—

" Here resteth the Body of | Elisabeth, the wife of | Richard Geater, | late of Melton, Gent., | and daughter of Francis | and Mary Folkard, | late of this town, Gent., | who died ye 9th October, 1759, | aged 61 years. | Here also resteth the body of Frances Geater, Spinster, | daughter of the said | Richard Geater | and Elisabeth, his wife, | who died the 20th March, 1778, | aged 51 years."

9. ALICE FFOLKARD was another daughter of ffrancis (No. 5) by the second wife. Parham Register contains the entry :—

"Alice ffolkard, daughter of ffrancis and Mary, baptized 7th October, 1703."

In her father's guardianship deed before quoted of August 9, 1718, she is stated to have then been "aged 14 years and upwards." She was a joint legatee with her sister Mary Punchard, of lands, &c., under the will (84) of her father of 1722. Among the marriage licenses at Ipswich (C.) there occurs :—

"Oct. 21, 1730, ffrancis Peachie, Gent., of Sweffland [*Sweffling*], to Alice Ffolkard, S[ingle], Parham, at Clopton."

She was evidently married at the latter place by her stepbrother, its rector. In 1735 she was exor. to her will (88), and was also a complimentary legatee under that of her stepbrother (95) of 1753. Her husband must have died before 1756, for in that year we find thus indexed a Fine (*F. Easter*) :—

"Thomas Newson vs. Alice peachie, vid., in Sweffling and Cransford."

Of her subsequent career and death we have no record.

10. FFRANCIS FFOLKARD, Rector of Clopton and Hasketon, was a son of ffrancis (No. 5) by a first marriage. Evidence to prove this has been given above.

No entry has been found as to his baptism. For reasons before given, this would probably be found at East Bergholt. His tomb informs us of his birth in 1688. The earliest reference found to him is in a rent roll of Baddingham Hall (*D.*) of 1705, which reads thus :—

"ffrancis ffolkard, Clk., for a chase way—2 capons, 2 shillings."

As he only took his A.B. degree in 1709, it seems probable that Davy has wrongly transcribed the date given. By his father's will (84), land at Baddingham is bequeathed. A Rev. ffrancis ffolchier took a degree at Cambridge in 1690 " by Order of the King," and there is just a remote possibility that this entry may refer to that man, but it is not known if he had any connection with Suffolk.

The degrees taken by this ffrancis ffolkard at Pembroke College, Cambridge, are dated, A.B., 1709, A.M., 1737 (*Graduati Cantabrigiensis,* 1659—1856). In the Institution Books (*R.O.*), there occurs the following :—

"ffrancis ffalkard instituted to Clopton, *alias* Claxton, in deanery of Carlford, 21st August 1721, on presentation of ffrancis ffolkard [*his father*]."

In the following year, in the Exchequer First Fruits Composition Books (*R.O.* xxviii. 42), is to be found the entry :—

"*Suff. R: Clopton, ffranciscus ffolgard Cl. p. Integris primitus pe: manibus £15, Octobris 9th, 1722.*"

Shortly before his institution to Clopton he must have married, his first child, Elisabeth, being born in 1720. His wife was Deborah, daughter and sole heiress of the Rev. Peter Chaplin, rector of Higham, Suffolk. She was born in 1698, and was aged 81 at her death in 1779. Her tomb (*see seq.*) is in Clopton church. She was left sole executrix to the will (95) of her husband of 1753.

The latter we find next named in the will (84) of his father of 1722, and by it is bequeathed to him the advowson, &c., of the churches of Clopton and Woodbridge-Hasketon, of both of which he ultimately became rector. He appears at some subsequent date, of which I have no record, to have sold these advowsons, for there is an old entry in the list of rectors of Clopton (*D.* x.) to the following effect :—

"ffrancis ffolkard, ye psent. Incmbt., sold the Advowson with that of Woodbridge-Hacheson to Mr. Close of Ipswich, who has jockey'd [*i.e.* gambled] them away, 9th November."

In 1727 our rector appears in the Poll List for the Knights of the Shire for Suffolk (*C.M.*) as having voted for Sir William Barker, Bart., and Sir Jermyn Davers, Bart. His wife had probably by 1727 succeeded to her father's property, for in that year he was concerned with consider-able property in Kent, Essex, and Bucks, as is evidenced by the follow-ing Fine (*F.* xxvii. *Pasch.*) :—

"Between ffrancis ffolkard and Allam Goodwin, plffs., and John Jeaffreson, gen., and Ann his wife, Cristofer Jeaffreson, Art, defts., of the manor of Sullingham with apptces., and of 5 messuages, 5 cottages, 5 gardens, 1500 acres land, 50 acres meadow, 130 acres pasture, 80 acres wood, 400 acres marsh and turf paying 20'- rent, cum pasture pomibus aivirs et libat fields, with apptces., in the Island of St. Christofer in Sullingham and in Sullingham Stockworth and Bourough Green, in County Canterbury, and of 1 messuage, 100 acres land, 20 acres meadow, 20 acres pasture, 10 acres wood, and cont. pasture pomibus aivis, with apptces., in Alphamstone, in County Essex, and of 100 acres land, 50 acres pasture, 100 wood, and cont. pasture pomibus aivys, with apptces., in Lilingstone Dayrell, in Co. Bucks. ffolkard and Goodwin pay defts. £1360 sterling."

The Jeaffresons (or Jeaffersons) named in the foregoing Fine were an old Suffolk family with which the Folkards became subsequently connected. The Christopher and John Jeaffreson named may have been, and probably were, the trustees of Deborah Chaplin. In a paper dated June 15, 1731 (*D.*) the subject of this notice is named as one of the trustees to a deed of feoffment for the support of two aged and infirm inhabitants of Hasketon executed by Thomas Timmse, of Hasketon. In 1734 he was left exor. with the Rev. Philip Candler, rector of Hollesley, to the will of the Rev. John Punchard (*Norw: Consis.* 149), rector of Hasketon, who was father to the John Punchard then married to his sister, Mary ffolkard. This testator was his predecessor in the rectory of Hasketon, and on the Rev. J. Punchard's death in 1736, he became the incumbent there conjointly with his first living of Clopton (*D. Hasketon Register*).

S — 2

His name is next met with in the will (88) of his stepmother, Mary ffolkard, of Parham, of 1735. In it he is referred to as " my-son-in-law," the old equivalent of our modern stepson. In 1739 he is indicated as the owner of the family residence at Parham by the advertisement relating to it before quoted. At a General Court Baron of Clopton Manor, held 12th August, 1749, the following record was made (*D.* xviii. 36) :—

" Reverend ffrancis ffolkard, of Clopton, Suffolk, Clerk, admitted on the surrender of Clopton Carr Millington, to land which said Clopton Carr Millington took up 9 July, 1742, as only son and heir of Edward Millington, decd."

In the Fine (*F.* xlii. *Trin.*) of 1743 given below, this ffrancis was probably concerned with a daughter of his sister, Sarah Blomfield.

" Between ffrancis ffolkard, Clrk., plff., and Ann Blomfield, Spr., deft., of 3 messuages, 4 barns, 4 stables, 70 acres land, 30 acres meadow, 50 acres pasture, with appurts., in Little Stonham Aspall, Stonham, and Combs, and of a moiety of 2 messuages, 3 barns, 3 stables, So acres land, 20 acres meadow, and 70 acres pasture, with appurts., in Buxhall, Ratlesden, Wallisford, and Rickinghall Infr. Plff. pays £220."

The following two notices, which come next in order of date, seem to show connection between the Folkards of Parham and those of Beccles (*See Ped.* 4). The earlier of the two (*D.* xx. *Dallingho*) is a deed by which

" ffrancis ffolkard, of Clopton, Clerk, and James Lyun, of Woodbridge, Surgeon, are appointed on the 5th April 1744, trustees to a marriage settlement on Rebecca Wake, on her marriage to John Wade, of Rendlesham, Gent."

This Rebecca Wake was daughter to Rebecca Wake (*nat.* ffolkard), as shown on Ped 4. The second notice (*Ibid*) runs :—

" Indenture between Jacob Chilton, Clerk, 1st part ; ffrancis ffolkard, of Clopton, Clerk, 2nd part ; and said John Clarke. 3rd part ; said Jacob Chilton did bargain, sell, assign, &c., all the said Premises, mortgage, &c., to said ffrancis ffolkard, in trust for said John Clarke, to attend the inheritance."

This John Clarke was probably the attorney of Beccles shown on Ped. 4, and both the entries seem to indicate the connection between the two lines above suggested, and the maintenance, even after their long separation, of intimacy between the members of them. Just before the death of this ffrancis a terrier of Clopton was prepared. This (*D. Clopton*) is headed :—

" A true Terrier of all the Glebe lands, Messuages, Tenements, portions of Tithes, and other rights belonging to the Rectory and Parish Church of Clopton, in the County of Suffolk and Diocese of Norwich, and now in the use and possession of Mr. ffrancis ffolkard there, or his tennants."

This Terrier is dated 31st May, 1753, the holding being stated at 13 acres and 2 roods. The will (95) of this rector is dated 5th September, 1753. It directs his burial in the chancel of Clopton church, where there is a monument to himself and his wife bearing the following inscription :—

" Here lieth the Body of | the Rev. Francis Folkard, A.M., | Rector of this Parish, | who died 23rd November, 1753. aged 65. | Here also lieth the Body of | Mrs. Deborah Folkard, | his beloved wife, | who was daughter and sole heiress | of the Rev. Peter Chaplin, | Rector of Higham in this County. | She died 21st August, 1779, aged 81. | Near this place | are likewise interred, | three of their children, | two of whom died infants. | The third, named Peter Francis, | died at the age of 9 years."

This monument is of black marble, and stands within the Communion railing. On a shield above it are the arms of Folkard impaling those of Chaplin, which are :—Erm. on a chief indented az., 3 griffins, or. The crest of the latter family is concealed by the chancel step (D. x. *Clopton*).

Of *post mortem* references to this rector there are several. The *Gentleman's Magazine*, in its issue for 1753 (*Fo.* 541), includes in a list of deaths for that year :—

"Nov. 23, Rev. Mr. Folkard, R[ector] of Clifton [*should be Clopton*], Suffolk."

At a General Court of the manor of Kettleburgh held 13th October, 1755,

"Montague North, Clerk, acknowledged free tenure of lands conveyed to him by ffrancis ffolkard, Clerk."

In 1761 (*D.* xviii. 36), certain lands and a house at Clopton, formerly occupied by the Rev. ffrancis ffolkard, Rector, belonging to John Jeaffreson, passed, by the will of the latter, to his son Samuel Jeaffreson. This John Jeaffreson was doubtless the man who was party to the Fine of 1727 above quoted.

Of ffrancis ffolkard's children, Elizabeth and Deborah are dealt with separately hereafter. The only records of his son, Peter Francis, and of two children who died infants, are those given on the monumental inscription above. The Parham Register has an entry which may refer to another child of his. This reads:—

"ffrancis ffolkard, buried 24th March, 1733."

I am unable to fix any other possible parentage for this individual.

11. ELIZABETH FFOLKARD was daughter to the foregoing, and, according to the inscription on her tomb, was born in 1720. The exact date of her marriage to the Rev. Montague North, D.D., is not known to me ; but she was single at the date of her father's will (95) of 1753. As that will refers to her intended marriage with Dr. North, it is probable that it took place shortly after her father's death. Davy writes of her that she died childless. Dr. North (*D.* xxv. *Glenham Parva*) was a younger son of the Honourable Roger North, of Rougham, Norfolk. His family was one of the highest rank in that county, he being great grandson to Dudley, fourth Lord North, who married Anne, dar. and co-heiress of Sir Charles Montague, from which marriage, no doubt, the name of Montague was given to the husband of this Elizabeth Folkard.

In 1749 Dr. North was presented to the rectory of Little Glenham, and subsequently to that of Sternfield, both places being in Suffolk. He rebuilt the chancel of the church at Sternfield at his own expense in 1764. He was also a canon of Windsor. Dr. North died in 1779, surviving his wife but five years. In 1769 this Mrs. North and her sister Deborah Folkard, the latter then unmarried, were guests at a masquerade given by Mr. Herbert, a younger son of the eighth Earl of Pembroke, at his seat at Little Glenham ; Sir Dudley North, who died in 1691, and who was a younger son of the fourth Lord North, having had his residence at that place. The following curious letter relating to this masquerade is preserved among Davy's collections (*D.* xxv. *Glenham Parva*), and was copied by him from a piece of paper in the handwriting of Mrs. ffowller, the wife of the Rev. Richard ffowller, rector of Dallingho and Easton. The Duchess to whom allusion is made in this letter was her Grace of Hamilton, who was, at the date of this party, remarried to the Honble. Richard Nassau, father of the Earl of Rochford.

"There were 24 Masques. Mr. Herbert was a Conjuror, but he could not be persuaded to tell fortunes ; for, as he said, he was an Astrologer, and the Comet took up so much of his attention that he could not spare time for such trifling employ. Mrs. Herbert was a Nun. Mr. Stratford, a Dutch Skipper ! Mrs. Stratford, a Shepherdess ; Mr. Lake, Mother Shipton ; Mrs. Lake, the genteelest dress among the Ladyes, a Venetian domino made of white Lutestring, trimmed with gold edging, and very fine in diamonds. Mr. Charles Long admirably supported the character of flirting fine lady, he was called Lady Bunbutter, he said very many clever things. Mr. D. Long was first Punch, then a Counsellor, and then Punch again. Mr. Lambart was the prettiest figure among the gentlemen—a shepherd with a lamb in a string. Mr. Thomas was an exceedingly good Country Squire, and Mr. Moore, of Ipswich, was Clod his man. Mr. Nelson was incomparably good as a Jew Pedlar, with washballs, &c. Mrs. Nelson's was a Turkish dress: her sister, a gray sister, an order of Nuns ; but the most attracting was Mr. Redman, the clergyman, as a child of two years old, in a white frock, back string and belt, dragging a coach with one hand and in the other hand a doll. Master Nassau's were called Cupids, and said many smart things ; some of the servants filled up the other characters : A pretty haymaker, a Pallas, and Barbary Lady, and two others, though I don't know what they were called. The Company without masques were the Duchess and Mr. Nassau, Mr. and Mrs. Long, Mr. and Mrs. Carter, Mrs. North, Miss Dyball, Miss Folkard, Miss Pretyman, and Miss ——. There was dancing on the Green, first minuet Mr. Lambert and Mrs. Stratford, the same gentleman with Miss Pretyman, Mr. Stratford and Mrs. Lake, the Country Squire and the fine Lady, and a few more. The characters then all joined and danced two Country dances. When it grew dark the Company went in and drank tea, and some pretty fireworks were exhibited on the green. The Company then went to cards, a Commars, and a whist table, after which there was Cake, lemonade and Orgeat ; when the Duchess and family, Mr. and Mrs. Long, went home, and the rest stayed supper."

Reminiscences of this Mrs. North are still preserved in Dr. Punchard's family. From him I have learned that his grandfather, John Baldry Punchard, who was second cousin to her, lost all hope of succeeding to any of her considerable property owing to some quarrel respecting her lap-dogs, for which animals she had a strong affection. She and her husband are both buried in Sternfield Church, in which two mural monuments are placed bearing as inscriptions :—

"To the Memory | of the Revd. | Montague North, D D., | late rector of this parish | and canon of Windsor. | He was the youngest son | of the honorable | Roger North, Esq., | of Rougham in Norfolk, | and died 22nd August, 1779, | aged 68."

Above the foregoing are the arms of North, viz :—Az., a lion passant, or, between three fleurs de lis, arg. The crest,—On a wreath a dragon's head erased, sa., purfled or gorged with a ducal coronet and a chain of the last.

"To the Memory of | Elizabeth North, | late wife of the Revd. | Montague North, D.D. | She was the daughter | of the Revd. | Francis Folkard, | rector of Clopton | in this County, | and died 21st September, 1774, | aged 54."

The arms above are those of Folkard, viz. :—Sa. a chevron between three covered cups, or.

In the nave of Sternfield church there hangs a hatchment (D) on which the arms of North and Folkard are impaled.

12. DEBORAH FFOLKARD was the younger daughter of the rector of Clopton (No. 10). We have no record of the date of her birth, but she was under age at the date of her father's will (95) of 1753. In 1754 we find her thus named in a Court roll of the manor of Kingshall, in Clopton (*D. x. Clopton*).

"Deborah ffolkard, the youngest daughter of ffrancis ffolkard, Clk., admitted under the will of sd. ffs., her father, as follows :—' I, ffrancis ffolkard, of Clopton, in the Co. of Suffk., Clk., do make this my last will and Test., &c. All the rest and residue of my real estate, whatsoever and wheresoever, and of what nature and kind soever, either in present possession, revertion, remainder, or expectancy, I give and demise the same and every part and parcel. thereof, with the rights, members, and Appts., to my youngest daughter, Deborah ffolkard, and to her heirs for ever '—to land which sd. ffras. took up 12 August, 1749, upon the surrender of Clopton Carr Millington."

A further entry on the same roll reads :—

"ffrancis ffolkard, Clk., free tenant, died since the last Court. Deborah ffolkard, youngest daughter of the sd. ffrancis, acknowledged free tenure and pg. a relief."

In 1769 she was present, with her sister, Mrs. North, at the masquerade above described. Davy, in his notes on the persons present at that entertainment, refers to her as

" Miss Folkard, Deborah, youngest daughter, and coheir with her sister, Mrs. North, of the Revd. Francis Folkard, Rector of Clopton. She afterwards married Frederick Keller, son, as I suppose, of the Revd. Frederick Keller, Vicar of Benhall. She died s.p."

We know nothing of her subsequent life or of her death, but it is manifest, from the way in which property held by her for life under her father's will is referred to in that (100) of her uncle, Thomas ffolkard, of Bedfield, of 1780, that she was living at that date.

With this Deborah the descent of the direct Parham line died out. Residence at that place was, however, entered upon by a branch from the Dennington Settlement, which has not as yet been in any way dealt with in this monograph. When this is undertaken it will include many of its members formerly and now resident in Parham.

The old Settlement was continued by a descendant of the Bedfield line, whom I now proceed to notice.

13. THOMAS FFOLKARD, of Parham, was son to Thomas, of Bedfield (*No. 15 of that line*). He was second cousin to the Deborah above dealt with. From his tomb we learn that he was born in 1767, but where is unknown to me. In 1780 he was named in his grandfather's will (100) and was legatee under it of the property held for life by the foregoing Deborah. I learned at Parham that before settling there he had lived at Spexhall. His eldest child, Mercy, having been born in 1793, his marriage probably took place in the year previous. His wife, as I learned on inquiry of a Mrs. Capon, of Parham, who is a grand-

daughter of that wife by a first marriage, was a widow named Sarah
Wayman. By the inscription on her tomb we learn that she was born
in 1756, and that she lived to the great age of 89, dying in 1845. She
was eleven years the senior of her husband, this Thomas Folkard.

In 1809 both husband and wife were parties to the following Fine
(*F.* lv. *Easter*).

" Between Jeremiah Wade, plff., and Thomas Folkard and Sarah his wife, defts., of 2
messuages. 2 curtilages, 2 orchards, 20 acres land, 15 acres meadow, and 15 acres pasture, in
Parham, £60."

Davy seems to have visited Parham in 1825, and (*D.* xxv. *Parham*),
then noted that the old family house " now belongs to and is the residence of Mr. Thomas Folkard." The same authority, on his pedigree of
the Folkards of Parham, informs us that the ancient gold ring with the
family arms before referred to (No. 2), was at that date in the possession
of this man, from whom it passed into that of the Gray family. In the
list of freehold voters for Knights of the Shire of 1830, this man's name
is included, and in that of 1841 he voted for land possessed by him at
Framlingham. The parish clerk at Parham told me that this Thomas
left no son, but had two daughters, who will be noticed hereafter.
According to information given me at Parham, he fell into straightened
circumstances in his old age, and had to sell the old family house, going
to live with his daughter, Mercy Gray, at Old Parham Hall, where he
died in 1853. His tomb in Parham churchyard bears the following
inscription :—

"In memory of | Thomas Folkard, | who died March 4th, 1853, | aged 86 years. |
Also of | Sarah his wife, | who died Februay 16th, 1845, | aged 89 years."

14. MERCY FOLKARD was daughter to the foregoing Thomas.
From her tomb we learn her to have been born in 1793, but the locality
of her birth is unknown. It was probably at Spexhall. She married
John Gray, of Old Parham Hall, one of the finest old baronial houses of
the county, but now only used as a farm-house. The Grays were an old
Parham family, and in the Register I found the following entry :—

"Ann Graye, da. of Sir William Graye and Ladye Ann, baptized 20 May, 1605."

Rumour has it that the marriage of this Mercy was not a happy one,
it being even suspected that the husband caused her death by throwing
her out of window into the moat which surrounds Old Parham Hall.
After her death, which occurred at the age of 72, in 1865, her husband in
1869 remarried, at the age of 79, to Rose Adams, who was the second
daughter of John Baldry Punchard, and an aunt of the Rev. Dr.
Punchard, from whom I received these details.

The tomb of John Gray in Parham churchyard bears the following :—

"Sacred | to the Memory of | John Gray, | who died May 7, 1872, | aged 82 years. |
Also of | Mercy, | his wife | who died February 22, 1865. | aged 72 years "

15. MARTHA FOLKARD was the younger daughter of Thomas
(No. 13). We have no record respecting her birth, which is probably

registered at Spexhall. All particulars known respecting her are those furnished by the following inscription on her tomb in Parham church-yard :—

" Sacred | to the Memory of | Martha, wife of John Smith, | (of the parish of Chelsea, | Middlesex, and daughter | of Thomas and Sarah Folkard, | of this parish), | who departed this life | April 17, 1822, aged 25 years.

> "Absent or dead, still let my name be dear,
> A sigh the absent claim, the dead a tear;
> T'is true the bud was nipt at early dawn,
> And life's sweet fragrance from my bosom torn ;
> But who, my dearest children, can foresee
> The time of death prescribed for you or me,
> Some replete with pain, and age decay,
> And some in bloom of life are snatched away.
> Yet blessed be that God who called me here,
> Fraught with life's burdens, anxiety and care,
> For now to me all grief and woe is o'er,
> And I am landed on that wished-for shore."

"Me hinc fata vocant, salvite eternum proles | Æternumque vale mihi, O dulcissime conjux."

I was informed at Parham that this Mrs. Smith left a son who was at that time living there.

Settlement at Wickham Market.

(Includes branches at Worlingworth and Darsham).

---

1. LAWRENCE FFOLKARD, of Wickham Market, was son to Thomas, of Bedfield (*No. 5 of that Settlement*), who died in 1627. We have but little information respecting him. Of his having settled at Wickham Market we know nothing beyond the statement to that effect on the Candler Pedigree. At the date of his father's will (45) of 1626, this Lawrence had ten children living, all being then under age. The only remaining notice of him found is in his brother Anthony's will (57) of 1656. By this, legacies are left to this Lawrence's son James, to four children of his son George, to his son Lyonell (evidently named after his brother-in-law, Lyonell Russell), and to his daughters Mary and Susan. This will only accounts for five out of the ten children we know that he had living in 1626. James and George are noticed hereafter, but of the others we have no additional record. A Laurence ffolkard, whom we find to have lived at Bedfield and to have been buried there in 1724, was probably this man's grandson, and is so dealt with below.

2. LAWRENCE FFOLKARD I believe to have been grandson to the foregoing, though there is no evidence of this. He resided at

T

Bedfield, and particulars respecting him have been given under that Settlement (No. 12).

3. GEORGE FFOLKARD, according to his uncle Anthony's will (57) was one of the sons of Lawrence (No. 1). Judging from the fact that that will only left legacies to this man's children, and not to himself, it seems probable that he was dead before the date of it, 1656. I have found no other certain mention of him. His children named in the will referred to were George, Anne, Mary, and Hannah. With reference to the first of these, it seems not unlikely that an entry to the following effect in the Bedfield Register related to his marriage (*D*. xv. *Bedfield*).

"G. ffolcard and Elizbt. ux. mard. 1670."

As to the daughter Anne, the following entry in the Frostenden Register may refer to her :—

"Thomas Gore and Ann ffocard were maryed August 19, 1641."

The will of her uncle of 1656 does not, however, refer to her as being a married woman. It may be further surmised that the daughter Hannah may have been the party named in the following licence entry (*Ipsw. Registry, Sundry Books*, xx.) :—

"11 April, 1643, License marriage between John Smyth and Anna Ffolkar of Melton, S.W."

A second entry of this license has the date 11 April, 1642, and spells the name " Ffolsar."

4. JAMES FFOLKARD, of Worlingworth, on the authority of his uncle Anthony's will (57) of 1656, was another child of Lawrence (No. 1). That will also supplies the names of three of his children, James, Anthony, and Thomas. In the will (60) of his aunt, Ann ffolkard, of 1664, he is named as of Worlingworth, and we find him about the same date assessed for two hearths in that place as " James ffowcard " (*L.S.* 183/612). His son Anthony also has notice in the will last referred to, but of his sons, James and Thomas, nothing further is known. (*See additional Notes.*)

5. ANTHONY FFOLKARD was a son of the above James. I have assumed this man to have lived at Darsham, but on the weak evidence only that a believed grandson of his, Anthony ffolkard, was born there in 1793. The original found of the following was probably executed by this man (*D.C.* i. 35).

"December 21st, 1723. To Sir (*Quære*) John James, Thomas Raynor. Recd. yn of Tho. Korridge, Esq., by ye hands of Sir Robert Kemp, Bart., the sum of twenty pds. in part of ys Bond by me, Anthony ffolkard."

6. ROBERT FFOLKARD, of Darsham, I believe, though without full proof, to have been son to the foregoing. The sole reference to him met with is in the following extract from Darsham Register (*D.C.* iii. 162):

"Anthony, son of Robert and Hannah ffokard (late Knoller) was born September 18, 1793, privately baptized October 6, 1793."

I find in the Framlingham Register a

"Hannah ffolkard, aged 17, buried 5th June, 1785."

This Hannah, failing all efforts to trace her parentage, may be assumed to have been a daughter of this Robert and Hannah. On examining the Darsham Register personally, the entry first quoted was found to be among those missing from it, nor could I trace therein any subsequent descendants as having resided there, though the rector told me of a child bearing the name having been drowned at Darsham some years back. This was possibly the child of some Folkards who lived close by at Yoxford, and who, there seems reason to think, may have been of this line of Darsham.

Settlement at Cretingham.

(Includes branch at Hollesley).

---

1. THOMAS FFOLKARD, of Cretingham, was a son of Thomas, of Ashfield (*No. 11 of that line*), who died in 1689, and he is named in the will (72) of the latter, of 1684, as his eldest son and exor.

In 1683 he was appointed exor. to the will (68) of his brother Jonathan, he being therein referred to as of Cretingham. An error in the Pedigree must here be acknowledged. From investigation made subsequent to the compilation of that Pedigree, there can remain no doubt that this man's wife, Margaret, was the Margaret Johnson assigned as the wife of Thomas, of Crowfield, who died about 1708. On the 3rd January, 1700, (*C.P. before 1714. Reynardson* 360)

"Thomas ffolkard and Margaret his wife reply to a bill of complaint (*Mitford* 362, *Indexed "ffolbard"*) filed by Thomas Scotchmere and Anne his wife, seeking as joint heirs-at-law a moiety of certain property at Diss in Norfolk. From that reply, and from a subsequent one dated February 12, 1701 (*Reynardson* 353), it appears that Robert ffoldgier, of Bramford, left this property, valued at £9 yearly, to his only child, Anne. About 1657 this Anne married Rowland Johnson, their daughter Margaret marrying Thomas ffolkard. Johnson dying, his widow remarried to Thomas Scotchmere, of Bramford and Kempsford, Suffolk, and had further issue—ffrancis Scotchmere, and a daughter who married another Thomas Scotchmere, the last and his wife being joint plaintiffs in the suit. The defendants say that Margaret Johnson was under age when her mother died in 1669. They plead that the 'said Thomas Scotchmere, before his Intermarriage with the said Ann, your oratrix said mother, in consideration of the sum of Five hundred pounds obtained by Thomas Scotchmere with the orator's mother as her marriage portion, the said Thomas Scotchmere, as a provision for the said Ann and the two children of the said Rowland Johnson then living, whereof your oratrix is the survivor,' settled the property in dispute upon them. It is also stated in one of the answers that Thomas Scotchmere, senior, on his death, left this Margaret ffolkard (*nat* Johnson), his stepdaughter, an annuity of £3. 10s. till 15 years old ; then one of £2 till 21 ; and £100 on coming of age. They plead that having held the property undisturbed for twenty years before the institution of this suit, that this is barred by the Statute of Limitations of 21 James I."

T 2

The verdict in this case has not been registered, but the property was eventually devised by the will of the wife of the subject of this notice, and the following Fine of 1709 (*F*. xxxii. *Michs.*), was probably intended to amicably settle the title upon her :—

"Between Margaret ffolkard, widow, plff., and Thomas Scotchmere and Ann his wife, defts., of 1 messuage, 1 barn, 1 stable, 1 orchard, 2 acres land, 2 acres meadow, and 2 acres pasture, with appurtenances, in Diss. Plaintiff pays defendants £60 sterling."

This wife Margaret is named in her husband's will (77) of 1706 as his executrix, as also in the will (80) of 1709 of her son Thomas. Her own will (85) of 1725, has been found, she being at that date of Pettaugh. From the date of proof her death in 1727 may be conjectured.

In 1702 we find this Thomas ffolkard named as of Cretingham in a Suffolk Poll list (*D*. liv. 36). His will above referred to was proved in 1706 or 7, and by it he appears to have been possessed of considerable property in Ashfield, Diss, and elsewhere. Of his children, Thomas will be found dealt with below. Of the six daughters named in his will, Lydia was the youngest, and was at the date of it unmarried and below age. Ann was probably " the wife of James Clough of Ashfield," referred to. Elizabeth, it seems likely, was " the aunt Welton of Framsden," referred to in her mother's will (85), and in that case had predeceased her mother. Mary, it may be conjectured from the fact of the eldest daughter of Joseph Godbold being so named, was married to that man after her father's death, and she had probably also predeceased her mother, her children being named in the will of the latter. The marriage of Priscilla to — Scotchmere must also have been after her father's death, his will referring to all his daughters save the wife of James Clough, as then unmarried. Susan, though named in her father's will, received no mention in that of her mother, and had probably died in the interval between the dates of them.

2. THOMAS FFOLKARD was the only son, apparently, of the foregoing Thomas, and at the date of the will (77) of the latter of 1706, was under age, though old enough to be left exor. to it with his mother. The last does not mention him in her will (85) of 1725; but the " Thomas and Ann ffolkard " of that will named as the mother's grand-children must almost certainly have been the issue of a marriage by him of which we have no other record. It may, however, be justifiably conjectured that the following notices in the rolls of the Sutton Manorial Court (*Add MSS*. 23,951) refer to this man. If so he was in 1712 living at Hollesley, and married to a wife named Anne or Anna :—

"15th November, 1712. Thomas ffolkard, of Hollesley, yeoman, admitted to land in propria persona on the surrender of Abraham Colman of South Leyham, Co. Norf., and his wife Maria."

"(Same date). Thomas ffolkard and Anna his wife surrendered a messuage to John Barker, of Wickham Market." (*Afterwards crossed out*).

"1st August (?) 1715. Thomas ffolkard and Anna his wife appear thereat to have surrendered the land they had from Abraham Colman to Mrs. Benington, of Orford."

"13 April, 1719. Elizabeth Barker pays tax for land called ffoufart, in surrender by Thomas ffolkard and Anne his wife."

The fact that the name of Ann was transmitted to his daughter renders the foregoing conjecture the more probable. It may be, also, that he was the same Thomas ffolkard who in 1727 was on the Poll List (*B.M.*) for Knights of the Shire as owner of land in Rickinghall Inferior. Nothing is known with certainty of the after-history of this man's two children.

3. THOMAS FFOLKARD was one of the grandchildren named in the will (85) of the mother of the foregoing in 1725. I have been unable to trace anything more certain of his parentage than has been given above, but the date would make it not improbable that the following will, abstracted from that in the Bury Probate Office, was his.

"Thomas ffolkard, of Yaxley, Farmer. Personal estate to be sold and the money placed out at interest. This to be paid to Rose ffolkard, my wife, half yearly. After her decease the money to be divided equally between Sarah, the wife of Samuel Bartram ; Alice, the wife of Robert Caston ; Margaret, the wife of Samuel Creasey ; and Mary, the wife of William Woods, my daughters. Robert Caston, of Yaxley, Co. Suffolk, my son-in-law, and Rose ffolkard, my wife, Executors, 13 September, 1774. Probt. 28 September, 1774, to Exors." (*V. Dalton,* 1774).

Settlement at Helmingham.

1. SAMUEL FFOLKARD was a son of Thomas of Ashfield (*No. 11 of that line*), who died in 1689. He and his wife Susan received prominent mention in that father's will (72) of 1684. This wife, who we know from her husband's will to have outlived him, we learn, from the following will (abstracted), to have been a daughter of Anne Dove of Gosbeck :—

9 February, 1691. Anne Dove of Gosbeck, wo., aged. To my daughter Mary, the wife of John Colchester. My daur. Sarah. My dar. Susan, the wife of Samuel ffolkard. Elizabeth, the wife of Daniel Bigsby. Penelope, the wife of Thomas Dove, gent. ' My daughter Elizabeth hath no child, nor is likely to have any.' To my son William. To Sarah and Ann Dove, the two dars. of my son John. To Elizabeth, Anne, Samuel, Penelope, Susan, and Thomas ffolkard, children of my daur. Susan. To Thomas, Anthony, Daniel, and William, children of my daur. Penelope. To Sarah Dove my daur. and Thomas Dove, gent., my son-in-law. Residue to son John Dove. He sole exor. 26 June, 1694. Commis. Sarah Dove, *fil. natural. et legal.*' (*Ipsw. Probate Office. Liber Candler* 1694—8. *fo.* 20).

In 1691 we find this man as bondsman for the marriage of his daughter Elizabeth (*Ipsw. Pro. Sundry Books* xxxiv.), the entry as to which reads :—

"29 September, 1691. License of Marriage between Benjamin Baldry, of Soham Combust, single, and Elizabeth ffolkard, of Cretingham, single, at Soham Combust. Samuel ffolkard's bond in £200."

It is probable that at the date of giving this bond this Samuel was resident at Cretingham along with his brother Thomas. His will (75) of 1704 states him to have been then of Helmingham, and it refers to his "being aged." The proof of this will points to his having died within a few months of its execution. Of his children, Thomas, Penelope, and Susan are apparently named in his will as being at the date of it unmarried, and we have no further mention of them. His son Samuel is dealt with below. Another child, Anne, "ye wife of Charles Covell," is named in his will, as is also her child, Anne Covell. This daughter received further mention in Anne Dove's will above given, and we also find the following entry as to her marriage (*Ipsw. Pro. Sundry Books* xxxiv.) :—

"19 December, 1695. Marriage License between Charles Covell, of Winston, Widower, and Anna ffolkard, of Helmingham, single, at Helmingham."

At the foregoing date this Samuel had doubtless left Cretingham for Helmingham. Another daughter, Mary, "wife of William Ladd," finds mention only in her father's will. The remaining child, Elizabeth Baldry, whose marriage license has been quoted above, also has mention in that will, and the Rev^d. Dr. Punchard informs me that a daughter of hers married a member of his family.

2. SAMUEL FFOLKARD, son to the foregoing, and named in his will (75) of 1704, we learn, by that document, to have been then married. He is further mentioned in the will above given of his maternal grandmother, Anne Dove, of 1691. It was probably this man who was included in the Poll Lists for the Knights of the Shire as a voter for land in Wetheringsett, in 1702 and 1727. If so, no doubt the following entry in the register of Coddenham (*D.* viii. *Coddenham*), affords us information as to his marriage :—

"Samuel ffolkard, of Wetheringsett, and Mary Blomfield, of Crowfield, married 27 Decr., 1720."

I deem it probable that the will (91) of Samuel ffolkard, of Wingfield, is that of this man. It was proved in the year it was written (1746), and mentions daughters Elizabeth, Sarah, and Susan, the first of these being married at the date of the will. The following entry in the Saxmundham Register may possibly refer to the marriage of the last named daughter :—

"James White and Susan ffolkard married January 29, 1747."

As no wife is named by the testator, she had no doubt predeceased him. I have traced no further residence of the family at Helmingham.

Settlement at Letheringham.

(Includes branches at Woodbridge and Ipswich).

1. JOHNATHAN FFOLKARD was a son of Thomas of Ashfield (*No. 11 of that line*), who died in 1689. In the will (72) of the latter, of 1684, he is referred to as being then dead, and his wife Margaret is named as having survived her husband. We know nothing additional repecting this wife, save that she was named in her husband's will, and that in 1697, in the admon. of her son Johnathan (*Admon. 17*) she is referred to as then living.

On a Hearth Tax Roll of about 1665 "Jonathan ffokard " pays a tax on five hearths in Bedfield, probably in a house owned by, if not occupied by him there (*L.S.* 183/612). His will (68) is dated 1683. In it he describes himself as of Letheringham, and as possessed of property in Crowfield, Ashfield, and Earl Soham. His two brothers are exors. to that will, which, being proved in the year it was made, 1683, is conclusive as to the year of his death.

As to his children, Thomas, evidently his eldest son, will be noticed further on. Johnathan is a legatee, under his father's will, of lands at Earl Soham, being described in it as under age. By his grandfather's will (72) of 1684, this son succeeded to lands at Ashfield. From the admon. (No. 17) of the latter we learn that he died in 1697, then being a bachelor and resident at Woodbridge, his brother Thomas administering his estate. A daughter, Elizabeth, is a legatee under her father's will (68) of 1683. We probably discover her marriage at Woodbridge at a later date in the following license in the Ipsw. Pro. Office:—

"24 March, 1689. License Marriage Benjamin Wade, of Sudbury, single, and Elizabeth ffoker of Ipswich, single, in Woodbridge church."

Another daughter of the subject of this notice is named in her grandfather's will (72) of 1684 as Margarett. She has no reference in her father's will, and this daughter must certainly have been born posthumously. Possibly the following license in the Ipsw. Pro. Office refers to her marriage :—

"July 6, 1736. William Voice, Widower, Mendham, to Margaret ffolkard, at Mendham."

A third son, Joseph, is named in both the wills above referred to as being under age ; a son, Samuel, also being similarly described in them.

2. THOMAS FFOLKARD was the eldest son of the foregoing Johnathan (No. 1). He is named in the will (68) of the latter of 1683, succeeding by it to lands at Crowfield, as he also does to other lands there and at Gosbeck under the will (72) of his grandfather, Thomas ffolkard, of Ashfield (*No. 11 of that line*). An error in the Pedigree as to

this man's wife has been acknowledged under the notice of his uncle
Thomas of Cretingham (*No. 1 of that line*). But a further error, it is now
apparent, was made by me when draughting that Pedigree. There is
now no doubt that this man, instead of being a brother, as thereon shown,
of Thomas of Woodbridge, was identical with him. The first error made
as to his wife led me to the conclusion that the two men were distinct.
In dealing with him in this notice I shall therefore amalgamate the two
Pedigree entries and those of the children.

The subject of this notice we learn from his tomb to have been
born in 1670. In 1697 he administered to the effects of his deceased
brother Johnathan of Woodbridge (*Admon.* 17). The next record of him
is that of his marriage. This was to Mary Oliver, who we learn by her
tomb to have been born in 1675. The entry of this marriage in the
Hasketon Register reads :—

"Thomas ffolkard and Mary Oliver married 9th April, 1701."

The name of Oliver is ancient in Suffolk, a William Oliver having
resided in Helmingham in 1272, but I have no information as to this
Mary's parentage. Among the Registers of dissenting chapels pre.
served at Somerset House, I found that of Woodbridge. An entry
therein reads :—

"At a Church meeting on October 15, 1713, Mrs. Mary ffolkard and the widow Dean
were received as members of this Church."

She was, at the date given, a widow, her husband having died in
1710, she being exor. to his will. We learn from her tomb that she died
at the advanced age of 75 in 1751, so having survived her husband 41
years!

In the year subsequent to his marriage, this Thomas is named in a
Suffolk Poll List as of Woodbridge (*D. liv.* 36), and in that following,
1703, he was a jurat at a Court of the Manor of Kingston, Woodbridge
(*D. xxi. Woodbridge*). His will (80) is dated 1709. He describes
himself therein as " being infirme," although then only 39 years old. In
it he refers to his mother, Margaret, as then living. Shortly afterwards,
in 1710, we find him named, with John Graygoose, as one of the church-
wardens of Woodbridge (*D. xxi. Woodbridge*). His widow no doubt was
a seceder from the Established Church when she joined the dissenting
community. His death, and that of his widow, are thus recorded on a
tombstone in Woodbridge churchyard :—

"Here lies buried the Body of | Thomas Folkard, | who died the 9th of March, 1710, |
aged 40 years, | Also Mary his wife, | who died the 31 July, 1751, | aged 76 years."

Of the children of this couple, Mary, Johnathan, and Margaret, we
know nothing certainly but what is mentioned respecting them in their
father's will ; but it is not improbable that with regard to the daughter
Mary, save for our knowledge that she was of weak intellect, the follow-
ng marriage license (*Ipsw. Pro. Reg.*) may have referred to her, Battisford
lying not far from Woodbridge :—

"March 15, 1740. Simon ffenn, single man, to Mary ffolgar, Single Woman, of Battisford, at Barking."

From an entry in the terrier of Bredfield (2 miles from Woodbridge), it may be concluded that the daughter Margaret married Philip Philpot. This terrier is of 1725, and the entry reads :—

" Lastly there are two other pieces of land, late of Thomas ffolkard, and now of Philipp Philpot in right of his wife, the one lying on the borders of Bredfield on the south side of the house of Richard Roe, and next unto Melton, and contains by estimation about 4 or 5 acres. The other piece lyeth near these thro' the yard of the sd. Rich. Roe, and contains by estimation about half an acre " (*D*. xxxvii. 112).

As regards the son Johnathan, we find a John ffolkard who lived at Bredfield, whom I think to be the same Johnathan, his name having been abbreviated. He witnessed a deed of the Manor Court there as " John ffolkeard" in 1770 (*D*. xxxvii. *Bredfield*) and is described as a farmer, of Bredfield, in a list of Suffolk freeholders of the same date (*D*. iii. 177). His will (99) is dated 1778, and was proved in that year. It only refers to one child of his, Elizabeth, who was then married to John Burrows and had several children.

While dealing with the Bredfield settlement it appears desirable to note that in 1378 a resident on the manor there named "fulcat" compiled a " *Consuetud. Villat hundr. p. fulcat factæ et capiit*," *i.e.*, " The Customs of the towns of the hundred by fulcat made and taken " (*Add. MS.* 14,849). It is also stated in Domesday Book that " In Bradefelda Falcus held of the Abbot 4½ carucates."

3. THOMAS FFOLKARD, the eldest son of the foregoing (No. 2), seems to have settled at Ipswich. There can be no doubt as to this, for in the list of freeholders of that town of 1770 (*D.C*. iv. 177) we find him entitled to a vote for the land at Crowfield left to his father by his grandfather. We learn from his tomb that he was born in 1704. He is named in his father's will (80) of 1705, succeeding under it to land at Gosbeck. His marriage to his wife Elizabeth must have taken place somewhere about 1730, for we find their daughter Elizabeth to have been born in 1732. We know nothing of this wife's maiden name, but from the fact of the name of Beger being given to one of her sons and to her grandson, I conjecture that it was Elizabeth Beger. From her tomb she appears to have been born in 1715. In 1774 she proved her husband's will (89) under which she was the sole legatee, being described in the Surrogates' attestation to it as " Elizabeth ffolkland." She survived her husband only four years, dying in 1777. Her will (98) is dated 1776. She lies buried with her husband, whose tomb bears the inscription given below.

The next mention found of that husband is of 1739, in which year the following advertisement appeared in the *Ipswich Journal* of April 7th and 14th :—

" To be Lett, And ent'd upon immediately, an Old and well-accustom'd Cooper's Shop in the Thorough-Fair in Woodbridge. Enquire of Mr. Thomas Folkard, Ironmonger in Ipswich, for further Particulars."

The above reference was, no doubt, to the shop of his father, who was a cooper by trade, and the advertisement corroborates the assump-

U

tion of his parentage. In 1742, thirty-one years before his death, he made his will (89), by which everything was left to his wife. In 1744 the house and shop of his father, above referred to, appears to have been again vacant, the following second advertisement relating to it appear-ing in the *Ipswich Journal* for December 29th of that year :—

"To be Lett. A House near the Royal Oak in Woodbridge with a Cooper's Shop. Apply to Mr. Thomas Folkard, Ironmonger in Ipswich."

In 1745 this Thomas subscribed £5. 5s. in "A List of the Subscri-bers of the County of Suffolk for the support of His Majesty's Person and Government and the peace and security of the said County in particular on occasion of the Rebellion." This rebellion was, of course, that of the Stuart Pretender. This list is in the "Tracts relating to Suffolk "[(B.M. 10,350). In 1767 he paid a fee of sixpence on a rent-roll of the manor of Kingston-Woodbridge for a cottage he possessed there. His death occurrred in 1773, the following being the inscription on his tombstone in the churchyard of St. Mary Stoke, Ipswich :—

"In memory of | Thomas Folkard | who departed this life | the 9th day of November, | 1773, | Aged 69, | Also Elizabeth, his wife, | who departed this life | the 22nd of February, 1777, | aged 62 years."

The latter is described in the Register as "Aged" and "from St. Lawrence" parish.

Of this man's children, Elizabeth appears to have been the eldest. From her tomb we learn of her birth in 1732. She is a legatee under the will (98) of her mother, of 1776. Her sister Lydia was born in 1745, she being also named in her mother's will. Both these sisters died unmarried. Their joint tomb is in the churchyard of St. Matthew's, Ipswich, and has the following inscription :—

"In Memory of | Mrs. Elizabeth Folkard, | who departed this Life | the 30th day of Dec-ember, 1814, | Aged 82 years. | Also Mrs. Lydia Folkard, | sister to the above, | who departed this Life | the 23rd day of September, 1815, | Aged 70 years."

The Register entry has "Elizabeth Folkard, Spinster," and "Lydia Folkard, Spinster." The *Ipswich Journal* of September 30, 1815, has this further notice of the last :—

"Monday died suddenly, in the 70 year of her age, Mrs. Lydia Folkard, daur. of Mr. Folkard, formerly an ironmonger in this town."

Mary, another daughter, is named in her mother's will (98) of 1776. The *Gentleman's Magazine* of 1782 (fo. 456), has this entry among its list of bankrupts for that year :—

"Mary Folkard (*indexed Folkhard*) Ipswich, Suffolk, Milliner."

The three sons are dealt with below.

4. THOMAS FFOLKARD, of Ipswich, son to No. 3, was born in 1740. He is named in his mother's will (98) of 1776, of which he was an exor. He filled the office of Collector of Customs at Ipswich. He had married before 1779, for we find the name of his wife Elizabeth (her

maiden name being unknown) in the following Fine of that date (*F.L.*
Mich.) :—

"Between Thomas Kent, plff., and Thomas ffolkard and Elizabeth his wife, defts., 1
messuage, 1 barn, 1 stable, 1 curtilage, 1 garden, 1 orchard, 12 acres land, in Crowfield and
Gosbeck. £60."

By this Fine we observe that the lands in the two places named,
which had been bequeathed by the widow of this Thomas's great-great-
grandfather, had remained still in possession of the family. This man is
in 1798 further described as owning land in Crowfield (*D.* viii. *Crowfield*)
for which he was taxed £1. 19s. He had then let it to Christopher
Groome. We find him included in an Abstract of Returns of Charitable
Donations of 1786 (*B.M.*) and named therein as of St. Lawrence Parish,
Ipswich. His death is thus noticed in the *Ipswich Journal* of March 17,
1798 :—

"Sunday died Thomas Folkard Esq., Collector of his Majesty's Customs in this Port.'"

That his death was by suicide is evidenced by the following entry in
the Register of St. Mary Stoke, Ipswich :—

"Thomas Folkard, Esq., Collector of Customs here, from St. Peter's, Ipswich, aged 58,
buried 14th March, 1798. *Occidit sua ipsius manu.*"

The tragic end thus recorded leads to a conjecture that it may have
been due to domestic infelicity, for we find his wife re-marrying within
but little more than a year after his sad death, her re-marriage being
thus noticed in the *Ipswich Journal* of 1799 :—

"Married, May 16, Mr. Robert Johnson, of Chesterton (*Cambridgeshire*), to Mrs. Folkard,
relict of T. Folkard, Esq., Collector of Customs for the Port of Ipswich."

I have found no trace of any issue to this Thomas Folkard.

5. BENJAMIN NATHANIEL FOLKARD, of Ipswich, was
another son of Thomas (No. 3). He was born in 1755, and was exor. to
his mother's will (98) of 1776. In *Tracts relating to Suffolk* (*B.M.* 10,350)
we read :—

"Mr. B. N. Folkard, of Ipswich, gave £1. 1s. on a list of subscription towards building
a ship of war for the service of the public in 1782."

In 1784 he was party to the following Fine (*F. li. Trin.*) :—

"Between Benjamin Nathaniel ffolkard, plf., and John Davis and Susan his wife,
Samuel Tovell, and William Gladdon, defts., of 1 messuage, 1 curtilage, 1 garden, 1 orchard,
and 2 acres land, in Stutton, £60."

His name is in the Ipswich Poll List for election of Knights of the
Shire in 1784, 1790, 1807, and 1820. In 1788 he was concerned with a
second Fine (*F. lii. Easter*) :—

"Between Benjamin Nathaniel ffolkard, plf., and Samuel Ewer, Esq., and William
Bennett and Mary his wife, defts., of 1 messuage, 1 laundry, 1 brewhouse, 2 coach houses,
1 stable, 2 curtilages, and 2 gardens, in Parish of St. Mathews, Ipswich. £100 sterling."

In the British Museum is a MS. petition of William Batley, of
Ipswich, Gent. (*Add. MSS.* 25,337. *fo.* 54), pleading that Ipswich had
been incorporated by several charters, and that the Bailiffs, Burgesses,
and Commonalty had granted leases of the ooze or waste tidal ground

of the river, "and that in January 1794 they granted to Thomas Fulcher, Builder and Timber Merchant, and Benjamin Nathaniel Folkard, lease of other parcels of the sd. ooze amounting to 5 acres, 3 roods, 20 poles, for a term of 99 years at the rent of £2, 10s." This petition further stated that Fulcher purchased out his partner's share. These leases were put in suit by John Cobbold, Esq., in 1810.

I have discovered no record of any marriage made by the subject of this notice. I, therefore, conjecture him to have lived and died single. His death is thus referred to in the *Ipswich Journal* of April 7, 1821 :—

"Thursday, died at St. Mary at the Elms, in this town, aged 66, Mr. Nathl. Folkard, once a reputable ironmonger in this town."

His retirement from business before his death may be assumed from this notice.

6. WILLIAM BEGER FOLKARD, of Ipswich, was a third son of Thomas, of Ipswich (No. 3). The first reference to him found is in the will (98) of his mother, of 1776. His second Christian name is not therein given. In the Poll List for Knights of the Shire of 1784, he is entered as William Folkard, of Ipswich, only. In that for Parliamentary members for Ipswich, of 1820, he is designated by his three names, and in that for the Bailiffs and Town Clerk of Ipswich, of 1823 and 1825, he is again given his full name. I have no other mention of him.

7. CHARLES BEGER FOLKARD, of Ealing, Middlesex, I surmise, from his second Christian name, to have been son to the fore-going. He was a civil engineer. In 1871 he administered to the effects of a sister of his, Sabrina Martha Folkard, of 20, Harley Street, Cavendish Square. He died 21st May, 1876, admon. of his effects being granted to his son, Charles Watson Folkard, of Elm View, Ealing, analytical chemist. The last named had letters of administration granted to him in 1881 of the personal estate of Catherine Duncombe Folkard, of 76, Sloane Street, Chelsea, spinster, who died 27 December, 1880, and who was probably a sister of his. Henry William Folkard, of Markham Square, Chelsea, proved in 1882 the will of his sister, designated Miss Folkard, of Woburn Place, Russell Square, London, and I conjecture both of these to have also been children of this Charles Beger Folkard.

Reference has above been made to Catherine Duncombe Folkard. Mrs. Russell has informed me that her grandmother was a Mrs. Folkard (*natus* Duncombe), and that she was married to a Mr. Folkard, of Sweffling, Suffolk, a sister of this Miss Duncombe being grandmother to Sir Charles Dilke. A Mr. John Folkard is at the present time a farmer at Sweffling, and is probably a grandson of the Mr. Folkard who married Miss Duncombe. The rector of Sweffling informs me that this farmer, or his family, came from Stratford, near Parham. He may, therefore descend either from the Dennington or Parham branches of the family; but I think it more than likely that the man who contracted the Duncombe marriage was a son of Thomas Folkard of Ipswich (No. 3).

Mrs. Russell further informed me that some of the Ealing family emigrated to America, and in that connexion it seems desirable to mention that letters received in 1887, from Mr. G. A. Lomas, of Albany, United States, asked for information "of a Mr. Charles Folkard, of London, who was brother of my mother. In my mother's family there were ten or more sisters of hers, and one brother—Charles. I do not recall what his business was. My grandfather Folkard was largely interested in stoves, &c. . . . My mother's name was Sophia Amelia Folkard."

I think it probable that the last was a sister of the Charles Beger Folkard, of Ealing, under present notice, as her grandfather would then have been Thomas Folkard (No. 3), the ironmonger, of Ipswich, who, as such, might have been "interested in stoves." I wrote details as to this to Mr. Lomas, but received no acknowledgment.

FINIS.

𝕬𝖉𝖉𝖎𝖙𝖎𝖔𝖓𝖆𝖑 𝕹𝖔𝖙𝖊𝖘.

(Obtained while passing through Press).

PEDIGREE No. I.

𝕾𝖊𝖙𝖙𝖑𝖊𝖒𝖊𝖓𝖙 𝖆𝖙 𝕽𝖆𝖙𝖑𝖊𝖘𝖉𝖊𝖓.

SAMUEL FOLKARD, of Wetherden. This man was presumably a son of Samuel, of Ratlesden and Wetherden (No. 1), though no record of his birth has been found. The Register of Great Barton, near Bury St. Edmunds, contains the following entry :—

"1663. Samuell ffolkerd, of Wetherden, and Sarah Wright, of Barton, were m. Novr. 19th."

Dr. Muskett informs me that he has searched the Register of Wetherden down to 1710, but that it contains no reference to the name of ffolkard.

𝕾𝖊𝖙𝖙𝖑𝖊𝖒𝖊𝖓𝖙 𝖆𝖙 𝕷𝖊𝖙𝖋𝖊𝖗𝖎𝖓𝖌𝖇𝖆𝖒.

SAMUEL FFOLKARD, named on page 143 as a son of Johnathan ffolkard (*No. 1 Letheringham Settlement*) was in all probability the "sun-in-law" referred to in the following abstracted will :—

"9 May 1724. Christopher Danford, of Wingfield, co. Suffolk, yeoman. To Elizabeth Smith, of Wingfield, my sister-in-law, £20. To Rebecca Sheppard, my sister-in-law, £40. To Samuel ffolkard 'my sun-in-law' £10. To Elizabeth, Sarah, and Susan ffolkard, when respectively twenty four years of age, all money resulting from the sale of my stock. To Gabriel Reeve, of St. Margaret's of Willkesin, [*Quare Ilketshall*] my kinsman. To Edward Reev's widd., of Badingham, 'if not remov'd.' Samll. ffolkard, my 'sun-in-law,' to be an executor. *Probatum* 29 Octr. 1725." (*Ipsw. Pro. Bishop, No.* 72).

No doubt the three girls named in the above will were daughters of this Samuel ffolkard by the marriage to a Miss Danford indicated, of which I have obtained no further trace.

Settlement at Wickham Market.

JAMES FFOLKARD, of Worlingworth. This man has been dealt with under No. 4 of the Settlement at Wickham Market (page 138). His children, James, Anthony, and Thomas, were then referred to. The following abstract of wills, since obtained, give us further particulars respecting these sons:—

"Christopher Godbold, of Ubbeston, lynnenweaver, 1677. To Anthony ffolkard, of Ubbeston, (*See No. 5 Wickham Market Settlement, there ascribed to Darsham*) my kinsman, £20. To my sister Susan, the wife of James ffolkard, £10, &c., &c. To my sister Anne, wife of John Carver, &c. (*Arch. Suff. Sayer, fo.* 312ᴬ).

"Susanna Godbold, of Ubbeston, widow. To my cosen Mary ffolkard, daughter of my cusen James ffolkard, of Heveningham. To Susanna ffolkard, daughter of cousen Thomas ffolkard, of Wolinworth, deceased, &c. Anthony ffolkard, of Ubbeston, my cousin, Executor, &c., &c. Cousins Ann Collett, of Heveningham, and Susan Osborne" (*Ipsw. Pro.* 1712—18, *fo.* 66).

It will be seen that all the three sons are named in these wills.

The last testator was married to the first at Dennington in 1668, the Register entry there reading:—

"Godbold, Christopher, Widr., and Susanna ffolcard, *soluta*, mard. May 14, 1668."

This Susanna ffolcard evidently did not belong to the wholly distinct line of the family settled at Dennington. She was not improbably a daughter of Robert ffolkard, of Ratlesden (No. 4 of that Line) and his wife Susanna; in which case the cousinships named would be correctly stated. No record of her birth has been found, nor is she named in her assumed father's will (63). The similarity of the mother's name, and the identity of trade between the father and this woman's husband, strengthen, however, the likelihood of the assumption made.

Index Nominum.

NOTES.

I.—The following Christian names in association with Folkard, Folcard, Folchard, Fulcard, and Fulchard, occurring as they do very frequently, have not been indexed in detail: *viz.*, Elizabeth, John, Mary, Robert, Thomas, and William.

II.—The old capital ff is invariably indexed as F.

III.—The addition of a terminal e to names is not noticed.

Abbreviations.—For P, read " Pedigree." For " Sæp.," read " Often."

Index Locorum.

NOTES.

I.—The old capital ff is invariably indexed as F.

II.—The modern spelling of names of places has been followed where known.

Abbreviations.—For P, read " Pedigree." For " *Sæp.*," read " Often."

Printed by R. Follard & Son,
22, Devonshire St., Queen Sq., London.